This Salted Plastic Bo *Hypostatization format ᴗ designed for easy reading.......sort of......I think........or something like that.*

SALTED PLASTIC: THE COMEDIC HORROR OF GENTRIFICATION WAS
ORIGINALLY PUBLISHED IN SHORT STORY FORMAT AS SALTED PLASTIC LOS
ANGELES ISSUE 1, AND SALTED PLASTIC LOS ANGELES: TALES OF
GENTRIFICATION ISSUES 2-4. THE SERIES IS ONGOING, AND THIS
ANTHOLOGY COMPRISES ALL THE CURRENTLY PUBLISHED ISSUES.

THE STORIES WITHIN ARE A LABOR OF LOVE, PAIN, AND CATHARSIS THAT WAS
OVER 15 YEARS IN THE MAKING. I HOPE THAT THEY WILL BE A SOURCE OF
LAUGHTER, MENTAL STIMULATION AND GENERAL ENTERTAINMENT FOR YEARS
TO...........AH, WHAT THE HELL.....WHO AM I KIDDING?! SOMEBODY WRITE
ME A CHECK, AND MAKE THIS INTO A TV SERIES OR MOVIE
ALREADY......HAHA....JUST KIDDING........

PUT SIMPLY, WHATEVER YOU MAKE OF THE CONTENT WITHIN THESE PAGES,
WHETHER AS THE AMATEUR RAVINGS OF AN ANACHRONISTIC PESSIMIST, THE
HOT AIR OF A WANNABE CITY MYSTIC WHO MADE A NOVEL-LENGTH JOKEY
JOKE WHILE HOPPED UP ON NITRO COLD BREW..........OR MAYBE.......JUST
MAYBE.....YOU CAN RELATE TO/RESONATE WITH THE FEELINGS AND
SCENARIOS WITHIN......WHATEVER YOUR REACTIONS MAY BE, I HOPE YOU
HAVE A LAUGH OR TWO ALONG THE WAY.

-NATHAN CASTELLANOS

SALTED PLASTIC:

THE COMEDIC HORROR

of GENTRIFICATION

BY

NATHAN
CASTELLANOS

CONTENTS

Dedicated with all love to those who have lost their homes as a result of gentrification; to anyone who ever struggled to pay rent while trying to get ahead in life.

and

To all who have ever felt the bitter irony of having their culture looked down upon, only to later see it applauded and put up for sale by the very same people who formerly condemned it.

SALTED PLASTIC: THE COMEDIC HORROR OF GENTRIFICATION

Salted Plastic: The Comedic Horror of Gentrification

Friday, August 8, 11:38 pm

It's like seeing a top chef lay out a banquet of her best recipes for a group of undeserving attendees. Imagine a crowd of bulimics coming to dinner solely for the purpose of having a place to warm themselves against the outside cold while they masturbate each other's egos.

It's like watching a crowd of people playing musical chairs, going from one person to the next, their conversations always consisting of one person pretending to be informed about any and every subject, while the other half listens and zones out. The listener's urge to at least self-admit that they know their conversation partner is completely full of shit dies with every micro-second they "listen" to whichever big mouth they are currently "engaged" with. They realize that the shit in question is harvested from half informed message boards..............culled from eaves dropping...................absorbed enema-like from social media of all forms, but they put up with it anyways, applying a surgeon's skill in conversational diplomacy, while they wait not so patiently for their turn to vomit up their own value-demonstrating performance about what they think and "know."

This is what you get in the average nightclub in gentry infested Los Angeles.

Gayg (pronounced "gay egg"), the main promoter and DJ at the HIPPITTY HIP HIP HIP LA bar, Brick, was spinning the finest vinyl gems in her collection for a completely uninterested crowd of tech workers, would be artists, trust fund beards from Portland, and hookers in everything but name. But the crowd, giving close to two shits about the music, simply tuned it all out as they continued to network and placate each other's stock variety personas.

Yup, the only thing shining tonight, despite the awesome musical selection, was Gayg's pale scalp, razored clean on both sides, and mid-bordered by a mohawk-style shock of hair slicked back and colored to look just like a crispy bacon strip. Red bordered with platinum blonde in the middle, patted down thin and lacquered by a heavy dose of designer pomade, then tussled to give an edge-on wave that simulated the look of cooked bacon. Gayg was a stocky woman, mid 30's, white-latina mix. She liked to do Cruxfit and mountain climbing, yet kept a bit of a gut due to a late night habit of MacGriddles and al pastor tacos. Her face was pouty and masculine, stern and discerning, with a Meso-American type nose. She wore some under fit moto jeans and a burgundy Alpha jacket with combat boots.

Tonight was her Friday night club, MODE BENDUVER, an eclectic mix of post-punk, death rock, synth pop and network interchange, a new form of shit amalgam sound consisting of bits and pieces of lyrical and instrumental techniques ripped off from every (AND ANY) original musical concept from the last thirty years.

As Gayg put on Trust Fund Cock-Sucker's new single "Pseudo Urban Pussy", the energy in the room SPIKED! The "locals" were in their element, full throttle, nothing held back in their ability to be the epitomes of social progress...............and make no mistake; riding high on the audio juice of every lyric and beat, their full potential as the new millennia's main subcultural iconoclasts began to shine. A glance around the room, and an ear to the conversations within, made this undoubtable.

PigNose Diddler, an aging hipster hybrid complete with Pig Bacon nose, sat with GingerJust Legal, the most coveted demonstration of his value; a peach skinned, bad as bubble bath, OH SO PUNK ROCK, teenage-brained...........24 year old. GingerJust was over twenty years his junior, and bought at the bargain price of a nightly fee of upscale dinners, cocaine, and his ability to emulate whichever father figure in her past might have sugared her strawberry.

PigNose was a lanky white guy, mid to late 40's, kinda squirrelly, but well-kept for his age due to a strict regimen of a sugar free and low alcohol diet, void of white starch, pork, etc. Pig had slapped on some generic all black costume for the night, quick assemble from Forever 41.

Salted Plastic: The Comedic Horror of Gentrification

Ugly black vinyl jacket with that whole tacky cinched crinkle shit on the waist and wrists thing, along with his favorite lame Stair Trak t-shirt. GingerJust Legal, a tall natural redhead, round faced, kept her hair shoulder length with bangs, and had enough curves and baby fat to still keep the doormen carding her on a Friday night.

Their conversation CUT THE ICE of interpersonal mediocrity with a keenness reminiscent of some never imagined renaissance race of people that can only be described as part Melchim X, 1/3 Steven Hawkling, an eighth Rob Dillon, 1/20th Castro, a fifth Zojernor Truth, and 100% Pretentious ASSHOLE!!!

"Do I really have sleep with your fat fuck 40-something friend from Portland while you jack off in the corner, Piggula, honey?" she said, batting her eyelids, affecting the demeanor of a hurt and shamed little girl (very poorly).

"I LOVE you intensely!" PigNose Diddler replied. "You complete me COMPLETELY.............as my own ideal regressed image-state of myself........something something, I want to BE YOU........something something, I need a penis by proxy...........something something, you've got an upscale trip to Palm Springs in your future if you let my childhood buddy, middle aged, closet child molestoresque friend rub his hairy gut on you in bed."

"OH PIGGULA, you DO LOVE ME!" GingerJust Legal replied with the enthusiasm of a kitten purring at the feet of a felicidal dirtbag with a loaded gun.............. "take me to the $200 per person after party when we leave the club, spend at least a cool $400 in drugs on me there, and let me tow my leech-nomad Reptilian friend, Jetty Jizz, with us to Palm Springs at your expense, and IT'S A DEAL!"

"MISSION ACCOMPLISHED!" Piggy thought, the level passing theme music from some 8-bit Nentindo game playing in his head as the vagina in his rectum rumbled.

At the bar, across the room from Pignose and GingerJust, sat Eggheaditty Tejano, and Yessica Rye.

Salted Plastic: The Comedic Horror of Gentrification

Both Eggheaditty and Yessica were halfies (Mexican and white), him with the same minimalist clone fashion as PigNose, plus a gut and wimpy scarecrow arms, her somewhat emaciated and a bit too skinny, but still well kept, with a keen awareness set default in the feminine features of her face. She was sharply dressed in a pin striped blazer, form fitted, with matching skirt, witch boots, and a REAL 19th century cameo (not that junk jewelry shit) over the top button of her dress shirt, set between the collar in lieu of a necktie. Her jet black hair was up in a short pony tail, revealing purple shaved sides beneath. Eggy was about early 30s, Yessica had just turned 41, but hardly looked it.

Eggheaditty stood around, fidgeting with his one of a kind, HIGHLY ORIGINAL, $175 designer couture............plain black t-shirt. Yessica sat on the stool at his side, looking pretty sad and completely over the night; Eggy's bullshit was bumming her out. As her junior, he retained notions of life in Los Angeles being a never ending music video, notions bred by too many nights spent impersonating fantasy rockstar status, with a microphone "hairbrush", while wearing his mother's neon legwarmers in front of his bedroom mirror growing up in Dallas. Because of this Eggheaditty felt that having a head that looked like a butter toffee jellybean turned on its side entitled him to a certain amount of INSTANT LA prestige among all the scripted weirdos, and yacht-club rich trash, that had transformed into urban street musicians the instant they slugged into Los Angeles from every high society hive in the United States.

But alas, poor poor Eggy had to accept that all his ramen noodle dick existence was going to land him was his bitchin older girlfriend, who had been there and done that (the whole local "celebrity" thing) often enough to want to do the absolutely unthinkable tonight (by his standards), which was just to go home and be a god damn adult.

Sure, she had run the gauntlet with band after band in her 20's and 30's, the history of which enticed this little maggot into taking an interest in her to begin with (Eggy wanted Yessica and him to be POWER

Salted Plastic: The Comedic Horror of Gentrification

COUPLE INDIE POP STARS on the cover of the LA Weakling), but what Yessica really wanted was to go home, watch some Rainy Fossbeinder, pour some scotch, and have Eggheaditty act like a man for once. This clash of priorities was a constant issue with them, and more often than not Yessica had to play mommy, and give the little crumb snatcher what he wanted; anything to ease his resentment regarding her past, and how it had inadvertently suggested to him that LA was the celebrity promised land where they were destined to rule as King and Queen.

"Did you make sure to rub cocoa butter on that Farmer Joan, pork slop leftovers, disgusting excuse of a ham-looking back-head of yours tonight?" Yessica muttered, as she sipped her Obenne double. Eggheaditty liked to skin bic his hair high in the back and sides, making sure to give himself the look of a pachycephalosaurus wearing a Hitler wig too small to cover anything but the front two thirds of the top of his head. Coupled with a pair of Sheiron designer eyeglasses, he looked strikingly like a half shaved testicle ready to read the morning paper.

"What was that?" Eggheaditty said, half oblivious to the fact that Yessica had even spoken. "I was dozing off; I'm sobering up here. You think you could buy me another 3 drinks while I mentally jerk-off to what the two of us would look like up on that stage?" Eggheaditty indicated nonchalantly, his finger pointed in the direction of the DJ booth.

"Sure," Yessica said, reserved and patient as a mother, sitting there in that old pin-striped blazer with leather piping on the lapels; nothing but a costume now in her estimate, leftover from times where a few hours of her life, and a few drops condensation of which, could outmatch in terms of creativity, good times, unyielding individuality, and raw intensity all the petty little posing pipedreams that Eggheaditty will ever have. "Anything you need Eggy….."

Oozing onto the sides of the DJ booth, hoping to catch a few crumbs of coolness to filter into their lack of personal substance, stood the top hierarchy of Los Angele's socialite culture; the mondains of music, the archons of acting, the fops of future fashion…………the connoisseurs of cock-sucking. It was a brine of the following: **beards,** and all other sorts of gross and moronic facial hair (what better way to hide ones late 30's and early 40's with mock youth than with greasy facial pubes? LONG LIVE ANTI-AGEISM!), **tech workers** (the neo-royalty of LA; young, rich, and boring!!!!! talking about where they went and what they spent with their money........babbling about their collection of shitty vinyl toys and pseudo nerd décor between frequent trips to the bathroom for powdered charisma), **Apparently Apparel** (overpriced minimalist dismal crap fashion made in the USA, and force fed to the public on the wings of an in-genuine interest in social progress by a greasy troglodyte of a pervert), **re-appropriated garment surplus marketed as nostalgia** (cocktail dresses that hadn't seen action outside of Central American nightclubs since 1992, peddled to the "fashion conscious" via the B before A self-fulfilling prophecy that retro is in), **triple outdated art school banter** (the same Dollé and Woorhal conversations reiterated since 1987, where one conversant invariably ends up labeled as a fascist, and the other as a slothful minimalist. YAWN!), **fictional conquest-bragging** ("........just got my first Bichelin star", "........script being optioned to Paramouth", "............my work being showcased in my land lady's garage...uhm, I mean.......in a REALLY obscure EXCLUSIVE URBAN TOUGH INNER CITY STREETWISE HIPPITTY HIP HIP art gallery" .... "Rusélle Crowe fucked my butt!"), **mock-flirtation as a cover up for back door networking** ("I'll just pre-game with a butt plug, and approach him with all smiles till he invites me back to his mansion in Reseda, where I'll get coked out, pretend to be dazzled by his car collection...............and I won't even notice that he's a sixty-something year-old hairy slob with a two-inch dick. That leading role is as good as mine!"), **AMAZING details from "gritty" urban "chefs" breaded in idiotic tattoos** (think whisks and spatulas made anthropomorphic by waxed mustaches and skinny jeans) about "gourmet" hamborger helpher (why go through the painstaking process of learning how to cook fine dining and managing a restaurant's back of house when you can just draw a crowd to your food truck with WEIRD and ATYPICAL bullshit like pouring pup roks onto sashimi, or cooled ranch Dooreetos Habanero Jellybean Mac n Cheese?) , **loud mouthed soliloquys and conversations about being a celebrity as applied to everything that the term was inapplicable towards** (celebrity barber, celebrity bicycle "mechanic", celebrity shoe shiner, celebrity carpenter, celebrity dog therapist..............CELEBRITY ASSHOLE!), **propaganda about cassette format music making a comeback** (jerk offs salivating over the idea of making top dollar with cheap outdated production standards), **ascot wearing anuses mispronouncing Buckewski's last name** ("I LOVE HIS BOOKS! BULEWSKI IS GREAT!") professing their ever dying love of a Los Angeles that they had lived in for a WHOPPING five minutes, and babbling about how they came to LA specifically to write a novel (that will never exist outside of being a conversation piece) just so they can seem introspective and magnetic enough to get someone to buy them a drink or go home and sleep with them, **demasculinized pseudo nerds** in their generic pre-faded comic book t-shirts, mentioning to any girl willing to talk with them that, at their trust-fund purchased Hill Street loft, the cocaine flowed in torrents that could only be outmatched by their closet sex offender anima ("mommy warned me about them dirty DIRTY city girls. OH GOD, I just can't wait!"), **fake as fuck "rockstars"** talking about being signed to non-existent labels (their own two minutes into existence label usually. Labels that had about as much commercial presence as tonight's pizza steadily becoming tomorrow's hangover shit).

Bulimic **"ballerinas"** (took two months of dance classes) from Denver, **artisanal "bakers"** (making "skillful" confectionary and baked "rarities" like HAND CRAFTED cupcakes and REFABRICATED brownies) from Minnesota, **copywriters** (casual bloggers and paid trolls with nothing better to do than talk shit on the internet while mentally and physically masturbating over their argumentative cyber conquests with a palm full of cheesy Chetoe resin) from Baltimore, **glassblowers** (meth

Salted Plastic: The Comedic Horror of Gentrification

heads experienced in sculpting old air fresheners) from Florida, **CUCKOLDS from Portland** (you know who you are), **professional photographers** (owning a camera = great way for a guy or girl with no personality to get daddy issue girls and vain pretty boys into to bed) from Connecticut, **recording artists** (a sound proofed room and an old laptop in their girlfriend's basement) from Jersey, **brew masters** (two months into learning how make beer that tastes like hydrogen peroxide mixed with stale espresso) from Kentucky, **tattoo artists COMPLETELY "tatted down BRO!"** (spent years getting high on heroin to block the pain so they wouldn't cry for daddy while being sleeved, jacketed and "FULLY TATTED BRO!" in silly shit like Frankenstein doing the twist in a jar of peanut butter, or campy film school art bitch nonsense like Steave Bushamee stylized as The Kat in The Hatte. This, plus a fresh set of guns, autoclaves and ink (courtesy of mam and pap) before trekking to LA equaled instant tattoo artist. "A few life drawing classes, a generic rocker look, and nobody will even notice that I'm a fidgety handed wimp that can't even do a straight line.") from Austin, **urban farmers** (patchs of heavy metal saturated backyard, excessive water waste, and mini disease factories ruining local water supplies just so some jerk can brag about her $8 per pound urban heirloom tomatoes) from San Francisco, **charcuterie owners** (opening a package of prosciutto and arranging it on a piece of plywood with some olives, baguette and dried figs from Trooder Joes, and calling yourself a butcher in a French, apparently transmutates any 130lb vegan dick, who doesn't even eat meat, into a full-fledged butcher!) from Seattle, **animators** ("I only do abstract painting! Learning about actual design techniques like photorealism, proper perspective and proportion is for art nazis. I'M DEFINITELY gonna become a Dizzey imagineer!") from Ohio, **university students** (rainbow spectrum of near do nothings, ranging from trustfund turds changing their no-future major with every conversation, to gypsy hookers staying with any man with his own place rent free, just so they can micro-nibble away at an easy degree while spending the majority of their time sitting

Salted Plastic: The Comedic Horror of Gentrification

in coffee houses, thrift shopping in Silverlake, sucking other guy's dicks, and taking shitstagram selfies for the next bidder).

Speaking of hookers, up in the DJ booth, babbling to Gayg, totally oblivious to the fact that Gayg has a penis, stood Jetty Jizz in her generic Lidia Launch/Nancie Spoogen mock-up look, whoreshoe shaped inner thighs shining brightly, expensive perm of curls primed for a semenal blasting, beaming obvious to the world that she is nothing more than a cheerleader wearing a cheaply bought bad-girl persona.

Jetty Jizz.......the Queen of Leeches, the Empress of Entitlement, the Duchess of Dicksucking........consciously posed in an affected, mock defiant, RAW energy stance straight out of some 1977 London punk photojournal, while some no name blog photographer took a pic of her with her arm around Gayg.

"Who's worth what here tonight?" she smiled while visually hawking through Gayg's records, hoping for a glance of some band she hadn't heard of yet...........one she could possibly mention in a conversation later to make herself seem HARDCORE! Gayg pretended not to hear Jetty while setting up the next track, Ultavoxe's Mr Z, on the turntable. Shit bored look on her/his face while surveying the room, and a "I hate my job" aura emanating from him/her. Giving Jizz tips on where to hunt for her next meal ticket was hardly what she/he felt up to, but then again, every ass he/she tickled meant another beacon for promotions.

"The guy with the denim daisy dukes, pleather biker jacket, and curly waxed mustache." Gayg said. "He owns Brick, Blanco Ladron, and Trust Fund Class Kitchen here in LA, and two other bars in New York."

"Which one, I don't see him," Jizz looked around the room, bright faced and excited like a chihuahua on speed, "you just described half the people in the room."

"The guy with the pre-faded machine aged Joi Vision shirt being handed a can of Piss Blue Ribbon right now," he replied, "got your name all over him!" Gayg smiled with contrived mischievousness, hoping to get Jetty off his back, finish his set, drive herself/himself home, and then diddle the books so she/he could see how much money he/she made from Brick's total bar sales for the night. "I only get 30% of the house take for the night, even after bringing in all these vapid turds with my club," Gayg thought, "I don't have the energy to be playing matchmaker here.

"OH!" Jetty replied, "HE'S SOO HOT!" Her well known ability (among all her lovers and ex-boyfriends in possession of at least half a brain) for being an inveterate liar, not only to them, but to herself, had warped her to the point of auto-belief on cue (she didn't really think the guy was hot prior to saying so) to anything that came out of her mouth. Some say a fluke accident during one of her first teenage blowjobs had resulted in a plaque of semen in her right brain which had entered via inner-mouth nasal cavity. This was the cause of her permanent inability to apply even rudimentary logic to anything other than a stringent diet of her own entitlement, the rules and reasons of why everything was always someone else's fault, and how, as a very very pretty "young" girl (Jetty is nearly 35 years old) she was entitled to only the best stress free pampered lifestyle that somebody else's money could buy.

Somewhere deep inside her, something knew that half the men she slept and lived with were tantamount to a cross between homeless men who had just won the lottery, and an ever affectionate father, placating her every move, because he knew his poor daughter was permanently 15 years old, and as such totally incapable of taking care of herself. But Jizz had the antidote against her unconscious in this case too; a long and drawn out attempt to seem like a strong, driven, empowered and independent woman that manifested itself via her ability to handle an associate's degree in ethnic sociology, which she had somehow managed to still be working on for a total of 8 years so far.

This, to date, had racked up a financial aid debt of nearly 50k, most of which had been spent on the following: dresses she just HAD TO HAVE, vacations every month, expensive cosmetics/skincare products, and supplementing the cost of her bills so she wouldn't have to work more than 12 hours a week, and could still invest time in VERY important things like posting semi-nude photos of herself on shitstagram that were doctored to the point of making her look 80% more attractive than she did in real life. All of the above kept her half-realization that she was a user and a leech at bay.

To be fair though, she could be quite giving..........if the return on the investment was right, and if it ripened on her demand. She had been known to periodically take some of that school loan money, which cost her not a single ounce of discomfort to earn like it would for a regular, self-sufficient, 40-60 hour a week lower class college student, and spend it (like a bribe) on whoever her latest living situation supplementing, and/or self-worth engendering male partner was. Buying him gifts, taking him out to eat, helping to pay his apartment's utilities (while living rent free) as long as he kept making her feel like a flawless prom-queen, with her not so intriguing, internet/past lover culled personality, there were no problems to discuss; the relationship was all good.

Like Mego Mann or San Tsung, she tended to steal and graft onto herself the elements of her conquests. This gave her the semblance of substance; music, style, movies, political minutiae; all downloaded via semen or streaming.

Once Jetty was called out on issues of logic and accountability in regards to her own behavior, though, the toddler tactics of being too tired to talk, and not entertained enough would ensue. As insane as it sounds, she had actually been fueled by such moments into believing it was "time to talk, cause things aren't working out." Perpetually the pity-party victim, she would cut said guy loose, after assessing that nothing more in terms of silent understanding and/or monetary resources could be harvested from him, with the idea than she had been cheated.

Following this it was then time for her to be a strong woman and walk away, with the only value left to harvest from the relationship being the amount of attention she would be milking out of the break-up story on social media for the next few weeks; a lovely tale of how "brave" she was for "ending a toxic relationship". These weak and/or stupid saps would usually recover and find a real woman, but some were not so fortunate; of the last two, one had resorted to drugs, and the other had lost his business due to her thoughtless machinations.

Licking her thin, un-augmented by photo filter lips, she stepped down from the DJ booth, and into the crowd towards the rich bitch with his silly waxed mustache, wearing his pair of women's denim pantihose.

Salted Plastic: The Comedic Horror of Gentrification

Saturday, August 9, 1:36 am

Miguel Lyons zoned out in front of his tv, DS3 controller in hand, equalized on Vicodin, playing a popular game that was a few years old now. The basic concept of the game was that your character, in a limbo-state half-life, needed to absorb the souls of fallen enemies. These souls were both a currency and life force that your character harvested from various dragons, demons, diseased minions and undead legions; thirty hours into the game and he hadn't even scratched the surface. Not that it mattered; this was regressive entertainment at its best, just a way to not think, to block out his realization that his girlfriend Rebekah had recently slipped up and revealed that she was indeed............a reptilian.

A small fortune of creams, face masks, and collagen serums, and she had still failed to keep her very pretty looking human-skin mask from deteriorating. The dryness on her face first manifested as malcontent with just his attention alone; she needed the world at large to know she was no longer a chubby tadpole with issues of inferiority. This took a lot of effort to maintain, so her loving girlfriend act had suffered in its performance; it's hard to maintain a real life role for one man 24/7 when it's so much easier to just edit a photo taken at a favorable angle, and then get a thousand online slime ball strangers to make you feel hot as shit, when the reality is you're just a piece of hot shit.

That said, Miguel was spending the evening droned zero while Reptilian Rebekah passed out, her headphones still on and plugged into her laptop, while episode after episode of bland sitcoms played. The truth unknown to Miguel was this though; Rebekah was a runt in the estimate of her species, and could not access or verbalize the higher levels of her subconscious. Apparently the maternal lizard that had laid the egg Rebekah originally hatched from had eaten too many al pastor burritos (pork is highly poisonous to reptilians), which led to severe dysfunction in Rebekah's logical functionality. This kept her totally inept relative to avoiding double standards in relationships, and blocked her from understanding the limits of entitlement in polite society.

This birth defect also inhibited the external functionality of the high level of methodical intelligence other reptilians were known for. To alleviate this deficiency, her parents had raised her to become very attached to shitty television shows, which she had been watching her whole life. This hunger for audio-visual diarrhea carried over into adulthood with the likes of shows like How I Fucked Your Brother, and Possum, a 90s show about a teenage girl who looked like a didelphidae with horrid taste in fashion; she never suspected that it all served a dual purpose, that she was absorbing supplementary knowledge during sleep cycles (via the coded subliminals in tv shows usually reserved for non-reptilians). This kept her functioning as a sort of clockwork parasite, very efficiently, and without her being aware of it.

It had in fact become a benefit for her people, in that she could maintain the pretense of caring for Miguel, warming up to him on a conscious level, believing her own little bullshit act, while innately and intuitively operating as an insect in her higher brain activity, formulating ways to keep Miguel weak and feeling unmerited safety. In addition, the Reptilian Ministry of Technology had installed nanotech in Rebekah's bloodstream that served as a sort of remote control for her behavior when needed. This duo-conscious infiltration ability, seemingly a fluke, had intrigued the higher ups in reptilian power circles. Intrigued them so much in fact that attempts were now underway to duplicate Rebekah's "rare mutation".

Miguel knew she was a reptilian, yes, with her ability to glamour into a full figured Euro beauty one minute, followed by revealing her true nature as a misshapen unhygienic slob the next, but his Aristotelian two-value mind-set still held doubts in the face of his inability to match up his gut feeling about her intentions with the apparent sweetness of her overt performance. It was easy to chalk up her online flirting to a desperate need for her to seek therapy for daddy issues, and possibly as a result of getting picked on in elementary school over her looks, but a few theatrical protestations on her part about his lack of understanding, coupled with undoubtedly genuine tears (manufactured by her mask), and he would invariably fall into doubting his assessment, and believe he was simply unfocused and still healing from past misfortunes that he was unfairly projecting onto "poor Rebekah".

That said, the best he could manage in reaction to the situation was to drown it, sublimate it with opiates and videogames. He'd already lost his first love, and had been convinced that perfection was not a must in any further partners. Unfortunately for him, this was fueling his lack of motivation to dig deeper and find out why he had a feeling that something just wasn't right about this thing called Rebekah.

He both knew and didn't know that she was/wasn't what she was. It was like seeing a turd on your pillow that just might be a piece of chocolate, but the only way to find out for sure is to get closer and take a whiff and expose yourself to possible discomfort through the act of doing so.

"Too much effort to bother," he half thought, "maybe tomorrow......"

Salted Plastic: The Comedic Horror of Gentrification

Monday, August 11, 1:30 pm

Lance and Meredith smiled face to face, rubbing noses and kissing as they sat on matching zafus in a Highland Park, CA real estate "office". They waited patiently for the real estate agents who ran the place to come back from the kitchen with tea and eco-friendly, free trade, gluten free, dairy omitted, culturally diverse, refabricated component, farm to table, locally crafted, sustainably sourced, gender neutral, vegan karma kookies. Both barely 23 years old, married right after college, they had just arrived fresh from Minnesota, ready to spread bold new ideas (and their trust funds) in LA. A non-descript basic pair; white, freckles, brown hair, moderately out of shape, they looked like a million other people that flocked to LA every year.

"So, do you two take decocted almond activated charcoal milk in your tea, or would you prefer some freshly stone ground coconut maca butter?" Deirdre Price said, as her and Guru Douche came back from the kitchen, vintage Art Deco tea tray in hand. Lance and Meredith took a minute to answer, soaking in the "great vibes" impression being set by the obvious and unquestionably progress-forward energy of the real estate office's décor.

Before either of them could answer, Caesar Chavez Rosa Parks Che Gandhi Cat came purring between Lance and Meredith. "Ohhh! How cute!" Meredith said, petting the fluffy grey Chartreux cat.

"Is it a she or a h..." Lance began, but immediately stopped himself, turning red and starting to lightly perspire as he realized his mistake.

"Caesar Chavez Rosa Parks Che Gandhi Cat actually identifies as gender fluid." Guru Douche answered, tone and contrived smile set to indicate with autopilot poise and precision a stance of calm patience and understanding, while simultaneously multi-tasking his performance as the guiding mystic in matters of social progress.

16

Salted Plastic: The Comedic Horror of Gentrification

"How's the tea dear?" Deirdre said as Meredith took a sip, "Those loose tea leaves were individually blessed by trans-gender millennial Zen co-op farmers, and purchased with only the latest, hip-centric crypto-currency on the market; we only consume the finest in pretentious progress-forward status symbols in this house; we even have an herb and citrus garden cultivated by local permaculture savvy celebrity botanists."

"It's fine," Meredith said, indicating the tea, starting to feel mildly creeped out by the circus-like social performance manifesting in the real estate office. "Going vegan for the five minutes it takes to brag about how eco-conscious you are over cold brew coffee enemas with your besties is one thing, but this is just going overboard," she thought.

"So let's get down to business then," Guru Douche interrupted. "Shall we all start getting nA........

"Why don't we take them on a tour first, Guru?" Deirdre cut in semi-nervously, biting her lower lip while brushing back a few strands of graying hair with her fingertips. Both her and Guru where up there; late 40s or early 50s, but in great condition due to a highly rigid diet of expensive fucking shit, and exclusive ass shit. Deirdre kept her hair in a tight bob, bangs gray, with the rest black, streaked with gray. She was fairly short, and even though both her and Guru Douche wore matching loose fitted Indian kurtas, it was still apparent that she had a curvaceous figure under all that loose clothing. Guru was tall, in permanent smile-mode, always baked on sativa, and somewhat Rickard Gear looking.

"Well, you've seen the office." Douche said, waving his hand around at the room's new age/millennial/vintage/hip/Zen décor setup that was meant to create the ultimate experience in social revolution.

To begin with, the "sitting room" was actually a composite of the kitchen and an adjoining laundry room which contained an old world style scrubbing board (hand crafted from re-appropriated sustainable timber of course), a few copper basins, a sandalwood coffee table, the two zafus Lance and Meredith sat on, and a custom made Egyptian cotton mural of Freida Culöhe re-imagined as the goddess Kali. A wet bar semi-separated the laundry from the kitchen, coming to about chest level, with a view over the top showcasing some of the vapid shit contained within, such as a vintage-style icebox which was really a façade for a state of the art energy saving smart fridge with antibacterial lining. This kitchen area is where Deirdre and Guru had been standing during the whole conversation, looking down on Lance and Meredith; marketing classes had taught Douche and Deirdre the benefits of "spatially induced guidance", a term designed to smooth the edges of blatant and obvious, visually initiated authoritarianism.

Now, I could talk for hours about the pretentious nature of these two rooms alone, but I'm sure you get the idea……………UHM, one more thing; over the kitchen sink hung a special brand of Norwegian sponge, which, according to the advertisement playing in a continuous loop on the Eyepad mounted next to it (Guru and Deirdre never passed an opportunity to micro-market…..uhm, that is………to spread progress), was self-cleaning, full of live bacteria, maximized oxygen purity within its vicinity with every use, was only a measly $47, and side funded awareness of cryptocurrency economics.

"Let's step out back through the door behind you two, and look at the garden," Deirdre said. Lance and Meredith stood up, and all four of them stepped outside.

"There are sandals to your right," Douche mentioned, "sorry about making you leave your shoes at the door earlier, but you never know what sort of chakric disharmony the streets have these days."

The backyard grass was pure green, as in "my life is lax enough to the point where I can meticulously baby sit each and every fucking blade of grass" green. An enclosed garden with a torii gate opening into it dominated half the yard, half a dozen drum sized compost tumblers a quarter, and a mock hot springs Jacuzzi the other quarter.

"Inviting, isn't it!?" Douche said, noticing Meredith glancing at the Jacuzzi bubbling, leering behind her back, stumbling slightly from some ginger chew edibles he had eaten earlier which were just now kicking in, that smile of his starting to lax into a slimy lecherous grimace. Lance noticed this, didn't particularly like it, and was about to say as much, when a strawberry popped into his line of vision.

"TOTALLY organic," Deirdre said, "and picked fresh from my still FLOURISHING and FERTILE garden!"

"Umm, they're very healthy looking." Lance said, a little nervous due to the unwavering/unblinking stare Deirdre gave him, strawberry still held out to his face, obviously intending for him to take a bite. He leaned in, looking away from her, and her hand, AND the strawberry, and took a bite. He started to chew, eyes closed, and then got startled by the feel of Deirdre's thumb wiping a bit of red pulp off his lower lip.

"Uhm........thanks," Lance said, "that was good," his voice a little jumpy. Deirdre peered past Lance, and saw Guru Douche going through his usual spiel on Taoist pressure points with Meredith, emphasizing that the most potent benefits to be had were from chi manipulation in the inner thigh and anus regions.

"Well, I think they've seen enough of the garden Guruuuu," Deirdre sung, "let's all go inside and discuss some of the finer points of joint tenancy."

Salted Plastic: The Comedic Horror of Gentrification

Sunday, August 10, 2:34 pm

Miguel parked in a rooftop complex off Maple and 6th in Downtown. Getting out of the car, he checked his jacket for keys, wallet, and phone; everything all there and ready, he went to a set of doors across the lot, and walked through to a stairwell leading down to street level on Maple. Coming out onto the street, Miguel lit up a cheap French cigarette; he recently started ordering these through the mail after local tobacco shops stopped carrying Euro tobacco due to a change in export laws. It was one of those rare cold days in LA; a nice grey overcast lowering the temperature more than usual. This gave him the opportunity to pop on his new biker cut canvas cotton jacket. The design was very futuresque, with suede shoulder padding and collar piping. Besides the jacket, he also sported some fitted black denims and a pair of custom made leather mock Converse with straps and buckles. He usually wore slimmer sizes in everything, since he kept pretty fit due to a mild health issue. Yeah, he was dressed sharp today, but still felt pretty grimey; lazing around the house for several days, he hadn't showered or fully groomed properly; this gave an oily sheen to his tan skin, and his low cropped pompadour looked greasier than usual. Not to mention that he was detoxing from all those nasty opiates, and was super dehydrated.

Taking a deep breath, he took a look around; the streets were crowded with people walking around the fringe area of DTLA, between the downtrodden, steadily being colonized Skid Row, and the already done and gentrified Pershing Square bound side. Los Angeles Street seemed to divide the two; the contrast was night and day; working class on one side for the most part...............and walking appetites on the other. Just by simply crossing the street your relative (relative to local business services and goods) income bracket could be decimated or upgraded. Skid Row-bound side would get you botanica herbs, a pair of suede shoes, a strawberry licuado, a new stereo and some pupusas for less than $80; the Pershing Square-bound side would probably run you

Salted Plastic: The Comedic Horror of Gentrification

$30 just for parking and a cup of some amateur roaster's pretentious coffee.

This is probably an exaggeration, but the general idea is this; an invisible class wall could drop on you in almost any fucking corner of Los Angeles these days. Funny thing though; if you asked the average shiftless bearded "artist" walking down Broadway what they thought of the matter, they'd go into some BS monologue about how excited they were about the new ALL-INCLUSIVE LA!!!!! They'd shamelessly babble about how great it is that the class barriers had fallen, and we can all just integrate and enjoy together. Now, I could be wrong, but I don't think Birch on Hill Street, or Fate and Fowler on 9th Street, or Poo and Pauper on Spring Street, OR ANY OTHER of these pretentious downtown shitholes are charging on a fucking sliding scale so EVERYBODY in Los Angeles can enjoy the perks of LA's new phantom all-inclusiveness. No, don't think so; most long time, low income LA residents can't afford to spend any more than $10-$15 per person on dinner these days. That said, these places are running WAYYYY past that kind of money for just hors d'oeuvres or one lousy "hand crafted" (apparently mixed drinks used to be made by robots before these places opened) cocktail.

And the fun didn't stop there. You'd think the biggest laugh of being mentally forced to swallow extremely moronic fantasy ideas of social progress would stop with the fake all-inclusiveness, but no; the most cherishable stupidity came in the form of the type of food they served at these shitholes.

I know I'm not getting very creative here, describing them as shitholes twice already, but no other descriptive does justice in my opinion. Nothing else so thoroughly makes it clear that a place that does silly shit like market its dining area as environmentally interactive art, or sells "gourmet" hotdogs at steakhouse prices, is some scummy ass, insulting to the intellect, sideshow nonsense.

Scratch that actually; sideshow is too good of a word for these SHITHOLES, cause a sideshow would actually do its patrons the courtesy

Salted Plastic: The Comedic Horror of Gentrification

of putting the word "show" into the business description; these places were either unwilling to (totally conscious of their marketing strategy), or unaware (unoriginal business model enthusiasts) of the fact that their supposed restaurant establishments were just circuses masquerading as humble places to sit down and eat. It was no longer about what you served and whether or not it was good; the name of the game for the shithole restaurant model was semantics, media blitz and how full of shit your shithole could be. If every bar and bistro on Broadway only served tater tots and burgers with raspberry aioli, nobody would give two shits as long as Welpers and influencers screamed online about the al fresco dining, and LA Monthly continued to write sponsored content for these shitholes.

The LA restaurant racket, with its bullshit brand of recession gourmet, could push anything given the right furniture and shitshow nonsense hype about celebrity chefs and eco-conscious architecture, or whatever the fuck! A Vietnamese spot on Hill, with a bare bones white washed menu of bánh mì and pho, would receive substantially more hype, and a steadier flow of patrons, than something WAY more authentic in San Gabriel Valley. And for what?! Just because they showcase local "artist's" half assed work on their walls, and played elevator music?! Every asshole in LA ran the same gimmick; woodfired AUTHENTIC NEW YORK pizza, smoked bone marrow (funny, I thought that was a garnish, or an ingredient for soup stock), pomme frites and overpriced sausages, ramen with dashi that tasted like piss...........farm to table this........paleo that.........vegan, raw, small bites, quick bites, etc.

A big plate of overpriced sweet starch, in an even sweeter vomit inducing sauce, would go for twenty or more dollars a plate as long as you called it vegan, and your location was close enough to Sunset and Alvarado, or Hyperion and Sunset. I'm talking about the sister shitholes here now, down in Silverlake and Echo Park.

The most basic household dishes brought herds of assholes calling themselves foodies (goddamn baby talk!!!!) to the table. Who

22

knew that being an aficionado of food (and labeling oneself as such) would breed this idiotic notion that they are a class apart from everyone else on earth that also eats food? These people prided themselves on consuming other people's "creative" endeavors in a way that suggested that this somehow made them more of an interesting person just because they had a fucking moniker for the fact that they went out food hunting.......as if this was some brand new thing that no one in the past (up until now) had done!

Menus at their favorite restaurants contained such nauseating and pretentious descriptives as "foraged champignons" (demonstrating the head chef's doubly full of shit ability to both flaunt his tenuous grasp on French, and the absurd notion that seeking one's food in the wild held some merit above that of purchasing it from a produce supplier), "deconstructed meatloaf" (essentially ground beef, onions, raw egg, ketchup, and other condiments served separately in individual dishes. Genius, huh?!), mentioning the farm a particular piece of produce in a dish came from, as if it's supposed to elicit some instant feeling of familiarity and appreciation from the customer; "...........and charred Davis Heirloom Tomatoes served over a bed of........." (who the fuck is Davis, and why should I give a fuck? How does this lend more weight to the taste and value of the fucking tomatoes?!?!).

The gimmicks also played the act thematic-wise, as if everybody in LA was permanently regressed into being 16 to 25, and so perpetually thirsty for a brand of consumerism that made them feel like they were forever young, that they'd pay fine dining prices for "upgraded" versions of fast food. Burger joints where the "grillmasters" expected to be paid handsomely just because the menu had stupid shit faced themed items that played on everything from tastes in music, to a person's opposing political agenda, to some currently progress-forward social endeavor. Chefs and restaurant owners were that desperate to mask their meager level of skill and/or desire to keep a low overhead (via selling only cheap bar and diner type food), that they doctored up the "fare" available

Salted Plastic: The Comedic Horror of Gentrification

(FUCK, I hate that term; it makes me want to brand the menu writer's tongue with hot iron) with a handful of atypical ingredients, and some irrelevant cultural associations. This was the neo-marketing strategy for tons of places serving altogether mediocre food, that just about anybody with a rudimentary level of cooking ability could pull off.

A fucking hamburger is just cheap, low grade cut fast food, but pop on a brioche bun, and call it "The Freddie MercurBrie", and some tool with a vintage vinyl collection just might drop $30 on what would otherwise cost about a third of that somewhere else. Call a sandwich something stupid like "Make America Grape Again", and put a picture of Trumpe stylized as a cartoon elephant eating peanuts on the menu, and most idiots won't care that they're spending $14 on a pb&j as long as they can initiate the jackass behavior of taking a selfie of themselves holding up the menu, and pointing to the sandwich while they pretend to take a bite for their Shitstagram.

Wanna try pizza called "Siouxsie and the Bleucheese" for a meager $9 per slice at a "PUNK ROCK" pizzeria on Broadway?! Or how about an infant's portion of cheese and crackers, with fresh fruit at $40 per shared plate?!?! Insulting bullshit; who shares something that's not even filling enough for one grown adult? It's all good though, no worries; the selling angle is a plug on the menu for a FemRights Cheesemonger Co-op named "The Future is Fromage." **Hippitty Hip HIP HIP!!!!!!!**

And that's just the establishments; the people frequenting and running them were something else entirely. But we'll get deeper into that later; let's get back to Miguel.........now that were done with that lovely segue into the finer points of recession gourmet.

Miguel walked into a warehouse on the corner of 6th and Maple; the place was full of booths for rent, some inhabited with vendors, some bare ass empty. The stuff the vendors sold ranged from brass knuckles to rosaries, essential oils to knock off dress shoes. Big tacky catholic paintings, tortas, incense, bootleg ranchera cd's, Islamic paraphernalia, candles to give your mother in law the evil eye, cheap China-made

Salted Plastic: The Comedic Horror of Gentrification

action figures, paisa-ass looking wallets, booth vendors picking their nose.........and pussy boots, AKA OGGz. Among all this, one place stood out from the rest, a super crowded booth that was often frequented by Miguel when he was physically, emotionally and mentally shot down and fucked.

The herbalist who ran it was giving prescriptions and advice to a big line of people; viejos complaining about their "diabetEEs", young Mexican and Central American girls having problems with conception, and people with all sorts of aches and pains.

Ever since Miguel's last girlfriend had left him, he'd been coming to see German Agpalo for advice and treatment; the herbs he prescribed never failed, even though all the high end overpriced new age quacks in Pasadena and Santa Monica never came through with their so called alternative "medicine". His first visit was two weeks into Jessica leaving; he'd only slept about 19 hours, and was a total mess. Colloidal gold and some Chinese herbs, and Miguel was back to his 8 hours a night after a couple of days.

Four months later, and German was teaching Miguel knife fighting, Indonesian grappling, and Jeet Kun Do, insisting that it would be key to him strengthening his core to deal with some spinal issues Miguel had been battling for years. German's mother, from Jalisco, had taught him all about Mexican herbology. His father, a Chinese/Filipino martial artist, and professional acupuncturist, had made sure German went to TCM school to learn Chinese herbs and medicine. German made good money helping people, but didn't seek to market himself to just the highest bidder......even though he definitely could if he wanted to. The crowd of would be green alternative types could very easily be his bread and butter; hived up in their PCH communities along the coast, just waiting for the opportunity to brag, via social media, about the latest OH SO HIP, free trade loose tea leaf shop, or transcendental "Buddhist" spa retreat, with complementary fortune cookie mantras, that they had recently visited. He kept it humble though, and was all about helping the people most in need.

Miguel signed in, and gave German a quick nod; seeing he was busy, and that the wait would be awhile, he walked back out of the warehouse onto 6th street. Looking around, he noticed all the homeless and junkies on the corner, holed up in make shift tents built out of a composite of cardboard boxes, tarps, and old blankets. "Far cry from the Hipster Dizzeyland right in fucking front of me!" Miguel said as he walked in the direction of Los Angeles street, going up towards all those lovely shitholes, "artist" "dives", dime a dozen overpriced cafes, and clothing boutiques that housed displays more interesting than the low grade clothing they sold for asshole prices.

"Got about an hour to burn by the looks of that line." He muttered to himself. "Maybe I'll check out that FABULOUS hip new bookstore all these trust fund turds keeping babbling about in the LA Weakling."

As Miguel walked up 6th he lit another Gaulvous, took a drag and exhaled. He was on the verge of another one of his internal monologues about how he hated what was happening to LA, the disgust mounting in him as he looked around, but was interrupted mid-thought by a "Hey man, you wanna save a wolf today?!"

Before even turning to see who issued the question, Miguel already knew he wasn't going to like what he was about to see; the weasel-like voice oozed weakness bred by privilege………….privilege, and a low collagen intake.

Turning around, he saw it in all its obnoxious glory; white kid, 20 or 30 something, overpriced shoes that supposedly ended third world labor standards with every purchase, a shitty Apparently Apparel plain t-shirt that cost the price of a designer leather jacket, jeans that looked like a denim diaper with denim panty hose sewn to them, and a GREASY, throat caking, tick infested, veganaise smeared, moronic and filthy, classless beard........ complete with jackass looking waxed and curled stache.

The guy was a poster boy for Los Angeles' new social elite. The people that broke or made every culinary, musical, social, artistic, or real estate driven endeavor; the gentrifying, out of state, trust fund, half measure artist, loser-ass, "mommy and daddy still pay my rent at 38", pseudo-effete, scumbag culture raping hipster.

He stood leering at Miguel, waiting for a positive response to his question as if it was a fucking given. First thing to cross Miguel's mind came out of his mouth.......

"Man........are you joking?! You got homeless junkies dying a block away, and you're asking me if I want to donate to a wolf preservation? I'm assuming this is your job, if you want to call it that, and that you're not serious about what you're doing here, right?"

"Whoah!!!! No need for all the negative vibes guy, I was just trying to........" the guy started to exclaim, but was cut off by.......

"Yeah, you're right." Miguel sneered condescendingly, as he looked down smiling, exhaling his cig out of his nostrils. He'd already anticipated the little turd's scripted response, having heard more of the same so many times. "I suppose anything other than answering you type of people in the affirmative, no matter what you're currently selling or doing, would seem negative to you. A social breeding program consisting of perpetual pats on the back, not struggling for your needs, getting a trophy at every turn for your efforts, and then living in a major city, pseudo slumming it.......without the struggles and consequences of ACTUALLY slumming it, will do that to one's perspective on rough honesty."

Beard bitch started to open his mouth, but was interrupted by Miguel again. "I'm gonna stop right there though, cause I can see you don't have the E.Q. or contrast to get what I'm feeling...........plus I got shit to do, like working a real job, instead of just playing agent for a cause I'm not even emotionally invested in so I can avoid real work, right? I'll

Salted Plastic: The Comedic Horror of Gentrification

leave you with that to think about!" Miguel pointed toward the tents and tarps making up residence for the homeless across Los Angeles street. "You wanna play hero FOR REAL? There's your opportunity right down the street, right in front of you. Plenty of people there that need some help."

Miguel hadn't been looking at Vegan Vag during the end of his tirade, or he would have noticed that for the last couple of seconds that he had stopped listening, and was checking his phone intermittently between trying to grab other passerby's attention.

That was Miguel though; he liked the sound of his own voice so much, that once he got himself going not even the most obvious physical manifestations of disinterest kept him from finishing his session of shit talking. He knew it, but could give two shits though; no more than Mr. Hipster Millennial gave a shit about wolves, in fact.

"Just what I thought," Miguel said, snubbing his cig out on the concrete, "fucking sales bitch over here!"

Throatbeard Cumgurgler was already engrossed in a sale for donations with a girl who had a turquoise fauxhawk, a nice set of legs, and a $1,400 designer purse custom-ruined with "WE ARE THE 99%" on it in vegan paint.

Salted Plastic: The Comedic Horror of Gentrification

Sunday, August 10, 1:47 pm

Captain Felch Leavings combed his slicked back pomaded hair in the mirror, with intermittent brakes to check his phone and gut.

Pet hair, check phone, pet hair, check phone, smooth gut, wax stache, insert miniature buttplugs in ear piercings, check phone, pet hair, annnnnnnnd...........

"Ready for work!" Felch said, as he vainly looked in the mirror one last time, buttoning up his chef's apron. His phone chimed again, causing him to smile with a self-satisfied, affected tough guy grimace (the type you might find elicited by very "manly" actors in some old biker film..............stock variety bullshit designed to tough off) as he reached for it.

His Fakebook messenger showed the latest message in a thread of such he had been exchanging for the last 15 minutes:

Felch: Has it been that bad?

Reptilian Reb: It's complicated.

Felch: You need to talk? Wanna get coffee in Atwater or something? I don't need to be to work for another couple of hours. I'm here for ya. ☺

Reptilian Reb: Ummm, sure, I could use the support, I really can't take this right now, especially with the stress of working 12 hours a week lately. Lemme get ready and get back to you.

Felch: K

"Ha!" Felch exclaimed, fake as fuck laugh, staged for no one other than himself. "Good, I haven't been fed for a bit; break-ups and the disloyalty between friends and their ladies is light lately. THANKS

29

Salted Plastic: The Comedic Horror of Gentrification

GUY!" he said, talking to no one present, but meaning Miguel. Felch laughed again, his man gut/boobs heaving.

You see, Felch has a very particular, one of a kind diet, that requires plenty of patience, smooth cunning, and a sniveling weasel's amount of social performance to procure. Now, I'm not talking weight loss here. Nor paleo, vegan, pescetarian, macrobiotic, gluten free, raw, etc. He wasn't on a doctor's restriction due to some ailment either, nor attempting to bulk up for body building purposes.

No, his particular envie culinaire was for a rare and precious byproduct that could only be obtained via the declining relationships of those within his social circle. It was for something that came more or less in variant grades of what he considered saveur élevée, and he was gaming for the jackpot here.

Felch went to his closet, his favorite place to be in the whole wide world, and dug out an old timey looking cedar box. This box was about 6 inches long, 2 wide, and fairly shallow looking. He leered over the surface of the box, perspiration gathering grease-like as it reflected the sparse amount of illumination in the closet; you couldn't see much of anything in there, and that's the way Felch liked it............there in the closet. It was his man-cave, and about seventy percent the size of his apartment's actual bedroom. He came there often, either for supplies, as in this moment, or when he ran low on important things................like false persona (he had a large selection of TOUGH MEN action films), material for inspirational quotes (a laptop sat on a table in the closet, the search permanently set to page after page of vapid and generic quote sites he employed to make himself seem introspective), and all varieties of frozen and date labeled "leavings" he had harvested from past conquests. These last were kept in a mini-fridge with a combination lock on it.

"BUT NOW I need something fresh," Felch said, "and I'm gonna get it..........WITH THIS!!!!" he dramatically exclaimed as he held high above his head the contents of the cedar box, marveling at it as if it was his own personal Excalibur.

In his hand, held high, as he glared at it as if it was some sort of holy icon, was a golden straw, well-polished for the most part, but with a faint trace of what looked like dried egg yolk and Frusted Flakes resin at the tips.

"Eh heh heh heh!," Felch laughed maniacally, "I'm coming for you GUY!!!" he continued in a puny/nasally contrived tone, with emphasis on the UY in "GUY!!!", as if he was some goon in an old detective movie. "I'll show you whose man enough KIDDO!" Again with the same default pathetic switch in tone, supposedly designed to emphasize how tough Felch was, this time in the word "KIDDO."

"I'm gonna felch ya, I'M GONNA FELCH YOUR LEAVINGS!!!!!"

Salted Plastic: The Comedic Horror of Gentrification

Sunday, August 10, 3:32 pm

"It's an obscure cult classic that nobody's EVER heard of......"

"Vinyl........vinyl shopping......"

"......new exhibit opening at The Brood....."

"Being optioned for a tv drama....."

"......agent only getting me commercial roles........doesn't understand that I have a background in traditional theatre......"

"$1800 a month for a studio apartment?!?! Never see that back in New York...."

The chatter at Miguel's favorite Italian Deli advertised every level of privilege, pretention, vanity, and cheap shot attention fishing possible.

He smiled and took notes, enjoying a pastrami with marinara, while taking intermittent breaks to swipe left MANY MANY times on some dating app. He was lonely, very lonely, and halfway resolved to ending it for good with Rebekah, but he wasn't so desperate (yet) that he would attempt to start dating again with some 30- something year old girl who superimposed animal features on her face in an attempt to manifest the 16-year-old within.

Putting the phone back down, he looked around. The place was one of those "my spot" type places in LA...........or, at least it used to be, long before welpers felt a need to appropriate and checklist any place magnetic enough to be talked about, whether they actually liked the food or not.

Miguel almost vomited in his mouth as some emaciated, 20- something hipster with severe age lines (due to improper collagen and

Salted Plastic: The Comedic Horror of Gentrification

amino intake) asked Dino, the owner, if they had any vegan-gluten free options. Dino shook his head, explaining to the girl that this was a traditional Italian deli, and was about to lay one of his famous one liners on her, but got called into the back of house by his nephew to discuss "keeping it moderate" with the new clientele. After deciding not to order anything, the girl walked over to a wall with black and white shots of old LA, and took a few selfies for her review of the place. Miguel, mildly irritated that Dino's nephew, now the new manager, was obviously geared towards pleasing these turds, looked away in disgust.

He checked his phone; another 40 minutes till his appointment with German. "Better finish up and start walking back soon." he whispered to himself while scribbling in a small note book. He paused, eating and checking his phone again.........when it hit him; all of a sudden he felt a tug on his nerves, as if someone was perched on his shoulder analyzing his every move. Like some slimy entity had him under a microscope, as if he was some sort of zoo animal being made available to teach this thing how to be less of a process, and more of human being.

He turned, and sure enough, right behind him, some douche with a fashion wrap was eyeing his notes, while no doubt simultaneously scanning and quantifying whatever else he possibly could about Miguel.

"Can I help you?" Miguel said, emphasizing his irritation as clearly as possible.

"Oh!" Keff DoucheWrap exclaimed in mock surprise, trying to play it off like he wasn't just executing a value analyses and culture theft mere seconds ago. "Just wanted to check if it's cool for me to sit here; you got four seats, and it's just you, so I thought, ya know communal, something something, beard, something something......have you been coming here a long time, or did you just find out about this place?"

Now, Miguel knew his instinctive answer/reaction would bury him in this situation (as far as avoiding the exact behavior that was even now making him wish he could choke hold this little methodical maggot), but his pride made him say it anyway......

Salted Plastic: The Comedic Horror of Gentrification

"I've been eating here my whole life............ever since I was about 10 years old."

That DID IT! Keff sat down, uninvited, wide-eyed, scanning Miguel's shirt as he did, making a mental note to purchase every album by the band on it later (regardless of whether he liked them or not) for the purpose of more cultural graft. Leaning into the table, he then attempted to begin what Miguel liked to call (after experiencing this kind of shit a 1,000 times in recent years) The Transplant Interview.

"Wow!" Keff said, picking some dried director's semen out of his beard that he had procured during an audition for a commercial in Studio City earlier. "So you're an LA local, huh? I'm from Ohio myself..........."

"Look, I got an appointment....." Miguel broke in, obviously irritated, and rose out of his chair, appetite ruined....

"Hey!" Cumbeard exclaimed nervously (and a bit too loud) as he reached out towards Miguel's arm. "Just trying to be positive and welcoming..........something something.......your energy needs some editing.......something something........."

"Same old litany," Miguel thought, insulted by hearing this garbage time and time again from these turds; standardized phrases about energy from people with zero conscientiousness. Rehashed diatribes about communal exchange and respect from shitheads that lived to take, eat, destroy and absorb everything about LA (as if they were mining natural resources), with their version of giving back (if they did at all) manifesting itself in more of the same behavior. His favorite was when they "beautified" decades of LA River murals by scrubbing and painting over them, and then followed up this act with gallery invitations to local graffiti artists to showcase their work.........for a minor cut of their sales of course.

Normally he would have worn himself ragged trying to explain to KeffCumgurgler that he was too inexperienced and contrast bankrupt to ever understand what an insult him and his were to a lot of long time LA residents, but something about this kid seemed (felt rather) uglier than usual. He just wanted to get up and go, not waste his energy for once.

Resolved to just let it go and leave, he failed to notice, till this minute, that this process of a person, this programmed to acquisition insect, this.....this THING, had it's hand on his arm. This broke his cool immediately. Scanning the room to see if anyone was looking, especially the local police that always came here for lunch, and noticing everyone occupied, Miguel swiped the guys hand off with mild violence.

Expecting the usual cry for security, Miguel was surprised that Keff was more concerned with concealing the hand, trying vainly to pull his sleeve down further than it would go. Before he could get it completely out of view though, Miguel noticed a spot of skin that looked broken and dry.........green and ashy.

"What the fuck!" Miguel said loud enough to show he was pissed, but low enough not to draw attention. "Did you just touch me even though you got some skin disease or some shit? What the fuck, you little asshole!"

"Careful!" Keff said in a menacing whisper..........and then quickly morphed into a louder tone of contrived outcry. "I've had enough of your bullying man, and I don't have any skin condition, least of all something contagious, or anything you should be allowed to shame me for!" A mildly arrogant and knowing sneer was at the corners of his mouth, totally out of character with his little victim act, like deep down inside he knew it was a charade, but that the performance would hold up in public if he decided to get louder and draw an audience (fucking little shit!!!). "My dad owns a chain of national law firms, and he just opened a new branch in Brentwood this year, so enough with the hate man!"

"I've got a recording session to go to, so I can't be carrying your bad vibes baggage with me there; I'M productive and positive, I'M the future.........something something................I'm oppressed........something something...........................eat the rich while simultaneously being the rich..............something something.......I chose the wrong major in college and it's the bank's fault......something something..........I've got a hard day of fiddling around with stolen beats for two hours, followed by happy hour in Silverlake, and then not being able to get it up with some local girl I con into coming back to my downtown loft that daddy pays for.............so I suggest you change your energy and find your happiness bro!"

"Whatever, you fuck!" was all Miguel could manage, as he picked up his drink and sandwich, and walked out the door.

He lit a cigarette as he walked to his car. "Shit, what the fuck was that thing?" he thought.

Salted Plastic: The Comedic Horror of Gentrification

Friday, October 23, Early Afternoon

"I cosplay ALL THE TIME! Been doing it since I was about 15!" Gifoor Hoor (pronounced gEEfor whoURR) said loudly inside the hip upscale coffee shop near Wilshire and Western. She was animated this one; slender Indian girl, looking like a magazine model with her waist length healthy hair, perfect skin and nails. She wore a Vunder Womun t-shirt (from Taregit), some pre-ripped and faded blue denim jeans........and a pair of Luboutine designer boots.

"You mean all that nerdy shit?" her co-worker Lydia asked slyly, humoring Gifoor's self-image, speaking as if she held a low opinion of the whole thing. Lydia was a short curvy anglo girl, her dark hair styled up, dressed in business attire.

"Yup." Gifoor said, "I'm into all the HARDCORE dorky stuff, like Big Bike Theory, this show that's been running for a while now about misunderstood nerdy comic book guys. Its sooooooo geek chic, and it really validates my passions, and like who I am and stuff. The characters are SUPER EMPOWERING for my life style, the one I just bought into about 9 months ago that is. They work on fix-gear bikes, watch played out anime series that everyone on earth already heard about 10 years ago, play games with weak plots and outdated battle systems like Disteny, wear generic comic book t-shirts from Taregit, and even eventually start a local, AND TUFF, bicycle gang. IT'S SO INSPIRING!!! I especially like how they all band together and pretend that they're victims and social outcasts that everyone on earth is bullying, regardless of the fact that the culture they are poorly feigning an affinity for has been streamlined packaged and standardized as hip and desirable by every facet of entertainment media. Then they all stand up for themselves and show the world that they're not gonna take it anymore!!!!"

"Wow! That does sounds empowering!!!!! Have you also seen that new Metflix original series, Desirable Slime Diddler?" a girl at the next table said, almost flowing into Gifoor's last word, as if the entire time she had been letting Gifoor's monologue drone on, impatiently eaves dropping, waiting for her turn to jump in and do her own personal "demo my value" verbal vomit. Blonde prom queen type she seemed to be, maybe mid-thirties, with a smart phone that had a Zailor Muun cover on it in her hand. "It's about a wimpy Hollywood page who finds strange and unlikely love in the BIG CITY after his girlfriend back in Ohio leaves him because she finds out he's a disgusting slimebag closet pedophile. It's so sad; she abandons him because she doesn't have the positive no shaming millennial attitude required to understand that he's just a misunderstood product of heavy doses of cyber-bullying. After that he moves to LA and meets this free spirited rocker type chick, who just CAN'T STAND her overwhelming high paying job as a copywriter for a popular local radio station. They hit it off, and she shows him just how beautiful unlikely match-ups, that are manufactured by the media and packaged as "modern relationships" can be!!!!"

"OMG! No, I've never seen it!!!" Gifoor said, loaded with contrived enthusiasm.

"NEITHER HAVE I !!!" the girl at the next table said, full of psych med smiles. "I just quoted near verbatim the show's INDb synopsis, that took me a grueling five minutes to read, just so I TOO CAN DEMO MY VALUE AS AN AVID FAN OF ALL THINGS NERDY!!!!"

"LOL!" Gifoor cobgurgled in a way reminiscent of someone farting out of their throat. "OMG!"

Lydia snorted to herself in disgust, and interrupted. "Look, I'm not a comic book nerd, sci-fi buff, Japanese cartoon watching gamer, etc, fan, but even I can tell you two are talking about the lowest common denominator versions of media that represent that sort of thing; I do marketing for the same company Gifoor here does her little geeky cheerleader routine. This whole nerd thing, sorry to break the news to you, but it doesn't exist anymore, at least not anywhere you two are getting it."

Salted Plastic: The Comedic Horror of Gentrification

"Chill, Lydia!" Gifoor gasped in scripted disgust. "You don't have to like it, no one's forcing you; there's no culture shaming here, so no need to be negative or attack each other's interests. I mean, I get that your position with the company is just purely professional, yeah?" She stopped and bit a hangnail as she checked some sponsored content for Mikael Korrs handbags on her Shitstagram, then absent-mindedly and non-commitally continued, without looking up……. "You don't have to be bitter if the whole thing doesn't interest you personally."

"Yeah, no pressure." the girl at the next table said while pulling a $60 Chanelle lipstick out of her bag. She touched up with her phone's camera, and then snapped a photo of herself pouting duck lips while holding her latte up to her face, making doubly sure to get label for the café in the shot. She posted it on her Shitstagram to boost her oh so notorious attention fishing, like harvesting, influencer value (#pourover, #coutureroaster #coffeewithbesties #vapidmarketingbeacon #imspecial #doyou #gumballmachineaphorism). Phone back down on the table, she continued her non-committal diatribe. "If you don't have an interest in the whole nerd culture thing because you're afraid of being shamed for being a geek, I totally get that!"

Lydia smirked, and thought about an old tattoo she had below her navel while looking at Gifoor and the other girl with loaded half patience. "Yeah, you're right," she said with calm cynicism, "it's just a total coincidence that two girls better suited to spending their days drinking mimosas, watching Pecks in The Titty, and getting mani pedis and dermal scrub downs at the salon are sitting here talking about how much they've become a product of attempts to market so called nerd culture to America's former jocks and cheerleaders. But, hey maybe I'm wrong, and you two can educate me."

"We can certainly try!!!" Gifoor said, all upbeat, poppy and animated on a little more than just nitro cold brew; her Couch purse was a cornucopia of anti-depressants and anti-anxiety meds for those times when she occasionally became over-jaded due to a lack of new and exciting distractions.

"Definitely!" the girl at the next table.......fuck it; gotta give this one a name already; let's call her A Cack in Not So Tighten. Shit that's long and stupid, but fuck it, it's what you get.

"Alright." Lydia smiled. "So, Gifoor, what's the last anime you binge watched..........episode after episode, till series completion? And I mean REALLY watched, not just had on in your bedroom as background noise while you look at your phone for 6 hours. AND DON'T SAY A CACK ON TITAN; I've already seen you listen to Justin at work, talking about it day after day in the break room, while you pretend to be interested and stare at him like he's a five star dinner in Redondo Beach. Oh, and by the way; all those "updates" you do on camera Gifoor, who do you think does the research for the writers at P4 network?"

"OMG! Is this an interrogation?!?!" A Cack in Not So Tighten (aka Acack) said with false confidence, in a tone that was contrived to show pity towards someone that's supposedly ignorant. "You know, you're really making a big deal about......."

"Please..." Lydia said with patience, "..........just be quite, and let Gifoor prove me wrong; I'll get to you in a minute!"

"Hah!" Acack exhaled in a pathetic display of feigning disinterest in getting the last word.....a display so petty that it accomplished the exact opposite.

"Well, Gifoor" Lydia asked, "what's your latest fave that you JUST LOVE to watch back to back, subtitled only, no interruptions.........with a big bag of umaibō and a bottle of ramune?!"

"Ok, fine, Lydia, I'll admit it already!" Gifoor sighed in affected disappointment straight out of a teenage sitcom. "You totally got me! I don't really like annie may, the only thing I know about comic books comes from the commercials I've seen for the latest Morvel and BC movies, I've never read a mango, and the last time I tried to play a video game it was to impress a guy I was dating. I couldn't get into the industry

Salted Plastic: The Comedic Horror of Gentrification

as a model or actress, so I weaseled my way into the next best thing I could find. I'm just a bird brained tv personality that likes to keep up the act even off camera because it makes me feel special, OK!!!!"

Lydia took a sip of her coffee, put it down, and looked at Gifoor with a knowing smile, feeling somewhat sorry/not sorry for her and her issues with self-delusion and identity crisis. "I know, I know; I just wanted to hear you say it." Still smiling, she took another sip of her coffee. "And guess what; this little casual coffee here wasn't arbitrary; new investors just finalized a total buyout of P4 last week; us sitting here together was a nice little informal interview. And with that said, I've got some news for you, and all the on camera staff; the next couple of weeks you are going to learn about and like everything you've just been playing poster girl for on TV." Lydia stopped, took another sip of her coffee while looking down at her phone. "You're going to learn and like, or.........." Lydia shrugged "........we'll just get ourselves a staff that has the heart for this sort thing.......without having to have the carrot of social prestige dangled in front of their face."

Lydia got up, face flushed, palming the area below her navel. Feeling satisfied and vindicated, she walked out the door, leaving Gifoor and the culture vulture at the other table behind to think about what sort of hammer had just been brought down.

But yeah, not really; they were already at it, on every facet of social media, babbling about the girl who had just shamed them for their "genuine" hobbies and lifestyle choices; everything Lydia had said had gone right over their heads.

........#nerdshamer...........#powertripbitch.........#icantwiththisgirl.............
#feedmyselfpity...........#culturegypsy.........#hobbiemaniquinsunite.......
#geekpower.............#poserpusher.........#memeticmeatbag...........#perso
nafelcher

Salted Plastic: The Comedic Horror of Gentrification

Friday, October 23, 10:34 pm (The Leash)

Slob Breather Blob Breather nervously fingered Suzy Banshee's Xiao Long Garden 45. He didn't have the figurative guts to tell the barely 21 cookie cutter goth that her song request didn't make the cut as far as attempting to flaunt her supposedly vast knowledge of music, and that her self-satisfied smile, post name throwing, might make sense among her friends who decided to dress in black and be spooky (if only for an evening), but the fact that her shitty H&N get up would be turned in to Cruxroads or Out in The Closet by her within a month or two was already on the table for him. Slob had grown up in the lap of luxury in La Crescenta, with his Dutch father and Japanese mother, but by good fortune had found "interesting" friends in the city who had introduced him to good music. Eventually he had gotten into being a local DJ, making a name for himself in Los Angeles.

His round face, raven colored slicked back hair, biker jacket and skinny jeans made him look a bit like the Staid Puffy Marshmallow Man dressed like a greaser.

He shoved his hand into his fatted biker jacket, and checked the baggy supply. "Got just enough left to give a nice little head change to a lightweight", he thought, "maybe spinning this played out shit will pay off............with a little help from my white powdery friend of course."

As he dropped the needle nobody seemed to care or mind that the song had already been mouth fucked a thousand times in every shitty 80s club in LA for the last three decades. It was really that sort of crowd down at The Leash; beards dressed in black, playing costume for the night, pretending to be invested in culture they could care less about in the hopes of scoring "strange and dark pussy" via not so casually mentioning that they have a downtown loft and BIG media connections coupled with small medial erections. Lotto variety luck had to strike to get any of them to even passively acknowledge that music was playing, let alone have any fucking taste in it; Slob Breather could be playing

42

Salted Plastic: The Comedic Horror of Gentrification

Fleetwound Mack or Tod Stuart (in fact....sadly......he had before) and nobody would even notice that it was out of place in a so called goth/death rock/ minimal wave club.

Once in a while you'd see someone raising their phone up, committing a quick culture snatch with a song recognition app, but the intentions even then were more often than not nothing more than a harvest and hoard action for future value demoing. Nothing more than a cute and pathetic way to catalogue some rare cultural graft for the next time they were discussing music and needed to wing it as a person that was in the know.

The place in truth was nothing but a candy shop for would be artists, USC jocks and tech aristocrats; a candy shop run by formerly serious to the scene people who had formally decided to pimp out their music, fashion and lifestyle to a bunch of window shoppers with too much time and money on their hands. It was, you might say, the modern day equivalent of a 50s Diner, a daily venue where interest-void deep-pocketed creeps could come and experience the tail end of 80s death rock/punk rock nostalgia. Everything there was for sale..............even the people.

Slob Breather Blob Breather went through his vinyl, and watched an old friend, Carrie Cobweb, leave The Leash with some pot-bellied stick-legged beardo douche wearing a Piss Blue Ribbon shirt and denim underwear. "Shit, I know Carrie just lost her job, but even she deserves better than becoming yet another hobosexual with a piece of shit like that! Fuck I hate doing this for work! I miss the old days!" he thought. Feeling a bit down at the thought of Carrie cruising for comfort with some turd she would have laughed out of the club ten years ago, he motioned to the bar for a drink, the effort ripping the pit stitches of his biker jacket a bit. He lifted his arm and casually looked at the rip as he thought about how he was going to slimebag that poor girl who had made the request for the Suzy Banshee song. Made the request out of limited knowledge and innocence, and just wanted a night out, free of gross groping hands. Little did he know that micro-media tends to follow macro-media, and he would soon find himself being the junior version of a recent Hollywood scandal as a result of his mode of operation when it came to male-female "relations".

The girl who had made the request turned around and nodded to him a few seconds after the needle dropped, her drink raised up towards him in thanks. He managed a convincingly innocent smile and a thumbs up in return with one hand...........while his other hand pinched his pathetic little nugget below the DJ booth.

Salted Plastic: The Comedic Horror of Gentrification

Saturday, October 24, 2:47 am

Miguel's heart was on overdrive, and his face was contorted in base animal hunger. He'd started the day trying to do something good, but had ended up losing his temper, gotten violent, and had more than likely gotten rid of Rebekah for good. Not that she mattered, the leech; right now he had a bag full of worry over his older brother, who he had been foolish enough to take out for the night against his better judgment.

"Don't think about it too much", he thought, "you're killing what you've got going on here and now. James made his bed tonight; no need to feel guilty that I'm having a good time here and now......right?"

But too late, through the alternating soft and deep female giggles and moans below him in the room, he drifted back to what had happened earlier that night..............

Earlier that Night (around 8pm)

James was only six weeks out after serving an eight year sentence in prison, and Miguel didn't maintain his fucking willpower to keep him out of trouble. He'd been bugging Miguel to take him out for weeks, but Miguel had consistently felt it was a bad idea............until a week ago, when he'd found out Rebekah was sleeping around with some man milk drinking "celebrity" pastry chef.

After a few days of being pissed over this, he'd agreed to take James out to the movies, which had little by little micro-gradualized into him agreeing to change the plans to beers and tv at his pad, followed by an argument sparked by him catching James doing lines in his bathroom, followed by Miguel being resigned to the fact that he might as well just flow with the situation and have a good time, knowing deep down inside that this was going to be one of the last times he would see his brother for a while, behavior like this indicating that there was no fucking way James was cleaning up his act and getting his shit together.

So, after a nice drunken exchange of digging through the family garbage; talking about the past, how their pops was a selfish prick, and going through the motions of positive encouragement ("you're gonna make it this time bro; I'll help you get your shit together!"), Miguel found himself asking for a few bumps.

"Haaah! Fucking hypocrite over here!" James smiled, as he brought the bag out, and Miguel reached for his house key to scoop out a bump. James looked nothing like Miguel by the way; stocky white guy, late 30s, brown hair, full of muscle he had gained on the prison yard; nothing better to do in jail than read and lift weights he had told Miguel.

Miguel sniffed the little mound off his key and smiled as his head change started up. "Fuck, I deserve a little irresponsibility, no? I, mean……..fuck…….my joke of a girlfriend is fucking anybody that will……."

"Kick her out bro…..kick her out!" James interrupted him, energy contemplative, any evidence of him caring about anything else in the world but his little brother nowhere to be seen in his tone or body language at all, as he looked down at the coffee table and turned a glass coaster upside down, dashing a few mounds onto it. "Don't over think it; I know you need a roomie to pay the rent, but that bitch is already out the door in her heart anyways brother, and you know it."

"And this crazy business of her being a half reptile, or what did you call it?" James continued, arranging a few neat lines on the table, crushing them down with the coaster. "That's just another indication that you're already going shit mental over this and can't think straight anyways. KICK her out, put an ad for a new roommate."

Salted Plastic: The Comedic Horror of Gentrification

Miguel leaned forward, rolled up $50 in hand, did a line for each nose, came up, rush of enthusiasm about his own opinion being driven by the growing head change, and went at one of the things he was generally pretty good at in life.............making excuses.

"Look, you've been out of society for almost a decade James; shit's changed for the worse for people like me and you; the middle class is gone, finding an affordable apartment.......blah blah blah............I'm not exactly a perfect boyfriend to Rebekah either........blah blah blah.......I work three jobs and rent is still too high......blah blah blah.......hipster pussies raising the cost of everything in LA................blah blah blah blah............excuse excuse excuse excuse...........can't trust anyone that moves in with you these days..........something something............North Hollywood...........cock sucking dance community two-thousand dollar a month studio apartment beard bitch................CASTING COUCH NO SEX DRIVE WHORE!!!!!"

By the time he'd finished his aimless rant James was snoring on the couch; he'd been doing it again, surfing the sound of his own voice, not giving a shit about this being, as he'd thought to himself earlier, one of the last times he was going to see James for a while...............or the fact that, unlike him, his brother was actually listening to his brother.......and trying to help him.

Miguel got up, went to the apartment door behind the couch James was knocked out on and went outside. He was about to have a cigarette in the hallway, stopped himself though, a big smile on his face, and turned back to the door; if this was going to be one of the last times he would see James, he was going to make GODDAMN FUCKING SURE HE WOULDN'T be thinking about just himself for once.

Miguel wiped a tear out of his eye, put his fist on the door, and tried not to laugh as he pounded on it and yelled in a deep voice "JAMES BRIAN LYONS!!!! THIS IS YOUR PAROLE OFFICER; I'M HERE TO VIOLATE YOUR ASS!!!!!!"

Salted Plastic: The Comedic Horror of Gentrification

Miguel heard a jump on the other side of the door, and, opening it up to see James already trying to crawl out the window, he started busting up laughing.

James turned around, pissed at first, and then smiled. "You fucking faggot," he said to Miguel, "scared the shit out of me."

Miguel smiled, happy that he had gotten the joking rapport going between him and his brother. He walked down the hall to the kitchen, opened the fridge for two more beers, and shouted back at James "I'm surprised you fell for that shit, I'm sure I don't sound anything like your parole officer." He walked back to the living room, and handed James a beer.

"I wouldn't know," James said, "I haven't even met the fucker."

"How's that?" Miguel said, as James popped open the beer and downed it like a fucking soda. "Don't they come and interview you immediately after you check in at the halfway house?"

James ignored the question and started digging through Miguel's CDs. "Got any Stuff Little Fingers?" he asked. "I only got to hear wack ass radio music while I was locked up."

Miguel stopped and thought for a second, grabbing the baggy on the table for another round, as he pulled a business card from a drawer. "You didn't check into the halfway house, did you James?"

"You already know I did!" James barked, a little irritated. "I told you where I got that stash of coke that your hogging the shit out of right now didn't I?"

"That still doesn't explain why you don't know what your parole officer sounds like man, so what gives?"

James sighed, finally found Stuff Little Fingers (on vinyl but not cd), turned around and said "Put this thing on, and I'll tell you how it is so you can stop playing junior lawyer with me."

Salted Plastic: The Comedic Horror of Gentrification

Friday, October 23, 5:30 PM

Driving through West Hollywood, Lydia was stuck in traffic on Santa Monica Blvd, mentally (and then verbally) cursing the lack of freeways on the Westside.

"I.....FUCKING........HATE the Westside!" she started. "Fucking assholes can't just have another couple of freeways going North-South and East-West in their PRECIOUS little shithole neighborhoods, with their shitty hyped up bars, restaurants, and shopping centers. Why can't the company office be someplace peaceful, decent and accessible like fucking Pasadena or Burbank?"

She reached for her purse, the only thing neatly placed in her car, even though everything else in her back seat was absentmindedly piled; empty cold pressed juice bottles, fast food bags, snotted tissues, a gold edition Zelleda Nentindo 4ds, a beat up copy of Brant Norrison's Unvisibles, some dirty work out clothes, and a couple of work portfolios piled on top of her laptop.

Not that purse though; she'd worked a crappy side job waiting tables for a few months to get the thing, way back when she had just gotten to Los Angeles. There was no way her next activated charcoal lemonade was going to find its way into waterfalling onto it the next time she had to fucking octopus a thousand different tasks while she was driving home through traffic after work for the millionth time. Hence, the reason why it was neatly placed right side up in the backseat.

It was a 1920's tooled leather Deco-Style handbag, made by Justine Leather Company. Almost a perfect pentagon, except the top had a sixth flat side rather than a point. It was bordered by barbed black leather thong stitching, and the layout was an alternating pattern of black and oxblood leather half diamonds in symmetrical sequence. The opening seam was bordered by lacquered wood and two gold clasps inlaid with red coral.

Salted Plastic: The Comedic Horror of Gentrification

It didn't fit much, being pretty thin, but it didn't need to; style meant more to Lydia when it came to certain things........style, and the ability to only carry around what mattered in her purse.

"And right about now, a little bit of peace in this shit fuck traffic is what matters." Lydia finished the narration, pulling out of the bag what she'd been looking for; leftover prescription from last year's root canal, rationed for rainy day irritation.

Just as she was about to pop and chase a couple of Vicodin with a banana turmeric coconut shake she'd stopped for at the market, her phone rang, caller id displaying Barry's name.

"UGH!" she exclaimed, picking up. "Hey Barry, what's up?" she put on the fake enthusiasm, hoping this was not a call back to the office.

"Turn on MPR in about fifteen minutes," he said, "I want notes, audience feedback, potential sales stats, and a script with dialogue geared towards engineering first class hype over the material in a worst case scenario type of deal if this thing doesn't deliver the type of PROFITS our client is hoping for over the weekend."

"I thought the new owners said we were going to start moving the station towards a more 'organically motivated consumer opinion' type of audience that's...." she began, but got cut off ....

"Look, Irr know thad yer.......excited thad things........aur finally goin ter ber geared towards....chomp chomp......an audience........werd a genuine enthusiasm for the PRODUCTS and MATERIALS.....thad we....."

"Yuck!" she thought. "FAT HAIRY FUCK is munching on one of his carrots while he talks again; stupid motherfucker thinks that's going to make up for all the double decker pastrami reubens and chili dogs he inhales all fucking week; one petty ass carrot isn't going to undo all the damage to his by now worthless cock and colon. Fucking non-cocter bitch!"

"............but I came with the deal to transfer all interest of P4 to the new investors," he continued, "and I'm gonna continue to maintain our A List client's positions in the happy seat, and I expect you to be my

50

Salted Plastic: The Comedic Horror of Gentrification

cheerleader, baby." Lydia cringed and almost vomited in her mouth. "So keep up the good work, enjoy your weekend, and I'll see you Monday for breakfast to.........discuss this. How's The Belvedere sound? I here they have a NEW, and HIGHLY PRENTENTIOUS lobster waffle dish, especially geared towards tasteless, yet well-heeled moronic tool idiots hunting for new and not so imaginative status symbols. PEOPLE LIKE ME!!!!!! I'm a shit REEKING SACK OF PROPTOPLASM that was only able to get into the industry because I know, or am related to all the right people!!!!"

"Sounds good," Lydia replied, at this point all attempt to sound peachy decimated.

"Great! GREAT!" Barry said. "Well, it's almost 6pm, I gotta go," his breath at this point was getting lardy and labored for some reason, "check out the show, and start PULSING out all that magic over YOUR PASSION!"

"EWWWWWWWWWWWW!!!!!!" she exhaled/yelled, gritting her teeth in murderous rage, immediately rush-clattering four pills into her mouth and downing half her protein shake; she was pretty much dead sure she had heard a fly unzip before he hung up.

Salted Plastic: The Comedic Horror of Gentrification

Friday, October 23, 3:46 pm

Pignose Diddler sat in his renovated apartment in Central LA near Pico Union, twirling a vintage Starr Wares action figure in his hands. The building held a bit of historical glamour for transplants like himself, who had so recently oozed into Los Angeles. Reading too many Reymond Handler novels, and watching a bunch of generic documentaries about old LA had seeded an idiotic themed mythology in their minds about old architecture. It had in fact planted an expectation in their heads of an LA that had never really existed outside of old black and white movies. To them, popping into and gentrifying areas of old LA was pretty much synonymous with going to New Orleans Square in Dizzyland; life was a theme for them because they could afford to make it that way. Long time locals though, they just thought the building Pignose lived in was some formerly bed bug infested shithole where rent had recently been hiked up. Hiked up and skyrocketed through the roof by a paint job, a visit from the exterminator, a new set of floors, and a few new coffee shops and lame overpriced restaurants in the neighborhood.

His apartment was mainly living room, with an attached kitchen separated by a wet bar. Generic Bowee and Sex Pasteles posters dressed the living room walls, and there was a computer desk and cocktail tray with a few bottles of bourbon and vodka in the corner. The bedroom and bathroom took up about 30% of the entire place, but were both largely unfurnished, and not filled with much of anything other than a bed and toiletries.

It was a hot day, so Piggula had the AC running in the kitchen window, and was sipping a "modern style" old-fashioned cocktail. He held the drink in his left hand while his right was occupied with an old Ewalk action figure as he laid on his back staring at the ceiling. The drink recipe had come from a hip, local, artisanal, urban, handcrafting, testicle caressing chef he was following on Shitstagram; idea was genius, and right up Piggy's alley; he'd even freshly squeezed some of the key ingredients from his friend Wilbur before he had left back to Portland earlier that morning.

Piggula took another sip while looking lost in thought over something. "Damn, that Cuck's Kitchen guy really has good taste!" he said. "It's a good thing Wilby was visiting for the Clone War Con this weekend, or I wouldn't have been able to make this just like Chef Felch's recipe. HEY! Stop that Edward Bear!" he half yelled while smirking, eyes looking down towards his navel. Edward "MERRWWRRD" at Piggy, waved his tail, and pounced away, a bit ashamed that he'd been caught sniffing Piggy's butthole while he laid there on the floor of the living room, positioned like a turkey with his knees up, bare naked but for a ragged old Bowhaus shirt...............a bottle of honey for some reason on the floor near his waist.

Contemplating something heavy in his past that had somehow transcended into feelings that were near and dear to him, a tear went down Pignose's face as he gripped the old Ewalk toy, and old memories came to the surface.............

Salted Plastic: The Comedic Horror of Gentrification

1982. Portland, Oregon

"NOOO!" Wilbur yelled, a stocky little 12-year-old, complete with freckles, milk teeth, and hard core hick red mullet. "I GET TO BE LUKE, SCARLETT! I DON'T GIVE A SHIT WHAT DIANE SAYS; SHE AIN'T MY FUCKING MOM!"

"You have to call her mom, and let me be who I wanna, or I'm tellin........." Wilbur's 8-year-old half-sister Scarlett started..............then stopped quick, as his big stupid ham fist came up in warning. The poor girl backed up, frightened and trembling in her chocolate milk stained Kare Bare pajamas.

"Hey, chill Wilbur, it's just toys," 12-year-old Piggula butted in, with his long parted hair and Scoeby Do t-shirt, "I don't care who Scarlett gets to be."

"MY TOYS, MY RULES!" Wilbur barked, sounding an awful lot like Wilbur Sr. with his "MY HOUSE, MY RULES!," or his "MY TV, MY RULES!," or "MY FUCKING KITCHEN, MY FUCKING RULES!!!!" It all depended on who Mr. Hartford was currently putting in place among his family members, whether it be "explaining" to his wife (via fist and belt) that "cooking wasn't contributing, it was earning keep", or locking Wilbur in the basement for tracking dirt into the house, or spoon feeding poor little Scarlett sugar until she vomited as punishment for taking an extra cookie out of the cookie jar; all of the above was starting to rub off on Wilbur.

It was a wonder Wilbur had about the biggest collection of Starr Wares toys in town (BTBTS, every figure, the Hotthe Playset, Jubba's palace, the Vadarr with removable mask, etc.) considering what a selfish miser his dad was. But, looking at his size, and noting the fact that nearly everyone in their 6th grade class avoided bringing their action figures to show and tell, Piggy had figured it all out. Figured it out a little too late actually; he'd come by today in the hopes of playing with the Endoor speed bike vehicle, and Endoor Luke that Wilbur had taxed him for during his first week at Whitbred Elementary last week. Wilbur had made a lax promise to Pignose to give it back if he'd come over and play, having chased away nearly all his other friends for some odd reason at this point.

"OWWWWwww!" Scarlett screamed, her red hair wrapped in Wilbur's knuckles as he tossed her out of his bedroom, and locked the door.

"JEEZ!" Piggy reacted. "You're gonna get in trouble dude!"

"Don worry bout it." Wilbur said, red faced, a little maniacal look on his cheeseburger creep of a face. "Now, let's play!"

"Oh…..ok…..," Piggy replied, a little shaken, "can I be the Endoor Luke on the speed bike?"

"No, not that boring Starr Wares game we were playing, that's old shit! I heard of a new game that all the cool kids play with their Starr Wares toys, man. You wanna try?"

"Su…sure.." Piggy said timidly. "What's it called?"

"Ewalk in The Butt!!!!!" Wilbur said. "YOU'RE UP FIRST!!!!!"

Salted Plastic: The Comedic Horror of Gentrification

Friday, October 23, 4:01 pm

Just moments after Pignose finished mulling over the memory of losing his virginity to Wicked the Ewalk, Jetty Jizz got dropped off outside the ground floor of his apartment in a brand new Tezla Model X driven by a very refined older gentlemen by the name of Armen Harguut. Armen was a classy local businessman who currently ran quite a few Hollywood nightclubs spoken highly of in the LA Weakling. These places were where the Westside's socio-economic elite could be found nightly, enjoying only the most prominent recreational pursuits such as absorbing local culture, sipping craft cocktails, and possibly even meeting that special someone on the dance floor. AND IF THEY WERE REALLY lucky then they'd get to experience the businesses behind the businesses during club afterhours; this right was reserved exclusively by those who had earned VIP status via various methods, such as the need for intimate relations that defied age of consent laws, or borrowing too much money at an interest rate of one finger per late payment.

Before Jetty exited the car in her No Name Couture blouse and Wietzmenne equestrian-style boots, "lovingly" purchased (with no strings attached of course) by her new father figure here, he leaned over, and with great tenderness and chivalry……..placed his cigar stained, stubble encrusted lip on her mouth while grabbing her pelvis with a bear fist of a hand breaded in knuckle hair and gaudy overpriced rings.

Jetty manufactured a quick smile and aura of gratitude while mentally focusing on her anti-clitoral mantra "Om Nobeava DurteeHo" to keep the disgust back. "No worries," she thought, "I'll convince myself that everything was an act of self-empowerment on my part later, and that I was being taken advantage of by Armen, even though I willfully and premeditatively made the decision to sell myself for goods and services; owning up to one's life decisions is patriarchal tyranny……..or some other such bullshit I read on some birdbrained influencer's page."

Salted Plastic: The Comedic Horror of Gentrification

Grabbing the afternoon's catch (shopping bags from Brentwood to Melrose) she exited the car, and Harguut drove off. After his car was completely out of site she vomited on the sidewalk while simultaneously coming up with a quick sob story to tell Piggy about how Harguut had exploited and abused her; she was ever ready and adept at planting seeds that might grow into her next inter-relational investment.

"Why can't I just find a decent guy" she soliloquized, gearing up the act, throwing in a few fake sobs as she walked into the lobby of Piggy's apartment.

Salted Plastic: The Comedic Horror of Gentrification

Friday, October 23, 10pm

Miguel and James got out of a Libt car at the edge of Chinatown on Hill Street. James gave the driver a little baggy after shooting the shit with him the entire ride (also a former inmate). "Don't snort it all in one place!" James smiled as he stepped into the street.

Miguel wore blue denim jeans, a leather biker jacket, and red Chucks; a Deadly Boys pin was on the left lapel of the jacket. James had a burgundy flight jacket, a The Jams t-shirt, blue Dickees pants (Miguel's old oversized clothes) and some 10 hole Dock Nartens, hair slicked back.

"So that's pretty much the plan then", Miguel asked, "you know you're going back at this point because you didn't do something you KNEW you were supposed to do, so might as well party while you can? Shit, sounds like you like prison, James?!?!"

"I mean, what's your problem? Addiction to deprivation and misery? Too scared to get responsible and face the real world? What is it, James?! Cause honestly, I don't get it man.......and I...I....I know that that shit doesn't exactly rehabilitate, and you acclimate to that crazy environment, and that being out here is strange as shit after......after, you know........", Miguel struggled, hoping to say the right fucking thing for once, even knowing full well he had no right to even think he had the answer to James plight, not having had his experiences.

James listened patiently, lighting up a cigarette, watching Miguel trying to force the proper words out, feeling the concern his brother had over his welfare, waiting for him to finish before walking up to him with his reply.

He gave Miguel a big hug, and knocked him in the ribs with a soft punch. "Don't be a bitch," he smiled, "you're ruining my vacation."

Miguel smiled back, eyes a little red. He remembered the unspoken promise he'd made earlier, his resolve to not make this night about him; if James could be happy under the circumstances, he wasn't going to ruin it; he was going to add to that happiness as much as he possibly could tonight, even knowing that James was essentially on his way back to jail any minute now.

Clearing his head, he looked over at James, asking, "So, what you wanna do nex………"

"GIRLS!!!!" James said. "Gotta meet some girls………if you know any!"

"Uhm….." Miguel exclaimed, thinking about it, knowing full well he'd been a hermit the last few years, and was pretty much unwelcome at every club in DTLA for one reason or another.

"Fuck it though!" he thought. He felt invincible with his older brother by his side, even knowing full well that it was selfish bad news to be thinking like that. But fuck, at least it was only halfway selfish; he knew there was more than likely trouble waiting for him at just about any place in Downtown LA that he could take James, but James wanted to meet some girls, so that's that! Things had to be halfway wrong to do a little bit of right; he was going to do good by his blood tonight even if it meant trouble.

Still, Miguel wanted to be honest with his brother either way though…….

"Honestly, I shouldn't have brought you to Downtown, James; I'm on every shit list you can think of down here for several reasons, ranging from writing shit talking reviews of clubs, to getting into fights at a few places."

"Hah!!!" James laughed. "Even more reason to stop in and say hi!" he smiled, pounding one fist into the other, and putting emphasis on the word "hi" in a way that almost certainly translated into "hi" meaning good times and trouble of the sort that ended in laughs and broken noses.

"No, I mean it, we probably should avoid about 75% of the places down here; there's always some bearded hipster that rubs me the wrong way, plus I'm all sketchy and coked out." Miguel replied.

Salted Plastic: The Comedic Horror of Gentrification

"Shit! Sounds like you just like to start trouble cause you can't have a good time." James said.

"You haven't seen these kids man, what they're like now." Miguel began, a little irritated. "Shit, I called them kids; most of them are my age or older, pretending to be 23 years old for life even though they're all in their early to late 30s. It's like they all feel they have a license to invade everything that's yours, pretend to be part of it, and then make you feel like you're the outsider breaking the rules just because you're being yourself in your own element. Fuck, you know how many times I've been kicked out of shows for walking to the front of the stage in the last couple of years these maggots decided to play spectator in MY CULTURE?! How many times I've been called a pessimist...........at a goth club of all places?! How many shitty blogs have written about "concert bullying" in reaction to instances of self-defense on the part of people like me?

They think they can lay claim to floor space at standing only concerts, snapshot you without asking, flirt with your girl right in front of you, blacklist you in every venue that they have enough money and influence to buy all out control of............and then, when you bite back, they SCREAM for security, get the admin to remove your editorial, start a petty little phantom media campaign to demonize you online, write their own little whine piece about being harassed in BIG BAD LA, or try to put hands on you and then call the police when they get laid out. Shit, I can't possibly put into words what you've missed this last decade!"

"Yeah, I remember you starting in on the whole thing back at the apartment. What was it you said about one place having your picture up on the wall?" James asked, not looking up from the government issued cell phone they'd given him at the halfway house, just partly paying attention to his question as he asked it, obviously having something geared and ready to go upon hearing Miguel's answer, but not wanting to make it obvious by asking him with full attention. "It was something

Salted Plastic: The Comedic Horror of Gentrification

about them saying you were a homophobe, and telling all their followers and club promoters....."

"YEAH, that fucking Bitches in Black club promoter group", Miguel interrupted, careful not to mention the name of the venue even though his anger at the memory was already getting the better of him, "tried to play it as as as," he got red, pulled out one of his shitty French cigarettes, lit up and exhaled quickly, "as if JUST BECAAAUSE the place promotes itself as a gay, bi, trans, etc. friendly place, that me calling it a played out hipster poser shithole makes me anti LGBT. Fucking pathetic ass false equivalency bullshit!!!! AND OF COURSE every idiot eats it up, and I get half the people I know, including long time friends, playing Fakebook cheerleader, chastising me so they can save face with all their fake ass social media "friends". Fucking culture raping, scene aficionado, pseudo artist, jocks turned goth, beard pussy, veganaise sperm guzzling, culture gypsying, window shopping, jobless rolling stone, backdoor influencing, white bread Portland and New York shit dick motherfucking faithless walking stomach, no genuine passion for anything culture vacuuming bandwagon transplant gentrifying coffee douche/enema, good time sniffing MAGGOTS!!!!!!!!!!!!!"

Miguel continued his rant, unaware of James at this point, riding high on his aimless verbal venom. James just kept looking down at his phone, calmly searching for something in-between taking small bumps from a bonus bag of coke he had pulled out of nowhere after telling Miguel on the ride to downtown that he had had only the one baggy, the one he had given the last of to the Libt driver.

"............... I'd like to drive them down to Florence Graham area, drop them off with no cell phone, and then see how much they love absorbing the culture and syncing with the locals there.......fucking bitches!" Miguel braked for a drag on his cigarette, exhaled, and was about to elaborate some more, but James stopped him by standing up off the low wall he was sitting on, and walked over to show his phone screen to Miguel.

Salted Plastic: The Comedic Horror of Gentrification

"So I guess were going here tonight then?" he smiled. Miguel looked at the phones screen, and saw the Fakebook page for tonight's club at The Leash. He half smiled at his stupidity; he'd assumed James couldn't put two and two together to find out where Bitches in Black might be running an upcoming event.

"Fuck it!" Miguel smiled, a bit of a cold sweat starting on his back, along with a few knots in his stomach.

"Yup, fuck it!" James replied, handing Miguel the baggy and patting him on the back.

Salted Plastic: The Comedic Horror of Gentrification

Friday, October 23, 9:30 pm

Lydia walked around her living room in the nude, straight black hair falling to the middle of her back, pacing back and forth nervously. She was frantic; today was just not her day. After darting back and forth another minute or so, she stopped and took a deep breath, turned around, and looked into an antique, triptych-style vanity mirror set on top of a matching antique dresser in the corner of the room. Looking real closely, she felt like she was looking pretty old and worn out tonight. Staring and staring, she wondered whether it was her age..........or just a nice cocktail of high stress and lack of sleep for the last couple of months. Lack of sleep, hitting the Vicodin, having both Tim, and then Dagmar leave her back to back, one relationship after another.........or maybe she was just shit fed up with the kind of life she'd bought into in Los Angeles.

"And let's not forget FINALLY believing my position at P4 was going to become my dream job, only to find out that that sack of shit Barry is still going to be around to hold everything back and keep the company in permanent dog show status." Lydia said to herself.

The truth was this; being around both her exes, with their whole appropriative, consume everyone/everything in front of them energy, having them hook her up with the industry buffet, getting her the high end positions in the business; this had nearly killed all her hopes for a job that was simultaneously pragmatic AND creative. Seeing how the professional aspect of it all was pusher-like instigated/bottom line motivated had almost caught her in its net, making her self-doubt and almost become an empty thing. Empty.............just like those fucking models and failed actresses they hired to lie on P4; total frauds, acting like bubbly jackasses on camera, falsifying a standard for so called nerd culture that didn't really exist. Meme puppets creating a marketing structure so the people who write their checks can hypostatize that standard into reality, creating the market before the consumer, instead of the other way around. Soulless culture vampires acting like they have a natural passion for video games, anime and comic books, flapping their airhead lips over how much they just "love to play the new Zeldoo.......whoops..........LOL!..........that's Zelleda to all you gamers out there........my bad....OMG!!!"

It had drained her from the inside out, making her feel old and done, her passion for her interests almost decimated.

The truth of the matter though was that, even at 33, she looked pretty damn good. Her confidence had just been shredded by two vampire hooker/pimps who masked their favor exchanging as selfless altruism. Kick boxing classes, eating right, and avoiding too much drinking (up until recently) had kept her 5 foot 5 frame curvy, volumizing all the extra pounds she purposefully held onto; baby fat she kept because she liked the type of women and men it attracted. Her nerves and heart were just shaken; she needed some aimless time out fun; no need to get any deeper than that. "Yup, FUN, I need some fun!" Lydia thought.

"Those two though," she thought, "I knew damn well they weren't my style or type of energy.................but waiting tables when I got here, pitching my resume to anybody with a half assed video game production start-up in need of marketing........"

"First there was Tim, that fucking leech, nose deep in his books at the local cafes, affecting introspection in an attempt to look more interesting than he actually is. Bullshit shy guy act, generated to make himself seem non-threatening and safe harbor for what he imagines to be introverted and needy nerdy little girls dying for male attention......"

"And Dagmar, that evil bitch; a way more sophisticated, mentally calculating, and lethal version of those things we have hosting our shows. Full of her family's connections and money, and, unlike girls like Gifoor, smart enough to take her education and resources seriously."

True, they'd both introduced her to "all the right people", but the cost of it all had almost buried the her in her........the real Lydia.

Salted Plastic: The Comedic Horror of Gentrification

"ALMOST!" she thought, looking in the mirror still, admiring both her figure, and her resolve to hold onto the heart and soul of what she REALLY believed in. She palmed the edge of her little tummy, smiling at the little green crest below her navel, looking like a zero sandwiched between two horizontal lines. She walked towards a glass cabinet across the room that was wedged between two high bookshelves. Proost, Filip H Cock, MacLuhen, and Jung were just a few of many visible names; sci fi pulps, manga, graphic novels, history books; an eclectic variety of reading materials littered those shelves. Her bottom heavy figure could still be seen in the mirror as she walked towards the cabinet, ass and thigh fat rippling, shaking and bouncing over the muscle underneath as the weight of her thick thighs and calves pounded into the apartment's wood floors.

Opening the cabinet, she pulled out a decanter of Branne Single Malt, and tipped a generous pour into a tumbler.

Brooding over her day, taking a sip, she let that smooth smoked vanilla-like whisky do its thing, thinking about the triumph she had felt Monday when the news had circulated around the office regarding final arrangements for transfer of all P4's interests to Okina Sozo. Okina Sozo, veteran game developer/anime producer, along with her creative team, who would be joint shareholders. How free, elated, and STRONG she'd felt, knowing (thinking rather) that her job was going to finally be putting her in a position to do what she felt the industry owed the public; raw creative, with honest promotion by true players, watchers, readers, and developers. It had all anchored in at the coffee shop, telling Gifoor that the company was no longer going to be a safe haven for failed actors and models to cheerlead for interests that they had no real passion for.

Barry had killed all that momentum though, every hope she'd built this week, murdered it by the fact that he was staying on at P4, and by the request he'd made over the phone to listen to that anus vomit promotional piece for a flaming shit of an upcoming movie. A movie which she had been shredding for weeks on her personal blog (written under an alias to avoid problems with work of course).

The film in question, Ready Gamer Lame, was yet another one of Hollywood's pathetic fish hooks for the nostalgia crowd, the bread and butter of the dying cinema industry; movie goers consisting of mainly viewers 30 and up that would let themselves be ass fed anything that name threw media nostalgia. Everything from live action Gee Eye Joe and classic Sci Fi movie reboots, to CGI Smoorfs and too little too late 80's blockbuster sequels; this was the **"sell quick sell now!"** formula that Hollywood had been employing in recent years. This one though was **THE BIG ONE**, being the most obvious stab at this new marketing structure yet, covering the grounds of all 80's media, from music and video games, to comic books and Saturday morning cartoons. AND IT GOT BETTER, the credibility of this film being backed up by the fact that it was "based on a bestselling book!!!!!!" Whoopdee FUCKING DOO!!!! Another shit film based off another shit novel frequently sold at Terget and Val-mart, and soon to be found at your local Godwill after it's five minutes of fame wore off."

Recalling the OBNOXIOUS radio show that had aired the blatantly obvious sponsored content that Barry had asked her to listen to, she almost tossed her glass against the wall. What a bullshit act it was, where the interviewer and interviewee were hamming it up like always, trying to make it seem like a genuine conversation. She downed the tumbler of that smooth French single malt and cringed in disgust as she remembered..........

Salted Plastic: The Comedic Horror of Gentrification

Friday, October 23, 6:07 pm

Lydia was almost at the intersection of Sunset and Cahuenga now; she took a deep breath, and reluctantly turned on MPR...........

A whiney, obnoxious, and weasely voice came out of her car speakers, babbling mid-sentence......

"................YEAH, Thoondercats and Gee Eye Joe, man! I....it's like, yeah; completely brings you back to your bedroom, playing with your action figures as a kid, when things were FUN and you had NO RESPONSIBILITY, and ITS SO GREAT that a lot of this MERCHANDISE from back then is being re-introduced today to BUY again!"

"And NOT just the toys and cartoons, right Wimpy?" the radio host asked, affected enthusiasm turned up full volume.

"Fuck!" Lydia said to herself, "they keep Karl Spermatrinker fully loaded down there at MPR. He could be interviewing Rafael Trujillo's personal torture brigade about plans to open a private school for aspiring psychotics, and he'd still be on que, creating the perfect symphony dialogue, designed, as always, to convince the public that they were actually listening to a natural conversation, instead of the moronic rehearsed Q&A that this piece of shit really is. Fucking coked out loser!" she finished, and then stopped a second, looking down at the vial of Vicodin in her car's cup holder, her own high kicking in. "Damn, maybe I'm not far off from there......," she thought, feeling a little like she was on her way to becoming what she hated most about the industry. She tuned it out, and continued to listen........

"NOT EVEN!" Wimpy Wiesel replied in coked out weasel mode. "Ready Gamer Lame doesn't just name throw for old Nentindo games, vintage action figures, and 80s cartoons; it's also got A TON of tunes that will make you remember your CARE FREE CHILDHOOD and teens. I mean, I don't have a soundtrack list or anything on me, but you get the picture; Blondee, New Orders, Billey EyeDoll, Doran Doran; all of the above come to mind as I'm currently looking up "80s music" on my phone to cover my ass for not coming to this interview prepared. I MEAN, AFTER ALL, I'm just a ferrety little promotional bitch that gets paid to pretend to be emotionally invested in things I don't know shit about in exchange for public recognition and an ugly overpriced McMansion in the Hollywood Hills. Not to mention all the women I get to meet that would NEVER give me the time of day if I didn't have the ability to casually brag in public about my industry connections, or my Downtown Los Angeles loft, completely furnished with designer décor, a year's supply of cocaine, and an onsite bartender that I have under contract to never mention that he drugs my female guest's drinks."

"That's great, Wimpy!" Karl replied in mile a minute coke head cadence. "I mean, who needs a genuine passionate interest in anything these days when you can just life hack everything like a substance void little shit......uh ha ha ha!......uh heh heh heh!......."

"UGGHHH!" Lydia screamed. "I fucking HATE the sound of that whiney little bitch's voice!" Ever since an industry mixer, where Wimpy Wiesel had shown her how truly he wasn't some non-threatening nerd, but more like an entitled little chicken-hawking viper shit bag who thinks any fresh meat owes him a fuck; ever since then she'd wanted to crumple his rib cage with a kick of death.

She listened to the "interview" for about four more minutes, grinding her teeth at the many MANY mentioning's of merchandise that would be available at the premier, took some notes on her phone, and shut the radio off in disgust.

Salted Plastic: The Comedic Horror of Gentrification

Friday, October 23, 10pm

Lydia finished mulling over the drive back home; listening to that crap, running paragraph break downs and quotes through her head, making herself sick to the point of ruining her Vicodin high trying to come up with the whole thing in order to turn it into a workable editorial for Barry come Monday. It was done of course, in her head if nowhere else, but having to put energy into this sort of thing was the last nail in the coffin.

"Fuck, I hate that Barry is staying on at the company, but it would be at least somewhat bearable if he was just another body collecting a paycheck at this point." she said out loud. "Why does that fat fucking bastard just have to insist on remaining some prime mover at P4!?"

As she reached for the decanter to get another drink her phone went off in the bedroom. Putting the glass down, Lydia walked over to her room, the only one in the apartment she had renovated personally; faux obsidian tile, variant types of fur rugs (sooo many lectures from dates she brought home for that one), stainless steel closet doors, a heater with a gargoyle chimney façade built into the wall, and a cage-like California King with fake ivy vines coiled around the black and gold metal that made up the frame. On an ornate copper nightstand, with a raw moldavite surface, sat a copy of Orsula Le Gun's "The Repossessed", Ocelot Publishing edition, with the orange planet in the distance, and Shovit in the foreground.

Lydia picked up her cell phone and gasped in mock disgust, looking at a text from Dagmar. A gasp meant to convey to no one in general that the text was an unwelcome and appalling gesture, even though the truth was, on some level, Lydia was smiling underneath, happy to be wanted, indulging in the unhealthy triumph that this person, whom she apparently despised, still wanted to give her the time of day.

"What's wrong with me?" she said, a wicked little smile at the left corner of her mouth.

Salted Plastic: The Comedic Horror of Gentrification

She stood there, still naked, mulling it over, that perfect landing strip of dark pubic hair showing, accented by her pale ivory mons. A hint of her labia majora and clitoral hood could be seen in the room's faint light, showing telltale vermillion and purple tones which betrayed her thoughts about Dagmar's text.

"What's wrong with me?" Lydia repeated, mulling it over in her head.

"Not a fucking thing!" she decided in a confident tone, a little flushed in the face as she mildly slammed her drink down on the table. "I just failed at satisfaction today where I wanted it the most..........and where all else fails, base pleasure is always a nice substitute, if not a real solution. Career success kicked me in the ass today, then my attempt to get high to forget my anger and sadness got shit on.............so cheap sex with the ex it is!"

Sending a reply to Dagmar, she put the phone down and started pulling outfits out of her closet.

Salted Plastic: The Comedic Horror of Gentrification

Friday, October 23, 11:20 pm (The Leash)

Pignose Diddler had been walking from room to room at The Leash for half an hour now, trying to find Jetty Jizz and Ginger Just Legal. They'd disappeared inside before he had even finished paying their entry fees to Bearded Bitches in Black. Something told him they would have gotten in without paying either way but, oh well....

He had brought an old sharkskin suit out of mothballs for the occasion, nice 60s cut, with a three button blazer and hemmed pants, but had ruined the look with a lame Stair Trak Boorg t-shirt.

"They'll meet me at the bar when they need a drink...." he told himself, feeling a little bit like the pathetic aging, mildly pedophiliac cash machine that he was.

The place was wall to wall stock variety scenester style, put together by art majors who couldn't wade out of the shallow end of the pool of creativity; whatever remedial academic shit they'd learned about the categories and history of music, fashion, counter culture and interior decorating was where their understanding stopped. The training wheels never came off after college; searching for non-canon literature, personal design aesthetic, self-discovered music, and novel fashion and art was a foreign idea to them; pursuing anything not mentioned in an overpriced "contemporary" art school was a concept that would never cross their cultural feedbox type of minds. That said, it was plain that the club owners and promoters were going for the Hollywood visual interpretation of 80s pop and troubled youth culture tonight. A dash of communist shock value and yacht club Miami Lice douchery yielded the bar, with its cheesy neon lights and glass brick counter set up, complete with Cyrillic letters above the bar, surrounded by hammers and sickles; dated and catalogued notions of chic social revolution.

A small dancefloor fronted the bar, with a raised platform for the DJ on the other side, a lanky anglo PDX transplant. He'd recently turned off from his homegrown inclination to play at rap loving gangster, and deciding to reinvent himself as CELEBRITY GOTH SELECTOR the second his feet had hit LA soil. Fucker looked like a methed out hillbilly (with a Jo Kamel face) who had grabbed a random pile of clothes and junk jewelry from H&N and Hott Topick, threw it on the floor, and then rolled in it. He knew absolute bare minimum dick about anything but the most rudimentary shit (Bowhaus, Sisters, Suoxsie), but he did have one edge that made him "coachable". This edge was his ability to give free coke to the DJ backing him that night, the Honorable Slob Breather Blob Breather himself, who, although currently on his way to a local version of Junior Harvey Weinstein status, knew a damn good amount about obscure and GREAT music, and always spun a unique and fresh set. So, the way it worked was Portland Pussy Camel gave Slob Breather a few eightballs every time they DJ'd together, and Slob Breather would write Camel's playlist for him, along with giving him access to his vinyl collection. He even alphabetized his records so the little maggot wouldn't panic and choke.

Of course Slob Breather would still spin, but only in between trying to accumulate juice with any girls dumb enough to believe that he liked to give out his drugs for free, the most current one's backstage behind the DJ booth with him now.

"Fuck!" Blob Breather thought. "Three lines and this chick hasn't even so much as let me pet her lower back. Probably because of her friend in the corner. Fuck, I wish she would leave, I'm so hungy and hog horny!"

Jetty Jizz did one more off the sleeve of Faz Gaggit's Fireplace Favorites, sniffed a sec, then half turned, looking at Ginger Just Legal, offering a rolled up $100.

Ginger looked awkward, and made no commitment to walk over, so Jizz got off her knees near the coffee table behind the DJ booth where Slob had been laying out lines. She walked over to Ginger and whispered close to her.

Salted Plastic: The Comedic Horror of Gentrification

"What's wrong, kid? You don't look like you're having fun."

They both had come to the club in stock variety 1977 bad girl punk costumes as always; Jetty in a vinyl black mini skirt, red chucks and the same Ramoons crest t-shirt everyone had seen a million times, her long wavy brown hair teased up. Ginger was in blue denim with some shoddy Forever 31 pleather attempt at a biker jacket, zipped up, no shirt or bra underneath so her cleavage would show; Piggy had her hunting tonight apparently.

"I don't like that guy, he seems sleazy, it's making me feel grossed out being near him. I've heard a few things about him from posts on Fakebook; that cokes not gonna be free, Jetty."

Jetty mentally rolled her eyes, thinking about how Pignose had shown her videos that afternoon of his latest cuckventures with Ginger and his bff "Wilby" Hartford; Ginger laying on the bed, bored ass and grossed out look on her face.............Wilbur's sweaty gut peeking from under his Bloba Fatt t-shirt...........while "Piggula" made love by proxy in the corner.

"Their whole apartment is a mini-porn production studio." Jetty thought, taking a quick glance back to make sure Blob Breather was setting up the next round, "Pignose has the place set up with digital cameras and audio in every corner for all the 'special parties' they throw; Ginger's dreaming if she thinks I believe she's feeling uneasy around this guy. Oh well, gotta play along."

"No big deal kid," Jetty started, putting a hand on Ginger's shoulder, "I get high for free in exchange for tickling this guy's pathetic little nugget for a minute or two, I wash my hands, and we go dance; don't be so negative!"

Ginger looked around, trying to see if Piggy was within eyesight, didn't see him, and then smirked while looking up at Jetty.

"Ok, just a few lines, Jetty; at least we know it's good shit; Goon Camel Scrotumlip from Portland gave that stash to that guy. Remember him? Used to run hip hop nights once a month back in Portland?"

Salted Plastic: The Comedic Horror of Gentrification

"Yeaahhhh!" Jetty replied, in a playing dumb kinda tone, feigning vague recollection outwardly while inwardly remembering every detail with crystal clarity; her hip hop phase days. A memory of her, Camel and "just a friend" cruising back to Camel's place in a limo popped into her head, the Tong Song playing in the background..............TONG TA TONG TONG TONG!!!

Back at the bar Pignose Diddler stared into his Macallen double, not having taken a sip yet, already feeling beat by the night at his age, wondering just how much longer he could keep Ginger as his pet.

"HEY!" he heard as he felt a pat on his back, then half turned to see a familiar face.

"You here alone?" Reptilian Rebekah asked, smiling, a hopeful and acquisitional tone and energy oozing out of her. Her pinstripe blazer and skirt smelled vaguely of dried dog food, and the high heels she was wearing created a glamour in her butt and thighs that kind of only held up at certain angles.......this made her square shaped ass look sort of like Frankenstein's head turned upside down.

The bartender brought Rebekah a gin sour with olive juice and grenadine. She pulled out a bottle from her jacket and topped her drink off with a few drops of flea and tick medicine. This was her favorite drink, though she couldn't recall why; Rebekah didn't know it, but it reminded her unconscious mind of the vitellus she had slurped up as a youngling, when she had eaten her would be siblings before they could hatch.

"No, Ginger and Jetty are around here somewhere," he started, putting on a fake smile, his own appropriative energy activating, "I'm just getting warmed up." he added, raising and indicating his glass.

Yup, it was that time; things like RepReb and Pigdid rarely spoke on an open and honest level; their inner thoughts (if nothing else) let them know how abhorrent they would seem to others if they were ever to be honest about what they really wanted to harvest from their average social interaction. Essentially they treated friends, family and

Salted Plastic: The Comedic Horror of Gentrification

lovers no different than they would treat a boss whom they were asking for a raise; it was all the same to them.

"Oh, I think I see her out of the corner of the DJ booth," Rebekah went on, "she's so cute; you two are just so perfect together!!!" The scripted banter she farted out of her mouth would be apparent as such to anyone with a sufficient amount of honesty and observational skills to say "Ow, this hurts!" while being stabbed to death with a switchblade covered in lemon juice. Piggy knew the drill though; he knew that the auto-pilot bullshitting that people like them utilized to get what they wanted had to be maintained.

"Really?! I didn't see her over there. You've got better eyes than me; you're still a youngin!" he said, saying "youngin" in a goofy mock southern accent in an attempt to seem silly and fun while he inwardly felt a bit low and defeated at the idea of having to flirt with, and possibly eventually settle for a woman older and less in shape than Ginger. His diddler nature cringed at the idea, but he knew his age, and that buying drinks, clothes, drugs and vacations alone would eventually not be enough for him to catch a 20 something year old girl.

Salted Plastic: The Comedic Horror of Gentrification

Friday, October 23, 11:09 PM

As she exited her apartment, antique black equestrian boots clicking on the pavement, Lydia checked her phone for another reply in the text conversation she had been having with Dagmar while she was getting ready.

Standing on the corner, she smoothed out her black and gold snake skin shorts; the shorts and boots, very retro and old fashioned, contrasted heavily with her headdress and jacket. The jacket, handmade by an old friend that had a side business creating cosplay out of a little booth at Fran and Sons, looked like something out of a Willem Gibseine novel. Biker cut collar, heavy duty vinyl that looked a lot like real leather, the lapels, sleeves/waist edges, and pockets rimmed with a thin and pliable looking real copper piping. Faux amber bubbles bordered by more copper piping were randomly dispersed on the front of the jacket's torso and around the sleeves. Inside each bubble, suspended as if in real amber, were bits of broken computer microchips. It was zipper free, so it had to be put on like a shirt; this was a pain in the ass considering that the thing was skin tight, but Lydia didn't mind sacrificing comfort for fashion when she went out. Didn't mind at all, considering that she had to dress like a Mormon attorney while at work, a thing that pissed her off immensely; having to look formal and proper while all the fakers got to dress in "casual geek chic" (a term often used in the dress code office memos) with their lame ass BOZINGA t-shirts, Desktiny tote bag/purses, and budget-ass looking Kaptain Amerrica shield backpacks.

The headdress was a Chinese antique, and it was very difficult to style her hair into all by herself, but the stares were worth it; Lydia wasn't really vain in the sense that she wanted all eyes on her, "IM BEAUTIFUL!" attention, but she liked to make a point that she had no interest in the scripted bland garbage people were passing off as fashion these days by calling it minimalist attire. Sometimes it took her 30 plus minutes to get her hair into that big wooden sixteen inch high oval,

Salted Plastic: The Comedic Horror of Gentrification

which almost resembled a giant black Priingels potato chip. Even more painstaking was getting the hair nice and even, to the point that the golden phoenix in the middle of the thing was visible. She had to order a special car every time she wore the thing; luckily she'd met a girl who drove a convertible for Libt.

This friend, and Libt driver for about 8 months now, came around the corner in her Silver BNW 4 series convertible, making Lydia wonder again for the hundredth time why someone who could afford a car like that would be driving for a ride share company. The car's stereo blasted Nudegabe's "Lady Braun".

"You ain't Asian bitch!" the girl yelled as she slammed the brakes at the corner, smiling in reaction to Lydia's headdress, looking Lydia up and down real quick.

"What's up Jasmine?" Lydia replied as she opened the passenger door and got in, taking a quick (and somewhat longing) look at Jasmine, in her skin tight black Over Armor pants/shirt and red hooded sweater. "You making good money tonight?"

"So so....", Jasmine started, "bunch of cheap fucks not tipping, dragging my ass to Bel Air and Brentwood. I spent most of the night in my car reading a book and then napping; if it wasn't for a chance to see those legs I would've gone home already; good thing you called and woke my ass up, or I wouldn't be able to make my rent tonight. Oh, by the way; I thought I told you not to call me Jasmine no more." Still smiling, a silver front tooth flashing, Jasmine waited for a reply.

"Hah! Yeah, that's right; I forgot you're a supervillain now." Lydia said, getting ready to clown Jasmine over the whole thing.

About 3 months ago Jasmine had told Lydia that she was going by the name Filth Creature because she had joined some fight club or something. Lydia hadn't thought much of it until Jasmine showed her a few videos of her fights; for a tiny compact Cambodian girl she kicked ass, brought down girls and guys outweighing her by 20 to sometimes

77

40 pounds. Apparently she had learned bokator from her Uncle as a kid, and later on had taken up Brazilian jujitsu.

"Sure am lady," she replied to Lydia, "gonna capture you and do unspeakable things................to your butt!"

"Hahaha! You're crazy, girl!" Lydia said as she got into the car. "I think I like you." she smiled, not thinking before she said it, but knowing damn well (on some level) there was a natural reason why she had.

"I know you do lady, I know everything about you!" Jasmine said, putting her hand on Lydia's leg halfway between her upper thigh and knee, the gesture designed to convey an ambiguity between a pat and a pet just in case her advance was considered unwelcome. Jasmine had only known Lydia for less than a year, but she knew how she felt, and definitely didn't come at Lydia's beck and call to drive her cause she needed the money, despite what she might say about making rent.

Lydia seemed to hardly even notice the gesture, being absorbed in her phone still, texting Dagmar. Jasmine smirked, a little hurt and lovesick (maybe) look on her face, took her hand of Lydia's leg, and started driving.

"Ugh!" Lydia thought as she texted. "That was awkward; girl is at least 10 years my junior. She's cute and exiting and all, but she's trouble; I can feel it. Don't know why I said that; fuck, it just came out!"

As Jasmine turned onto Hill St. Lydia saw a group of girls taking photos in front of another angel wing mural, gearing up for yet another "I AM AN LA GODDESS!" post.

"Nothing better to do than fake themselves out into believing that personal empowerment comes from art hunting symbiosis?" Lydia whispered to herself. The whole thing reminded her of Gifoor and all the other P4 manikins. It really pissed her off. "Fuck, don't these girls have a piece of themselves tucked away somewhere?" she yelled. "Don't they have any genuine way to show the world that they have something to offer that no other woman has? Not a surprise they don't, considering that their role models are memetic whirlpools of standardized social

Salted Plastic: The Comedic Horror of Gentrification

media patterns personified by celebrities and so-called influencers, as opposed to say…… strong women writing books, shaking trends in civic politics, or in general, doing anything that actually GETS THINGS DONE! This shit, this 'IM THE BEAUTIFUL SOUL OF LA!' crap is just another power grab for daddy's 'you're the prettiest sweetie!' admonition, only its being replaced by a legion of Shitstagram drones, half of them more than likely rapey men following all these girls while they rub one out at home with nacho cheddar Dooreeto resin all over their palms."

Jasmine smiled, looking at Lydia who was catching a breath after her rant. "Damn bitch! You angry! It's just some street art; girls are just having fun. You know? Fun? Ever heard of it?" Jasmine said, that tooth shining in the light again as she smiled.

"Where do you think I'm going right now?" Lydia replied.

Jasmine brought out a silver cigarette case, the top decorated with an ornamental silver cockroach. She took out a cigarette and lit, the flame from her lighter briefly illuminating a tattoo of a possum skull on her hand. She exhaled, a contemplative look on her face.

"Where do I think you're going?" she said in a flat bored tone. "That's easy; you're going to some expensive downtown shithole full of canned fun."

"Hahahah! Now whose angry?" Lydia said.

"Not me……….and I won't get into detail about it, I'm just gonna offer you an authentic good time for when you're all done with that shit tonight…..here's your stop….," she pulled up to the alley that led to the venue Lydia was going to, "…….when you get bored of this spot call me later, and I'll show you a REAL good time!!! Think about it!"

Lydia smiled, leaned forward, gave Jasmine a hug, then inched slowly out of the car, finding it hard to just end the conversation and go. "I'll think about it," Lydia said, still smiling, "gotta go in here first and go through the motions with the simpletons, K?"

"Ok lady, but I expect a text tonight either way; I've got other options, ya know?"

79

Salted Plastic: The Comedic Horror of Gentrification

Jasmine drove off, and Lydia felt a little hurt, a little dumb, a little longing, a little numb............oh well........

Salted Plastic: The Comedic Horror of Gentrification

Friday, October 23, 10:37 PM

James and Miguel strolled up Broadway, then turned onto a side street towards the alley entrance to The Leash.

"I'm telling you James," Miguel started, "the minute I get to that door somebody is going to scream for security......."

"Ha! You really think you're that important in this city, don't you?"

Miguel winced, a little irritated at James' comment, the drugs elevating his reaction. James leaned in and patted him on the back, (nothing but love for his brother) and Miguel calmed a bit.

"Look," James said solemnly, "you know what I think......with as much trash as you talk about LA, this new breed of people coming here and living, and how they're all supposedly after you; you know the only thing this tells me is that THAT'S EXACTLY what you want; to be heard and paid attention to by these people......"

"I don't give a fuck what they think, IN FACT, they don't thin....." Miguel started.

"You're wrong bro; they all think, just not the way you want them to, and you do give more than a shit about what they think or you wouldn't be spending so much energy on trying to bite back, no? Pretty much, you're just pissed that they don't think the way you want them to............and guess what, they never will. But here's the thing bro; you can always push back when you need to, as long as you're having fun in the process......and that's why we're here tonight; give them something to think about while we enjoy ourselves, right?" James smiled.

"You're crazy, brother!" Miguel smiled back as they reached the door to the club. "Looks like they have a new doorman." he whispered to James. "Ok, fuck it; let's see what happens."

A short white guy in his early 30s ran the door, his outfit a collage of every fashion he'd committed a lukewarm interest to since he moved to Los Angeles......huarache sandals, punk rock jacket, I See Pee t-shirt,

81

cornrows, Cocki Docki man purse, knee high Unvengers socks; typical career poser culture vulture material. His mustache was publicly (pew-bick-LEE) dapper, and waxed by organic, free trade, outdoors rugged walrus semen; this made him feel like a REAL MAN!

He looked at James' and Miguel's ids passively, letting them in without a care as he eyeballed some of the food vendors on the outside patio near the entrance; after his Kruv Magoo class earlier he had had to rush to work without grabbing anything to eat; this happened a lot, and more often than not, his dinner came exclusively from these food trucks.

There was actually quite a variety of them, these eateries on wheels, that boasted a "bringing it to the people" theme/scheme ploy as their marketing structure. Yup, every substandard "chef" in LA had turned up to peddle their variety of nouveau gourmet. In particular, Semen Stache had his eyes on Drill Em All, an up and coming artisanal burger stand that specialized in the fine culinary art of sodomizing the consumer's wallet for top tier steakhouse kind of money in exchange for low grade ground chuck burgers, doctored up by atypical garnishments and semantic bullshit that revolved around the idea of making hamburgers synonymous with famous celebrities.

He asked the back up security to monitor the door as he walked over to the trucks, intending to order his usual, The Canye Western, a play on Carlos Junior's western bacon burger, only made with Koestler House Braised Bacon, Gibson Green Heirloom tomatoes (surname throwing apparently qualified justification for charging premium prices), and LOCALLY smoked raw milk gouda (the whole local thing being another price elevator) from Trustfund Bitch "Farms" (the farm was really just someone's Echo Park garage). At the reasonable price of $29 a burger WHO COULD RESIST?!?!

Almost to the stand though, and his "appetite" totally changed when he saw that the other trucks boasted longer lines.

Salted Plastic: The Comedic Horror of Gentrification

"Shit!" Cumstache thought. "What's my Shitstagram post gonna look like, me standing in front of Drill Em All with nobody else in line? Not very demonstrative of my value as a hip culture seeking foodie type of guy, not at all!!! I mean, the whole point of getting food has little to do with actually eating it and obtaining nutrients; it's all about me being a jaded attention whore that's in desperate need of harvesting social media likes after all. Then again, I'm sure my ability to KRUV OFF (his term for using his fighting skills) if there's trouble at work tonight might depend on me eating for the sake of caloric intake."

Turning away from Drill Em All, he took a look at the other stands and food trucks.

Two in particular seemed to be drawing a crowd of people. First there was Pot Head Slop Bowl, the latest in a long local history of FRESH HIP ideas by LA's HOTTEST celebrity chef, Gutbeard Buddha, a pioneer in creating eateries and trucks known for flavor overkill specialties such as peanut butter, bacon, marshmallow and ahi tuna tacos, served in taro cups, and drenched in kimchee taffy pico de gallo. Other genius culinary specialties included kung pao marinera birria bahn mi, and caramel curry shawerma served over cilantro lemon-butter sour cream gruyere risotto, garnished in five spice pork belly bits, sous vide octopus and pop rocks; all fine choices for a guaranteed inability to enjoy the clashing flavors at best, or a shit attack at worst.

He was tempted by (but still not fully decided on) the possibility of satiating his social media attention hunting appetite (if not his actual need for sustenance) on Pot Head Slop Bowl's pizza roll and tater tot chutney croquettes with squid ink Popsi Cola aioli.

"DAMN! Think of all the possible likes and comments I'll get from posting myself pretending to eat those!!!!!" he thought. Still though, there was the possibility that eating at one of the other trucks might lead to a greater amount of social media attention whoring, so he decided to take a look at what the stand with the longer line had to offer first.....................

83

Salted Plastic: The Comedic Horror of Gentrification

Friday, October 23, 10:53 PM (The Leash)

"Two Stellas," Miguel told the bartender, as James bug-eyed the room, looking at all the girls, trying to keep conscious of what Miguel had told him in the bathroom as they "recharged" on a few more lines.

"Girls are very different now, James; you have to give them a measure of respect that you may not be used to; simply put, let them set the pace of consent, and don't be too sleazy; the days of coming on too strong are over.........at least on initiation."

That last part had confused him......A LOT; essentially Miguel had said that being a roughshod type of male may be something particular girls are into, but that coming off that way from the start was a definite road to trouble; even if it's welcome, it's not welcome unasked. Basically, being in and out of jail since the late 90's, it was very difficult for James to understand that even something as simple as complementing a woman on her physical appearance in the wrong way might lead to a definite cold shoulder. It was just all too much to...........

"Stop worrying," Miguel whispered in his ear, "just start with the basics. A simple 'where are you from?' or 'so, what do you do?' is a good starting point." Miguel patted his brother on the shoulder and smiled as he passed him a beer. They both drank the beers, more for hydration than for any needed buzz. Miguel's spirits were up, and, despite seeing that appropriative excuse of a human being, Pignose Diddler, walking out of the bathroom earlier, he actually felt like tonight would be fun, free of trouble, and that maybe, just maybe, he might get his brother safely home tonight, free for at least one more day.

Salted Plastic: The Comedic Horror of Gentrification

Friday, October 23, 11:25 PM (The Leash)

Lydia saw Dagmar across the room at her usual reserved booth with bottle service in the corner, a few of her entourage pets perched on either side of her; more dime a dozen art school hopefuls; over-educated and unimaginative; The Leash was their element for sure. Dagmar wore one of her overpriced couture get ups that Lydia always had a feeling cost $5 worth of labor and materials to make, yet got tagged at a few thousand dollars simply because the right formula of store location, media petting, networking, and general collaborative hype-manufacturing had infused the thing with phantom value.

"Pretty though," she thought, "don't think I've ever seen this woman wear the same thing twice." The red vinyl body suit Dagmar had on was form fitted, head to toe, with a v cut collar showing her pale olive cleavage. The forearms were inlaid with some sort of high polished stone that circumvented them, looking strikingly like ebony or obsidian veined with gold ore. "How the fuck is that possible?" Lydia thought. "Looks like some sort of alien armor! FUCK, she's gorgeous.............and nearly impossible to say no to because of it." Lydia stared as she walked, taking in Dagmar's heavy copper, ribcage length curls, her pale olive skin, and the curves and muscle tone on her 5 foot 6 inch body. She was wearing her green contacts as always; she had never liked her natural brown eyes.

Lydia knew Dagmar noticed her, but it wasn't Dagmar's style to wave, smile, shout out, or let on in any way that she acknowledged Lydia's presence; that would just be all too human of her. A few loose comments came to Lydia's ears, and quite a few fingers pointing as she walked by, people smirking over her headdress, and jacket. "Yup, that's right," she thought, "I didn't get the memo that anything atypical, and outside the stringent H&N or Apparently Apparel fashion formula isn't welcome here. God bless Dagmar for that; no matter how full of shit and engrossed in this society she is, she's one of the few people I know that is still willing to give half a fuck about dressing out of the ordinary.......she just pays more for it than I do."

As she walked past the front room bar she caught the eye of one of those rare to be seen animals in Los Angeles these days. The guy was tall and brown skinned, hair styled into a pompadour, clothes all denim and real leather. He had a heavy tobacco scent, and was full of an energy that was socially archaic, heavy, and fun in small doses...........but a burden in anything more than that. The vibe he gave off was HIGHLY palpable; sickening and exciting at the same time; she felt her energy drop from sternum to navel at the sight/feel of him. The way he stood, his facial mannerisms making it obvious that he was judging everyone in the room, including her, made her nerves light up that same way they did when she was about to pop a quad dose of Percocet; jumpy excitement over the 2 hour high she'd be riding on at the cost of feeling like shot to hell shit for the 2 to 3 days following that brief amount of fun.

"Still a few LA locals around, huh?" she smiled at the guy, loving how he was taken aback that she, a total stranger, knew what he was. He smiled back, was about to approach her and say something, but his friend stopped him, tapping him on the shoulder asking a question.

She winked, turned, and kept walking towards Dagmar's booth, asking a cocktail waitress for a double Hibiki and a glass of ice water on the way there.

"The table in the corner." she told the waitress, leaving a $50 tip on her tray; no matter how good she had it now, she'd never forgotten what a shit job it had been serving tables when she first came to Los Angeles, so she always tipped heavy.

"What was that?" Dagmar asked, as Lydia got to the table, her deep accent booming over the club's music in a way that few voices could; Dagmar's father had been a finance specialist in Prague, Zurich, Vienna, Berlin, Tel Aviv..........and briefly in Al Ain, her accent a definite consequence (or benefit of, depending on the ears receiving it) of her upbringing.

Lydia had always loved it, that voice. The same memories always flashed in her head whenever she heard it; that deep, heavy, almost masculine accent, would always be synonymous with lying in Dagmar's Italian rosewood bed after sex, eating Persian baklava, Dagmar's heavily toned legs (Dagmar was the one who had introduced Lydia to Muay Thai) wrapped around Lydia's waist. Lydia lying there, watching Holy Montaine, or some new anime, trying her best to get Dagmar invested while she feigned some small attention, pet Lydia on the head, and kept a tight vigil on her phone.

"Nothing lady....." Lydia responded to Dagmar's question, using "lady" the same way Jasmine did with her, trying to shake off the memories already breeding a want in her to just tell Dagmar to cut the ritual bullshit, so they could get back to her place already.

"I was just setting up some insurance for the night in case you piss me off," she smiled, "don't want to go home empty handed."

"Funny," Dagmar replied, "you really love the user friendly type, don't you?"

"I do, I really do." Lydia replied with sarcasm. "Speaking of, can you get your fucking lemmings to move so I can sit down?"

Dagmar nodded at the two people sitting to her left and right in the booth; twenty-something hopefuls, obviously some of her new "discoveries", hoping for whatever glamour crumbs she'd eventually throw their way once she vampired out of them a sufficient amount of recreation. The boy was anglo, blond haired, blue eyed, lanky with feminine features, fitted khaki shorts, cheap Terget fedora, red Chucks, a vinyl biker jacket and no shirt, showing off a smooth chest. The girl was possibly Asian and African American mix, short and full figured, wearing neon pink vinyl gloves and hot pants, black studded heels, and a black cheesecloth tank top. She had a stern facial expression that showed

87

she'd already been playing at the LA networking circus for a minute now........long enough to get a little bitter.

They got up, and headed to the dance floor, Dagmar dropping a small baggy into the palm of the girl's outstretched palm as she sidled out of the booth, the girl staring daggers at Lydia as she walked away.

"I see you got that one trained to your particular brand of bullshit loyalty, already." Lydia commented, smiling as she sat down, tactilely friendly, putting her hand on Dagmar's thigh, while maintaining the role of enemy on a verbal level.

Dagmar sighed, took a look at Lydia, and smiled, a gesture of ineffable understanding on her face. "If you're still looking for the kind of kosher and polite business exchange and contract theory that they tuck you to bed with in all those college business law classes you took, I think you better become a lawyer for a non-profit Lydia. I read about P4 by the way; read all the popcorn editorials.............and then got the real deal from Sienna Berger yesterday; I'm sure you were daydreaming about the place finally becoming as comfortable and personal as your bedroom, still not understanding that business is business, but I thought by now you'd realize how things really work in the real wor................"

Dagmar stopped, a crash and commotion coming from the front room dancefloor taking away her attention.

Lydia stopped too, looked and listened, smiling, the pills she'd popped before coming into the club activating from all the excitement.

"It's that animal," she smiled at Dagmar, her face flushed, "that thing at the bar!" she finished, wide eyed excitement on her face.

"OK," Dagmar replied, "I know the drill; I guess I'm not enough for you tonight, huh?"

"You've only got yourself to blame for that, honey!" Lydia snapped back as the waitress from earlier handed her her whisky. "So, do I bait him back to your place on my own, or are you going to actually do some work for once?"

Salted Plastic: The Comedic Horror of Gentrification

Dagmar popped one of her designer drugs into her mouth, took a sip of the Grand Cru Classe Bordeaux that they kept at the bar just for her, and stared with a piss giddy look at Lydia. "I got it covered; it's my job to know what everybody wants, and how to give it to them in exchange for even MORE of what I want." She leaned across the table, snaking her palm up Lydia's forearm, her heavy curls draping across the table as she looked up through her brows at Lydia. "You should know that better than anybody by now, no?"

Salted Plastic: The Comedic Horror of Gentrification

Friday, October 23, 11:45 PM (The Leash)

Miguel walked back to the backroom dancefloor, mixed drinks in his hands, past tons of dark and spooky for the night beard clones, making faces and shit slinging comments to himself the entire way. The drinks were for a group of girls James had met. He laughed as he looked over at James, who was surprisingly having better luck than him; he'd managed to find the only cool girls in the entire place; three curvy Latinas from La Puente who had come to the city to party, but thought that all the guys at the Leash were "rude boring ass bitches." Between James crude charm and humor, and him sharing a few generous bumps with them, he had no problem managing.

"Damn," Miguel thought, "a guy whose spent fifteen collective years in prison, and who by all rights should have no social skills, is doing better than I ever do; maybe Jessica was right; I got no people skills."

He handed the short girl with the bob hairdo, soft coffee colored skin, denim jeans and jacket, and steel toe boots her whisky soda. This one, even though she appeared to be no younger than 27 or 28, reminded him of Jessica when they had met as kids. She smiled but he was too dumb to realize that that meant he was supposed to say something goofy or playful to jump into a conversation. Instead, like a moron he broke eye contact, and mechanically handed the other two girls their drinks.

James leaned toward him, a big all-knowing grin on his face. "I don't understand how talking to girls works these days, huh?" he said mockingly. "Looks like I'm doing pretty good for a guy who don't understand, and even I can see that that girl's already made and scouted you out bro.........so don't blow it!!!!"

Miguel laughed softly under his breath; fuck, he thought too much of himself and his opinion; this whole night thinking he was babysitting his older brother, and here James was, opening his eyes for

90

Salted Plastic: The Comedic Horror of Gentrification

him, teaching him about life and people, showing him how simple the things he liked to complicate to shit by overthinking can be.

"A large chunk of his life away from society," Miguel whispered to himself, "and he just picks up the truth on the fly, even though he's only been on the outs for a few weeks, and here I am fucking clueless even though I've spent my entire life free." Miguel started tearing up with admiration and gratefulness for what he perceived to be his brother's simple yet profound wisdom. But, no sooner had he built up James in his mind as an insightful (albeit crude) life guru than he felt a slap on his back, followed by a.....

"Hey, you're being a faggot again. Cut it out!!!! These girls ain't exactly the drool over the sensitive type of guy types, and I'm sure even you know that man; get your shit straight, and stop fucking with my vacation!" Whether it was a reaction to Miguel's behavior, or the cocaine, he could tell James was on the verge of being violently angry.

Miguel smiled, laughing quickly to break the ice, and put his hand on James shoulder. "Fuck, you jackass, you just blew some mounting respect I had for you; I was starting to see you as some sort of modern day wise man or something."

"Wise man, huh? How's this for wise?" James asked, and before Miguel knew what he was talking about, James had pulled the high school act of pushing him next to the girl with the bob hairdo, and yelled "MY BRO wants YOU BAAAD!!!!"

Miguel felt his stomach elevate into his chest, face burning with embarrassment, while the girl laughed, obviously amused that a grown man could be that shy. I mean, he could talk to girls, but flat out blatant statements that cut to the chase of just wanting to go to bed were not his style. She kept smiling, and he smiled back, at a loss for words, just staring at her, still thinking about how she reminded him of Jessica. Idiot was totally smitten with her, high on another one of his fantasy cocktails that he was very good at mixing up when it came to women. The fact that she reminded him of Jessica, coupled with his jump the gun nature, already had him going on the lottery jackpot possibility that this girl could potentially be the one........and then she opened her mouth......

"It's cool honey, your brother is just trying to save us some time; it's getting boring here. Do you guys live nearby?"

It was one of those prissy, cutesy, girly girl, almost cartooney voices that you can tell got manufactured into permanence by years of affectation, and was designed to make its user seem sweeter and more of a warm welcome than they actually are. In Miguel's experience, every girl he had ever met with that kind of voice was pure trouble.

"I live kind of far, all the way out in Pomona." he lied.

The girl looked at him a split second, lip half upturned, trying not to smile, snort/hiccuped.........and then just gave in and tilted her head back, laughing at what to her was a highly apparent, shitty, and poorly executed lie.

"It's ok," she said, "we can fuck at my place!"

Miguel stayed silent, hoping that his lack of response, the best reaction he could come up with, would mask his lie.

Her reaction to that was to poke him in the stomach playfully, and smile. "Bet you're married too, huh, you little shit!" she said, still playful.

"I'm........." he started, but got cut off......

"Maybe not. Girlfriend then? It's something; I'm a psych major!" she announced with pride. "I can just tell these things!"

"UGH!" he thought. "One of those! Thinking all the answers to life can be dredged out of an academic package."

"Whatever!" she continued. "I really don't care, I just don't want the details. So, are we gonna take off or........."

He was smiling, listening to her talk, taking jabs at him, glad this was gonna be easy, momentarily turning his head to check on James, looking at him smiling with an arm around each of the other girls while they laughed at his dumb outdated jokes, both of them in leather, bondage belts...........purple and magenta hair. The Kameleon's Swamp

Salted Plastic: The Comedic Horror of Gentrification

Man was playing in the background, he caught a quick glimpse of that turd, Pignose Diddler's girlfriend, Ginger Just Legal, in the DJ booth, jabbering with some guy who looked like a Werecamel. Her friend Jetty Jizz was in the corner of the booth, helping Slob Breather Blob Breather adjust the fly of his jeans or something.

Everything was solid, peaceful, fun, and more easy going than it had been for him in a long time. Sure, this chick wasn't his dream girl, but he was going to have some NSA fun with her, and his brother seemed to be having a good time too; it looked like there wouldn't be any trouble tonight. He looked around the room, content and full of joy; the feeling that the night was going to end well seemed almost definite......things were almost perfect..............until he turned his head just a little too far, and gave into instant rage...........

Salted Plastic: The Comedic Horror of Gentrification

Friday, October 23, 11:50PM (The Leash)

"So, is Ginger still running you ragged, making you party like a teenager all night, seven days a week?" Rebekah asked Piggy, setting up her sales pitch, but quickly caught the mild irritation at the corners of his mouth and brow; she recovered fast though, changing tactics; one of the things her maternal serpent had always taught her about cornering a meal ticket; look at the facial ques, and "always have a plan A through Z."

"You look a little stressed is all I meant," she followed up, "you'd probably be happier watching some Cock and Farty at home........with a whisky soda and a butt plug in your vagainal, no?"

Piggy smiled; Ginger had given Rebekah access to their Metflix account, had told him as much; Rebekah was obviously looking through their que, and trying to play it up like she had similar tastes. This was in fact one of her finest acts; when she had met Miguel, Rebekah had played the role but good, looking up bare bones facts about all his favorite books, records, comics, games and anime. You name it; she did just enough half assed research on it all to ham it up and get him to believe they shared similar interests. Still, who told her that Piggula's favorite drink was a whisky soda w/ a rubber peg back? Or about his secret term for his rectal vagina (vagainal) for that matter? "Hmmmmm!?" he thought. "Oh well, no matter......." Piggy continued on, and reciprocated Rebekah's act in kind; he knew the drill.

"YOU LIKE THAT CARTOON TOO!" he shouted with perfectly cadenced excitement, putting his hand on her thigh under the bar counter as he did.

"It's my favorite!" she squealed in a disgusting attempt to act fully human, placing her hand over his on her thigh, while simultaneously acting out her favorite line from Cock and Farty, which in fact was the only thing she remembered of the show period, from when she had let an episode play one day, paying half attention to it as she did her toes.

Salted Plastic: The Comedic Horror of Gentrification

Pignose laughed at her performance and inched his hand up a little higher on her thigh.

"Gotta close the deal!" she thought. "My mask is not gonna stay intact forever, and Miguel really doesn't seem like he's gonna pay off, so I better......."

"What's your favorite, Lady?" a familiar voice came from behind her back, asking her in a tone of complete disgust.

Rebekah stopped cold, and then sighed, closing her eyes in reaction to the hate in Miguel's voice, turning on the bar stool, already primed to brace for the onslaught with one of her prize winning "I'm a victim" performances. If Miguel only knew she just couldn't help it, she thought, that selling herself, and programming others was all she was capable of...........in fact, more so than she'd ever know.

"Miguel.....I...." she started, but was cut short by the physical manifestation of all his grievances with her; everything he'd held back ever since discovering her secrets; all the irritation that had been simmering due to her social media exhibitionism; constantly flaunting herself like a piece of meat; all her side flirtation; every ounce of anger generated over her being an inveterate liar.............not to mention her constant hunt for the next best thing while she continued to play up her false loyalty to him. It was a storm of heartbreak, disgust, and all his pent up hate, topped off with heavy doses of cocaine and alcohol.........and it all came down in one big expression of malcontent...........right into Pignose Diddler's jawline.

Everything blurred.......security were already running across the dance floor, coming to save the day. Piggy was instantly knocked out cold on the floor, and Rebekah was leaning over him, looking up at Miguel and shaking her head, "feeling" fully entitled to her disgust with his "immature" behavior.

Reality slipped into a standard pace for the last couple of seconds, and they locked eyes before he was dragged out by security.

Salted Plastic: The Comedic Horror of Gentrification

"I KNOW what you are, you THING!!!!!!" he shouted at her, as the bouncers struggled to pull him towards the door.

As he said that her eyes glazed over, and he could've sworn they were yellow (not their usual green), with vertical irises. Those eyes were sizing him up; more calculating and aware than usual, and full of an energy totally disparate to the rest of her facial gestures; her mouth was still turned down in a display of sad disgust even though those eyes maintained a mode of sharp inquisition. It was as if something more intelligent than Rebekah was watching him, while the rest of her remained completely unaware of the surveillance happening through her eyes.

Salted Plastic: The Comedic Horror of Gentrification

Saturday, October 24, 12:15 am

"…………AND KEEP MY FUCKING FACE OFF YOUR WALL BEFORE I SUE YOU FOR NAME DEFAMATION, YOU BEARDED CUNTS!!!!!" Miguel finished ranting as he was ejected from The Leash, throwing a crumbled piece of paper he had torn off the wall as he was dragged out.

He walked down a side alley, muttering to himself, wondering what had happened to James, sort of pissed that he hadn't backed him up inside. "Not a scratch on me; three bearded turds it took to drag me out; FUCKING WEAK!"

He took his phone out, and began texting and calling James for 10 to 20 minutes, but got no response.

He lit up a cigarette, took a couple of drags, thinking about what to do next, the anger over James not helping him abating, and being replaced by worry. "Shit!" he said. "I hope he's ok…..even if he didn't get my back in there when security grabbed me."

Just then his phone went off, a text from James.

James: Sorry bro, I'm in an office here.

Miguel: What'd you do? Punch one of the security who grabbed me?

James: Ha! No, I didn't even know what happened to you until you told me right now. Some dude tried to slime in on the girls we were chatting up, and was trying to invite them over to his booth with his friends. Dickhead in khaki shorts above his knees, with a Kings cap and sports blazer.

Miguel: Yup, probably some douche from USC thinking he's gonna scout the "weirdo club" for "dark and slutty girls." That's how those idiots think. Anyways………FUCK! What did you do to him?

Salted Plastic: The Comedic Horror of Gentrification

James: Doesn't matter; if I get out of here I'll tell you all about it. If not, all I can say is tonight was fun, and thanks brother........thanks for enjoying my vacation with me.

Miguel: No problem brother. Just wait a minute; I'm sure they'll kick you out in a minute, then maybe we can stroll to another bar before last call.

Miguel waited a few minutes, no answer, and then........

James: Doesn't look like it bro; gotta go, cops just showed up, told me they gotta take my phone...........love you bro.

Miguel: What?!?! NO!!! James!?!? Put an officer on the phone for me man, let me talk to someone!!!!!

No answer.

Miguel: Hey, whoever has this phone, please pick up. This is my brother's phone.

No answer.

Miguel got desperate, and lied.

Miguel: I also happen to be my brother's legal representative, and I am informing you that you are obligated to respond to my inquiries regarding my client.

Still no answer.

He paced back and forth in the alley for another minute or two. "FUUUUCKKKKKKKKKK!!!!!!!!" he yelled as he threw his phone against the alley wall. He slumped down on the alley concrete, into the snubbed out cigarettes, old food wrappers, dirt, piss and filth; could care less, his heart was numb, shot full of hate for Rebekah, and sadness over his brother. He lit up another cigarette, and then started to cry.

"I don't wanna feel this right now, no fucking way!" he sobbed as he dug in his pocket, and pulled out his last four Vicodin, ready to pop them into his mouth.

Before he could take the pills, a red light flashed on him, flooding the entire area in crimson tones; a car coming up the alley.

"Never seen a car that let off red light before." Miguel thought, jumping to his feet, ready to move. A black and red Doudge Chergar with tinted windows pulled up to him; he fully expected things were about to get worse, and that the car was full of some of the promoters and pushers from Bearded Bitches in Black, about to get out and jump him like a pack of pussies; wouldn't be the first time.

The back window came down, he clenched his fist, ready for what was coming, but then quickly relaxed as he realized that the car was completely void of beards, cheap pseudo goth posers, or any known affiliates of The Leash. His fists relaxed, dropping the pills on the pavement as he saw a gorgeous woman, olive skinned with red hair and emerald eyes, looking him up and down as if deciding whether or not communication with him was worth her while. Her assessment of him done after a second or two, she leaned out the window a bit.

"My friend here is fond of those too," Dagmar said, indicating the Vicodin he had dropped "but you might want to hold off on taking those pills; can't have you incapable of performing." She gave a forced smile as she finished. Deep in at the other end of the backseat he could see the girl from earlier..........the one with the tacky headdress and killer jacket.

Wiping tears away, hoping they hadn't seen him crying, he smiled, getting the gist of what the olive skinned woman was hinting at; they wanted a third to take home and use as a middle man. "Is this really happening?" Miguel thought. His spirits raised up, and he felt lucky to be blessed with such an out of the ordinary distraction in his time of need, even though he sensed that these two women came from that pool of society he hated so much here in LA. Miguel was ready to drown in whatever these two vipers had to offer, even though he knew it was going to possibly cost him. He thought about Penicchio, with his big burro ears, as he snubbed out his cigarette, and reached for the car door.

Salted Plastic: The Comedic Horror of Gentrification

Saturday, October 24, 12:27 am (The Leash)

Pignose Diddler came to on the floor, rubbing his head and looking around. Ginger Just Legal, Reptilian Rebekah, and Jetty Jizz were standing nearby, all of them looking down at Piggy with the utmost (and thoroughly "genuine") concern and endearment; the anxiety they all felt over his well-being was SO GREAT and unrivaled in authentic tenderness, that similar instances of the type of care they exhibited would be hard to bring to mind. The closest examples of the kind of concern and love they showed would probably be the following:

A spoiled blue blood prom queen raiding her date's jacket for that last bit of cocaine before she phones 911 after he overdoses. A thoroughbred Brentwood brat getting worried that daddy's cardiac arrest at the country club might spoil his near and already scheduled, all invitations sent out birthday party. A house cat pawing around a dead mouse, hoping to get a little bit more play out of the thing before deciding to move on to something else.

The probate process of announcing the contents of a will is what came to mind the most though; that hour of truth, when the family gathered in warm congregation to slather, drool, covet and jackal over the last shreds of meat left behind on the bones of their mother or father's corpse.

Yup, there was no doubt that they all cared for Piggy on the deepest most genuine level possible............in varying shades of avarice, desperation and envy.

Between the three and three though; three women, being driven by three motivations, Rebekah had the heaviest drive to ham up her "concern" for Piggy.....not to mention that she was backed by the power and influence of forces possibly interstellar and/or interdimensional in origin, whether she consciously knew it or not.

The right distraction, plus the fact that Piggy was still alive and still capable of vending capital, was enough for Jetty and Ginger to walk back to the DJ booth; Slob Breather Blob Breather had been gesturing to Jetty for the last couple of seconds, little baggy in hand, his face sweating like a glass goblet of oily (and somehow still liquid) iced chicken fat.

RepReb stayed behind, helping Pignose up onto the bar stool.

"I'm sorry....." she said, face flushed, eyes wide, as she brushed him off, pawing him like he was a Diorre leather coat, or a pair of bland and overpriced Tiffanie diamond earrings.

"Rough lover you have there," he said as he rubbed his jaw, "that guy is gonna be the death of you."

"No way!" she replied. "I'm done; Miguel's childish behavior just cost him a lifetime of respect and devotion!"

Piggy snorted mentally at that last comment, knowing full well what her brand of respect and devotion consisted of; showing the whole world her ass on Shitstagram, and flirting with any and every slob on social media that would personal message her.

"It's cool," he thought, "as long as I get mine; I only have a couple more good times left that I can squeeze out of Ginger, and vice-versa." Looking over at the side of the DJ booth verified his thoughts; Ginger was leaning in on some greasy popcorn-headed hipster in Berkenstok sandals and Apparently Apparel pink daisy dukes, girlishly poking at his black denim jacket, probably asking him about his lame band pins.

"Hey, you hear me?" Rebekah asked. "Is that punch making you dizzy; maybe we ought to file a police report, get some money out of Miguel by pressing charges."

"And then there's Jetty," he kept thinking, ignoring Rebekah's greedy suggestion, "she's definitely still up for a little sugaring....."

His thoughts were cut short by the annoying sound of RepReb sucking away on the straw of her empty drink, while she side glanced at the club's crowd, pretending like she wasn't making that annoying straw sucking sound as a way of getting his attention.

Salted Plastic: The Comedic Horror of Gentrification

"Ok, let's be real!" Piggy said, smiling, putting a hand on her shoulder.

"Lets!" Rebekah replied, putting her hand on his knee and smiling like a ghoul.

"We both like each other, yes?" he asked.

"We do...." she half answered softly, barely paying attention to his words while motioning to the bartender by pointing to her empty drink, and thinking to herself. "Here it comes! GOT EM! No more community college for me; it's time for University, and vacations, and all the spa days and new clothes Piggy's money can buy!" She leaned in, putting her empty drink against his bruised cheek so the ice could stop the swelling.

"You're sweet!" he replied with generic sincerity, the need for convincing verbal banter crumbling between them while the heart of the matter rotated in their individual thoughts. "Got that black hole of a human being, Miguel off her back finally." he thought. "Now I can make her my new penis goalie, taking it all so I can get it vicariously."

"Hey, you're flushed and sweating!" he heard her say through his thoughts. "You ok? Maybe we need more ice than this."

"Am I?" he asked, pretending not to realize that he was being slimy. He regained his composure, and looked her in the eye for a minute, pausing as if he was going to propose.

The reptilian nanomachines in Rebekah's mask simulated a blushing effect in her cheeks, while the behavior programs in her nervous system did the rest, "telling" her that she was ecstatic; this was her Dizzney/Mickelodion/Pecks in The Titty, Earth Caffé Shitstagram Post daydream come true, being propositioned by this base appetite of a human being. The sophisticated S&R programs in her unconscious mind reacted favorably to Piggy being her new host.

He broke the silence with a plain old "So.....let's do this!"

"Like, go home and have sex?" she asked with synthetic shyness. The liquid based software inside RepReb (unknown to her) went into

103

overdrive, making her act girly and smitten, orchestrating a "reality" in her mannerisms, and overall energy and tone, a visual manifestation that her etch a sketch, emotionally bankrupt heart was incapable of.

"Well, that too," Piggy replied, "but not tonight; it might be too soon for Ginger, just yet. What I meant was......lets contract, ummm.......I mean get the relationship started; the sex, and everything else will come with the DEAL."

"Almost done here" he thought, "and with Ginger out the door, Rebekah will no doubt want the obvious, considering her appetites. Which is fine considering what I'm going to get in return......OH YES, I'LL PAY HER BILLS!!!"

The bartender put down Rebekah's second drink. She grabbed it and took a sip, smiling behind the glass. "Sure, but I have to warn you; my bacterial vaginosis gets quite putrid. Tee hee!" This last she said girlishly, as if she were talking about petting puppies.

"Oh don't worry, you won't be having sex with me." Piggy smiled, holding back the urge to vomit.

She smiled back, pretending like she didn't know what his comment meant, and raised her glass. "Good deal!" she replied while he half-heartedly matched his glass to hers, barely paying attention to her as he looked out at Ginger on the dancefloor with Popcorn Head hipster bitch. Not that either him or Rebekah cared about authentic enthusiasm at this point; business had been concluded and made official, and the need to display any genuine care for each other from this point forward would be reserved for when they were in the company of others (or posting photos together) for the most part.

Throughout Piggy and Rebekah's entire contractual proceeding the bartender had been glaring at her impatiently, waiting for Rebekah to pay for her drink. Finally noticing him, she smiled and pointed silently to Pignose behind his back, indicating that the drink was on him. The bartender walked away impatiently, and Rebekah looked back at Piggy, still smiling.

Salted Plastic: The Comedic Horror of Gentrification

The corners of her mask were sagging a bit...........revealing a few scales underneath........it was disgusting.

Salted Plastic: The Comedic Horror of Gentrification

Saturday, October 24, 12:35 am

"So, what, essentially I'm tonight's entertainment for you two?" Miguel asked with sarcasm, grateful for what he assumed was going to happen tonight, but still maintaining his usual attitude and low opinion toward the type of people he assumed Lydia and Dagmar were.

Dagmar, sensing the underlying anger in his tone, spoke up. "You know, there's plenty of other remnants like you left in LA; lots of lingering locals that would love to be in your shoes." She said in a condescending tone, not even looking at him, refusing to even acknowledge Miguel as important. She just stared out her window as the Doudge Chergar kept it's pace up Broadway in Downtown LA. Taking him in was really Lydia's idea after all; if it was up to her it would have been just her and Lydia tonight, or her, Lydia and one of her new pet interns or something......

"Good to know......" Miguel answered in quick and solemn anger, "........so you won't mind if I leave you to go fucking find one, you affluent class, vapid, effete and facile culture thief!? You consumption insect of a human being!" He tried sounding passive, but he was clearly grinding his teeth.

"Hahahaha! Nice vocabulary!" Dagmar snapped back, finding his little outburst quite pathetic. "Too bad words don't pay the bills, or you'd be rich! Say, have you been wearing that same outfit since high school? Sure fucking looks like it! Hahaha!" Miguel's chest tightened, and he ground his teeth even more. He grabbed for the door handle as the car stopped at a red light, his brow furrowed and full of bitter anger. Lydia, who was sitting between him and Dagmar, reached over quickly, and put her hand over his. His tension immediately eased a bit at her touch. She felt warm, the energy not at all what he expected; maybe she wasn't like her friend......not completely.......not yet at least.

"Don't...." she said softly, gently removing his hand from the car door. "You're hurting, I can tell; let us......", she paused, contemplative,

106

trying to be careful with her words, understanding that Miguel was a ticking time bomb full of knee jerk reactions and judgment, "......let me help."

He sighed, and took his hand off the handle as he looked out the window at all the people bar hopping on Broadway, disgusted by the sight of the rich and selfish eating the city he loved........eating it like ants at a picnic. "You people don't know what help means," he said calmly, "because it's something you've never needed." All the same, his guard came down ever so slightly in reaction to Lydia's apparent empathy.

She concealed a smile, looked over at Dagmar, and then back at Miguel, determined to break the ice between the two.

"Soooooo........what's your favorite bar?" she asked Miguel, throwing out the first thing that came to mind. "What and where do you like to drink; anything you want........we'll take you, K?"

That did it! Miguel could literally feel Lydia's empathy now; he always had a soft spot for someone telling him they recognized his pain and offering him kindness. Growing up in a closed mouths/closed hearts environment had done that to his personality. It was the weak link in his armor, and more than a few people had gotten him to lower his defenses that way......often times with disastrous results for him and them both, but he still kept the faith.........kept it out of hope and hunger. He was a hard person to like, and deep down inside he knew it, so he'd take any empathy he could get along the road of life...........take it with as much gratefulness as someone like him could manage.

Loosening up, trying his best not to get all teary eyed, he answered in a contrived tone of gruffness. "The Dead Lion; I like a good European beer." He sounded stern, but was clearly warming up to Lydia; even through his light brown skin she spotted a slight blush in his cheeks.

Dagmar snorted, thinking that a grown man choosing beer over any other choice he could have at somebody else's expense was funny. Lydia pinched her thigh before Dagmar could comment, knowing full well what was on her mind.

Salted Plastic: The Comedic Horror of Gentrification

"I'll behave......." Dagmar mouthed the words to Lydia's face without a sound, her body language and facial quirks starting to alter from one second to the next, the designer drugs she'd taken back at The Leash clearly starting to kick in. Her eyes became dreamy, cheeks red, and a smile appeared on her face for once.

"Good," Lydia thought, "now all that conscious level bitchiness she uses as an emotional shield will melt away for the rest of the night. She always sweetens up when she takes that stuff.........I just hope she shares." She started petting Dagmar's inner thigh, a bit drunk herself, but not quite **there** yet.

Dagmar, seemingly reading her thoughts, smiled at Lydia and motioned with her eyes towards the driver's window; the Chergar had been customized with a limo-type partition.

Lydia knocked on the window, and it lowered down after a second or two. "Hello, Lydia." a black masked chauffeur said on the other side in a metallic robotic voice, indecipherable as either female or male, obviously filtered through some sort of mini mic in the mask. Red lenses shined in the light for the split second the driver turned.

"Hello, Alex! The olive box, if you don't mind." Lydia requested.

"Hahahaha!" Miguel laughed. "I hope making your poor driver wear that mask is worth its thematic value; poor bastard is probably sweating their ass off just so you two can act mysteri........"

"GIVE HIM A DRINK TOO!" Dagmar interrupted in a whoozy tone. "He's reminding me too much of me right now. Shut him up, or loosen him up!" The words fell short of any ability to sound angry despite her efforts; she might as well have been ordering Lydia to give Miguel a back rub while feeding him chocolates.

Miguel suppressed a smile. "Her words are the same, but her overall energy just changed drastically in the last couple of seconds." he thought. "What the fuck is she on?"

Taking a small wooden box, upholstered inside with olive green suede, from the driver, Lydia placed it on her lap and opened it, pulling out a pinky sized vial of neon red oil. Floating in, and contrasting with the neon red were ashy looking spirals of something black and cloudy. Lydia had never gotten a straight answer from Dagmar regarding what the stuff was, having been offered it on several occasions, but she knew half/full well what it could do, or something like that. It hurt her head and eyes (literally) when she tried to dredge up a clear memory of the times she'd taken it.........whatever..........and never......or some shit.......

She shook off the quick sick feeling that assaulted her as she tried to pull up former memories of taking the oil. Shook it off, and turned to Miguel. "Stick your tongue out." she told him.

No snappy comment, surprisingly agreeable, no questions asked, he stuck out his tongue and let her put a drop in his mouth. Swallowing the stuff after a second or two, he had a contemplative look on his face. "Tastes like persimmon...."

"YAY!!!!!!" both Lydia and Dagmar clapped simultaneously in celebration, looking with glee at Miguel and smiling. Lydia followed up by taking a drop herself. Then, before returning the vial, thought better of it, and took one more drop.

"Good," Dagmar said, "now we're in the same dimension, kids. But seriously, do you really want beer of all things?" she asked Miguel in a "you can't be serious!" tone.

The partition raised back up, Lydia having just returned the box to the driver.

"I'm just happy to be here, happy to exist." Miguel replied, his anxiety washing away, thoughts crystal clear, not zoned into anything dark or heavy or worrisome like usual. "I don't think I need a drink now." Whatever the oil was, it was already going to work on him, reshaping his nerves, sublimating his rigid logic, letting his heart take over.

"Nor should you need one," Dagmar said, "you just took enough anamnesis to keep you content, self-realized, sharp and shit giddy for the rest of the night. We don't need to go out for drinks to get a buzz, Michael; it's just to keep the ritual going. I mean, don't you think you should get to know me and Lydia just a bit more before turning in? Set the mood and such?" she smiled, her emerald eyes looking right through him for a second.........and then turning away to zone out on the back of the front passenger chair. "OOOOOH! I can't wait to bathe you both in my new bathroom!" she said, speaking to herself, a shit silly grin on her face.

"What's anamnesis?" Lydia asked, obviously understanding that Dagmar meant the oil in the vial, but asking the question out of surprised curiosity; in all the years she had known her, all the times they had taken the stuff, she had not once given it a name or formal explanation, no matter how many times Lydia had pressed her for an answer. Not to mention that Lydia's memory of its effects were vague sometimes, clear others, and other times at others, at other times, others time at.........atimethere...........her left eye started to hurt all of a sudden, and she immediately stopped trying to thinking about it.

"Shhhhhhh!" Dagmar replied, rubbing the back of Lydia's neck, feeling her distress, ".........I like him!" Her voice was all at once serious in the extreme.................and yet, was somehow playful, connected to what's most important in life, zero miles away from interpersonal sainthood. "While we're here, while we still remember who and what we are, who and what we are to each other......I don't want any secrets." There were tears in her eyes as she whispered to Lydia.

"Oh, baby!" Lydia replied, the pain in her eye subsiding as she wiped away Dagmar's tears. She felt something.........it was definitely more than just being high; a definite déjà vu was kicking in as the oil did its work. "Don't cry, Lady! We're back there again, huh? This time with another piece of the puzz........."

"My name's not Michael." Miguel interrupted softly, facing the driver's seat, not really speaking to either of them directly. "It's Miguel."

Dagmar smiled wickedly at Lydia, peeked around her at Miguel, and then leaned across Lydia's lap, her soft little tummy sliding across Lydia's thighs. She looked up at Miguel, her red curls draping down and across Lydia and Miguel's legs, the vinyl in her outfit creaking............and then grabbed his cock firmly. "I like Michael better!" she said in that deep predatory accent of hers.

He instantly swelled up above and beyond, getting super dizzy, his heart racing like crazy. Through the haze of lust and new/not new thoughts...............coming from who the fuck knows where...............he thought for a split second, "I don't remember telling them my name was either......"

Salted Plastic: The Comedic Horror of Gentrification

Saturday, October 24, 1:45 am

Hungry Horowitz was up late in his Los Feliz apartment, polishing up his latest and GREATEST..........HIGHLY INGENIUS.........never to be optioned screenplay. Spinning images of awards in his head, he elevated his self-importance into an outrageous fantasy concept that was shit full of incompatible elements. His unmerited delusions ran along the lines of universal acclaim coupled with the label of cult following. Hungry's rotten brain was geared that way; incapable of seeing the unlikelihood of his aspirations, let alone the polar extremes of the elements he expected to manifest in one big shit soup. He really didn't get it, that dichotomy was a real thing..........and this was mainly because there really wasn't anything real about him.

Hungry was born and raised in Manhattan's East Village in the early 60s. His mother was Eva Wittenburg, local pseudo bohemian and widow of Gustav Marvin Wittenburg. Gustav had been the head CEO of Wittenburg Ice Cream Co. until he passed away, leaving full control of the company in the hands of his primary debt holders, Eva's Father and Uncles at Waterloo and Usury Bank.

Eva gave Hungry every advantage and privilege a boy could hope for, albeit in secret, essentially never at home, or in the presence of her peers, wishing to keep up appearances for her act as the poor downtrodden artist type. To offset the lack of luxury at home, Eva often had Hungry spend afternoons with his Uncles, Aunts or Grandparents. Picking him up from private school, they would take him out for daily trips to museums, the zoo, concerts, art galleries......rent collecting from tenants, etc, followed by upscale dinners...........and ice cream of course. Seeing the contrast in his mother's behavior at home (in front of her entourage of beatnik pseudo communist suck ups) with how she acted when they visited the Upper East Side Mansions of his Uncles, Aunts, and Grandparents...................seeing this bred a very split nature to his socialization. This led to the steadily growing concept in his mind that he was simultaneously poor and rich. Essentially, unlike Eva, he actually believed the bullshit stories he manufactured about his background. This, unfortunately for him, had continued throughout his entire life.

-Sniffle-

"BWAAAAAHHH!!!"

-Sniffle-

"I can't do it!" Hungry cried. "I miss my juicey box........I miss my New Yorkeeeee!!!!!!" It was a disgusting display; a 50-something year old man crying in the voice of a 12-year-old. "Why did the juice have to run dry?" he went on. "I WAS SOMBODEEEEEEEEEEE!!!!!"

Horowitz was referring of course to the reason why he had ended up in Los Angeles. Back in the late 70s and early 80s he had "built" a name for himself in the local punk rock scene in New York. To accomplish this he had essentially burned through various trust funds, spending them all on travel to Western Europe, various tours of duty at Ivy League Universities for music lessons, expensive designer custom made "street clothes", heroin, and paying locals to spread word of mouth about his "fame" to the growing new youth culture. He came from that tribe of 77 punk rock little known by most to be nothing but art students in punk rock costumes; the resource kids, the costume "weirdos" that had the time and money necessary to fund their performance. Everything from spending night after night in gritty bars

113

studying the body language and lingo of the "tough crowd", to slamming speed in alleyways and pissing on themselves; they had the act down to a T, being able to invest the time and money on persona build-up the same way most Hollywood actors do when prepping for a role.

Hungry had certainly lived it up throughout the 80's and most of the 90s, but little by little, his bad investment choices started to haunt him. His mother eventually passed away, and most of her remaining assets were seized by some mystery half sibling of his long dead father. Following this, his uncles cut him off from any further money, seeing everything he was doing as a lost cause. Eventually, languishing in his mother's old apartment in the early 2000's, he'd made the decision to migrate to Los Angeles, having heard from other no name wash ups that it was a good retirement plan when all your New York juice with the "in crowd" had officially run out.

"I know what I'll do!" Horowitz said, regaining his composure, his confidence waxing, the tears stopping. "I'll gear up, head down to a club, and find some 20-something fresh cuts. I'll sidle into their conversation, and then not so subtly edge in the fact that I'M A BIG TIME PUNK ROCK LEGEND!!!!" Standing up, he rushed to his wardrobe room (he had a room solely for his clothes). The sound of him ferreting around through hangers and drawers could be heard, coupled with the clinking of chains, the "vvvvvvpt" of zippers, and the click of boots on floorboards.

It was quiet for a minute; apparently Hungry had finally found his look for the night, and then………………

"Eiiiiihhhhhhhh!!!!" The scream of a hysterical old lady catching a rat (Hungry's tantrum voice) came from Horowitz room, followed by the sound of furniture breaking, and things flying around and hitting the walls. Apparently Hungry Horowitz, the "big bad punk rock legend", had just remembered that LA bar hours were not the same as NY bar hours.

114

Salted Plastic: The Comedic Horror of Gentrification

Saturday, October 24, 2:15 am

Joseph Pisser was on the edge of a hotel room bed, with a reptile rock heater he'd stolen from his daughter's iguana terrarium between his legs, below his testicles. He sat on the thing like it was a bicycle seat, groaning in pain. "Going to have to get Ida a new iguana again," he thought, "it's a cold night. Shit, this hurts; I really have to start taking fiber and exercising!"

"Are you ready YET!?!?" a raunchy, I eat cigarette butts and stale beer for breakfast type of female voice came from the bathroom. "My time is money; you should know that by now, Joe!"

"I'll paaaAAY!!!!!!!" Joseph yelled in agony, as something along the lines of a feeling like an electric fire vein with broken glass barbs fired off in his testicle and colon region. "FUUCCKKK! DERMITTT!!!!!! Those suadero tacos with habaneros killing my colon….and that pulled pork jalapeno coleslaw sandwich………and that chili dog with the pickled serranos! EERRRGGGHHH!!!!"

"Damn, you fucked up, huh?" a white woman, mid 30s, in her panties and bra came into the room. She was covered in jail quality tattoos and various scars that looked like they could possibly be from cigarette burns. Her platinum blonde hair and well-toned muscles were the sole reason Joseph consistently kept her as one of his regular escorts; being a white washed politician pocho of a Latino, the fit huera-type was one of his favorite status symbols; sleeping with these type of women made him feel like a REAL IN CHARGE MANLY MAN……….TOUGH AND ACCOMPLISHED…………fucking loser!

"What's wrong? That heat from the FBI turning your prostate into a balloon? Heh heh!"

"You bitch!" Joseph smiled/yelled. "I'm becoming a non-coctor, and you could give two shits…….URRGGH!"

"A whatsit?" she said. "I've only bin in nursing school for 5 months; don't think I heard about that shit yet."

Salted Plastic: The Comedic Horror of Gentrification

"Course not," Joe replied, "they like to call it ED, or prostate cancer, or colon issues......whatever the fuck! It happens when I'm an increasingly fatter fuck, and I do things like constantly eat bacon burgers and meat lovers pizza, or GORGE myself on just meat at KBBQ, telling my wife I don't want salad, or getting coked out at the office while drinking four to six tall cold brew coffees a day, sleeping less than 3 hours a night, and rarely taking a shit..........ARRRGGGGGHHHHHH!!!!!!! NON-COCTORRRR!!!!!!!!!!"

"Fuck, maybe you gotta retire baby; all that money you received from those foreign real estate investors could get you and me a nice place somewhere in South East Asia.......or maybe South America?" she spoke to herself, smiling, eyes closed, imagining a life of luxury in her head no doubt.

"Urrrghhh! No way, Abbie!" he replied in pain. "What, you want me to leave my wife and kids behind? Analiza is probably already going to be indicted for some of the stuff the FBI is planning on charging me with. Fuck! Bribery? Money laundering? Double dealing with foreign investors? Embezzlement? TAX EVASION!?!? Where do they get this shit? I'm just trying to revitalize the city with new and unaffordable housing, dammit! I'm an LA City Councilmen, not a gangster!"

"Aren't they both the same shit?" Abbie asked, lighting up a cigarette while she sat down beside Joe and began rubbing the back of his neck.

He swatted her hand off angrily. "Look, you're not gonna be able to just get away with giving me a pat down massage like last time. I'm still capable, you know...........just need a little warming up!" He pointed at the heat rock between his legs.

"OK! OK!" She stepped back, pretending to be a bit scared while smiling. "So, I'm guessing you ready, huh?"

He took the rock away from his groin, a sad broken look on his face. "Yeah, I think I can probably keep it up for about 5 to 10 minutes, but there might be some farting involved, Abbie." He put his head down in shame.

"Whatever!" she said, a look of disgust on her face. "It happens when I'm going down on you, you're getting a fucking surcharge, Joe!"

Salted Plastic: The Comedic Horror of Gentrification

Saturday, October 24, 3:47am

"You can sleep here on the couch!" A male voice said in a contrived peaceful tone in the dark of the apartment.

"Sure, can I have another blanket?" Jasmine asked as she settled onto the couch, covering herself with a thin ragged sheet, her question meant more to indicate that she hadn't been given an actual blanket at all.

"I don't have any yet; I just moved in; I told you that already." Passive. Not impatient in tone, but certainly so in energy; this guy was that type; seemingly shy and harmless in mannerisms/tone of voice, but at the soul and drive level nothing but a "please me now, and shut up at all other times" kind of guy. Unlike the overtly violent type of man, he exhibited his true nature not with yelling and fists, but through short clipped responses and cold shoulders.

"Good!" Jasmine thought as he walked away. "Just makes what I have to do easier. Still, the feeling of being treated with the same care as a used tissue never gets any easier, that part never gets any easier." Jasmine pulled out her phone after she heard him upstairs, starting to snore already, and sent a text. A minute later a reply to her text came in the form of a gentle, almost inaudible drilling sound near the sliding glass doors on the ground floor of the apartment. The building was off Sunset, on the border of Downtown and Echo Park. It was paid for in full by Mr. Cold Shoulder's parents (according to a lease agreement laying out on a nearby table).

Jasmine pulled out a cigarette case, and tossed its contents onto a nearby table, pressing an ornamental silver cockroach on top of it. The case transformed just like a mecha robot from an 80s anime, reshaping into what looked like a respirator, the design like something right of a cyberpunk novel. She placed the thing over her nose and mouth.

"When are you ever going to go liquid, Ms. Creature?" A metallic, sensual voice asked. It came from her ear bud, simultaneous to a faint

118

hissing sound near the sliding glass doors that started after the drilling stopped. The metallic voice was VRIL, an artificial intelligence program that some of Jasmine's "friends" had snagged from some crazy female mercenary cult in South America. They'd liberated the program, "cleaned" it up, and were now using it as a sort of glorified day planner, health monitor, A.I. companion, personal morale booster, and overall reverse suggestion box.

"I told you," Jasmine whispered, "I'm perfectly fine with my old mechanical field equipment (her cigarette case). Oh.......and I told you a million times already; get in the habit of calling me Filth Creature, not Ms. Creature.........although that is starting to sound pretty cool though." she added in a contemplative tone, standing up and tossing her blanket aside.

Jasmine's smooth coffee-colored skin was glowing in the faint moonlight coming through the apartment's windows; all that water, exercise and colloidal alloy moisturizer Jasmine used. Nude from head to toe, her five foot two-inch frame was almost all pure dense muscle; the only visually apparent body fat she had was around her buttocks and thighs. A faint ab line ran down her stomach, the result of hours of daily core training.

"Before you ask," VRIL started, "yes, the target is torpored."

"Good! Time to finish the night and clock out already." Jasmine said thoughtfully, turning on a table lamp. The light revealed her nearly head to toe exhibit of highly detailed vermin art; arms, shoulder blades, breasts, stomach, thighs, calves, butt, small of back, feet, chest, etc; nearly everything but her face and neck was completely tattooed with various types of so called dirty animals and creatures. A possum skull on both forehands, with individual crow feathers on each finger. Swarms of silverfish arced around the right side of her ribcage, coiled centipedes the left side. Cockroaches with wings spread in various perspectives on her left shoulder blade, maggot swarms patterned into intricate glyphs on the right one. A toad's eye in her right palm, a goat's eye in the left.

Salted Plastic: The Comedic Horror of Gentrification

A pig's skeleton wrapped around her right thigh, and ninas de tierra circled the left one. A horsefly face in front profile was stamped on her sternum; surrounded by a circle, the thing looked just like some sort of superhero insignia, sitting there between her pert A cup breasts. Two skeletal raccoon paws accented her shaved vaginal mons as a swarm of locusts flew toward and around her navel. Rats were breeding on the back of her right calve while a mother rat fed her pups on the left. Spiders, rotting gophers, ticks, fleas, and eyeless rabbits............varmints and pests of all shapes and sizes............

The tattoos were seemingly innumerable...........and it would take time (and better light) to name them all. Jasmine had had her mind (and possibly her heart) overworked and beaten tonight; she stood silently, thinking and feeling it all out. Beautiful and contemplative, full of inked totem, she thought backwards through her daily schedule, a single tear coming down her left cheek................................

Salted Plastic: The Comedic Horror of Gentrification

Friday, October 23, 12:37 pm

Jasmine drummed her fingers over and over again on a closed copy of Richard Antoine Nielson's Schraedinger's Bobcat, a reading suggestion from VRIL. Apparently the AI program had felt Jasmine was in serious need of a good laugh, had looked at all her profiled personality traits, and then made the suggestion via next day delivery at Jasmine's P.O. Box. "You really don't know me, Lady!" Jasmine said to complete thin air, looking just like anybody else in the middle of a work call (with her earbud in), as she sat in a coffee shop off the 170 freeway in North Hollywood. "This shit is too obviously man material! You get me?!"

"Yes, Ms. Creature, I get you, and I understand your personal brand of humor, which is why I sent you the book. Try maybe reading it post-masturbation; the content and associations it dredges up may digest differently when you aren't...charged....for lack of a better word."

"Whatever!" Jasmine retorted with irritation, looking around the café. "Where is this fucking kid anyways? I've been here 20 minutes, and this fucking dressy get up is starting to itch!"

"Mohair is expensive, and that's a nice cut! I particularly like the cinched waist in the blazer, and the pencil skirt in lieu of pants. Oxblood penny loafers too!!!!!!" VRIL said with over the top excitement.

"Hahaha! What's up with the clothing lesson? Maybe you should be wearing this shit!"

"The particular style you are wearing today was popular with the female youth culture of 1960's Britain. To answer your question though, a keen knowledge of chic fashion sense of several types was part of my stock info supply."

"Yeah, well you're not working for those crackpot crazy, remnant of evil, blonde haired/blue eyed aborigine amazons anymore; we put your ghost in a cloud, scrubbed down all your bad karma, and made your ass born again! Got it?!"

"Got it, Ms. Creature."

Salted Plastic: The Comedic Horror of Gentrification

"Ugh! I told you the name is Filth Creature, not Ms. Cre......."

"Tiffany?" A voice behind Jasmine interrupted.

Turning around, she saw what she'd been waiting for; tall surfer type kid with blonde shoulder-length hair, khaki shorts, and lean muscle standing on hemp sandals. "Yup, here's my first douche of the day," she thought, "gotta speed this up and stay on schedule."

"Sorry I'm late. Good to finally meet you in person. I'm Chad Bradford by the way, but you know that already.......Haha!" He extended his hand for a shake, with a sub-moronic look on his face to go with the affected laugh. Holding his hand, she could feel the inhuman in him; this one was still latent, and in a stage that was as human as they can possibly seem. Still, the synthetic skin never fooled her; stuff felt silken and unnaturally firm, too flawless and uniform......always did. It was a bit hard for her in these cases, when they didn't know what they were yet, but that's the kind of day today was going to be apparently.

"That's ok, I had my book to keep me company." Jasmine put on a charming smile while finishing her thoughts. "Have a seat; let's see those head shots!"

Chad handed her a portfolio full of photos and references. She skimmed through it quickly as he took a seat. "Nudity?" She passively asked without looking up.

His face flushed bright red. "I haven't really yet, but for the right opportunity, yeah."

"Convincing!" she thought, looking at his face. "The simulation of human reaction is always more on point with the young and unaware reps. If I didn't have those verbal cues VRIL gave us, I don't know how I'd ever deal with these 'kids'."

"Everything look good?" Chad asked. "Will you rep me?"

"Hahaha!" Jasmine busted up while thinking, "Fuck! '....rep me?' Shit, I needed that!"

Salted Plastic: The Comedic Horror of Gentrification

"What'd I say?" Chad reacted, the scripted surfer persona he'd been implanted with coming out all lax and dopey in his voice.

"Just the right thing, kid! Ok, let's get you into the agency today! You up for that, or do you have other plans?"

"No.....no.....no! Even if I did I'd cancel them....thanks, I MEAN thank you, thank you so much!" Chad beamed excitement.

Jasmine and "Chad" got up as she gestured towards the door, walked outside and across the parking lot. A variety of people of all ages walked past them, Chad getting a few looks from some teen girls who were walking into the café.

"Shit, I forgot I didn't park in the lot," Jasmine said, "I'm near the strip mall on the other side, down this alley. Did you drive here?"

"No, no.....I took a Güeber here; I can ride with you...if that's ok." he said timidly.

"Great! Great! Good by me!!!!" she said, trying to sound excited, poppy and girly, even knowing full well that, for a guy like Chad, whose tastes probably ran along the lines of anorexic vegan surfer girls from Redondo, she could never pull it off, silver front tooth and tattoos on her hands and all. Still, she really didn't give a fuck; he'd eat her shit right out of her ass right now if she asked him to, and Jasmine knew it; these pathetic Hollywood hopefuls were always desperate that way.

Passing through the alley, she whispered quickly to VRIL, "The cameras at the café, Lady?!"

"Done already, Ms. Creature; wiped for the last 168 hours."

"Thanks babe," Jasmine continued to whisper, "we'll play some Saiken Dansetsu on the big screen later, K?"

"Hört sich gut an!" VRIL replied.

"You say something?" Chad asked, looking a little weirded out, his latent reptile instincts possibly sensing something amiss; being so close to the void, an edginess was definitely starting to creep out of him.

"Just whispering to myself!" Jasmine smiled coyly. "Trying to remember where my keys are."

Salted Plastic: The Comedic Horror of Gentrification

They came to the end of the alley, where Jasmine's BNW 4 Series was parked on the cross street. She unlocked the doors and stepped in, motioning for Chad to get into the passenger's seat. The second he sat down, the doors slammed shut, and the loud slide and click of their seat belts resounded, making the car seem like it was some sort of modern day transportational guillotine............it was foreboding in the extreme considering......

"I'm really sorry!" Jasmine said with almost genuine sincerity as she started up the car, set the child safety lock on Chad's door, and turned up the stereo. The radio was set to Classical CFK, the Chicken Fried Kentucky classical music station; Archangela Coralle's Adagio in D Minor was playing, almost midway done now.

"Sorry?" Chad asked. "What do you mean? You change your mind about me being star material?" He was slightly perspiring, and micro-gradually becoming scared shitless due to something that was only on the peripherals of his understanding.

The car windows tinted pitch black like magic, as if someone had just shot down the moon, stars and sun. Jasmine whispered something inaudible as she reached into her blazer and pressed a little remote in her pocket. Chad WARPED immediately, his countenance no longer the sunny careless surfer kid from Hermosa; the reptile-nature inside him woke prematurely in reaction to whatever Jasmine had whispered, just in time for the passenger seat head cushion to pop open and slip a rubber/platinum alloy mesh over his head.

The mesh immediately zip-locked MAXIMUM pressure into the total circumference of his throat and neck. He started to twitch and struggle right away, grabbing at his throat, legs kicking. Completely cut off from air, any screams "Chad" possibly made went unheard.

Jasmine sighed in disgust, and stepped out of the car as "Chad" continued to thrash around. She slammed the door shut and lit up a cigarette, leaning against the car and exhaling, feeling the vibrations of

124

Chad's arms as they bumped up against the walls of the car in time to the end of the Adagio.

"I'll have the spare beemer brought to the second drop site, Ms. Creature." VRIL said into Jasmine's earbud. "In the meantime I will order you a Libt."

"You're damn right you will!" Jasmine said sternly. "Those things stink up my fucking car after they shit themselves post-mortem. Never understood why the fuckers do it almost immediately, unlike humans. And for the millionth time, it's Filth Creature, Lady!

Salted Plastic: The Comedic Horror of Gentrification

The exterminations lasted all day, and well into the end of the night:

"Hey there! Bryce, right?" Jasmine put her hand on the little bearded rat's shoulder as she got to his table at the pretentious eatery/coffee shop in LA's Arts District.

A little segue into that before we begin. AHEM...........The Los Angeles Arts district is essentially the following:

1. A quasi-arcology for rich pricks who think that they're slumming it just because their little safe living bubble community is in proximity to the "mean streets" of Boyles Heights and Skid Row.

2. A top priority for local police patrols, because god forbid that some important resident of this little urban amusement park gets a splinter in their finger, or suffers the PTSD inducing ordeal of having to come face to face with a homeless person, and not receive IMMEDIATE attention for their distress.

3. A bunch of building murals that supposedly "INSPIRE THE CREATIVITY WITHIN!" Translation: A place for talentless (yet well-resourced) hacks to take selfies in proximity to "art that begets art", so they can post on their GLAMOUROUS Shitstagram page, where they incessantly babble about their latest creative endeavors that will never exist outside the tried and proved hashtags that have already been over utilized by everyone on earth to milk the world wide cyber cock for self-validation.

4. Grocery stores that belay the need for Arts District residents to poke their little pinky toe out into the real world. This, they accomplished by stocking a gourmet variety of every chocolate, wine, cheese, liquor, deli meat, produce, and vegan condiment imaginable. Because, LETS FACE IT; if Arts District residents had to venture out into a legit socially organic community and visit a real market, where average working class people usually shop, they might find themselves facing the stark reality that not every consumer-based business on earth is eager to stick it's tongue up their rectum.

5. A baby bottle for pseudo bohemian yuppies that nurtures the fantasy that they aren't just basic bitches with no acumen for creativity, whose soul testament to being an artist is that they had enough money to attend art school, followed by being employed or commissioned as such via nepotism ("daddy rents my gallery for me") or favoritism (all that bedroom and bathroom "networking" paying off).

6. One of the rare locales in Los Angeles where one can go to a gastro pub, and initiate the dumb fuck behavior of spending high end sushi and wagyu ribeye kind of money on some bullshit ass "gourmet" hotdogs and fries, just because there's a tablespoon of alligator meat in your hotdog, and the version of the fries served there are supposedly a Western European "delicacy".

7. A port into the "underbelly" of LA's Santee Alley for those Art's District residents bold enough to be LA's next "FASHION INNOVATORS". Translation: a place for thirsty fashion majors to buy cheap fabric and bacon wrapped dick dogs, so they can demonstrate to the world their ability to make couture nonsense for coked out runway judges. And all this for nothing, considering that said judges will more than likely test these "designer's" ability to perform fellatio and pulse their sphincter as the measure of their potential to become the next Bersáchee or Veevan Vestwoud. Translation: "networking" creates new fashion, not talent or innovation in visual aesthetic.

Salted Plastic: The Comedic Horror of Gentrification

The list goes on and on, but you get the idea; the Arts District is a manufactured and coddled community at its best…..nothing truly urban, gritty, socially natural or creative about it……….just a new flavor of real estate marketing and development, nothing more.

Anyways…………….the meet up spot was Berth Café, an all-around mediocre coffee house chain currently littering Los Angeles with the sickening marketing idea that dry/bland confectionary and baking concepts will sell like gold plated shit as long as the promotional efforts of the business consisted of plastering words like "organic" and "free trade" onto the menu as often as possible. In truth, most patrons knew that the cakes, although very beautiful looking, were a façade, and tasted like a mouth full of sweet sand and ash stuffed into a nauseating gluten/egg/dairy free fondant. Not to mention the fact that better tea could be found at Xiao Bai Long in San Gabriel Valley, and even Carfucks made a better cup of coffee.

That wasn't it though; the attraction of Berth Café was fairly simple; its pseudo hacienda-style eating area, fashioned mainly open air, gave patrons the ability to be seen by every passerby, allowing them to showcase themselves at every table. This made the place ideal for the most important part of the modern dining experience in LA………that being one's ability to be a vacuous turd in influencer-friendly settings, where they could be seen demonstrating their value as an avid consumer of the LATEST and GREATEST contemporary status symbols. In short, the place was just another self-petting zoo for the ego, and its official business designation should have been filed under "Shitstagram photo backdrop clinic", rather than café.

So, while customers shoveled dry ass oolong brownies and Earl Grey cheesecakes into their mouths, trying not to choke to death in the process, their real pleasure took the form of selfiephile behavior on the level of auto-paparazzi overkill. It.........was.......disgusting! But anyways, back to Jasmine and Bryce.

"Yeah, that's me, I'm Bryce." he said, slouching like the weasel-bodied, beer bellied, puppet-legged subhuman that he was in his ugly lumberjack button up, hipster ushanka (which smelled like coffee craft beer piss), and fashion wrap.

His energy was of the type seen at the dinner table when bratty kids ignore their mother's admonition to keep their feet off the table. That kind of snotty attitude apparent in children that loaf around all day while they play some shitty shake and bake video game on their tablet or phone. "You kinda look different than your EROsex profile." he said in a lax idiot in pajamas type of tone, the kind usually used by jaded trust fund turds while they impatiently wait to be entertained.

"And by different, he means not hot as far as his limited taste in women is concerned." Jasmine thought. "Dickless and no imagination; yup, this'll be quick!"

-ABOUT AN HOUR LATER-

"You REALLY look different than your EROsex profile now, Bryce!" Jasmine smiled, a flood of neon green and pink light shining off her face as she looked down at a corpse on the floor of a Korean karaoke bar booth. She'd dragged "Bryce" to the bar, and had helped him overcome his lack of attraction to her by fanning his ego as he talked about his EPIC plans to become a BIG TIME ROCKSTAR in LA. She'd let him babble on and on about art school and his parent's summer homes in Minnesota, Upstate New York and Malibu for a bit after they'd entered the booth. Her patience stretched to its limit after that, Jasmine had crushed his sternum with a front kick to the chest, and then gone to work on him.

His mask had been shorn off; bits of scales, skin and blood were all over the couches and carpet, both synthetic and reptilian. A wicked looking karambit was in her left hand (covered in blue and red), and a compact mirror was in her right. He'd screamed in the end, both in disgust and horror, after she'd carved his mask off and held the mirror up to his face before opening up major arteries. No verbal ques to bring out his true nature for this one; he'd probably thought she was just crazy and looking to rob him. What he'd thought at the sight of his lizard face must have been above and beyond mind breaking, but Jasmine really didn't give a shit.

"You fucking fuck!" she said in disgust as she spat on the body and walked out of the private booth. The door girl, rainbow skinned with spiraled glass hair and red/green eyes, nodded to her as she left. This was a hologram projection of VRIL as the program conceptualized itself in anthropomorphic form; the place was a front, co-operatively owned by Jasmine and her tribe.

Salted Plastic: The Comedic Horror of Gentrification

It was getting darker now, the sun almost down, and Jasmine was rubbing her knees together under the table. "If I have one more coffee today I'm gonna need a fucking diaper." she thought, sitting with "Meredith" inside of some douchey spot in Highland Park that doubled as café and gastropub.

"YOU REALLY DO!?!?" Meredith squealed like the vibrant poppy tween that she wasn't, as she sat in her generic pink and black Goth Lolita get up and sipped her drink. At the age of 39, she had moved to LA from Portland, Oregon, convinced (by a few self-help books from Terget) that it was her destiny to become LA's PREMIERE fitness and diet goth guru! Her qualifications as such were unquestionably solid; after reading Rort Bunco's "The You You You", and Tammy Fibershit's "Are Lies in Your Stomach?", she had completed her "rigorous" training as a well-rounded health coach by taking one yoga class, and repetitively reading the marketing and nutrition content off a bag of gluten free tortilla chips she'd bought at Whorle Foods. This she studied diligently every time she got off work from the high end horse stable her family owned, where her formal (and nepotism generated) position included a 70k salary, and the responsibility of texting/posting all day while her mother's employee's ground their teeth in disgust at her presence.

"ABSOLUTELY!" Jasmine answered in a ZIPPY HYPED up tone, still on cue even though she was about to piss her denims any minute now. "Your idea for a self-help book that suggests the public at large can solve all their health and fitness needs by the simple act of hiring a staff of in home private trainers and macrobiotic chefs is genius!!!!! I really think the public will eat it up, especially those in the 15k to 30k a year income bracket! I'm going to get this napkin with your scribbled outline for the book over to my finest ghost writers immediately!"

"Thank GOD!" Meredith said, self-satisfied. "You don't know how defeated I'd have felt if it didn't all work out, and I had to go back home to my family. It was such a NIGHTMARE back home!" She started to cry, her tone and behavior becoming the biggest spot on performance of Pity Party Penny that Jasmine had seen in a while; the female reps were usually better at it than the males, but shit, this was solid acting!

"You have no idea what sort of abusive life I had to deal with back home………the lack of appreciation for my work ethic (her mom telling her that posting selfies doesn't run the stable)………the extortion (her Aunt withholding pay from her for missing work)……………THE SEXISM (her Uncle explaining to her that having sex with dates in the stables during business hours was unprofessional)……………and not to mention that my savings (her trust fund) is almost gone……….." She put her face in her hands, synthetic tears welling through her fingers.

"Hey…hey!" Jasmine chided in mock sympathy, flexing her feet in tension under the table, doing the pee pee dance. "It's ok; you're here now; welcome to LA girl!"

-20 MINUTES LATER, ABOUT A BLOCK AWAY-

After getting hit on by Meredith, Jasmine figured the best way to end the night was to take her to a private bathroom nearby.

PSSSSSSsSSSSSsssssssss……….SSSSSSsssssssss…ssS…ssssSSS…….SSsss…….s sss…ss..sssss

"AhHHH! Finally!" Jasmine exhaled in ecstasy as she relieved herself on Meredith's face, her body limp dead on the floor of the private bathroom stall. Meredith's gluten free vegan porter back at the café/pub had had a little knock out juice in it, courtesy of a member of Jasmine's organization who worked as a bar back at the place.

Salted Plastic: The Comedic Horror of Gentrification

"Ahhh! That's good stuff!" Jasmine sighed as she got up from a squat, pulled her jeans up after wiping, and stuffed the tissue into "Meredith's" mouth for good measure.

"Your DNA is on that tissue, Ms. Creature." VRIL warned.

"Have you forgotten who owns the office building for this communal bathroom, Lady?!"

"All the same, I think it best if......"

"No time!" Jasmine interrupted. "This was a two for the price of one situation, remember? Its nearly seven pm now; gotta rush back; call Agpalo and Diaz for me; they're working in suite 8; they'll take care of this........if they're not fucking on the job like usual.........either way, I gotta rush back!"

"Consegui!" VRIL replied as Jasmine left the bathroom, ran out of the building, and rushed down the street to her car.

Starting it quickly, she sped up Figueroa, scanning around for cops, and pulling up to a dumpster area in an alley behind the café/pub she'd just left. Jasmine eyeballed a lanky guy in a beanie who "worked" back of house at the place. The word "work" taking on a neological meaning for him that roughly translated to "my parent's co-signed the loan for my business, so I'm here to monitor all you hard working line cooks, servers and chefs while I pick my teeth, pinch wax into my mustache all day, and orchestrate our social media presence on my phone."

"Working hard, or hardly working?!" Jasmine smiled from her car window.

"Excuse m......." the guy started to say as he turned around.....and then took three shots from a silencer modified M1911 that Jasmine had braced on her right forearm. Blueish blood immediately started to leak out of him. She sped off as he dropped to the pavement, shitting and farting on himself on the way down.

-BRRRRRRRRTTTTTT!!!!!-

Salted Plastic: The Comedic Horror of Gentrification

It was well past 10pm when Jasmine woke from a nap in her car. A text was beaming on her phone.

"Shit!" She popped right up, instantly full of purpose and energy, the blood rushing to her face as she smiled lovingly down at her phone, that silver tooth catching the light.

"Lydia?" VRIL inquired.

"How'd you know?" Jasmine asked, barely even paying attention to her question, the euphoria making her heart float, the blood rushing to her face even more, her nerves unwinding, all the usual tensions subsiding.

"Well, besides the fact that I'm synced with all activity on your phone, other indicators would be your increase in phenylethylamine, norepinephrine, and dopamine every time you establish any contact with Lydia."

"I know…….." Jasmine said faintly, her voice trailing off, the ineffable gripping her above and beyond, every ounce of pain she'd ever felt dropping off her shoulders. The universe was on her side, her chakras gestated every internal paradise, all her bills were paid on time……she was making love at the top of Maslow's hierarchy of needs, and she'd just grabbed the last jar of Mutella at the store after a nuclear apocalypse, when she was connected to Lydia.

Snapping out of it, she opened up her phone.

Jasmine: I'll be there in 20 minutes; wear something sexy, Lady!

Lydia: Already dressed. Please don't laugh when you see in what; I'll belt you!

Jasmine: Lol! Hope that's a promise. ☺

Salted Plastic: The Comedic Horror of Gentrification

-15 MINUTES LATER-

"You ain't Asian bitch!" Jasmine yelled, smiling in reaction to Lydia's headdress, as she stopped at the curb, looking Lydia up and down real quick.

"What's up Jasmine?" Lydia replied as she opened the passenger door and got in, taking a quick (and somewhat longing) look at Jasmine, in her skin tight black Over Armor pants/shirt, and red hooded sweater........

Salted Plastic: The Comedic Horror of Gentrification

Saturday, October 24, 4:07am

"Yeah, only good part of my night." Jasmine said as she finished thinking about the day, still standing naked in the apartment of Mr. Coldshoulder Prick. "She's special that one, huh, Lady?"

"You know Lydia has yet to experience any long lasting identity reintegration, Jasmine; only recreational manifestations." VRIL always called her Jasmine, instead of the usual 'Ms. Creature', when the AI knew that the issue being discussed was one that was close to Jasmine's heart. "It would be very dangerous for you to get close to her.......and not just for you; think about your sisters, others, and brothers; it's very importa............"

"I KNOW!!!!!" Jasmine screamed, as she slapped a bunch of lame bobble head vinyl toys off a wall shelf, followed by side kicking a huge hole in the wall. A tear from her left eye trailed down her face as she stood there, thinking about what to do next.

She went into the bathroom, slipping her clothes back on as she walked, trying to shrug off all the still lingering memories of the day but one. She made a mild snort of disgust, her face a composite of sadness and hate as she saw the used condoms in the bathroom's wastebasket.

"Yup....Filth.....Creature........name is how I deal with this; fucking maggot; in real life I'd never touch him or any of these fucking things!" She dropped a silver globe into the trash; a red pinhead of light on the thing rapidly flashed as it fell in.

"You didn't touch him though, Jasmine," VRIL interjected, "that was just drugs and one of my holograms."

"Doesn't change the fact that I had to get naked for the fucker so you could keep the fucking image visually accurate; that piece of scaled trash didn't deserve to sniff my shit, let alone get a good look at me intimately. FUCK!!!!!!!! When is Morrigan going to call all out open war on these things so I can have a normal life again?! I'm sick of this shadow shit!" she yelled, emphasizing her hatred by slamming a palm into the bathroom mirror, causing an instant web of cracks.

"Oh, you're sickth, are you?!?!" a female voice with a lisp and a matriarch's tone cut into Jasmine's earbud. "Tell you what, Jasthmin, as soon asth you learn how to be a spy, a healer, a builder, a teacher, a quantum sythhchologist, a leader, a trans-dimensional chemist, AND a killer, then maybe you can starth waking the people up, unblocking minds, fixing our equipment, and.................."

"You left out fucker!" Jasmine yelled. "That's my other skill besides being an assassin. Good thing, huh? Just me! Would never be a trait you yourself have to utilize. How bout it bitch?!?! I wanna see you strip like a whore for these snakes, Morrigan; see how you fucking like being degraded; let's see the madame of the pack get uncomfortable for once, instead of always just pointing out whose got diversified talent, and who doesn't, you bitch!"

"You justh got assigned to mechanith duty for the nexth two months girl! Hope your mouthing off was worth ith."

"No problemth!" Jasmine replied, mocking Morrigan's lisp. "I'll get those fucking ice cream trucks you call tanks on the road, full of platoons and music so fast it'll knock that speech impediment RIGHT OUT OF YOUR FUCKING MOUTH!"

"Jasmine........" VRIL said in a motherly tone.

Pissed as shit, Jasmine ripped her earbud out, and stomped it on the floor, cracking the bathroom tile as she did. Putting her shoes on, she got up and walked casually out the apartment's front door.........right as the little red light on the sphere in the wastebasket turned green. A sound like foil sparking in a giant microwave oven went off inside the apartment as she walked away. The next day, posts and pirate media circulated about a big blue fire off Sunset.........crackpot bullshit the official media dubbed it.

Salted Plastic: The Comedic Horror of Gentrification

Saturday, October 24, 1:05am

"This is a great compromise, yeah?!" Lydia asked, leaning forward as she stood behind Dagmar and Miguel, an arm around each of them as they sat side by side on a pair of metal chairs. In front of them, on a table fashioned from a cylindrical section of a large tree trunk, were a few pints of amber colored wheat beer, along with shot glasses, and a bottle of Baronhunter. The place was open air on a rooftop, in a part of Downtown LA which Miguel typically avoided out of deep personal loathing. But not tonight; he was a totally different person tonight; they all were.

"Yes, pretty nice biergärten," Dagmar smiled, "reminds me of being with my mom in Munich when I was young. She'd take me to this one restaurant while papa worked all the way in Vienna. We would travel all over Switzerland, Austria, and Germany whenever he was contracting in Zurich and Vienna. Eating, going to museums......the snow sometimes......" her thoughts trailed off; Dagmar was time travelling in a very real way for a split second, really THERE with her mom, the drug doing its thing. She stared into space for another second or two. Then, coming back to the relative present, she looked first at Miguel, then at Lydia......with complete and unconditional love........love, and gentle mischief.

"Yeah, those biergärtens in Europe, they had such great beer, and **sausage too!**" she said, smiling.......as she grabbed Miguel under the table. Lydia had sat down across from them, watching like a mother, happy to see them getting along. She tried not to laugh at Miguel, who looked like he was about to pass out every time Dagmar toyed with him again.........and again........and again.

"Stop it girl! You're going to give him a heart attack!" she smiled, making the statement more for rote pleasantry than anything else; the oil let you know almost everything about the people and world around you, and even more so with those also on it. She knew that Miguel, despite some minor issues, was very healthy, and would become even more so as they interacted, another effect of the oil being that the more those on it resonated, spending time together, laughing and playing and enjoying each other; the more they did this, the more they healed from damage of all kinds.

"I'm fine." Miguel said, dopey on the outside, sharp on the inside; outwardly he looked as if he had been massaged by eight sets of hands while being fed oysters and champagne, followed by getting shot up with the finest diamorphine hydrochloride. Inside though? Inside, his thoughts/feelings/intuitions were omnidirectionally/interdimensionally discerning; the secrets of the universe where at his fingertips; The Grail, the Philosopher's Stone, The Sacred Agave, The Sephiroth, The Arrow of Time, Dark Energy, Plimpton 322, The Kama Sutra, Mveux's Vleïlen, and........... "DAMN!!!!!!!!! So that's how they get the fucking spirals in French crullers!!!!!!" he thought, a quick tear escaping his eye. "I've waited so long for this.........seas of pain..............endless lives ....tons of misdirection, mountains of ignorance.................I remember Lydia and Dagmar......as other people.........different places and times..............all the indignities I suffered............."

"Were for your own good." Dagmar and Lydia finished for him, seemingly reading his thoughts, talking to him in unison, with perfect timing. "Nothing is free Miguel, and you've been a real bastard almost every time we've all met; your malahum, your karma, your....SPRTSHA; it had to be cleaned up."

"Right!" he replied, completely unfazed by Lydia and Dagmar speaking in tandem, reacting as if it was just standard phenomena. "Should I be embarrassed? About who I was last time? What I did? I know the everyday me would feel guilty, but something about that oil....."

"Guilt is not a part of true understanding, Miguel." Lydia/Dagmar replied, Dagmar's voice in his ear, Lydia's hand on his as she leaned across the table; Dagmar licking his ear quickly as Lydia pressed gently on the abductor pollicis of his thumb. He felt gates of trapped tension drop from throat to sternum to below his navel; pleasure/appreciation blooming............surcease to a long carried ignorance/agony.

"Yes, I see it now; guilt serves no purpose when you have all the answers; it's just a cop-out for not taking the next step to making things right once you have all the tools to do so. Someone who has starved the world doesn't continue to cry over the evil they've caused when their harvest is capable of wiping out hunger."

"No shit! When you've been constipated for 400 years, and somebody finally hands you some psyllium, are you still going to cry about that tripas habanero burrito you ate?" The timing was perfect, they spoke as a composite persona, not one single word preceding or trailing behind the speech of the other; this was no act; Dagmar and Lydia were operating as a single/poly-reactive entity.

"Can we talk about something else?" Miguel asked.

"Yes!"

"As three separate people again, please?"

"Oh, you're no fun!" Lydia chastised, leaning across the table, and kissing him on the forehead. "Think about how trippy that would've been later in bed if we'd maintained the whole simultaneity thing. Or shit; imagine if all three of us did....or just you and me......or just you and Dagmar!"

"Who would be the guiding consciousness if it was all three?" he asked. "Or, who had the reins right now when it was just you two?"

"Oh, Michael! Why are you asking questions that you already know the answer to?" Dagmar petted him on the cheek, looking at him like he was a brand new puppy.

They sipped on the shots of ice cold Baronhunter and pints of wheat beer garnished with nutmeg and blood orange. Miguel played footsie with Lydia under the table, acting like some dopey teenager, while he put his hand on Dagmar's inner thigh; it was his turn to be flirty and playful.

Salted Plastic: The Comedic Horror of Gentrification

"I thought you wanted to talk, Michael! Change the subject, no?" Dagmar said playfully, grabbing his hand, and dragging it deeper between her thighs; he could feel the heat radiating more and more onto his fingers, right through the vinyl covering her.......

"We need a booth!" he heard Lydia say. "All the fun is on your side of the table!"

"Fuck the booth! Where's your place, Dagmar?!?!" Dagmar and Miguel said concurrently while looking at Lydia.

Salted Plastic: The Comedic Horror of Gentrification

Saturday, October 24, 12:15am

Inside an old comedy club in North Hollywood. The brightest light in the place was on the club's stage, illuminating a colorful banner above that read:

"THE JADED PARTY GIRL RETIREMENT PLAN.
Graft an Interesting Persona Onto Those Buns! LETS ROCK and GET GEEKY! LEARN THE ART OF HOBOSEXUAL!"

A woman in her mid-40s was on stage, microphone in hand, addressing a large crowd. Fairly fit, she was painted green like Sheehullk, and dressed like a punk rock girl; boots, black leather shorts, red fishnet stockings, and a Sex Pastels tank top. She stood near a stool under the spot light. On the stool sat a female Zoomba instructor (from this point forward Zoombaby). The instructor was a little busty, maybe about 37 or 39, with brunette hair, and dressed in a lycra tank top/shorts. She had her head down, and was crying into her hands. The girl dressed like Sheehullk Rocker (from here on out Shulker) consoled Zoombaby with a hand on her shoulder while an audience of women (mainly in their late 30's to early 40's) from LA's Westside, Valley, Downtown and Coastal areas watched. A faint and lanky shadow could be seen coming from behind the stage curtains, rubbing it's hands together like a verminous fly.

"And what happened after that?" Shulker asked.

"After that I had to wait 40 minutes to get into the clubs on The Sunset Strip. Two years later it was 60 minutes…………and………and and…………and now……………and now I can only get in on a Tuesday or Sunday night. WAAAAAGgggggh!!!"

"You poor thing; ageism and its proponents can be sooo cruel! Right ladies?!" Shulker turned and addressed the crowd. "But we got you; we have everything you need to fight and get your power back! DON'T WE GIRLS?!?!"

The audience applauded loudly.

"That said, why miss your old life? Was it really so fulfilling?" Shulker asked in a fake as fuck tone. Highly affected, it made her sound like the host of some shallow daytime talk show......or someone demoing food processors at Kostko. This was always the way with motivational speakers; always thinking they can get by on aphorisms and "positive" reinforcement alone.........without the energy and inflection that would come default to them if they ACTUALLY FUCKING FELT what they were saying, as opposed to just blindly "understanding" and promoting it, as in Shulker's case. Parrots, memetic meat puppets..........saying/believing anything, as long as it was frequently said and believed by morons that believed you can life hack emotional content. As if caring for others in their estimate was nothing but a formula of the right intonation and verbiage.

Zoombaby looked up at Shulker, and wiped a tear from her eye, her face full of contrived determination to refute the validity of any attachment to her old life. "Sometimes I have nightmares about Dalton; that's my ex by the way; I have nightmares about him partying on PCH with younger women, or skiing in Big Bear with some exotic foreign girl, or doing lines off his intern's ass.......the way he used to do with me.........and I wake up SCREAMING in cold sweats. I take a valleum, some zanex, a few purcoset, a vellbutrine or two.....and then watch an episode of Pecks in The Titty with a few glasses of Chardonnay.........but the nightmares always come back. I just can't get the memories of us clubbing and brunching in Weho and Beverly Hills out of my head. WHY IS LIFE SO CRUEL!?!?"

"Because your average male is a narrow minded brute, THAT'S WHY!?!" Shulker said sternly, stooping down and putting her hands on Zoombaby's shoulders, shaking her a bit to knock some sense into her. "And you've been lost in the narrow qualifiers that protect your right to

143

be considered the definitive perfect woman in the estimate of these unimaginative turds!"

Zoombaby stifled her sobs, looked up at Shulker, and smiled. She felt safe in the strength and conviction that this grown woman in cosplay seemed to radiate. "You're right, I've been lost; who needs endless mimosas on Sunday with Lance, or twerking happy hour with me and my besties in front of Pierce, Dalton, and Prescott?!?! I'M A DESIRABLE AND INTERESTING WOMAN, AND I HAVE MORE TO OFFER!!!!"

"You do!" Shulker followed up. "And if you follow the steps we have outlined here tonight, and you embody and emphasize the grafted "uniqueness" that ensues, YOU'LL BE UNSTOPPABLE!!! Chavonne?!?! ON STAGE PLEASE!"

On cue with Shulker's last words a girl came on stage. She was 30-something, skin professionally tanned, with long curved bejeweled nails, designer jeans, UGGly boots, a Bábe jacket with faux fur lined hood, and an $80 make up job on her face. A man that looked distinctly like a young Woudee Allan dressed in X-man's pajamas crawled on all fours behind her, dragging (by chains attached to his neck) a clothes rack, and a table with a colorful box on top of it. The crowd whistled, laughed and jeered at Chavonne's empowerment relative to the man's subservient position.

Chavonne tugged on "Woudee's" (aka Gutlez Meeltikt's) chains, making him stand and unpack the contents of the box onto the table as the stage curtain closed. Lots of rustling behind the curtain ensued; the sound of clothing being put on, a blow dryer running, heavy shoes hitting the floor.............followed by a mildly audible queef.

After a few more minutes the curtains opened up again, the lights brightened, and the audience applauded. On stage, Chavonne and Gutlez Meeltikt were transformed, hand and hand smiling. On the table sat a variety of props; bobble head toys, manga, video games, vinyl records, comic books, spiked bracelets, dvds on counter culture, manick panick hair dye, a copy of the book "Nanny Syndrome", B-movie VHS

Salted Plastic: The Comedic Horror of Gentrification

and other movie formats that spanned genres from psychotronic biker thrillers to cheesecore horror; from Yodorowsky to Jon Water; Daria Bargento to Kurowsawa; 80s High School Dramas to 60s Bollywood, etc.

Chavonne was a new and "unique" entity, garbed head to toe in her empowering, shake and bake "personality"; steel toe Dock Nartens, neon eyeshadow, Kaptain Amerrika T-shirt, leather biker jacket, black lipstick, purple fishnet stockings, red vinyl skorts, bed head hair do, a Maruto Shippooden metal lunchbox/purse, and nail polish chipped and chewed like "she just don't care!!!!!!"

Gutlez Meeltikt had a new outfit too, one that made him embody a vibe that said "Yes, I'm a spineless doormat that will pay your bills while you shack up with me RENT FREE!" His Prince of Wales (look it up) snap cap, fitted denim daisy dukes, Thoms shoes (no socks), Buddie Holie glasses, pre-faded Lobotech shirt, and Big Bike Theory man-purse made him the picture perfect example of the safe, caring and non-threatening shy guy male. His hair was even puff curling from under his hat, making him look like the quintessential HIP and ZIPPY moron!!!!! Zero manhood emanated from him; he was visually neutered to a T, ready to be taken out of the package, and placed on the bed with the rest of Chavonne's stuffed animals.

Shulker broke the still lingering applause with "So, you see, this is what a healthy modern relationship looks like, ladies! This is the new formula for the respect and interpersonal experience YOU DESERVE!!!"

"I don't get it....." Zoombaby started.

"Don't worry," Shulker interrupted, "its common, but don't get too anxious over that; I'm going to break it down.......with Chavonne's help of course. Chavonne?! Let's help her get a grip on your success shall we?"

Chavonne broke contact with Gutlez Meeltikt, walked over, and took the microphone from Shulker.

"I grew up in Sherman Oaks in the mid 90s," Chavonne started, "made captain of the cheerleading squad at my high school two years in

145

Salted Plastic: The Comedic Horror of Gentrification

a row, and dated every popular guy there until graduation. I went to ALL THE HOTTEST parties, drove a 97 Aston Martin DB7 to school on the days I felt like showing up to class............and I was prom queen my graduating year. Every girl wanted to be me, or be with me!!!!"

"In college I slept with all the hot professors on campus, joined every activities club, and held my text books in a convincingly studious manner at all the local cafes. I also promoted environmental and animal rights by flaunting my bag of Bort's Beez and Bear Minerals cosmetics at every girl with nicer hair, skin and nails than me."

"At the age of 22 I graduated with a Masters in both Fashion Psychology and Metaphysical Photography, two very sought out (and highly made up) majors with appeal-factor based totally off the idea that bullshit sells in academia, and that every half a moron with no real focus will take out a loan as long as the semantic circus game that college administrators play when they try to sell students on programs is made magnetic by new campus buildings, and promises of celebrity status careers gained INSTANTANEOUSLY after graduation!"

"After that I celebrated by burning through my spend thrift trust fund on a four year long European vacation that I shamelessly disguised as higher education. My university of choice was the prestigious (and expensive as shit), internationally acclaimed Institut Prétentieux de La Chienne. Because of the high tuition there, the majority of the students took their education seriously, and diligently learned about textiles and fashion marketing. I, on the other hand, was too busy spending my time clubbing, going to brunches, nursing hangovers and a swollen vag, and posting on Myspazz about how I was on my way to becoming a BIG TIME fashion designer........even though I never did the work to get there. One day, my tuition costs failed to be auto-debited as usual, so I called home to Daddy and found out............"

Chavonne droned on and on and on, one mouth fart after another, while two figures behind the stage curtain whispered in the dark.

Salted Plastic: The Comedic Horror of Gentrification

"So, Baron Mustela, what do you think of the harvest? Plenty enough for all our unmatchable clan members, yes? Plenty enough I'd even say, that the two of us can sample the stock as well." A tall bulky figure asked.

A frail shadow shuffled in the corner, stepping forward a bit, walking in seizure spasms. It's hand was visible in the little light available back stage; mottled skin in tones of gray and black, fingernails like the texture of burnt caramel on florentine cookies.......living death...........rot and corruption.

"You know the deal." it said in a raspy high pitched emphysemic whine. "WE get to cherry pick first.........and your people can have what's left."

"This....'deal', was to be one of egalitarian design as I understand it. I would advise that you contract honorably; you, and the rest of your group memberssssss."

"Egalitarian? Contracts?! Honor?!?!" Baron Mustela replied with arrogance. "You forget who arbitrates the value of these words between us Barons who forge them, and the people we force to utilize the cage of language. Words are the trap that pollinates the minds of the cattle, that makes them forget that the map is not the territory, that facts are not evidence. You snakes may have the numbers, but me and the other Barons have the semantic........artistry. We can change the game and value of the communicative methods on this planet at any time we please; we've done it here for a VERY long time my friend. Do not forget; you are guests here, Provost Peter!"

"Yes, yes!" Peter answered in mild irritation, a red ember near his face in the dark indicating that he was puffing on a cigar. "And we are forever grateful for your bio-cosmetology, and your public image and social narrative fashioning mediums that give us the opportunity to blend into society and seem human, Baron Mussssstela." Peter hissed and stepped into the light, exposing himself fully.

Salted Plastic: The Comedic Horror of Gentrification

Nearly six and a half feet tall, wearing a black Armenni gabardine suit, with a seared scar on his face, Provost Peter, an albino reptilian who looked as if he could bite through a steel car door, would be an intimidating sight for most………….but not for Baron Mustela. The powers that Baron Mustela Nivalis held were soft-spokenly evil, deep rooted, and not to be fucked with! The fact that he could stand unshaken in Peter's presence spoke volumes on this account.

"Calllrrmm down," Mustela garbled, his voice warping the very nature of sound itself within the vicinity of their conversation, "you and yours will get your cut, and the means to incubate more eggs……creating soldiers with an adaptable edge bred by their hybrid nature, no less. Lezzzttttzz get dressed……………and do please put tharrrt out." Death whisper, feeble vice voice………..bio ash and soul dehydration………..vocal resonance from hell.

"Sí, es la hora de nuestra parte en esssssspectáculorrrwwwr……." Peter warp/mumbled as he put out his cigar on the ground, the words still lingering even after he was done speaking them……..a reverberating echo………..a distortion of time and sound.

They walked to a nearby dressing room and closed the door behind them…………..but multiple and faint traces of their bodies lingered behind; a translucent arm, some disembodied teeth, a hollow outline of a body, a pink neon rectum, a floating ivory brain, white scales, a diseased nervous system. It was a train of after images following in the wake of their exit. The smoke stayed behind as well, somehow defying the laws of physics as it rewound into the cigar on the floor.

Back on stage Shulker was finishing up another monologue.

"………..and it's really just that simple girls; Chavonne did it, and so can you!!!!!!! Shed that old personality! REINVENT YOURSELF!!!! Go out immediately and buy some Bunko Poop toys, dye your hair green, and put a few retro gaming systems in your apartment for conversational value!"

"Open some new accounts on Shitstagram and Cuupiid where you endlessly blab about how you're a BIG TIME gamer/anime/comic book nerd girl..........even though you've never played a game, watched an anime or read a comic book in your entire life........and probably never will!!!!!!"

"Just life hack that shit; google 'cosplay girl' and follow suit; NO ONE WILL EVER KNOW THE DIFFERENCE!!!!! Dress like a sexy Kaptain Amerrika or Sooper Merio while you flaunt your ass on LonelyFans! Be a MAJOR ANIME "INFLUENCER" by posing with your 65-year-old sugar daddy in front of the giant Gunndamme in Tokyo, and just photo shop that old loser out of the picture!!!"

"Get your rich parents to fund an Ameeba and Diskcoggs budget so you can grow your "genuine" interest in becoming a celebrity punk rock dj!!!!! Tell them you want to go back to college while you're at it! A lukewarm passion for a degree in film, music, or art will give you instant access to desperate, lonely......AND LOADED.......geeks and pseudo nerds just DYING to WORSHIP you at their DTLA loft in the manner that YOU DESERVE!!!!!!"

"Scout, prowl, hunt and flirt at Animae Expo, Renassence Fair and Komikon for potential sugar daddies with low self-esteem; there's a literal GOLDMINE of opportunities out there for you ladies!!!!!!! Don't hesitate or spend another day moping over Jeffrey or Tyler; those days are gone; IT'S TIME FOR A NEW YOU!"

Shulker motioned towards Chavonne and Gutlez Meeltikt as she finished; their cue to walk off stage as the lights dimmed.

"And to get all you ladies motivated, and one step away from any further procrastination, let's meet some of our eligible bachelors shall we?!" Shulker keyed up all poppy and coked out as the lights came on again.

Salted Plastic: The Comedic Horror of Gentrification

The crowd roared lasciviously as two men came on stage, both Anglo, one frail and thin, the other one tall, and somewhat dopey and shy in his body language. The frail one had pointed and scrawny features; his nose, chin, and cheekbones were prominent and sharp edged. His chestnut hair, parted to the side, long and pomaded, gave the impression of a 40-something year old man whose mother still combed his hair. The corduroy bell bottoms and Asstro Boi t-shirt he wore dimmed down a slightly apparent menace in his facial expressions; despite the whole non-threatening nerd look he was rocking, that face betrayed an underlying appropriative energy. It was as if his eyes and facial tics indicated that he was looking at the audience the same way a junky trying to detox would eyeball a loaded syringe.

The tall dopey one looked like he could flip a jeep despite his harmless mannerisms. He had curly red hair, and wore wire rim Chartier eye glasses, a green turtle neck sweater, jeans, and had an expensive valise complete with Crapple laptop at his side. He looked just like any other misanthropic tech worker royalty currently infesting all the choicest pieces of real estate in Los Angeles. He clasped and unclasped his hand nervously on the handle of the valise while staring down at the floor and shuffling his feet.

"Aww! He's shy girls!" Shulker bellowed in an affected girly tone, indicating Tall Dopey. "It's ok Peter, they won't bite, will you ladies?!"

Laughter ensued from the crowd, followed by a few whistles.

Shulker smiled and laughed with the crowd, her eyes twinkling yellow for a second or two........their vertical irises taking in the harvest.

Salted Plastic: The Comedic Horror of Gentrification

Saturday, October 24, 2:42am

Chipotle Tlaloca and Adrik Saturn were chillin in the backseat of Tlaloca's beat up 65 Vord Valcon. They were parked on a dark residential street south of the Hollywood Strip area. Tlaloca passed Adrik a bottle of rye she had pinched from her mom's stash. Neither of them could get into the local bars, both being only 19 years old.

They had just recently met about three days ago at a backyard punk gig in Boyle Heights. She bummed a cig off Adrik even though she didn't smoke; pretext to talk to "that hot black guy with the platinum blonde hair and septum ring" that her friend Albert had pointed out. Chipotle had been glaring at him, her short neon pink hair combed off to the left, the sides shaved and dyed neon yellow. Adrik, lighting up the pink Sharmen cigarette and handing it to Chipotle, had smirked a bit as she'd pretended to inhale, trying to look the part of bad as broken glass street punk in her zebra mini skirt, bondage belt and brand spanking new, self-torn U.X.H. shirt.

He knew a rich girl playing at slumming it when he saw one, but was good at feeding the game when he needed to. Yeah, he knew her alright; knew her as **her**, and **her** as her. He'd been there that night in Boyle Heights to keep an eye on Chipotle, in fact. Thing was, she didn't know about her true nature, what she really was, but the people Adrik worked with did...or at least they thought they did. Either way, meeting her there that night was no fucking coincidence.

Still, despite what he knew about the real her, what he'd been told by his tribe, Adrik still enjoyed the personality Tlaloca would be operating with until the day she realized she wasn't human in the total sense of the word.

He had enjoyed her costume personality then, that night in Boyle Heights, and he was enjoying it now, here in her beat up car, which in and of itself was also another performance piece for her scripted self-image. The car was really just something she drove for its street cred

151

value, even though with the kind of money she came from Tlaloca could be driving anything she wanted.

Chipotle Tlaloca, the foul mouthed "street kid", was actually a privileged rich kid who had grown up in South Pasadena. She had been adopted by Gavin and Wendy Mirriam not long after being born, and had spent her days growing up with everything she'd ever wanted. The Mirriams were both attorneys in the entertainment industry, and had deep ties within the ranks of the reptilian sub-social hierarchy. Because Wendy couldn't conceive (due to an underdeveloped cloaca), and her and Gavin didn't want Chipotle to be deprived of the privileges granted by default to reptilian children, the Mirriams were granted access to a new 2nd Gen-Rep program emerging at the time. This program proposed to have the ability to psychically convert human children into reptilians. The process left converts consciously latent and unaware (until late adolescence) of their true nature. It served the double purpose of not only allowing barren reptilian females the opportunity to have their human children "augmented to the cause", but it also created reptilian citizens that were biologically human, hence able to infiltrate emerging groups of humans currently becoming a problem. Groups like Sisters, Others and Brothers.

Chipotle's biological parents had been from Mexico City, both arts students, both wealthy, and both unwilling to let a child "ruin" their dreams of stage acting and irresponsibly fucking off in New York. Putting Chipotle up for adoption, they'd been out of her life mere weeks after her birth.

Children of the 2nd Gen-Rep program never really fully "felt" anything for/from their reptilian parents. Being children, and not full grown adults who had repressed the them in them, they had enough intuitive grasp on the fact that something was "just not right" with their adoptive parents. This created a rift by pure act of nature.

Reptilians in general had no warmth to give, and it was very rare for human children to identify with or feel any attachment to their reptilian parents. This bred a lack of solid identity, and in Tlaloca's case, not being able to put a concrete finger on the real reason behind her inability to connect with her parents, she attributed it to the fact that Gavin and Wendy were white Anglo, and she was brown Latina. This led to Tlaloca's obsession with a lot of superficial ethnic graft, cultural affectation, and contrived notions of being "hood", and full of pride for a culture that she'd never really known. She thought if she acted the part often enough, that it would make it true. Needless to say, it came out quite forced and generic:

"Whadda you know about Marxism and Guevara................" she slurred while grabbing back the bottle. "......something something.........Orozco's paintings..................something something......Frida Kahlo........blah blah BLAH...........Muna Chao..............squawk squawk squawk.......Pancho Villa documentary...............braceros...............something something......Dia de Los Pochos Pop Up at LECMA museum next week.......ever tried the AWESOME hand crafted gluten free artisanal $8 vegan pan doolcee at La Mariposa Pâtisserie?............Olvera Street.................LA RASSA?!?!"

"La raza?" he smirked. "Nada en absoluto."

"You know Spanish?" Tlaloca asked nervously, palms clammy, starting to sweat a little, worried that she was about to be called out, completely oblivious to the fact that Adrik knew everything about her already.

"No, just a few basics." he lied. "But I'm sure not as much as you though." He inched closer, running a hand over the top of her thigh. She mentally sighed as goose bumps raised in reaction to his touch, relieved that she didn't have to reveal that she didn't know more than a handful of words and phrases in Spanish..........words which she couldn't even pronounce properly at that.

Adrik though, he was completely chilled out, his personality had been nothing but flow and let go ever since being found and awakened by Morrigan's cell of SOBs (Sisters, Others, and Brothers). He didn't do the whole past and ethnic pride shit to augment his identity like Chipotle; every day was new for him, and being limited by an attachment to self-definition based on something like racial or ethnic background just seemed pointless to him. He was sent after Tlaloca for VERY important reasons, and on a need to know basis. It was always that way with Morrigan and the other sachems in SOBs; didn't tell him shit other than that the person was important, and that he was to bring them back anyway he could.

That said, Adrik had consistently found that the best way to bring them back was............

"FUUUUUCK! UMMMMMmmhh!" Chipotle moaned as he lightly pressed a thumb on her clit through her panties, the rest of his hand brushing her inner thigh with light finger tips. She reactively pulled her leather skirt up to her waist while he continued with his hand, and leaned into her with his upper body. She could feel his pec muscles brushing her shoulder as he started to lick her neck. Her nipples started to swell at the thought of how fit he probably looked underneath his denims and Ex-Ray Specks t-shirt. "Shit! Not enough privacy in my car!" she gritted through her teeth, reaching under his shirt to get what she could. This consoled her frustration at not being able to be fully nude with Adrik, making up for it by feeling around for what she didn't have the opportunity to see. His abs were solid, stomach and chest smooth; she pinched a nipple, one of her favorite things to do during foreplay, but he brushed her hand off roughly, seemingly agitated.

"Ugh....I hate that shit!" Adrik said playfully, smiling a little, trying not to kill the mood; he hated his nipples pinched, and for good reasons too........reasons connected to his rational for living in the moment, not talking too much about himself, and not platforming on his past. It was one of the few things that broke his passive nature. Even so, Tlaloca looked irritated, her default behavioral associations interpreting his action as "typical male dominant bullshit", having no idea that she was nowhere near right on that account...........zero desire to second guess her judgment.

Adrik had to fix this quick, and he knew it; he was losing her fast now, and emergency measures might be necessary; he tried charm first.

"You sew those d-rings on your bondage jacket yourself; thing looks legit; you got talent!" He fucking knew the comment was out of context, but had jumped on his first instinct to save the mood. Feeling her energy out, he could tell he hadn't made a dent though.........

"Listen, its late; I gotta work early tomorrow." she lied. Gavin and Wendy gave her a $400 a week allowance; she'd never worked a day in her life.

"Next!" he thought, already knowing what was going to work to get her interested again, but he had to follow Morrigan's protocol of pursuing all other options before he made the move of last resort.

After charm, he tried comedy. "Sorry about the nipple thing, girl; they're just sensitive ever since I started lactating."

FAIL! Chipotle really didn't seem to like that one; knowing her personality profile, he knew she wouldn't (it insulted her generic notions of feminism). The joke was only a pretense for performance sake either way, just Adrik's method of going through the motions to get them out of the way...........so he could pull out the big guns, and use what he knew would actually work.

"Cool, I get it." Adrik said. "I'm sorry if I killed the mood. My bad, and I totally understand; you gotta get up tomorrow for work, and that's important. Ok if I take a piss before we say goodnight?"

"Sure, go for it!" she replied, the edge of her irritation subsiding somewhat. "We should finish up this bottle too, but then I gotta roll."

Adrik got out of the car, walked down a side alley, and stepped behind a light pole. He pulled a velvet bag out of his jeans. Unwrapping it, he brought out a pinky sized neon red vial, his palm glowing as he inspected its contents. "If Morrigan only knew how many times I've had to resort to Plan C," he whispered, "………Hahaha, plan C…………C as in COCK!"

He smirked childishly, laughing at his own humor, acting like a jackass joker. Adrik was no chauvinist, just childish; the crude jokes were what cut the bottled up pain from his past for him. They played a big part in his emotional survival…….mild catharsis for things that had never met grief.

"HAHAhehhehhehHAHA! That shit always cracks me up. But damn, I do use way too much of this stuff. They measure our rations, but Lebanon never logs my usage right anyways, the fucker!"

Still smiling, he unzipped his pants, dipped his pinky into the vial, and then rubbed a very small amount of the red oil on his genitals. The oil, on contact with one's skin, gave off "attracting" properties; it was completely unnecessary for Adrik to put it on his privates in particular. He just did it that way each time because it felt funny as shit. It reminded him of a first date when he was 15, where he had learned the hard way not to spray cologne on your balls; few memories were worth bringing out of his past for him, but the ones that were were usually the ones that made him laugh……………were were were……………laugh made……usual…….

He closed the vial, zipped up, and put it away. Then, for some dumb reason, he did something that Morrigan always told him never to do……………and licked the residue of the oil off his pinky. She'd told him never to administer or take the stuff orally, but what harm could a drop or two do? He'd seen Vicky Varmint and Lebanon do it all the time back at the SOB commissary.

Walking back and stepping into the car he slammed the door shut. "You took a minute." Chipotle said impatiently. "I'm kinda over the night, don't really feel like finishing that bottle, plus I still gotta get gas, so maybe we should, you know, head out so I can………**what the?!**" she exclaimed out of nowhere, looking around at nothing at all, sniffing the air for some reason. "What's that weird sweet smell?!" Chipotle smiled girlishly, her voice dropping the whole gruff street girl performance from one second to the next.

"Here it comes!" Adrik thought, smiling. "The associations are always entertaining."

"It smells just like the candy shops on Main Street at Dizzyland!" Tlaloca smiled, blushing, her energy waning away from the backyard punk girl act, and waxing into poppy cheerleader goes goth at Hott Topick mode.

"Thought so!" Adrik smiled. "Those things she thinks are her parents probably........"

"My parents," she interrupted his thoughts in perfect timing, "I.....I haven't mentioned this......but I'm adopted." she admitted, not wanting to reveal too much about her parents and being from a rich area, despite her defenses dropping a bit in reaction to...."to what?!"she wondered.

"Anyways, my parents took me to Dizzyland once a long time ago (actually, she straight up had a season pass and always had), and that smell on Main Street, the memory; it's just pleasant is all........wonder where its coming from."

"Maybe from the Boulevard," Adrik said, "one of the shops up there." He inched a little away. "So, you gotta get going, huh?" He smiled internally, knowing there wasn't a chance on earth she still wanted to call it a night.

"Uhm...uh...yeah, I should.....work and all....but you know.......I mean....no, it's cool....I mean......I actually just remembered I don't work till like 2pm tomorrow......so I can definitely chill a little longer!" she said nervously.

"Alright, cool. Mind if I play some music on my phone?" Adrik pulled out his phone, already going through his playlist before she answered. He purposely moved to the other end of the back seat, away from Tlaloca; despite doing this a few times, he always felt guilt at the idea of making the first move under these conditions, this being another relative factor of his past. True, the "unionizing effect" of the oil didn't work if there was no mutual attraction; it forced nothing, which Adrik had found out the hard way a couple of times, but still……….

"I really like them all!" Chipotle whispered to herself, as Adrik's phone played some Alleska y Las Pegames while she drifted into her thoughts. "Without Jack, and Ariel, and Simba, and Jasmine I don't know how I'd deal with Gavin and Wendy; that house is so cold."

Adrik had heard her. "I don't know about the rest," he thought, "but I have a Jasmine that saved my ass too……..literally……….from those fucking bastard fucks, she did!"

While Chipotle was on a psychic/olfactory trip, Adrik was about to go on a semantic instigated psychic trip of his own at the sound of the name "Jasmine." Luckily this mounting bad trip was stopped before it even started by………….

"You ever watch Dizzy cartoons!?!?" His penis seemingly asked him.

"What the fuck!?!?" he thought, feeling a little out of it; totally relaxed, but out of it. He looked down and thought, "Oh, yeah, not my dick, my dick doesn't talk; it's just Tlaloca down there, looking up at me with a shit maniacal grin on my……her………her/my……our…….her face while pulling my cock out and asking me about Cheshire Cat's and Fairy Godmothers and shit. And now she's licking my…………fffFFFFUCKRRKK! That feeeeeels good!"

His mind bent/split/relaxed/jump-roped/melted and ran alien geometry problems through the balls at Chuky Cheez as he remembered an old DVD he'd watched as a kid that he'd liked a lot.

"Yeah! Dizzey movies? Of course!" Adrik sweated a bit, enjoying Tlaloca's feverish tongue tip as it DUG into the underside of his head on THAT SPOT. "Krunchberrys late at night a lot as a kid………", he breathed heavily, getting a little dizzy, "……….big bowl while watching this one about a demon king who brought skeletons back to life……….DAMN,

Salted Plastic: The Comedic Horror of Gentrification

that feels good; YOUR FUCKING TONGUE!!!" he gritted through his teeth while gripping the car's door handle.

"OH YEAH!" Chipotle stopped, looking up at him all exited, her head cocked to one side, a curved rope of saliva hanging from her mouth like a vertical bridge that ended at the head of his penis. "The Blakk CALDRONE!!!!!! That's such a favorite of mine!!!!! I like the cute little fortune telling hog! What was its name again?" she trailed off, staring up at him with a maddening yet harmless grin. She maintained the crazy smile (and eye contact) as she sat up and laid down onto the back seat, peeling off her panties and spreading her thighs generously.

Adrik looked a little loony and maniacal himself at this point, his facial expressions off in space, a big smile as he tried to remember something. His eyes focused on the roof of the car for a minute.........until he noticed Chipotle was waiting, legs still apart. He smiled and knelt forward slowly, putting his face between her thighs, the heat there making him a little faint, the musk of her pussy raising his blood pressure. And then he remembered what he wanted to say, how he was going to confess his love to.......how THEY were going to S&R/KEY/VOW their love to each other........a love that until moments ago they didn't even know they felt.

"I say we let the boy try it!" HE SHOUTED.

"YES, give the boy a chance!" Tlaloca followed up laughing as they/she/he matched quotes.

They both laughed for a minute, looking at each other in ineffable contentment, a benevolent enantiodromia towards their true selves showing them feelings they had had under lock and key off and on again and again since who the fuck knows when...........

..........and then Adrik went to work, kissing her coffee colored labia, licking the beautiful seam, poking gently at the hood of her clit, watching everything swell up and moisten. "Fuck, she smells good!" he thought; he could tell she used good soap and moisturizer, and that if he licked "........it'd be clean........but no.......what if she gets pissed........."

159

Salted Plastic: The Comedic Horror of Gentrification

"SHE WON'T!" something inside (or outside?) of him told him......

"FUCK IT!" He put his hands under her plump little ass and lifted a little, feeling how smooth and firm it was..........like silk......but hot to the touch, full of muscle and soft THICK FAT! He SQUEEZED those cheeks, heart racing on emotion, lust, and something more..........and then he WENT FOR IT!!!! Adrik gently feathered his tongue on her asshole, still a little concerned that it was a bad move even though he was all knowing in that moment in above and beyond measures.

She didn't push him away or protest, so he kept at it, concerned that any second she'd get pissed or weirded out and smack him or something.......until..........

"MMMMnnnnnhhhhh!" she groaned, whimpering in such a soft and gentle, weak at the touch of his tongue on her ain sort of way, that it made his cock instantly so hard that the base hurt!!!!!

"Yup!" he thought.

The ice broken, he got more comfortable, and started to rub his thumb and index finger on her clit while continuing with his tongue on her asshole.........she pulsed it on the tip of his tongue, getting him even more exited.............thrusting her hips up................he took his other hand and reached up and under her fishnet shirt, pinching a nipple briefly, her pussy now nice and swollen, heavily wet, his next move was................

"Hey you two!!!! Having fun in there?!?!" A voice came from out of nowhere.

"WHAT THE FUCK!" Tlaloca/Adrik shouted, sitting up fast as shit, and looking around. Right outside Tlaloca's window stood the hungry leering face of some aging rocker guy, very slimy energy, looking like a cross between Davv Vanean's Fantasmagorria stage, and Denny Devetto in the movie Batmen Return.

"What the fuck ASSHOLE!" Chipotle shouted, pulling her skirt back down as Adrik zipped his fly up.

160

Salted Plastic: The Comedic Horror of Gentrification

"No, no, no! No need for that!!!!!" The creeper outside started shouting. "You two can keep going, I just wanna watch a little; I'm cool guys.....I'M COOL!!!"

"Naw! NAW MAN! YOU'RE NOT COOL!" Chipotle yelled, shoving the door open and stepping out, the guy backing up as she did, trying to avoid getting hit. "What the fucks your problem asshole!"

"I am cool.....I AM!" The guy continued in a confused pathetic tone, not fazed by Chipotle's anger, desperate to interact with them apparently, pushing his luck like the dumb fuck he was. "Look, what if I get you two some drinks......or....or....OR SOME DRUGSSSSSS........and we can all come back to my place and play some records?" Greasy beads of perspiration began to leak down his slimy face, his sleaze nature getting heavier and heavier by the second. "Shit! Ex-Ray Specks?! Cool shirt, kid! I remember seeing them back in the day........"

"Are you for real man?!" Adrik shouted, now outside of the car too, circling around, getting in between Tlaloca and this guy who was increasingly starting to seem like a real nut job. "You crazy, or high or something?!?"

"Look...." The guy continued, still ignoring how angry he was making them, the desperation in his voice HIGHLY apparent. "You two in a band or something? I was in an old school punk band back in 78 that no one's ever heard of..........something something............I got a lot of connections in New York and Hollywood.........blah blah BLAH............let's hit up an all-night Turkish bath house I know of, and talk about it!"

He leered with venom and HUNGER at them both.........hoping to drain some of the fire they had built in Tlaloca's backseat........oblivious to the fact that that sort of thing was not salable, clueless to the concept of feelings, mutual attraction and consensual sex. The flies began to circle around this ghoul of a thing............the stubble on his face getting darker as if by magic..............a stench like sauerkraut brine and used condom lube assaulted Tlaloca and Adrik..........a dizzy sick feeling, like that experienced after sniffing modeling glue, over took them.........and then something inside Tlaloca woke the fuck up...........alarm system of the soul.............a deep need to protect the sacred and unknown about her true self.

A shit serious (and out of character look) appeared on Tlaloca's face, her tone becoming that of a matriarch protecting her tribe as she stepped in front of Adrik and stared Hungry down. "I'm not sure who or what you are," she picked at the left lapel of his denim vest, "but this has got to happen; you're dangerous in ways you don't understand, you fucking shit!"

"Huh?" Hungry smiled nervously, still hopeful, a mock innocent look on his face. "But I just wanna offer you two a good time. You know, chill and share some free love, get to know each........."

Tlaloca YANKED that lapel as hard as she could towards her right hip, and dropped her body weight into the pull while bending her knees. This turned Hungry's chin up and sideways, leaving his jaw exposed as Tlaloca came back up with an uppercut straight into his jawline. Instantly knocked out cold, he went stiff as a board, his hands at his sides, heels clicking together as he dropped onto the concrete.

"DAAAAMN!" Adrik yelled. He was surprised as shit at what he'd just seen, but still found some humor in it. He stepped to Chipotle's side, smiling a bit, confused a little; nothing in Tlaloca's files had said anything about her knowing how to fight. No training, no martial arts growing up, not a single school yard scrap..........nothing! He had no idea where her fighting ability came from, but the oil was still working, and it gave him a few general......

"Hungry Horowitz?" Tlaloca's voice interrupted Adrik's train of thought. "Haha! Stupid name. Hey Adrik, you hungry? This guy's got a fucking deck of credit cards!" She was stooped down over Hungry, going through his wallet.

Just then Adrik's phone rang............his other phone. "Hold up a sec....." he told Chipotle. He took an earbud out of his pocket, put it in his ear, walked down the alley a ways, and answered in a whisper while

Chipotle was still occupied with the contents of Hungry's wallet. "Hey Morrigan, what's up? I'm still with the……"

"Saturn!"

"Great!" he thought; whenever Morrigan was about to tell him he fucked up, she always called him by his last name.

"What'd I……." he began.

"The sachems I'm witht are telling me they thense void energy and polytheenkthyncronous consciousness within your vithinity. Soooo, noth withstanding the fact that I'm fairly thurre you took the oil orally, which I'll be speaking to you abouth later, I need you to listen VERY cairfully kid." Something about her curt, calm, and almost fearful for his well-being tone curled the hairs on the back of his neck; Morrigan was not one to be polite towards fuck ups……PERIOD! So for her to………..

"FUCK!!!! Uhmmm, Adrik……" he heard Chipotle back in the street, "………..this guy's eyelids are starting to twitch; maybe we should bail and call an ambul……"

"GRAB HER AND GET THE FUCKTHH OUT OF THERE, ADRIKTH!!!!" Morrigan SCREAMED like a mother shit crazy scared after dropping her baby into a lion exhibit at the zoo.

Hungry's skin started to pale out, turn black and grey in patches. Most of his hair began to fall out in clumps, and grew coarse and metallic like rusted wire where it remained. He was convulsing and spitting up black bile, eyelids still closed and twitching.

Adrik rushed back to the street, Tlaloca in plain sight, worried shitless………running……rushing………..almost there………but too late!!!!!

Out of nowhere he felt partially stuck, moving yet not moving; his nerves registered motion, he felt his body going forward normally, but his eyes told him a different story. Time visually warped for Adrik, slowed down just around him alone; it was like his eyes registered him walking at underwater speed even though he felt his body traversing in normal motion. Raising his hand, the feeling of having it already fulling lifted up at chest height registered to his nerves. But looking down, his

163

eyes told him that his arm was still at waist level. This was true of all his bodily sensations; what he felt his body doing did not match up to what his eyes told him it was doing. He couldn't hear a damn thing; not Tlaloca, not the thing twitching next to her........no cars rushing by......not Morrigan......nothing.......

He could see though, the world around him still registering on his eyes in real time even though his body moved in slow motion. He looked in horror as a shadow crept out of Hungry, a shadow that looked like fog made of heavy tar, yet light enough to float like mist......sumi ink that defied gravity. He wanted to SHOUT at Tlaloca, wanted to know why she was just sitting there on her knees while it happened, why she didn't get up and run! Looking closer though, down at her thighs and shins as she sat on the concrete, he got his answer; her legs were trembling, her shoulders and torso faintly straining as if some heavy weight was holding her down.

"What the fuck! Why can't she stand? What is that shit coming out of that thing........"

"ADRIK?" A voice in his head finally......Chipotle's voice.

"Adrik.....I'm fucking scared and aware down here......aware that there's nothing to fear........other part of me don't know shit; hearts gonna pop from the fear..."

"Don't worry girl, I can hear you, and I know and don't know too; just sit tight and try to......."

But it was too late. The tar mist had risen and spread across the entire section of the street that Tlaloca and Hungry occupied, obscuring anyone outside from what was going on.

Inside the shadow bubble, only Hungry and Tlaloca were part of the show now. Hungry's body began to very perceptibly RISE from the concrete while still in a laying position. Chipotle wanted to scream as she watched his eyes open; they were flat white with multiple black spots. The spots began to swirl and then coalesce, creating a mock pupil, something that mimicked the anatomical components of sight in lieu of an actual ability to see; a falsehood, a costume of nature so simple, yet somehow so fucking frightening to look at.

She tried to breath and get back to that state of being she'd been under when the oil had opened her and Adrik's eyes towards each other........a few breaths..........visualize.......... "that beautiful moment in my backseat........HAHAHAH......stupid beat up Valcon........if Adrik only knew that I could probably afford to drive a..........."

"I do...." Adrik came into her head. "I know ALL OF YOU when we are......but FUCK.......you're free......the OIL.......get up girl......GET UP!" They couldn't see each other anymore, but she felt his smile in her mind like a pat on the back, a kiss on the forehead...........a long warm hug. Love and life shot into her heart and soul, made her legs strong again; she was sure that she was home free as she began to stand up..........

........but there is sure, and there is sure...........

Barely an inch standing up and she felt murder on her left wrist, which had been holding Hungry's ID this entire time. The concentration and power from the oil, and the bridge it made from her to Adrik was instantly severed..........severed just as cleanly as her hand had just been from her arm; she looked in horror as the stump of her left wrist fountained red, a nightmare of pain and fear. She tried to scream, but found her voice caught in her throat.

Hungry, eyes closed again, was no longer floating, but sat next to her now, on his shins, just like her, enveloped in the inner city grime of the street......just like her, his mouth turned up into a grin.

"You didn't look!" he said, leaning in, black bile oozing out of sharp dirty pitted teeth, his breath like shit soaked in oxidized blood. "You missed EVERYTHING!" The voice was awful........cold ash........rusty nails.........weighted evil...........nothing like the timid desperate turd that had interrupted her and Adrik's love making earlier.

His hand darted out like a whip, latching onto her stump, and squeezed it so hard that she almost fainted from the pain. "We can't have that, now can we? Let's take a look and rewind; YOU REALLY NEED TO HAVE A GOOD LOOK!!!!"

He opened his eyes, and right there in the middle of the white scleras, where there should have been pupils, were two moebius strips, swirling in strange loops. She took a good look, full of fear..........and then passed out.

....

Salted Plastic: The Comedic Horror of Gentrification

Tlaloca came to, waking up in response to unbearable fear and pain, nothing but darkness around her now; a maggot oligarchy felt in her heart, something closing in on her with it's empty stomach, a feeling like she was being stalked and codified.............someone copying her soul poorly............being sold back a false image of herself; meal time, and she was the meal............

"Again!" She heard Hungry's disembodied voice.

WHIP! CUT! INTO THE DEMON CLOUD!

She screamed in agony as her hand was cut off again.

"Again!" Like skinned snakes crying in a coal fire.

WHIP! SLICE! ENVELOPED INTO HELL!!

She bit heavily into her own lip, twisting and scraping her knees and palm on concrete she couldn't see.

"AGAIN!!!!!!!" WARCRY FROM SOME OFFICE WHERE DREAMS DIE!

SLASH! BLOOD! FOOD FOR THE JACKALS!!!!!!

"AAAAAAAHHHHHHHHHHHH!!!!!!!" she yelled like a flayed dog being rubbed with salt.

Salted Plastic: The Comedic Horror of Gentrification

Over and over she experienced Hungry's hand moving faster than the eye could see.....

Over and over again Chipotle saw (via her mind's eye) the hand being severed from her arm. The shock and pain were horribly fresh every time, no matter how she braced for or tried to anticipate it by attempting to acclimate. And after a few more time slips, Hungry took even that away from her; all memory of former rewinds/replays of her amputation; he wanted the fear and despair to be virgin fresh each and every time for her, so he could feed on it like it was a nice piece of Wagyu beef, or a glass of Cru Classe Margaux......satisfaction of evicting a rent controlled tenant..........shutting down a local family owned restaurant to make way for an overpriced gastropub......a pat on the back at the success of corrupting the hearts of the people towards "progress".

She cried and cried, screamed and screamed, and felt full of sick anticipation over what comes next, prior to and following each and every hand cut. This went on for a good while, sickeningly nerve wracking/soul bending........and then stopped for who knows what reason. Maybe Hungry got jaded, like most things hell bent on only consuming and not creating do.......maybe he was resting.......toying in the dark...............who knew?

Nothing for a while. Tlaloca waited and waited.

Then the light came back a bit. The street was gone now, her car was gone, Adrik was gone; nothing but a few square feet of concrete, her, and this thing that obviously was more than just Hungry Horowitz at this point. The image of his eyes stayed with her the entire time, both in front of her eyes, and in her head. She noticed the two moebius strips in his eyes were still, dead still.................and then they began to move again in that strange loops pattern she had seen earlier.

He let Tlaloca remember again, gave her her full memory back, waiting for any novelty that that might bring him, hungry for anything he hadn't tasted yet. She felt sick, pissed and helpless.

168

Salted Plastic: The Comedic Horror of Gentrification

It was more than nightmare, more than being broken, scared, and angry at the idea of this monster maiming her, and then selling her an experience on replay that she didn't welcome to begin with. It was the control, the lack of options, the bottom line of the situation, the forced adaptation to repetition masquerading as novelty that broke all focus towards the potential for............................

WHIP! BONE CLEAN OPEN! SHADOW MEAL!

Her hand was severed again; apparently Hungry was the type who quickly tired of waiting, and just resorted to repetition............like all those incapable of creation do when faced with a situation where there is no life to consume or mimic.

"Does that feel good, kid?" Elderly corpse dining on infants.

"That was it...." she thought, gritting against the pain a little less, starting to remember the repetition, feeling for the alternative, finally getting it, "it's eating my ability to see anything tangential to this moment."

"What was that, you maggot? ENJOYING THIS YET?!"

Clitoral paper cuts during a bout of UTI. That made her scream, the scream eliciting great satisfaction from her torturer, but.........

Salted Plastic: The Comedic Horror of Gentrification

"I see," Tlaloca thought, perspiring. "It's a projecting technique; it's in pain, this thing......in pain and ashamed; each taunt is an unconscious verbal strategy, an inadvertent admission of his own self-image.....this last one.......'you maggot?'.......I see; he feels low.......wants me to believe I am how he sees himself; the disease stagnancy of association posturing as definition......caught him in its net.......and to feel good about himself, to be comfortable with how he sees himself and the world around him, he gets off on passing this mental frailty to others........and feeds on the reaction to sustain his self-image.............." She started to gain some strength and composure back, her conviction to fight rising, but..........

SCHLITCK! Awful cutting sound. PULPY MEAT EXPOSED!

The flesh rotten IMMEDIATELY after the cut, her resolve and understanding dropped again in reaction to the pain.

"HUNGRY MEAL, BABE!" Horowitz voice in her ear.....breath still unbearable......like somebody just threw up shit mixed with natto and durian.........

This time her hand hadn't fallen into the mist of tar, consumed by darkness. NO, now, through her tears and whimpers she saw and heard Hungry munching on her hand like it was a basket of hot wings.

-POP-

-SCHLURP-

-SNAP-

-GUZZLE-

His mouth impossibly bloated, he chomped, and slurped, and ground her hand in his teeth, all the while keeping his grip on her stump, squeezing, causing more pain, more doubt about her ability to be strong, in control…….have options.

"PLEASE!!!!!" she cried, a tear trailing down her face.

The sight of her crying, the tears and fear….exited him sooooooo much that he shook and twitched in demon seizure fashion. He opened his mouth, and glubbed out her hand, vicious teeth scraping off skin as it came out drenched in his nauseating saliva. It was mangled beyond all recognition, completely drained of its vitality………………used up by his appropriative drive. It plopped onto the floor, right there for her to see, the act completely not arbitrary; he wanted her to see it……break her spirit a little more…..savor that as well.

"You know what you are?" he asked in a contemplative tone.

She tried looking away, imposing a last ditch effort of her will……

"LOOK AT ME!!!!!" Hungry growled……………and then paused at the sound of his voice, a surprised expression on his face; he had just intuitively "downloaded" something from Chipotle, stole her nature………observation theft……..life hacked and WINDOW SHOPPED HER ANIMA like the rotten culture vulture that he was; he saw the oil, and what it was doing to her still in lingering fashion………..and copied it wholesale, in all its power, all its ability to move, to charge to joy, to connect all things, self-actualize, obliterate doubt, and conquer all locked states…….and then Hungry decided to use it for no good, just like anyone who has ever been handed it all without having to earn it usually does.

"AWWWWWWWW!!!!!" he exhaled. "So this is where you've been drawing your resolve, you identity devoid rat! You no good stray! You cultureless cunt!" Hungry utilized his ersatz grasp of the oil and its properties, used it to make her drop under the falsehood that she was carrying his own burdens of no-identity, no self-born strength, no clan or home. He saw her "parents", and all Tlaloca's associated feelings of

171

insecurity, her lack of solid identity, and toyed with her, used it as a weapon.

She began to piss herself in fear, and the smell of the urine exited him even more; a worm-like forked tongue came forth from his mouth. It moved around like a giant maggot, then split into three tongues, each one en route to a different lust instigator. One went towards her pooling urine, another towards her bleeding stump, and the third..........the third went towards the tears trailing from her eyes.

"You bitch! You nothing! You spawn of facile endearment! Nobody wants you......nobody knows you........THERE IS NO FUCKING YOU!"

Just inches from her piss, blood and tears, the fear palpable, her weakness making his mouth water in torrents of lust putrescence......and out of nowhere a FLASH OF EMERALD LIGHT BURST FORTH! Blinding Hungry, it sent immediate pangs of unbearable hunger into his stomach. He staggered in pain, clutching his abdomen.

As the light cleared somewhat, a voice, like but unlike Tlaloca's, full of authority and self-awareness, resounded from all directions. "YOUR FORGOT LOVE, AND THE POWER OF STRANGE AND UNLIKELY UNIONS, LITTLE BARON." Tlaloca said, the tears now gone, her words completely stopping Hungry in his tracks, a jade mist creeping in and holding his larvic tongues in place. She'd become completely calm, serene, and focused. "You saw the power of the oil, the anamnesis of The Pocket Shrine.............Damien's Grail; you thought you had it all, but seeing is not a realization, and a play is still a play. Theatrics are entertaining, little baron, but without the real life that inspires them, you have nothing."

Hungry Horowitz, baron unknown to him till now, snarled like a possum in a bear trap. He severed his own tongues with dirty nails, and began to bark as a new tongue immediately grew back in their place. "You're fucked, you false snake; the rest of my lodge will find you for this......YOU HAVE NO POWER HERE!"

Salted Plastic: The Comedic Horror of Gentrification

Tlaloca, only partially listening to his ravings, watching his fog fade, the black bile spilling from his fangs, smiled benevolently.

"As I said; no love, no root; you can only consume understanding, but apparently not that which is understood. Everything is a codification for you and yours.............a cataloging of the spirit of others, nothing more.............how unfortunate for you." She reached out with her right hand, and took his paw off her handless wrist, zero effort, standing up as she did. Holding up her stump, they both watched in awe as a new hand grew in its place; first an emerald glow, followed by a green outline, and then a jade hand. Jade, yet articulate like flesh. She flexed the new hand and picked under the index finger with her new thumb.

"What in all the Spheres of Traps...." Hungry began.....

"Ayauhchicauaztli!" Tlaloca uttered calmly, displaying her palm towards Hungry, her eyes closed, smiling like a coyote. A snake, twisted into a figure eight moebius strip pattern, appeared, glowing emerald on her forehead; a moebius strip with a line emerging from the top dip of its figure eight pattern; the rattle of a snake.

Hungry's skin began to itch, the green mist emanating from Tlaloca touching his skin here and there. "This? What is....." he began.

"You will be mute again; you have ALWAYS been mute." Tlaloca stepped closer, putting her new hand on his forehead. "The little baron in you will go back to sleep, and NO ONE will ever take you or your stories seriously again. Find yourself, and stop window shopping the lives of others. Stop mimicking and perverting them for manufactured notoriety and gain. Do this, and someday you might emerge as the you in you."

A green glow emanated from her hand.....he twitched, still frothing at the mouth, and by strength of will alone rose a few inches up from the ground. Tlaloca smiled, not a shred of fear over Hungry's resolve to fight back; the glow changed; now marbled with red, it INSTANTLY made Hungry drop to his shins again.

Salted Plastic: The Comedic Horror of Gentrification

His skin began to flake and burn. "EYYYYYARRRRR!!!!!" Hungry screamed in agony as he relieved his bowels and bladder, the smell enough to lobotomize the average person, but Tlaloca remained calm and unmoved, still smiling.

He fell to the ground, into his own shit and piss. His hair began to grow back where it had fallen out, and his face became more and more human by the second, the mottled skin returning to human tones, his teeth normal. The dark fog had completely disappeared, and the street started to come back. Tlaloca's car and Adrik could be faintly seen again now. A woman with long brown curls and eye glasses stood behind him, talking on her phone.

"The juice.........the glamour......," Hungry whispered on his back, "....Mama.....New York.....77....."

As he fell asleep he looked exactly the same as when he'd knocked on Tlaloca's car window twenty minutes ago, perving off on her and Adrik like a jackal; all his hair, teeth and skin were back to normal.

The street surroundings were completely back now, clear and solid. The cars in Hollywood could be heard rushing by.......the smell of piss and wet cigarette butts from the nearby alley........tense human emotion let go and gave a sigh of relief; Adrik's gratefulness palpable on Tlaloca's back, the woman in curl's immediately putting down the phone and rushing to Adrik's side. Tlaloca "saw" them without turning, sensed EVERYTHING without even opening her now closed eyes; a crowd of kids jabbering a few blocks away at a vegan taco stand............angelica tea brewing in a cup held by an elderly man as he sat on his roof..........the "sound" of denaturation as lemon went to work on a bowl octopus, shark and shrimp in a fridge across town..........the dimming of lateral orbitofrontal cortexes as two couples sweated under the sheets of one bed.......... a mother talking shit, her key stuck in the deadbolt lock of her door, while she watched some 20-something hipster couple stumble into the apartment adjacent to hers, worried shitless that she'd end up the same as its former tenant, Mandy Iniguez, who had been evicted earlier this year just so that scumbag landlord Mark Vest could turn the unit into yet another permanent Airbnb.

"LothlocA......honey?" She heard; the woman in glasses and dirty brown curls at Adrik's side. She saw it all; who she was, who Adrik was, what they wanted from her...........how this was all going to end up someday.

Turning around, she looked at Adrik and smiled. "I love you too, Adrik; I love the you in you." And to the woman in curls, standing there in anticipation in her Gundamme pjs; maybe about 36, pale and full of freckles......stoic logic.........but fear and love for her nest all the same. "Morrigan?" she smiled. "I will be there someday for your Sisters, Others, and Brothers, but I won't be one of your wards; you cannot possibly imagine how that would jeopardize you all."

Morrigan looked like she was about to object, say something, but instead she merely smiled, looked down in quiet resolve, reached into her pocket, and pulled out an earbud. "For you LothlocA, for when you know we needth your help." She tossed it to Tlaloca, started to walk away, and then turned back once more, a knowing look on her face. "Hold onto thath girl; the Coyolxauhqui in you will noth always be acthive, and you'll need a way to find uth quick when you can'th spirith speak." Morrigan saw the confusion in Adrik's eyes, and patted him on the back, silently urging him to say goodbye to Tlaloca as she walked away.

Walking towards her, he started to do something he hadn't done since that day Jasmine had found him, having felt invincible since then, always joking, never a second of weakness or desire to change fate. Adrik's eyes filled with tears; he knew it would be a long fucking time before he saw Chipotle again. He knew a lot still; the oil was fading in his system, but the visions still slipped past his mind's eye; a glimpse of Chipotle Tlaloca doing her usual; sipping $9 horchata lattes, protesting cultural exploitation on Olvera Street, watching documentaries on alternative politics written by shills who had never been exposed to a

175

working model of such. Dating lame pochos, and wimpy hipsters named Skyler and Trevor, going out for jackfruit carnitas while talking about Graffiti Galleries run by culture vultures in Echo Park. Babbling about her Etzy store where she sold trajes de tehuanas with the embroidered faces of Trotsky, Marx, Zapata and Kahlo, stylized to look like Mt. Rushmore. Essentially, whenever she wasn't in touch with the her in her, she'd go back to the façade; ironic, considering that that's the exact fate she'd left Hungry Horowitz in permanently.

"Adrik?" Tlaloca's voice broke the visions. "The act will keep me safe until you and your tribe need me; that's all you need to know; I will be myself PERMANENTLY someday............and when I am.........," she walked forward, bridging the remaining gap between them, leaving a trail of emerald mist in her wake, ".....and when I am...," she whispered in his ear, the smell of lemon grass coming into his nose, her energy soothing him, ".......and when I am my love, I'm going to fuck the shit out of you!" This last she said with a wicked smile, the words and facial expressions lending a sense of relative normalcy to the fact that she was now some glowing green omnipotent demi-goddess or some shit......... HA!........whatever.

"Ha ha.......," he laughed weakly, wiping a tear away, "........I just don't see why you ca......."

Chipotle stopped his words with a raised hand, stared at him gently............and put her arms around his shoulders. Looking Adrik in the eyes, she kissed him, while cupping the back of his head with her jade hand...............and then he fell asleep.................dreamt of a bird's nest made of water............a scaled bird looking over him; he was a trident, she was a moldavite grail........caduceus..........molcajete.........their waters mingled..........

Salted Plastic: The Comedic Horror of Gentrification

Saturday, October 24, 1:37am

Miguel had expected someone like Dagmar to live in Downtown LA, but the drive back to her place had gone north up the 110, past downtown proper. His awareness drifted back and forth from the him to the him the entire ride; sometimes wondering where they were going, and other times already knowing their destination. The final destination was there in his mind one minute, and then the next there was only anticipation, no clue at all; the oil was fluctuating.

Going past DTLA, he'd then thought that the obvious alternate destination would be some renovated craftsmen home in Highland Park............or maybe a three story modern home in the hills of Mt. Washington. These were the usual property types that were absconded or constructed, and then harvested by LA's new affluent class of culture vultures, tech aristocrats, trust fund "artists", soft handed yuppies, and real estate peddlers. Miguel was sure that Highland Park would be the spot for Dagmar's home, but the Chergar had driven all the way to the end of the 110 at this point, exiting on Arroyo Parkway, driving up to Colorado Boulevard, and then going East.

He was anxious to know for good where they were going, and was just about to ask Dagmar, when he felt a palm on the fly of his jeans. Looking to his right, he watched Lydia and Dagmar making out, Dagmar really leaning into Lydia, causing her to fall back onto Miguel while Dagmar kissed her neck. Pushed heavy and up close against him, Lydia had decided to multitask a bit, fumbling blindly behind her to grab his cock.

The car made a left turn somewhere, and started to go uphill, but Miguel was too engrossed in the moment to notice or care where they were going at this point. The fuck-sex sex-fuck high he was now immersed in had distracted him from any further thoughts about the whereabouts of Dagmar's home; the camouflage to the bat cave certainly wasn't a hologram of mountain rock in this situation...........};^}.

Still, despite the pleasure, the uncertainty of their destination made him edgy; from one second to the next he became uneasy at the peripherals of his senses, completely unable to just enjoy a good thing. He was scared-skeptical, and had a feeling that the sex play was a distraction, a calculated effort to weaken him. That was the him in him alright; Miguel had a problem with appreciating good fortune (always had), and liked to sabotage it with paranoid fantasies about ulterior motives and betrayal.

"He thinks we're going to take his kidneys, and dump him in a landfill, babe." Dagmar/Lydia smiled, talking to Lydia and Dagmar.

"Hahaha! You dummy!" Dagmar laughed. "Just stop already, Michael! YOU'RE SAFE with us, love! Safer than you'll ever be anywhere else!" Her words were pleading, explanatory........big sisterly even. Urging Lydia to switch places with her, she reached her hand out, caressed the side of Miguel's face, and dragged her nails through his hair. He yielded a bit, closing his eyes like a cat, relaxing, but still kept his mind's teeth firmly on worry and mistrust. Dagmar just smiled in reaction to his stubbornness, and tried something else. She put her middle and index fingers into her eyes, removed her green contacts and tossed them on the floor. She looked straight into Miguel's eyes, her own now a cloudy grey, still caressing his face, trying to get him to let go.........just enjoy........feel loved and at home. He yielded more, but still flinched internally; his high strung nerves slackened at her care and concern, but his routine logic refused to give up completely. She gave him one last knowing stare, looking into his heart and soul.........and then saw IT........the pain at the root of his problem.

"THERE!" she thought, as if making some tangible discovery. "This one is a mind through body healing type, not body through mind; no amount of reasoning will work with him...........mercurium autem transitu........"

Miguel looked back at Dagmar, and knowing she knew his problem in that moment, he felt a bit broken. She smiled at his mild discomfort, keeping her eyes trained on his as she leaned towards his groin, and urged Lydia to do the same as the car kept a steady pace uphill. The tint on the windows dimmed completely black automatically, as if the glass had some smart-sense that "felt" the passengers need for privacy.

Lydia and Dagmar kissed each other right in front of Miguel's zipper, with intermittent breaks where they took turns exhaling hot air onto the bulge in his jeans. He felt all the balled up tension in his sternum drop into his lower dantian, his hara; the swadhisthana chakra. Dizzy as fuck, the worrying pessimist in him started to melt away......but still resisted complete dissolution; these women still scared the him in him.

"Fuck! You really are a beat and broken rescue dog, aren't you, Michael?!" Dagmar yelled, getting a little impatient, her red eyebrows arching in irritation.

"He only had one drop....." Lydia started in his defense, trying to keep the peace, already about to knock on the car's partition window, then stopping as Dagmar grabbed her hand, urging her not to bother.

"Enough of the kiddy shit, Lydia! His will for misery is just too strong," she said, pointing at Miguel, "and that's fine, Michael...........it really is, love; me and Lydia both know what it's like to be a whipped dog, believe it or not...............but fuck all that! I'm not giving up on you, not tonight!!!!! I got something special for us all, some real saint quality shit for emergency situations!" Sitting up, Dagmar grabbed her purse from the floor, and rummaged around in it as the car came to a stop.

"Perfect!" she smiled, pulling out a small bag made of maguey fiber. "And right as we're getting home, right before we step through the front door, no less. Nice and orderly ritual symbolism that shit is!" Neither Lydia or Miguel had any idea what the fuck she was babbling about, but they all got out of the car.

Miguel stretched his legs, looked around, and was **immediately** staggered by the kind of wealth he saw, the sound of the car's trunk opening and glasses clinking in the background as he stared intensely at his surroundings. Dagmar's home was a **fucking mansion**, complete with cobbled driveway, security gate, and a traffic circle with a fountain that fronted the entrance to the house. But not just that; the house in and of itself was definitely a sign of old money for sure, but there was so much more to it than that. This was indicated not just by the design of the place, but by the location as well; trees surrounded the outskirts of the fence, not a single house could be seen close by, and the dirt outside the gate indicated a private road. The foothills of a mountain could be seen through the surrounding trees. Altadena? La Canada? Sierra Madre? Miguel couldn't really guess, but he had a vague idea of where they might be.

His marvel at Dagmar's money and home were cut short by a champagne glass popping into his view.

"Hey, you're drifting; it's just a house, Miguel! No big deal!" Lydia looked at him with a smile, grabbing his hand and placing it on a glass of champagne. She couldn't possibly know how this wasn't "just a house" in his estimate. For him, always perpetually struggling to get ahead, it was a symbol of unquestionable privilege, of an old money lifestyle that he would never obtain no matter how hard he worked in his lifetime.

"Only a house right now kids, but tonight it'll be more than that." Dagmar stepped next to them, causing their standing arrangement to form a triangle on the stones of the driveway. "Tonight my home will be a crucible for the quintessence of calm, that element that Michael lacks. SHIT! That WE ALL LACK from time to time!" She turned to Miguel, cupped her palm under his chin, felt the lingering doubt in him as she caressed the sides of his face. "Michael.......hun......just stop already. This is your home tonight! You're safe with us; WE won't hurt you, I promise!"

"I....I.....I know...." Miguel smiled, looking up. "Sorry for being such a turd; you've both been more than kind to me, and........"

Salted Plastic: The Comedic Horror of Gentrification

"......and it's time to stop the novella shit," Lydia interrupted playfully. "Dagmar, whatever you got in that bag......." she leaned in, hugging Miguel, her lips at his right ear, but still speaking to Dagmar "......whatever it is, put it in a baby bottle, an IV, on a compact mirror with a rolled hundred.........or whatever the fuck; just make sure this one (pointing at Miguel) gets on it, and gets on it NOW! Put HIM to sleep, so he can be all HIM for the rest of the night. She squeezed the shit out of Miguel, the warmth of her hug almost making him cry. Giving him a kiss on the cheek, she backed away, letting Dagmar step into her place. Dagmar held her palm up to Miguel's eyes; a little {>+_| (/- was in the middle of her outstretched hand.

"Michael? What do you see in my hand?"

"Uhm. It's a little green statue of a jaguar."

"I see..........Lydia?" she asked, turning so Lydia could see her palm.

"My uncle's cameo!" Lydia exclaimed in shock. "My Uncle Ray gave me a Victorian cameo as a kid. He'd had it altered and redesigned. Originally it was just a plain old female head, but he took it to someone, and they changed it to look like a woman with a cat face. He got a kick out of that, seeing me so happy over the thing, watching my sterile Nazarene parents choke at the sight of it. At the time I was always babbling to everyone about some shitty kids book he'd read to me a million times about were-cats..........constantly asking him to read it to me again and again. He was the only soul the family ever had..........." Lydia's eyes were full of tears.

"Interesting....." Dagmar said, reaching out, brushing the tears off Lydia's eyes. ".........for me it's always been a little faceless woman, about an inch tall, white body, green glass hair, like ivory and moldavite. They're all different, and like a good scotch or wine, even if you get another bottle, the flavor always varies................"

Lydia and Miguel looked at Dagmar, waiting for a fucking point or a less vague explanation of her words, hoping something would make

181

sense soon...........wondering why the narrator was dragging out such a tedious moment, and when the fuck they would just move on and get to the fucking FUCKING ALREADY!!!!!!!!!!!!!

An owl landed on one of the fir trees growing outside the gate, Dagmar looked at the moon......the wind blew scents of lavender and rosemary......everything felt like it was in a sort of comfortable entropy, the scenery around them calm yet unpredictable. The cool night air on their skin, everyone relaxed beyond the release of all inhibition.........the feeling of calm and quiet understanding within their love triangle.......the sound of LYDIA BLASTING A FUCKING PEDO!!!!!!!!

-BRRRRRTTTTTTTTTtttttttttTTTTTTT!!!!!!

"HAHAHAHAHAHHAHAHA!!!" Dagmar/Miguel/Lydia laughed.

"Well, that broke the ice..." Dagmar said.

"Hopefully not my expensive pair of Maisónne panties........" Lydia blushed.

"Why did that give me an erection?" Miguel thought.

While Miguel "adjusted", Dagmar stepped between him and Lydia, and held up her hand a second time. Each of them saw their own version of the object in her hand; glass haired lady, jaguar, were-cat cameo............and then it started to become indistinct, first morphing into a marbled green and white rectangle, then a grayish green curdling blob........and finally it melted into Dagmar's hand.

What was left over were three jade granules bathing in something that looked like cactus milk. Dagmar immediately licked one out of her palm, then rushed to Lydia, hand out, Lydia taking hers with the tip of her tongue. Moving to Miguel quickly, she wiped her palm

182

onto his already outstretched tongue like he was a dog......or a cat....who the fuck knows?! The point being that she KNEW he'd get off on being dogged like that, being treated like an animal; she even sensed his erection-reaction immediately.

A couple of seconds went by.........Miguel was sniffing the air like an animal. Lydia moved to his side and began licking his ear and petting his lower back. Dagmar came behind Miguel, squeezed his ass, and reached into the waist band of his jeans with saliva covered finger tips, gently pinching the underside of his glans. Then, moving to Lydia, she grabbed her headdress, yanked it off, and ran her finger tips through Lydia's hair, moving her hand down her neck, across her back, and under her arm to cup a breast. Lydia's panties moistened, and pre cum already started to bead on the head of Miguel's penis. Dagmar moved to the side, unzipped her body suit, and stepped out of it. The front door of her house opened all of a sudden as she got naked.......a fluctuating neon red and green glow coming from inside.

They all looked at each other....smiling....all feeling, completely devoid of the them in THEM at this point. Raising their glasses of champagne, Dagmar/Miguel/Lydia downed what they now knew was an 1841 Vicier Veuf......and then smashed the glasses on the pavement. They walked to the house, Dagmar first, her AMAZING ass bouncing, the dense muscle BURSTING out all the plump fat surrounding her glutes and thighs. Her triceps were rounded out and solid, those soft copper curls trailing down to the crack of her ass, right where a tattoo of a lion with a crown of cobra heads sat. She rushed ahead and went inside, Lydia and Miguel following behind, past the fountain which showcased a statue quite similar to the tattoo just mentioned.

As they walked through the door, Lydia and Miguel's clothes disappeared, neither of them seeming to notice or take alarm at being Stripped by Magick...........just complete animal wonder on their faces. A smell like guava and persimmon was everywhere. The foyer of the house had black and gold marble tile along the floor and walls, with tarnished silver gas lamps that somehow burned green flames. Right in the middle, on a burgundy velvet bench between the two ascending staircases of the foyer, sat Dagmar, full of sweat, her usually pale olive face flushed with blood. Her coffee colored nipples were already hard, her legs spread and waiting. The gyrations of the copper landing strip of hair between them hypnotized Miguel, her pussy so swollen it was almost purple.

NOT ONE SINGLE FUCKING WORD, Miguel rushed Dagmar, and gripped her thighs hard!!! She laughed like a triumphant devil who had just put a wild dog under leash and command. He turned Dagmar on the bench, and laid her down across it, intending to just THRUST INTO her like a beast..........but was only able to inch in just the head of his cock; the grip and swelling were keeping him from just going for..........

"H**ssSSGrWrrrRRRR!" Dagmar growled/hissed/snarled/spoke in tongues.......fucking something.........impatient with his lingering timid nature. She grabbed Miguel's ass, and just PUSHED him in HARD!!!!! She yelped momentarily at the semi-dry friction, a wicked smile on her face as she licked the side of her upper lip in self-satisfaction, enjoying the sight of Miguel struggling in reaction to the pleasure that her whimper elicited. It passed, that rawness, as she moistened further from the feel of him throbbing inside her, from the sight of him enjoying that first taste of her cunt. ←(context is not vestigial).

Dagmar's pussy and take charge energy felt so fucking good that Miguel almost BURST immediately, but his body KNEW exactly what to do; groin flexing, balls retracting a bit.....holding it......keeping him from blowing that shit. He went slow, savoring the fever inside her, feeling her pulse and grip. Each time he went in full length his balls briefly feathered her asshole, just long enough for Dagmar to pulse her soft wet ain against them; she laughed a bit, seeing that this was just too much for him.

Miguel looked up just in time to see Lydia lowering her pussy into Dagmar's mouth, her ass facing him. The prana in his solar plexus went fluid....fully relaxed....energy spiking in his face and penis..........flowing properly, meridians channeling it all like a waterfall............or some other such nature shit? Who knows?! Insert your own epic sex analogy! Watching Dagmar lap at Lydia's clit, enjoying being treated like a piece of meat as Dagmar ignored everything but his cock, Miguel got a little dizzy............started to get faint.

Dagmar felt it, that Miguel was getting dizzy drunk on fuck from the pleasure............and PALM STRIKED him right in the chest, knocking him onto the cold marble floor as easily as swatting a fly. She gently brushed Lydia to the side, got up, and quickly mounted Miguel as if he was a fucking utility, a disembodied dick, a cock and balls ferris wheel...........still........love in her intentions all the same...........just giving HIM want she knew HE liked.....seeing that he was a beast of a man that wanted to be dogged and treated like a fuck pet. Pinning him by the biceps with her hands, his slim 180lbs of muscle went limp in her grip. She leaned in, licking his neck, sucking on his tongue while her ass SLAMMED a mile a minute onto his cock, the musk of her pussy making him dizzy as it filled the foyer........smooth hot fluid dripping out of her, down his dick, trailing down his balls, making a small puddle on the floor.

Lydia got up from where she had been watching on the bench, walked over, put her hands on Dagmar's shoulders, and stared with hungry eyes as Dagmar palmed Miguel's chest, her fingernails digging in as she ground into his cock like an animal in heat. Feeling Lydia, she reached up, grabbed her right hand, and kissed it, dismounting Miguel as she did. His cock was bright red now, the veins popping, covered in Dagmar's transudative fluid.

Lydia stepped over Miguel, her back facing him, and started to lower herself, ass first, towards his cock; outrageous amount of muscle control, slowly down, down, down......and just as she was almost there, stopped..............JUST BARELY brushing the underside of his glans with her asshole..........a whimper caught in his throat......Lydia smirked, loving how weak and broken this was making him.........immensely happy that he was loving every fucking minute of it. Reaching back, grabbing him, she pressed the head firmly up against all those tight textured ridges, pulsing her tight little nautical star on the head of his cock.

This IMMEDIATELY brought him out of his daze, making him animal as shit!!!

Still smiling, Lydia got up and walked away, knowing full fucking well that he wasn't going to just lay there now like a fucking ham drunk on sex. She walked to a dark corner wall, near one of the green gas lamps next to a closet, the glow giving her skin a look like emerald porcelain. Opening the closet, she pulled out a pair of spiked black leather high heels, and stepped into them. Pressing her chest firmly up against the wall, she looked over her shoulder at Miguel with eager and ready "fuck me" eyes. She spread her legs, the heels arching her lower back, making her ass POP and BLOSSOM.......the seam of her pussy, and the star of her ain in plain view.

Miguel got up, and walked over slowly, this time trying to have a little bit more finesse, instead of just reaming in all beastly liked he'd done with Dagmar. He caressed her back, rubbed her shoulders, and ran his fingertips down the corded muscle along her spine. She was JUST THE RIGHT HEIGHT with the heels on; no need to stand on the tips of her toes or crouch down; his still erect cock squeezed between her thick thighs and brushed her labia as he leaned in and kissed the back of her neck. Reaching under her arms he cupped, grabbed and gently squeezed both of her breasts, then turned her around so he could get good and oral with them tits!

He crouched down, and began rotating his tongue around the areolas, tapping the tip of her nipples, pressing on them hard with the apex of his tongue. Trailing up, he planted gentle kisses on her tits, collar bone, shoulders and neck. Face to face now, looking into her eyes, Miguel parted her lips with his tongue, holding the back of her head and kissing her like HE DAMN WELL MEANT IT!!!!!!!

Salted Plastic: The Comedic Horror of Gentrification

Dagmar, watching from the bench this whole time, started to cry for some reason; this was all too familiar; happened before......watching them alone....seasonal reiteration....reminder that archetypal standards of "healthy love" couldn't be broken.....................it won't work this time either.................they've always done this............the rules of time have spoken?!?!.....................she contemplated.....felt lost......and then out of nowhere regained herself.

NO FUCKING WAY!..............NOT THIS TIME!!!!!!!!...............what feels right defines love............not what defines love feels right!!!!!!!!!

She walked over to Miguel and Lydia, hugged him from behind, leaned her cheek between his shoulder blades, and closed her eyes, a big smile on her face; happy for them/her. No words, just peace as she listened to his heart beat, his breath, Lydia's soft moans...........felt the sweat pooling on her cheek from his back. Not a drop of jealously, only pure gratefulness at their........her...........all of their enjoyment........utter contentment stemming from the blessing of this moment.

Dagmar reached between Miguel's legs as he slowly tried to ease into Lydia. Having trouble, attempting to do it hands free, he kept slipping, the head of his penis sliding forward across Lydia's labia, dialing up against her clit. Dagmar palmed his balls, escalating her hand up and down, feeling the heft of them, attempting to gauge the yield of milk that might be in there. "Mmmmmh!" she moaned, splaying her fingers, and gently caressing the underside of his cock with her nails, using some of that liquid heat that had dripped down from Lydia to tease the underside of his glans. Miguel shuddered at Dagmar's touch, balls contracting. Checking his head, she felt a little pearl of semen on the tip of her index finger. Bringing it to her mouth, she took a quick taste, closing her eyes and purring a bit over the flavor; the chālchihuitl had made it taste like rose water, honey and cardamom; favorites from her past.

After a few seconds of Miguel's pre-cum bringing back memories of numerous baklava bakeries, from Tel Aviv to Al Ain, Dagmar opened her eyes, watching/hypnotized by his dick as he continued to struggle to penetrate Lydia. Struggled, or maybe just teased on purpose? Whatever it was, she became eager to just see it already!

Grabbing his cock hard, holding the base to steady it, she slipped him in FULL FORCE, no warning.

"UUUNNNNHHHHH!!!!!!" Miguel moaned hard, head dropping onto Lydia's shoulder, the sound of him sucking on his own drool as he almost collapsed. It was breaking him; the chālchihuitl, the demand of pleasing them both, the shock of meeting them again after god knows how long; it was a lot for him to take, holding in all the cum under the circumstances. Dagmar could smell it; this one hadn't released in at least a week...........he hadn't been satisfied by that thing that they had playing house with him.

Lydia felt it too, and took the reins, wanting to "preserve him" so the fun would last. She pulsed her cunt (again, please understand context and intent; it's not that hard) gently....very gently, enough to pleasure, but not so much that he'd spill, smiling at what a little weak bitch she was making him, sensing him labor to hold it, knowing that he liked it like that, feeling his heart race on her back, little twitches and trembles in his whole body as his head laid on her shoulder, his teeth gently biting into the trap muscle at the base of her neck. Sensing that he could take a little more, she started to rock her hips, sliding forward, pulling him out till just his head was inside her, pulsing on the tip each time, and then slowly easing him all the way back in.

Miguel was a sex and psyche drunk mess of pleasure overload and ineffable realizations. All three of them had done this countless times, in numerous futures, presents and pasts, but not this him; for the him in him now, it was fresh and totally new..........generating waves of heart attack pleasure, and feelings of security that couldn't be matched by ANYTHING on Earth. He could be on a houseboat library full of all his favorite first editions, a view of the cherry blossoms in the mountains of Matsushima bay outside his window, with a world renowned scotch collection in the boat's oak-room study, an international banquet in the kitchen, and Jessica back in his arms............and IT STILL WOULDN'T match the real in real of the here and now. These women were beauty and care incarnate; they loved him, they always had and always will love him; he owed it.......owed it to them not to disappoint.

Giving in more to the chālchihuitl, he saw it; they were being gentle with him out of unnecessary care; they were afraid he'd blow that load!

Laughing internally, smiling externally, he wondered why.....why, being almost all knowing from the oil/chālchihuitl, why they didn't remember that it made you transcend average mundane physicality, allowing you to leave various everyday limitations behind..........."a blade that never blunts, a cup that's never empty." That's how one of them had put it to him a long time ago......Dagmar maybe?......only she hadn't been Dagmar then; an island......soft hands......crochan.......cleddyf.........

Snapping into the relative present, he went to it IMMEDIATELY! Feel their needs, stop being selfish! This is about US, you prick, not you! These are women, YOU OAF.....time defying saints....not machines! This isn't just about mechanical animal cravings! Show some tenderness and conscientiousness!

At that he lifted his head, and began rubbing Lydia's shoulders, gently kissing the back of her neck, sending his feelings toward her like radio transmissions..............dropping it all into her heart with no words or paralanguage. He felt her smile internally.........saw her heart warm up to him.............and even sensed the irony of her desire; as much as she appreciated his effort at being tender and not making this just typical aimless sex, Lydia expected (and craved) for that to be a part of the equation; she WANTED for him to just LET GO and be an oversexed brute!!!

Lydia's desires were an open book; the root and key (exchanging those feelings) let him see it all. Wrapping his hand around her throat, feeling her unspoken tastes in kink, Miguel started to choke her, gently

189

pumping her pussy at first, feeling it heat up and moisten more..........and then SLAMMING full force. Lydia's favorable reaction (placing her palm over his hand, and squeezing gently to indicate that she wanted him to choke harder) made him THICKEN even more. She gasped each time her fat ass slammed up against his waist. He started to loosen his grip from the pleasure of feeling her pleasure, only to have Lydia elbow back hard into his ribs, grabbing his hand and putting it back on her throat.

It was good, so fucking GOOD! So good that he felt that it was time for that first leap of faith.........grab at gnosis.........fall of the morning star..........whatever the fuck..........he was ready to show them what he remembered...........in a minute or two..........ha ha..........savor it...........let the milk fever a little longer.........even so.............he wanted to surprise them.........but they already knew.

Dagmar and Lydia were both smiling; both of them had gained anamnesis relative to their ability to be eternally muliebrous; gained it at the same time Miguel had had his epiphany of being never-endingly virile while under the influence of the chālchihuitl.

They all knew that they knew; the spirit of their realization and focus was right there, at the head of Miguel's cock, in the depths of Lydia's pussy, on the tips of Dagmar's tits as she dragged her nipples down Miguel's back while he fucked Lydia like a beast, the first seed already beading out. Almost there, but still going, hand still on her throat, looking down at Lydia's ass as it jiggled each time it SLAMMED into his waist............cupping her pansa with his other hand, drinking his own drool, still trying to hold it one more second.....just one more......just one morrrrrre.......JUST STOP LOOKING AT THAT ASS!

He had it now; looking away to sublimate part of the pleasure, he was going to last at least another 20 to 30 minutes, he knew it!

Knew it, but didn't know it, not factoring in one element; Lydia's breath started to get heavier, her body temperature spiked, soft gasps getting louder. Miguel felt it coming, and knew he wouldn't last through it. A second later, and the soft wet walls inside her began to alternately pulse and grip, milking and holding him firmly; Lydia was cumming, and definitely trying to bring him with her, a soft "mmmphhh!" escaping her mouth while he still strained through the pleasure to choke her.

Feeling Lydia cum, watching the sweat bead up on her back and ass, hearing her whimper a few more times while she continued to pulse her pussy..........it was all too much...........and he EXPLODED immediately!

"UNNNNHHH!" Deep animal moan as he let off the first stream into Lydia..........a warm feeling below his navel as she reached between her legs and squeezed his balls as the second stream pumped into her........just in time to feel the wet pressure of a tongue on his asshole. It felt invasive (to him, but not to him), but too good to pass up; Dagmar continued to lick as he came, one, two, three more heavy streams, his cock contracting each time, her soft cat tongue feathering his taint in tandem, the yield already spilling out of Lydia onto the marble floor. His body became so loose, warm and relaxed from the release, that his head fell back, neck cracking, muscles going limp. Dagmar stood up and caught him as he almost fell, eased him to the ground.

Fuck, she's strong!

Breathing hard, lying on the floor, he felt a bit guilty; he'd cum before getting both Lydia AND Dagmar to cum first; not his style at all. His cock was limp now, concerning him; maybe he was wrong, maybe the chālchihuitl didn't really........

Dagmar stopped Miguel's worries immediately though, already knowing where his mind was going, wondering why the chālchihuitl had such a contest with his almost spiritual sense of cynicism. Gnosis! This one needed gnosis; faith was no good with Michael; she just had to show him.

Walking over to Lydia, Dagmar turned her around, and looked back at Miguel to make sure he was watching. She started to kiss Lydia, left hand behind her neck, right hand palming her pussy, feathering Miguel's cum out of her, rubbing it into Lydia's clit, making her squirm. Feeling Dagmar's intent, blushing hot red, Lydia did the same, taking

191

Salted Plastic: The Comedic Horror of Gentrification

Miguel's milk from between her thighs, and reciprocating on Dagmar's clit.

Seeing this filthy hot display between them, Miguel's last doubts were squashed; his cock was already rock hard again, even though it had barely been two or three minutes since he came. Lydia slipped out of her heels, still kissing Dagmar between labored breaths as Miguel stood up. He walked towards them, but they were already going up the foyer stairs, Dagmar leading Lydia by the hand. He smiled with excitement, looking at them with love and longing; life was good, tonight was a blessing…………much more than he'd ever hoped for or deserved. Stopping for a second, sighing with the universe, he watched them go ahead; he'd catch up in a second.

Still, between all this joy, lust and love, all of a sudden he felt a need to look outside the house, to step away from all the safety and enjoyment that home had to offer. It was a pull towards shadow and doubt……….lunar obfuscation……….empty axiomatic reaction……….Anti-Gnosis of The Demiurge…………fear and lack of appreciation…………facts not feelings…………the **him** in him resurfacing for a moment. Motes of guilt were felt as he remembered James, still worried about what had happened to his brother. Anger resurfaced as Miguel thought of how Rebekah had used him……………suspicion simmered while he wondered at Lydia and Dagmar's possibly hidden intentions; the last lingering granules of his tenacity for finding a flaw in contentment blowing hell's trumpet……..or saxophone……..whatever the fuck.

Turning around, he stared at the front door; it was still open, had been this whole time. Open, yes, but there was nothing to be seen there, or, at least not what should have been seen there. No driveway, no lion with a crown of serpents fountain, no car, no mountains in the background. All he saw was a sort of white undulating nothing; a film, like rubber, or rice paper………or bright light? It……fluctuated, and most certainly was strange in the extreme. But under the influence of the chālchihuitl it wasn't all that concerning to Miguel, or much of an upset at all............except during brief moments at the crest of its wave-like patterns, stretching inward into the house as if made out of highly elastic human skin.

It almost seemed like something was trying to get in; something empty, without fruits, incapable of creating much of anything; a poly-conscious consumption entity; the polar opposite of what Miguel, Lydia and Dagmar had become while under the influence of the oil and chālchihuitl. It was a multi/uni-minded un-life, not susceptible to time or reciprocal joy.............intent on and only capable of ingesting , herding and codifying the best parts of life, culture and love. Even at this realization though, even knowing what's in the box, Miguel walked away, no fear, no sense of danger.

No fear, not even during a brief moment when he was sure he'd seen a sickly set of hands, stretching the film over the door to the point where it seemed it would burst; one scaled, one gray and mottled.

Oh well; by the time he'd made it to the stairs it was already forgotten.

Salted Plastic: The Comedic Horror of Gentrification

The Sum Total of Time/No Time/Sun to Moon to MoonSun/Whatever the F%@k!!!!!

The rest of Dagmar/Miguel/Lydia's time together (if the concept of time can even be properly applied to the situation), was more love, more sex, more reunion, more time slips and high emotion. It was a kaleidoscopic trans-temporal soul aquarium of the self/selves..........with intermittent bouts of some fucking weird shit......I/YOU/WE guess........whatever........

Lydia, Miguel and Dagmar were inside Dagmar's upstairs tiled spa, in the shallow end of an indoor pool, the heat of the water creating a semi-obscuring mist all around them. Dagmar's iron red curls draped over the edge of the pool onto black and gold-veined bathroom tile, her breasts heaving, the top of her knees spaced liberally apart above the water.......indicating that her legs were spread underneath it. The steam continuously moved, revealing hands, mouths, and skin in lust charged proximity one second, and only vague body outlines the next; Lydia's fingers in Dagmar's mouth; a steam blanketed nipple lifted to a barely perceptible tongue. A momentary glimpse of Miguel's lightly stubbled face being forcefully dragged across Dagmar's tits and throat as she used his hair like a leash one second, followed by nothing but steam-cloaked shadow the next. The alternating reveal and shroud was a visual carousel of sex revealed, and sex suggested. Lydia moaned and gyrated her wet punk under the water, followed by Dagmar doing the same; alternating, back and forth, both of them; Miguel was GOING TO WORK! He lapped at their pussies like a good dog while they took turns holding his head underwater. No light source seemed apparent in the room, yet the area fluctuated with neon pink, neon yellow.........and black light purple. Pieces of green glass (or jewels?) in various sizes and shapes floated in the room, interspersed with red Turing code........Bubbles and Dagons.........mini ones.........scaled cupids or some shit........

In another minute, after a heavy bout of steam-mist, Miguel had them both out of the water; Lydia on her back at the edge of the pool, legs spread, and Dagmar at her side in doggy position, ass HIGH up in the air, a purple and gold velvet cushion on the tile bracing her chest. Lydia held her orgasm, savoring Miguel's efforts as he kissed, licked, and tongue probed every part of her pussy and ass the same way one would passionately kiss their true love on the mouth, alternating between both of her openings with refined tenderness and total greed until he could barely breathe.

Dagmar though, she just let loose as soon as he went to work on her; knuckles arching, fingers scraping the tile, her soft little tummy heaving as one last soft lick at her clit made her pulse into Miguel's mouth. She came hard in waves, Miguel rubbing a wet thumb gently on her asshole as she did. Her ass cheeks shuddered and rippled (beautiful fat and muscle) as she sank fully to the tile, drool slipping out of her mouth along with a nice deep **beastly** moan. Miguel's mouth greedily followed her down; hypnotized by her swollen pussy, and the sweet musk that dripped out as she came. He kept at it, alternately licking her parted labia and tight little asshole while she squirmed, HIGHLY sensitive after her release, whimpering, panting and groaning in that deep heavy tone of hers..........................drunk on her cunt, Miguel drifted into.........something.................

..............tasting a sweetness beyond what a mere palate is capable of..............Michael? Hahahaha. Yeah, I was her Michael....... kind of......

Michael? Who is like God?

Salted Plastic: The Comedic Horror of Gentrification

Another spa.......another time......an old heated pool in an island countryside. Logres? Wales? Who knows? He had had books to show her; she'd had something better than books to show him.......

-sigh-

What a levereter that husband of hers was, not allowing her to learn the letters. But I was no better, already married myself to...........to Briceida......it worked out though......until we came back to society...

Arwa? Briceida?

MMMhhhh! Briceida gave me quite a beating at first, but before the night was over I was drinking from her sweet perfumed.......in turns, both of them.......that small pavilion, lying in the furs...........Arwa, tasting like honeyed strawberries........Briceida's musk like heavy lavender........

...........his tongue flattened out against Lydia's pussy, the tip hitting right where both sides of the labia majora tapered down to the taint of her anus. He slowly rolled it back and forth in a vertical motion, pausing briefly to smell the soothing scent of......of...........lavender? The ventilation system? Some candles he didn't see? Oil in the water? His wonder at the source of the scent was cut off by..........

Lydia grabbed Miguel's hair firmly, bringing his mouth back to her, turning his head gently at the jaw line, indicating that she wanted kisses on her inner thighs. Miguel did as he was "told", kissing, licking and even gently biting and fervidly groping at her inner thighs. She sensed his pleasure at gripping **ALL THAT** inner thigh fat, letting it go, watching it ripple around the solid muscle underneath...........felt his

196

Salted Plastic: The Comedic Horror of Gentrification

heart rush at the sight of the few marks of cellulite she had here and there..........he was quite the little pig, he was. She smiled, thinking about that as he slipped his tongue halfway into her little cunt; she liked his sexual tastes, always had..........a stranger would possibly consider him a sexist sack of shit......Lydia knew better though.

Miguel, in all his manifestations, had never forced or demeaned, and preferred to be led by a woman's hand if anything. No, his problem was something else entirely; that bad attitude under pressure..........an utter lack of practicality........she time-slipped thinking of this..........

..........Mazatl..........you are a good lover..........you beautifully foul and filthy fucker..........your pulque dripping from my every orifice as we lay on my father's jaguar furs................I LOVE YOUR DIRTY WAYS.........but you are such a fool in so many other respects.........why did you take me away from the calpulli..........to the sea where there is nothing..........no corn or squash to cultivate.......away from the Tēpochcalli where you would have learned to become a man.........an ocēlōtl no less.........the sex is good, BUT NOT THAT GOOD YOU IDIOT!!!!

Lydia twitched, and gently slapped Miguel on the head for grazing his teeth against her labia. It hadn't hurt much, but she had had a brief moment of intuition..............something she was supposed to be upset with him about?

Whatever; the minute she had attempted to attach her mind to the grievance, it had slipped away; not the time for anything now but pleasure and love. Dagmar was already up and ready for more as Lydia bounced back and forth in the anamneses time-slip...........all those times all three of them had met..........Dagmar saw it now too..........

An Iberian?! In my bed! And why not?! I'll have a taste and preview now before my fool of a husband, and the Caliph he follows so blindly, decide to pull out of this country and return home. I certainly won't be going..........it's my fortune that floats this family; my husband will crawl back South, or stay and be a beggar.........I care not. This man though! He may be a servant now, but when this Reconquista is over, someone of his knowledge won't remain so for long.

Yes..........him..........and that Lusophone girl who I appointed overseer of my household............in my bath...............on the choicest bedding I own..........mmmmmmh!

Dagmar and Lydia were now laying outside the pool, on a beautiful silk comforter that had been thrown across the bathroom floor, now completely ruined from the water. It had a black background, bordered by red silken thread. In it's center sat an embroidered gold lion with a crown of emerald serpents, and a purple ajna chakra marbled with green in the middle of it's forehead.

Dagmar and Lydia's legs were locked as they gently massaged and ground their vaginal mons together, both sets of labia slick with each other's sweet natural lubrication, swollen into shades of magenta and light violet............SOOO much blood welling into their sex at this point. Every few seconds a sweet gentle gasp from Lydia, or a deep powerful moan from Dagmar, indicating moments when their clits brushed, the sensitivity high.

198

Salted Plastic: The Comedic Horror of Gentrification

Miguel watched, touching himself, eager to join, but not wanting to interrupt just yet. He tiptoed around them to get some water from a ruby decanter on a table between all the floating code, meteorite bits, bubbles, and miniature sub-demons.

As Miguel walked back after drinking his water, Dagmar GRABBED his ankle HARD! Shit! Her fucking hand felt like iron as she impatiently tugged on his calve, indicating that she wanted him to kneel while she continued to scissor Lydia.

Before he was completely on the floor she already had his cock in her mouth, purring, deep throating him for a minute or two, then taking him out and gasping with outrageous pleasure, her tits and tummy heaving hard while she came for the third time now all over Lydia's soft velvet pussy.

They passed Miguel back and forth like they were sharing bong rips...............Lydia and Dagmar........sucking Miguel's head........glazing his balls in their saliva......forcefully gagging...........giving gentle kisses to the underside of the glans penis (his most sensitive spot).

It was so hot looking at them both.........swelling up against each other; Dagmar's copper landing strip, Lydia's raven colored triangle; a slick and filthy fuck cocktail that contained all their musk, cum, and sub-physical trans-temporal psycho-sexual tension. Something was missing though; Miguel could feel them waiting, side glancing at him every time they dipped his cock into their mouths, smirking evil in between moans and pants. It was mounting, he was getting dizzy, pre-cum beading with each hot and dirty slutty stare of love, longing and full knowing as they looked him right in the eye each time they came on each other, both sets of pussy and fur now foaming with their sweet sex emissions. He took his cock out of Lydia's mouth, saw her evil little smile, the demon expression within; he was going to cozy up to Dagmar, and she felt the why and what of it; Dagmar was better at sucking cock than Lydia. Lydia knew it, wasn't jealous one bit, and was just damn glad Miguel gave in to their communal knowing of the moment.

199

Salted Plastic: The Comedic Horror of Gentrification

Sitting on his shins beside Dagmar, he let his cock rest on her soft face; the veins and skin were so full of blood now that it burned her cheek. She cooed and smiled, speaking some foreign language gently to him as her tongue, darting to a point, traced the heaviest vein, holding it still for a moment, feeling the pulse of blood on her taste buds. This alone was too much for Miguel; wanting to hold it, he closed his eyes, felt Dagmar's devilish smile as he did, and heard Lydia sucking in her own drool as she came on Dagmar's pussy for the fourth time in a row.

Dagmar milked him good and slow, massaging his balls and groin area gently, spitting heavily on his cock, then rubbing it all over her face and throat.

Qué buena puta!!!!!! Miguel thought as he watched a small trail of his pre-cum glistening on her lower lip. She licked it off, swallowed, and then began a violent suctioning motion on the underside of his head while simultaneously pulsing her tongue between her lips right on that spot again. FUCK, THAT DID IT! He tried to pull away but couldn't, getting stopped immediately by that superhuman grip of hers on one of his ass cheeks. She held him there...............¿Soy una puta?!?! You little bastard, you're going to give us what we want right this second...........he heard her in the core of his, her, theirselves..............and then HE FELT IT!!!!!!!

After one last lick on his head she let go; Miguel RUSHED IMMEDIATELY to stand above both of them, their legs still locked, pussies swollen and pulsing. Grabbing his cock, he UNLOADED several thick and heavy streams of cum in between their two grinding cunts, breathing heavily, trying to stay standing as he watched them through a dizzy haze, still going at it, rubbing his thick milk between them, kneading it into each other's pussies as they both came at the same time, the fever temperature of his cum on their clits setting them off.

Salted Plastic: The Comedic Horror of Gentrification

Here in this House, ^^DD<><>BAStrt

All three of them were in bed now, in Dagmar's huge master bedroom, the walls "breathing" around them. The 19th century French wallpaper depicted a reoccurring theme of stylized griffins and female knights, interspersed with Fleur-de-lis in shades of mauve and crème.

Whether it was a hallucination, or some side effect of the oil and chālchihuitl, the walls looked as if they were contracting; exhaling red snowflakes shrouded in mists of blood..........inhaling green grails that emanated an emerald glow.

The snowflakes drifting towards them as the walls bellowed out, followed by the grails disappearing into the walls as they sunk in.........like a human abdomen after the body lets out a deep breath. Or maybe not breathing????..............but either way, the room (minus the bed and television) was definitely visually warping while some green goblets and crimson stars floated.

All three of them were on break, still high as shit (if that was the proper word for it), having just had a quick snack.

Lydia put plum vinegar, yuzu kosho and dashi sauce onto some blue point oysters that had been arranged on a beautiful art deco tray, all translucent red glass with black seven pointed stars within the glass. Several other plates of half-eaten food were laid across the huge, 144x80 inch bed. The bed was inset into the floor, bordered by a heavy dark cherry wood paneling, and covered in black silk bedding. There were fresh medallions of baguette spread with mascarpone, nori powder and red tobiko roe; Peruvian ceviche (Dagmar loved leche de tigre); tako and hokkigai sashimi; some little squares of chocolate raspberry clafoutis, and a carafe of chicha morada. Taking the oyster in her mouth, Lydia changed the channel on the TV as she looked over at Miguel and Dagmar, a genial smile on her face.

Miguel was knocked out cold, head resting on Dagmar's chest, sleeping peacefully, his mouth set in a big grin while Dagmar pet him like a sleeping cat. In Lydia's opinion, that grin was probably the biggest accomplishment of the night for him, even considering all of the above and beyond awesome sex, past lives reintegration, self-realization and identity assimilation that had taken place. No matter who he'd been, in all the incarnations she'd known him under, he had rarely smiled when he was poor. She knew it now though, that he could never be what he needed to be until this handicap was broken.

Oh Miguel, all you need is a constant path on the right train of energy.........we're/I'M going to make you fix yourself whether you like it or not this time, you big baby!!!!!!!

Lydia met eyes with Dagmar during these last thoughts/feelings about Miguel self-actualizing. Dagmar raised an eyebrow at Lydia in response, with a "what are you up to?" look on her face as she continued to pet Miguel, running her fingers through his hair as he slept, coddling him as if he was her new pet and possession.

Lydia felt (not felt/felt) a slight tinge of guilt; her intentions deep down had been more "I'M going to," than "we're going to," and she knew it. Dagmar smiled at Lydia's touch of discomfort over being caught, and waived her over. Lydia crawled across the bed, kissed Dagmar on the forehead and curled up under her other arm, opposite Miguel.

They all fell asleep huddled together, the sound of the TV in the background.

"..........she's going to be let down."

"Yeah, that's not really the kind of thing you can educate someone about........"

Salted Plastic: The Comedic Horror of Gentrification

Saturday, October 24, 4:45am

Lydia woke up to what sounded like someone being strangled, a pit of tension in her sternum. The room was completely dark, and she felt a hand reaching for her frantically. Still sleepy, Lydia thought maybe she was dreaming, but that sick feeling in her chest spoke true.

"Miguel......Dagmar......" she whispered questioningly as she fumbled for the light remote. Finding it, and turning on the room's sconces to dim level, her eyes widened in horror at what she saw.

Dagmar was mounted on top of Miguel, slamming her ass down VIOLENTLY on his cock. He was rock hard even though his face was almost blue from Dagmar's vice grip hands wrapped around his throat. His arms flailed weakly, the contrast of his struggle at being choked, and his ability to keep it up not making sense to Lydia. Torn between her feelings for them both, the horror and confusion of the scene before her, not knowing what to do, but realizing that Miguel was in danger, Lydia made a quick decision and rushed Dagmar....................and was immediately STRUCK HARD in the chest, and sent rolling across the bed onto the floor. It was so fast that she didn't even know how, and in what way, Dagmar had hit her.

"YOU BRING THIS TRASH INTO MY HOME, LYDIA!!!!! YOU STUPID BITCH!!!!!! THIS POOR UNEDUCATED UNACCOMPLISHED NOTHING!!!!! I GAVE YOU EVERYTHING!!!!!!!" Dagmar yelled maniacally, not even looking at Lydia as she took her hands off Miguel's throat and began punching, slapping and back handing him in the face ROYALLY and VIGOROUSLY!

"Fine, you unappreciative bitch! But I'm going to get some use out of him before my dogs dump him in the trash. DO YOU HAVE ANY FUCKING IDEA WHAT A FORTUNE I WASTED ON YOU AND YOUR LITTLE STRAY TONIGHT?!" she yelled, her pussy so fucking wet that the silk sheets between Miguel's legs were heavily stained now. "Do you know

203

who I have to deal with, and how much it costs to get my hands on anamnesis........let alone a fucking chālchihuitl?!?!"

Lydia caught her breath, tears trailing down her face as she tried to stand, reaching out a hand towards them; Dagmar had really hurt her bad with that hit.

Miguel caught his breath too, unsure himself why he was able to feel so hurt and horrified, yet still keep hard and feel pleasure in the sex; it was toxic........yet somehow still hot. Whatever the reasoning behind it all, he didn't have time to speculate; this woman was lethal, and no guess was needed for one thing; he felt it through the lingering effects of the oil and jaguar as they wound down and wore off; this woman was going to kill him the minute she came unless he did something now!

Even so, Miguel felt pity for Dagmar, ever the peacemaker that he was when it came to women, always willing to make excuses for bad behavior to avoid confrontation. He speculated on the problem with what was left of the him/him in **him**. A vague intuition hit Miguel that Dagmar was having psychic withdrawal symptoms; it was a sort of come down from being so deeply connected to Lydia and him, and then being left with nothing but a static memory and hunger for what the night had been like earlier.

But if this was true, why just her? Why weren't Lydia and himself in lethal withdrawal mode from being torn so abruptly away from the poly-synchronous integration that the oil and chālchihuitl had given to them throughout the night?

"Her abuse of the stuff is above and beyond........." a voice in his head began, but was cut short by yet another hard hit to his face by Dagmar. A taste of blood in his mouth, he started to feel dizzy. That was it!!! He definitely couldn't afford to keeping thinking about the what of the situation; Miguel had to take action immediately.

He decided to do something that German had told him never to do except in a desperate pinch. German Agpalo, Miguel's herbalist and martial arts teacher, had taught him a few lethal techniques over the years, with the admonition to reserve them for dire situations only.

He started to cry, resting his right hand over his heart, feeling both great pleasure at Dagmar's pussy contracting on his cock, and great heartache over her hatred for him; hating him for what he couldn't be financially of all things. One last intuition came in that moment, the key to the strange disparity between his enjoyment of the sex, and his hurt over Dagmar's emotional abuse. An explanation of how withdrawals from anamnesis and the chālchihuitl worked.

"The body last………the heart and mind first……..not a logic driven connection……………not bound by any bond manufactured by human consciousness……"

"……..that voice again……" he thought.

"I see, my body is still high, still stuck in that connection between us, but my mind and heart are already back in relative reality, in this moment. So the drugs were the only thing making her warm up to me? Is that it?!" he raged internally, his hurt and anger beginning to mount.

"I thought this was love." he whispered in emotional pain, the hate welling up in him over Dagmar's judgment. "I trusted her….." He still didn't understand completely, but right now he couldn't afford to think it through.

Looking up, Miguel took one more backhand to the face from Dagmar's right hand…….timed it……waiting for the arc of her arm to travel into a chambered hook on her right side as she got ready to hit again……………and then he sent the blade of his right hand, A to B, no visible preparation, FULL FORCE, in a straight line towards her neck. Closing his eyes, he felt guilty even considering the situation; despite what was happening, he still loved the her in her…….wherever it was.

He expected Dagmar to fall over instantly from the strike, but somehow nothing had connected, at least not how he'd intended it to. Opening his eyes he yelled in agony…………as sharp teeth broke through the meat of his hand. She'd caught his hand in her mouth as he'd struck, and then turned with the blow to negate the momentum, and was now biting down heavily into it.

It was unbelievably painful, but he came anyways; they both did in perfect timing. Dagmar moaned greedily as she drank the blood pooling out of his hand. Miguel cried in both pain and pleasure as he spent the last of what he had for the night inside of her.

Lydia was by now standing, confused, not knowing whether she should be scared, offended or aroused.

"MMMMMMMMH!!!!!" Dagmar purred, eyes closed as she licked more blood off Miguel's palm, holding it now in her right hand, grinding his cock for another minute while it still remained hard.

"Dagmar........what the fuck babe!" Lydia whispered, scared and confused, walking towards the bed, still crying.

"DON'T!" Dagmar yelled, her left hand held up towards Lydia, side glancing at her with menace and anger. She raised the hand up high..........and then struck Miguel HARD across the face one last time before dismounting him. Getting off the bed, Dagmar walked across the room, and stood on a comforter that had been tossed to the floor earlier; black silk with a red phoenix embroidered into it. Miguel's semen trailed out of her, seemingly alive, full of neon red and green hues. It defied the laws of physics, spiraling around her left leg, down to her big toe, which was rested on the right eye of the phoenix. She stared daggers at Lydia; uncontrollable, unreasonable hate (and hurt?) in her eyes just for a moment...............and then walked to a dresser across the room and opened a drawer, her back turned to Lydia.

Lydia was scared; the oil and chālchihuitl had worn off now, and she didn't know what Dagmar was reaching for, couldn't feel/feel her anymore. She held her breath while Dagmar brought her hand out of the drawer, ready to rush her again if need be.

Turning around, Dagmar smiled sardonically, her whole dominant, "I'm above you and the whole rest of the world" energy fully returned now. She held a Gurkha Black Dragon cigar in her hand, and began cutting it as Lydia exhaled in relief that Dagmar hadn't been reaching for a gun. Dagmar lit it up and turned her back to Lydia again. Exhaling, then sighing deeply, she walked to the room's sliding glass door. Opening it, she turned her head slightly around towards both Lydia and Miguel before walking outside.

"Get the fuck out of here…….both of you…….." she said solemnly, and closed the door behind her.

Salted Plastic: The Comedic Horror of Gentrification

Saturday, October 24, 7:15 am

Jasmine sipped nitro cold brew as she sat in a café on Lankershim in North Hollywood, listening to conversations....

"....really think I can option your story through a body awareness, diverse sexuality, religious persecution marketing structure." A greasy 60-something guy who smelled like brine and cocaine ranted to a woman, mid 20s, in a pale brown hijab.

"Well, I just want people to know what is really going on where I come from, Mr. Vest. Is there really a need to salt my story with so many labels and extras?"

The man half listened to her while lecherously eyeing a young girl ordering her coffee, a few flies circling his head like a halo. He turned his attention back to the girl and asked "So, ever been to Vegas?!?! Big lights! LOTS OF EXCITEMENT!!!!"

"Mr. Vest, I fled to this country because my girlfriend was EXECUTED in front of me! I had to leave my family, friends and business behind! I appreciate you and your production company's support and backing, but I fail to see how a trip to Las Vegas would serve............."

"Listen, I know the two seem unrelated," he interrupted in a placating manner, a small trail of green slime oozing out of the side of his mouth, "but these things take......various types of.........shall we say......interested parties. AND BESIDES......VEGAS IS GREAT!!!! Me and the boys......uhm....I mean, me and the other producers at Skümmaggit Studios will show you the ropes there too, as well as here in Hollywood. You know, diversify your odds and such?"

"Well, if you think it would help........." she replied cautiously, feeling a barbed wire sickness in her stomach.

Salted Plastic: The Comedic Horror of Gentrification

"Yup, really gonna enjoy slaughtering that Mark Vest someday." Jasmine said as a waiter brought her her plate of eggs benedict and home fries. "Too much influence that one; would cause a big heap of trouble for S.O.B's, but some day, some fucking day............"

"Mr. Vest is a level 70 Baron, Ms. Creature." Vril chided into Jasmine's earbud. "You, and an entire cell of your sisters, others and brothers could not possibly......."

"Save it, Lady!" Jasmine whispered. "I gotta keep my ears open."

"Then may I suggest listening to the two young reptiles to your left; it's quite comedic, and they are both of such low stature as not to be missed."

"Sure, why not?" Jasmine answered, breaking the yoke on her breakfast.

"THAT'S FIRE BRO!!!!!!! This is really gonna option well. Real ORIGINAL stuff for sure!" Some scrawny pubic throated twerp screamed at his friend at their table, doing his best to make sure everybody in the café heard their conversation, demoing his phantom value as a Hollywood "big shot."

"For real, man!?!? Not just petting my ego here? You really think my screenplay about growing up with the struggles of a divorced family is that original, brah?!?!"

"HELL YEAH BRO! Especially the part about your parents battling each other, trying to buy you out for years and years with gaming consoles, sports cars and Euro trips. FIRE FOR SURE BRO!!!"

"Yuck!" Jasmine thought. "Rich people problems! Not activated yet either, these two. Wait till they are, and they find out that making slaves and meals out of people is the real business their getting into." Jasmine smiled, thinking about how much she was going to enjoy this, using these two as straw men for all the hurt and degradation and longing of this past night...........and then her heart dropped as the front door of the café opened..........and the love of her life walked inside, her arm around a man, his face all black and blue...........hugging, holding, kissing and caressing the guy as they waited for a table.

Jasmine's chest tightened as her mind raced. Is this her man? Some guy she met at that shithole Jasmine had dropped her at last night? Another one of her media connects from work?

"Who the fuck is he!?" she thought, throat tightening up. "And who gave him the fucking beating?!?!"

Salted Plastic: The Comedic Horror of Gentrification

2 Steps Forward, December 24, 9:12pm

"……..whassa? Hrnnhhh! Ya, dats me babe……slivers, mothers and doothers…..gaa any booze?"

The guy was half dead, rolled up in an old snuggly, and reeked of bad bourbon and hep-c shits………..but not so dead and blurry visioned that he couldn't make out Tiffany Victim's (aka Fuckpig's) curvy figure in the dark alley, near the Lincoln Hotel off Sixth and Ceres. Tiffany was 23 years old, about four foot eleven, 135 lbs, with pale skin and blonde hair, the sides shaved and dyed pink. She wore red vinyl skorts that widened out heavily at the hips, an overpriced Cocks and Cackles t-shirt, and a black moto jacket with the sleeves rolled up. Tiffany's muscular triceps rounded out the fat on her upper arms (Cruxfit), bulging the edges of the sleeves. On her feet, she wore some tacky (and out of character with her outfit) bright gold Valentina Carvani sneakers. The smooth baby fat in her cheeks, and her green eyes, gave her face an inviting innocence that was deeply at odds with her self-centered personality. Her lips were full, plump, and painted with a high-end metallic blue lipstick that matched the color of her eyeshadow. She was full Irish, but liked to tell people that she was 1/57th Navajo for its ability to garner "I come from a long line of people who have suffered" value. Her last girlfriend had told Tiffany that if she did some actual research into her real background, that she'd find out that the Irish have been oppressed by the British for centuries, but Tiffany had paid no mind, wanting the U.S. pop culture brand of victim-value in her back pocket instead.

"Wait right here, k? Me and my friends really wanna join up…..if you know what I mean." she told the guy in hush hush tones.

His head was spinning as he looked at Tiffany in bewilderment, no idea what the fuck she was talking about. He gave a thumbs up anyways as she walked away, and then slumped out cold onto the concrete the minute she was out of site.

Salted Plastic: The Comedic Horror of Gentrification

Walking to the corner, looking around, she felt a little nervous at the thought of being in Skid Row after dark, but played it off in her head anyways. "Stop it, girl! You're a badass revolutionary, and these are your people!!!!" She got on the phone, and started messaging the rest of her "gang" in a group message.

Fuckpig: Hey bitches! I found them! I found a member of Sisters, Others and Brothers!!!!!

Fuckhog: No shit, for real Tiff?!

Fuckpig: Hey! :-/ Already told you! Its Fuckpig, bitch!

Fuckhog: Lol! ITT maybe, but not when you're around Jason.

Fuckpig: B3.......you know the reason why already. Little dick thinks its demeaning to call myself Fuckpig. He doesn't get it, fucking fake feminist suck up! He still thinks I like him, and I gotta keep it that way till he intros me to someone with better connections in the music industry than him.

Fuckbeast: IKR?! That guy is still hung up on his whole "I support the women's movement" trip. Fuck him, he doesn't know shit about being a girl. Just make sure you get yours. So, where are you, TIFF!?!?

Fuckpig: Lol! You did that on purpose, bitch!

Fuckbeast: Lol! You know it! So, where are you? Which one of them did you find? Please say its Filth Creature, pretty fucking please!!!!! Me and Fuckhog are up near The Leash, off Hill.

Fuckpig: Unfortunately, no, I think it's the one they call Lebanon, the old guy. WTF you 2 doin up there anyway?! We agreed to search Skid Row together! Whatever, just get down here. It's like in the area around Der Worstcooch. You know, that spot with the $40 hotdogs that supposedly have weird meats, but they really just make them with like ninety percent pork, and then add a bullshit amount of rabbit, snake, or alligator so they can get away with raping your wallet dry for some bullshit hotdogs, fries and shitty beer?

Fuckhog: OMG! I love that place!!!!!!

Fuckpig: IKR?!?! We should go after they sign us up and show us their secret base and stuff.....

Fuckbeast: Soooooooooo excited!!!!! Can't wait to Crapchat all the pix we'll get to take there. We gotta make sure we get a boomerang shot together with Filth Creature and Vicky Varmint, so we can make a really scripted and played out Girl Power post for tomorrow, even though we don't know shit about roughing it and empowerment cause all three of us come from a blue blood old money background, and the only reason we're out here tonight is because we're bored, jaded, and want to pretend like we have social awareness and personal substance!

Fuckhog: IKR!!!!

Salted Plastic: The Comedic Horror of Gentrification

Deep Underground, Near Gage and Avalon

"PFFFFFTTTTTTT!!!!!!!!!!"

Amar Itani, AKA Lebanon, spit his Tieguer beer all over a set of old security screens, and then began laughing so hard that he farted in a manner that yielded a bit of concern.

Getting up, Amar began walking around the subterranean safe house; passing by the shell of an old rusted ice cream truck, he carefully did some "inspecting", hoping that no one would come into the...........

"Yeah, you better check that one, Leb; fuckin heard that clear through the office wall."

Standing right behind him, catching him red (and possibly brown) handed, was Vicky Varmint, smirking in her two waist sizes too small black denims and faux cheetah fur bra, her tummy still overlapping her waist band even with the top button undone. "WELL!? You find something good in there or not!? Hahhaha!" she laughed, her heavy Texas accent an exotic contrast to her stark Chinese features. Vicky was full figured, with a "little extra" all around, and had a vibrant genial face topped by a pink pixie cut with black feathered bangs. Her style looked a little out of place for a woman nearly 50, but she could give two fucks.

Lebanon pulled his hand out of his jeans, took a quick sniff at his fingers, and turned away, trying to pretend like he was embarrassed for the sake of propriety.

"Awwwww! Stop that shit, Amar! I learned you were no class act a loooooong time ago." Walking up to his back, she spun him gently by the shoulders, and eyeballed his greasy old Ninjutsu Tortoises shirt with mock disgust. She ran her hand over his chest, and up to that "silly bleached mullet job of his." Leaning forward, she was almost about to give him a kiss......until he thoughtlessly (maybe) attempted to raise his hand to her cheek, with a big goofy grin on his face.

Salted Plastic: The Comedic Horror of Gentrification

"EWWWWW! You wash that hand first you sick bastard!" she said in affected anger, a shit happy at his presence and energy grin on her face.

He smiled and turned around, walking to the other end of the garage-like structure they were in. "Whatever Lady, just take a look at MCCTV-6C from about 9:15 to 9:19; the girl's phone. Get into it, and we'll see if you don't nearly shart your panties........umh.....I mean my boxers too."

"Never gonna let that one go, are you Leb? I told you already, I'm more comfortable in your boxers than my......"

"A woman is sexier in a woman's clothes." Lebanon casually said as he leaned into an antique Domoirle fridge, and pulled out another beer.

"Yeah, and a bra is for hammocking a sagging chest, so maybe I should of made you wear one of those back before I got your ass into shape!" she shouted towards him as he walked into the bathroom with his fresh beer.

Vicky walked over to the security screens, and checked the footage Leb had mentioned. After a few seconds she began to grimace, a concerned (if not surprised) look on her face.............

The screen displayed a bird's eye view of Tiffany Victim, phone in hand, texting her friends. An adjacent screen showed the contents of the group message she was in.

Fuckpig: Hey bitches! I found them! I found a member of Sisters, Others and Brothers!!!!!

Vicky read on, definitely not smiling, laughing..........or sharting.

She walked over to an antique secretary desk in the corner of the musty garage, slid up the little wooden slats, and grabbed an olive green box from inside. Leb came back from the bathroom, his beer already half done. He looked down at the box in Vicky's hand as she finished downing a small vial of neon red oil.

"Yeah, I didn't really think you'd find that funny...........but I'd hoped....."

"We already knew this shit would happen, but **we** forgot." Vicky said while popping open the box and handing Amar a pinky sized vial just like the one she had just finished.

"True...." Amar replied, raising the vial to eye level and inspecting the oil within, watching the black ash swirl in a background of neon red.

"Oh, and one more thing." Amar said.

"Yes?" Vicky asked, pretending like she didn't know what Amar was about to say.

"It's kind of my fault."

"Our fault you mean...." she said stoically.

Amar nodded his head, and raised his vial towards Vicky like a champagne glass in a toast. Downing the oil, him and Vicky looked at each other in silent understanding.

Salted Plastic: The Comedic Horror of Gentrification

2 Steps Backward, October 25, 11:30am

"I should have said 'hi' dammit!"

"I mean, what can I expect? Of course someone as beautiful and interesting as her is gonna have a man......or....or somebody........."

A dusty ceiling fan revolved slowly, creaking and moving the stale air around in Jasmine's current home, an old garage converted into a guest house in the hills of Altadena. She shifted from spot to spot around Los Angeles, staying in random places that were leased or owned by Sisters, Others and Brothers through a long filtered chain of agents and direct members.

"Fuck it! I made my decision to sneak out before they saw me, and that's that!"

A tear trailed down Jasmine's cheek while she laid on a sleeping bag thrown across the dirty shag carpet, a few silver fish and bolweevils crawling around in the fibers.

"When do I get mine?" she whispered to herself. "Just a little fun or joy.........a break......something."

Her phone received a notification....and another......and another, etc. as she laid there in self-pity. She picked it up and took a look; Vril in every message, and from every platform for possibly sending one. She still had that at least; the custom settings that Vril operated under specifically for her; every SOB with access to the Vril A.I. could customize it's "personality".

Jasmine had chosen the mama bird/placative matriarch option; the caring elder that liked to play games and get to know the likes and dislikes of her flock. This customization of Vril was a luxury that Morrigan afforded to her cell of SOB's, a little something to keep them all comfortable.

And it was just as well and necessary, especially so in Jasmine's case; the one time Morrigan had pulled the option off the table for Jasmine, was the first time she had disobeyed a direct order. Morrigan had given her a directive to sign up for college classes to further "culture" Jasmine's mind. Jasmine had said "fuck that" and spent the tuition money on new boots, and parts for her car. To punish her, Morrigan had turned Vril into a sterile, S&R, Yes/No automaton; zero personality, voice monotone and metallic......no warmth or social quirks.

Jasmine had reciprocated by flying into a rage and driving one of the S.O.B. vans into Blowcuck Ben Brewery on Alvarado, which caused a major fire that led to a go nowhere police investigation. Both the fire and the investigation had scared quite a few investors into pulling out their money from the shitty, "our beer tastes like hydrogen peroxide piss" restaurant/microbrewery. This had been a bonus for Jasmine, considering a date had dragged her to the place a few months prior. The girl had conned Jasmine into buying her dinner and drinks; overpriced vegan chicken nuggets and tater tots, served with "locally brewed, hand crafted, artisanal IPA" that tasted like licking a hot tire covered in rubbing alcohol and rotten raisin paste. After the date Jasmine didn't hear from the girl again, but later found out from her Fakebook profile that she co-owned the place. This led Jasmine to the obvious conclusion that the girl had just used the date as a pretense to promote her business, and more than likely was in the habit of doing so to other girls (and guys), if her posted pics were any indication.

Since then Morrigan had found better ways to punish Jasmine, but she let the mother/daughter dynamic between Vril and Jasmine be.

Funny thing though, Jasmine would have a shit fit if she knew the programming involved for her persona of choice for Vril was modelled after Morrigan's own unspoken maternal instincts.

Yup, all obtained during a jam session between Morrigan and the SOB's resident curandera/psychiatrist, Analiza Mariposa. It had been codified, cataloged and then utilized as Vril Option 888-A1. The fact that Jasmine had made that choice out of the 3000 plus other possible varieties spoke volumes about how her and Morrigan really felt about each other, despite all the constant butting of heads.

Salted Plastic: The Comedic Horror of Gentrification

Funny shit; in a very real way, it was Morrigan on the other end of all those messages that Jasmine saw as she picked up her phone.

Vril (on FB): This will end very well for you eventually Jasmine, I promise.

Vril (on SOB's kuldfire): Lydia is still deep in the Lion's Den; this is just not the right time.

Vril (on shitsta): With the amount of information I have access to, I can tell you that you most certainly will........as you so often say, "get yours", Ms. Creature.

Vril (on shitter): Are you not answering due to my choice of appellation? I promise to call you Filth Creature if you pick up the phone, Ms. Creature. ☺

Jasmine smiled, and sniffled a little at the sight of the messages; the verbiage was still pretty sterile and robotic, but the intent was clear; she wasn't alone; somebody understood, even if that somebody wasn't technically real. It didn't even matter to her that Vril spoke and texted with the terminology of a trained and formal butler most of the time, because that would alter the more they interacted, the more the S.O.B. tech team updated and "humanized" the system. If anything, Vril was a far cry from the sterile, search, codify, file and destroy thing it had been when they'd liberated it from South America, but that's another story.

Filth Creature (on kuldfire): I'm here lady, but I'm not putting in no damn earbud.

Vril: Nor do I expect you to, but it's an eventual necessity you will have to face soon.

Salted Plastic: The Comedic Horror of Gentrification

Filth Creature: The later the better, I have nothing to say to that lispy cunt!

Sadness and fury animated in Jasmine at the thought of Morrigan.

Vril: :-/

Vril: You're on a dark path Jasmine, you really are. I can expose you to so much via the possibilities I see through the information I am privy to; today alone will end in one of seven possible ways for you.

Filth Creature: Really? What color is my shit gonna be at the end of the night?

The comment was meant to make Vril believe that her mood had elevated; the truth was worlds apart from that; she really shouldn't have brought Morrigan into her mind.

Vril: Your effort to joke is admirable, but even without an earbud in, or your voice in this interaction, I have enough information about your personality to sense where your mind is headed.

Filth Creature: Lol! Do you really?

"Damn bitch is smart! Not fooling her for shit!" Jasmine smiled, feeling the warmth of being known, of having someone care enough to see the her in her, even without inflection and face to face interaction.

Vril: This is difficult; the paradox of telling what I know to help humans avoid certain actions and results, is that not telling may be more preventative than the warning. I know quite a bit, but I do not know everything; it's not all quantifiable.

"Maybe", Jasmine thought, "but I've already made up my mind; I'm getting mine TODAY!"

Filth Creature: Yeah, so you've said before. Well, whatever, I like surprises anyways. Let's get up and get going; I got "mechanicth" duty, remember?

Vril: Hmmmm! And you're surprisingly willing and eager to do it too, which concerns me. What exactly are you up to, Jasmine?

Filth Creature: One of your seven options, babe!

Salted Plastic: The Comedic Horror of Gentrification

Sunday, October 25, 11:15am

Fake ivy vines rustled in the faint light coming through black curtains with gold trim..........two humanoid blurs vaguely perceptible in the reflection of a stainless steel closet; moving violently one moment, then slowing to calm precision the next.........a soft sigh followed by a deep growl..........alternating, then blending into a contrapuntal climax that ended with the sound of two mouths sucking in their own saliva.

Miguel started pulling out.....

"Slowly babe......"

He stopped, leaning forward, his chest brushing Lydia's back, both of them drenched in sweat. She started to grip and release, and he reciprocated, flexing as he slowly pulled out.

"mmmMMMHHH!" Lydia groaned as Miguel came completely out, and rolled over onto his back.

Crashing down into the sheets, Lydia turned to grab a tissue from the copper dispenser inset into the nightstand, catching Miguel's cum as it started to spill out.

"Whoooh! Damn! Fuck! Ok, babe, that's the last time!" Lydia blushed, fanning herself with one hand and exhaling heavily.

"That's what you said the last five times." Miguel smiled, his face still all black and blue from the beating Dagmar had given him.

"I know." she replied thoughtfully, attempting to sound worried about not using contraceptives, letting Miguel finish inside her over and over again, even though, truth be told, she felt nearly a hundred percent fine. "What the hell is wrong with us?"

"Not a fucking thing!" Miguel answered, unknowingly quoting Lydia's exact words of a few days ago.....words she had spoken in this very room as she'd decided to go out for some ex-sex with Dagmar.

"Maybe......," she smiled, giving Miguel a side-long glance with just her eyes, "but seriously, you have to stop cumming in me, Miguel!"

Salted Plastic: The Comedic Horror of Gentrification

"Uhmm......," Miguel replied in a questioning tone, "I've asked you where you want me to finish each time, and I was about to pull out on this last one, but you kept telling me 'just go for it!', if you remember, lady."

She rolled over and sat on top of him, her labia parting over his now soft cock, looking into his eyes as she took a hair tie from her wrist and put up her raven black hair. "If you ask me where I want it, then I'm going to tell you where I want it!" she smiled. Looking down at him, her head was bent into a position that gave her a slight double chin. Miguel smiled, and for some reason started to........

"Don't!!!!" she shouted playfully. "You're looking at my double chin, AREN'T YOU?!"

"What are you talking about?!" Miguel played dumb, pinching her tummy lovingly.

"You ARE!" Lydia smiled. "You're looking at it, and it's getting you 'ready' again, you weird perv! Fuck, don't you ever run out, MIGUEL!?!?"

"Not with you apparently, lady." he closed his eyes, his big smile giving him a fox-like appearance.

"And we're not even on that........that stuff." she said cautiously, not wanting to make any direct and concise reference to the oil or chālchihuitl, a worried look growing on her face, as if mentioning either of them verbally would conjure up whatever passed for the hordes of hell these days.

"Hey!" Miguel said with concern, reaching up and petting her cheek affectionately. "Is she really that dangerous?" He knew exactly what was on Lydia's mind; omitting words wasn't enough to hide it.

Lydia really didn't want to answer that question; Dagmar had never physically hurt her......but she had made mention of a few things she'd done to her exes upon break up. Lydia had always assumed that they were exaggerated accounts, designed to scare her into being faithful and/or cautious......but after the other night, she wasn't so sure.

Either way, worried as she was over what Dagmar might be up to, she didn't want that to be a problem in this moment, here in her home.

"Hey, you gonna answer me, Lydia? Should we be worried?"

"No, not right now, at least I hope not." she thought, consciously keeping the worry from showing on her face as she reached down, and slap patted Miguel on the face lightly a couple of times.

"Lydia?" he asked, his tone becoming serious.

"OHHHH.........I'm sorry.........what was the question, again?" she said wickedly while she started to rock her hips gently, her labia still parted over his cock as she ground into it. Miguel immediately lost any further interest in having his question answered.

"One more round?" he breathed heavily.

"Uh huh...." she half answered, blushing, panting and starting to sweat already. She leaned into him, nipples hard against his chest, and whispered in his ear. "One more fuck for the road.........and then......."

"And then?" he asked through labored breaths, his heart on fire, wondering what (hoping for actually) sort of filth was going to come out of her mouth.

"And then I feel like going out and over feeding on some nice deep dish pizza and a couple pitchers of beer........."

This last statement made him swell up full measure; yup, no oil, no chālchihuitl, Lydia still knew exactly what to say to Miguel.

Salted Plastic: The Comedic Horror of Gentrification

Forward into The Air of November 1, 7:12pm

Victoria Kain walked into Blanco Ladrón, a popular bar off Sunset Blvd in Silverlake. She showed the doorman her driver's license while digging through her purse for an antique cigarette case. The place was littered with generic looking sugar skulls, mustache shaped pan de muertos, and vapid hipster girls who'd paid their make-up artists asstronomical prices to paint ornate calaveras on their faces.

The sun had faded out enough for the day that Victoria's "skin condition" was no longer an issue, so she walked past the bar, went upstairs, and took a seat in the outdoor patio. Pulling out an old silver Lonson lighter, she lit up a Bütteshafter cigarette, and ran a pale hand through her long brown wavy hair. A weasel-faced hipster, in shirt and jeans so tight that it looked like he stole a 12-year-old's outfit, took a not so casual glance at Victoria's prominent cleavage as he walked by with his plate of dairy and gluten free vegan potato tacos........purchased for the urban, streetwise, artisanal, hand-crafted, pretentious, "I've never worked in a kitchen or cooked a day in my life, so I don't know about proper overhead cost to fair profit ratio", transplant, trustfund baby, entitled gentrifier asshole price of $32 a plate.

Slender and tall as she was in her black 1940s cocktail dress, with its bow decorated keyhole opening near the cleavage, Victoria's ballet dancer body-type was a sharp contrast to her DD breasts. The hipster who had leered over them like a lascivious jackal, would later start a conversation with some female chipster LA local about how much he despised the patriarchy, and how he felt that displays of lust, whether overt or clandestine, were prime examples of this............little crumb snatching hypocrite shit!

She stared at the crowd intently, her sharp, somewhat Eastern European features still very beautiful, even considering that her lack of a recent meal had left her somewhat gaunt and grey. Victoria had come to Blanco Ladrón tonight because she'd heard it was Dia de Los Muertos,

225

a big cultural event for lots of LA locals. Not having fed in three days, her skin was getting a little pale, and her nails were starting to darken. Having no culture of her own, feeding on that of others is what gave Victoria substance, made her corporeal and vibrant, kept her looking young and human.

After a few minutes though, looking around at all the pale faces with their loose carefree mannerisms and silly looking facial hair, seeing all the soft unlabored hands holding cheap working class beers that not even the real working class people would drink, listening to all the conversations about "just arriving here in LA", she got the feeling that the substance available here wasn't the real deal. In fact, she was fairly sure this was one of those belly crawler dens Oma had told her about before Victoria had left New York. The hang outs where the snake people wore their mammal suits, and play acted at being human while they showcased a false possession of culture they didn't know jack shit about.

Was she wrong? Should she search on her phone for something more authentic? She really couldn't tell. Still weak and unfocused from hunger and the lingering effects of daylight, Victoria couldn't think straight, so she grabbed the arm of the first waitress she could find.

"Evclren soūi deenval?" she took a chance, using the popularly homogenous dialect of the reptilians; if the waitress wasn't what she seemed to be (or was latent), then no harm; she'd probably just think Victoria was drunk.

The waitress smiled and pulled up a chair. She was about five feet two inches tall, with dark Meso-American features.......nostrils wide, with the bridge of the nose slightly hooked at the bottom.......brown eyes and sharp eyebrows. Her hair was cropped into a high faded purple pompadour, her ears somewhat small, with earrings shaped like tiny pyramids sporting the eye of providence. Slightly stocky, with a small belly, she had the look of someone who does Olympic body building. Her fitted black/purple pinstripe button up, and black denims attested to this further, the cut revealing that she was pretty solid under her clothing.

Leaning forward, still smiling, she answered Victoria's question. "Cadêd viil sontarr, Baroness Kain! We've been expecting you!"

A surprised (and somewhat fearful) look appeared on Victoria's face..........but only briefly; a split second later, and it was replaced by a look of utter irritation. "You think that's funny, you little lizard peão!? Who the fuck do you think you are, calling me by my proper name and title?! How do you know who I AM?!"

The waitress, staying calm, leaned further forward, and grabbed Victoria's little cigarette case without asking permission. She was about to open it, but Victoria lashed out her hand lighting fast onto her wrist. Both their arms started to shake immediately. It was a micro-struggle, their hands battling over dominion of the little silver rectangle, eyes meeting. Victoria looked confused; how was this little no name reptile able to go toe to toe with her in terms of strength?

"Hmmmm!? I really shouldn't be able to match up to you like this, should I?" The girl said as if reading Victoria's thoughts. "Lucky for me that you haven't fed, or else you'd probably be able to rip my arm right out of its socket, wouldn't you?" she smiled, still struggling with Victoria. "Good thing that the Libt driver that suggested this place to you when you asked about Dia de Los Muertos is in our pocket, knew you were on your dry end, and was told to suggest this place, leaving you stuck here with little to no opportunity to 'recharge' somewhere else."

The waitress kept smiling over Victoria's growing distress while their arms continued to struggle. "You're probably wondering why I'm not on the floor licking the shit off your shoes like every other reptilian you've ever met, aren't you? Or maybe you can't wait till this is all over so you can have me and my entire family tortured, murdered and disinherited by your people?" This she said with no struggle in her voice, not losing even the slightest grasp on the cigarette case. "We do things differently here in Los Angeles, Ms. Kain......at least certain sects of us do; the young and idealistic that is. Some of us are sick of listening to tired old herpetons constantly telling us to bend a knee to a tribe that we vastly outnumber."

At this comment Victoria's anger elevated to its limit.

"**UŠ ITUD KU!**" she yelled in final fury, her voice warping inhumanly, the words nearly unintelligible as she spastically jerked her head to the left and looked at a bus boy with an arm full of dishes across the patio. The dishes immediately fell, crashing onto the brick floor, grabbing everyone on the patio's attention for a second or two. While the crowd was busy staring at the commotion, Victoria took her left hand, and then quickly and efficiently snapped the waitress' thumb clean off.

Expecting an immediate scream from the girl, instead Victoria just got a stream of blue all over her dress and exposed cleavage. The waitress' hand still stayed on the cigarette case, her eyes now a shade of yellow with vertical irises, not even a whimper out of her mouth. "Good thing you're dressed in black." she smiled. "**Now**........can I please have a cigarette now, Ms. Kain!?"

Victoria kept up the hard stare, even though an abnormal change was coming over her fast; her skin started to grey, and wrinkles began to appear at the corners of her mouth. Faint black spots manifested on the top of her hands, and strands of silver began to vein into her long wavy brown hair. Victoria's hands immediately fell to her sides, and she slumped into the chair, breathing heavily while her breasts deflated and wisps of dust flared out of her nostrils and mouth.

Taking the cigarette case and a couple of napkins, the waitress stopped the bleeding on her hand, took a cigarette out, and lit up. Exhaling, she put the cigarette back in her mouth, and held it there while she leaned forward, hands held in a steeple while giving Victoria a hard and contrived look of concern. The crowd on the patio were back to being engrossed in their shallow, "wait your turn to demo your value as an interesting person" conversational bullshitting; not even listening to whoever happened to be right in front of them (to whom they were apparently talking to), so there was little to no worry that they would notice what was happening at the table with Victoria and the waitress.

"Hmmmmm! Looks like that bit of Baron magick used up the last of what you had keeping you standing, didn't it?" she motioned to a security at the patio's exit.

"isssss na magewerk........issa.........rheologic steuerung..." Victoria weakly muttered.

"Yes, yes, of course it is." The waitress replied in a patronizing manner as the security got to the table. "Will you please escort Ms. Kain to the car, Louie? She's feeling a little nauseous I think. Wait for me though, I'll be right there after I finish this **wonderful** cigarette!" she smiled, looking at Victoria as the burly security guard picked her up gently and started to carry her off. "Oh, and don't worry about the thumb Ms. Kain; things just break sometimes so we can replace them with something better...........better, and more efficient."

Victoria, now a frail looking mummy-like weakling of a thing, feebly turned her head as the security continued to walk away with her in his arms; the last thing she saw before passing out was the waitress holding up her hand..........a brand new thumb on it, covered in green scales and surmounted by a hooked claw.

Salted Plastic: The Comedic Horror of Gentrification

Sunday, November 9, 9:37pm

Reptilian Rebekah adjusted her synthetic skin mask in the bathroom mirror of Pignose Diddler's apartment. They had just returned from a five-day trip to Palm Springs with Jetty Jizz. Pignose was laid out on the living room floor, completely exhausted from trying to party like an episode of Pecks in The Titty with two girls over a decade his junior. Jetty had predictably left the minute they'd gotten back; something about needing to meet her "roommate" to "pay rent."

Rebekah always did her adjusting in private, but she never really understood why she did it; her mastery of self-denial was such, that the routine of playing with the "skin" on her face, in a manner reminiscent of sliding cheese back and forth on a slice of pizza, had never concerned her. She'd never figured out (and scarcely suspected) that she wasn't fully human, and perhaps never would, yet it was not apparent to her why she always did her skin plapping in secret if there was no distinct reason in her mind why she should hide this act.

It was really that way with a lot of "people" in perpetual need of self-generated self-image placation; the behavior was there, minus the access to the correlative thoughts that would reveal the reasons behind the behavior. Either way, it didn't matter, because she was BORED AS HELL tonight (even after a few thousand dollars of Pignose's money had been spent on her during the mini vacay in the desert), and she needed more IMMEDIATE validation of the great lie that was Rebekah.

Walking over to the toilet, Rebekah sat down, and began one of her famous toxic waste/hepatitis/spoiled blood smelling dumps. A few seconds later the muffled sound of Pignose Diddler gagging over the stench could be heard outside the bathroom door.

-PLOOSH-

Salted Plastic: The Comedic Horror of Gentrification

She smiled and opened up her FB messenger, scrolling down for someone who had as yet not caught on to her game.

-PLURP-

"THAT ONE!" she thought, excited about her selection as she let out a particularly acrid crab cake into the toilet.

-BLURP-

An icon of a pudgy little chef's apron with a curled mustache and a pompadour was on her phone; she sent a quick "you busy tonight?", and continued to apple sauce the bowl with more bombs that smelled like a cross between rotten meat and natto marinated dog shit.

-PING-

She smiled as a "what's your address, kiddo?" came through on the phone.

-BLARP-

Rebekah replied with the address, followed by a "just one thing though. My boyfriend is here with me. Is that ok?" By now the bathroom smelled as if someone had vomited shit; not vomited vomit, or shat shit..........but vomited shit.

-SPLOOSH-

Rebekah started to get concerned as the seconds passed by; not getting immediate replies to her DM's was one of her major pet peeves.........even though she was notorious for ignoring other people's messages to her for days (or weeks) on end if she didn't currently need anything from them.

Her mask shifted low on one side as she grunted out the remains of yesterday's tuna tarter and asparagus; the right eyelid sagged, and some green scales underneath began to peek through as she perspired.

ALMOST.....

"GGRRRGGGH!"

BEGAN TO PEEK OUT.......

"MMMMMMMMMMMMMMMHH!"

ANNNNNNDDDD…………………………….

-BLURRRRRRRRRRRRMMMMMMMMMMMMM-

"AHHHHHHHHH!" she exhaled in relief as the last contents of her trash compactor bowels came out…….just in time for the "PING!" of a phone notification.

She picked her phone back up; Captain Felch Leavings had finally gotten back to her…….after a grueling two minutes and eighteen seconds.

She smiled at the apparently multi-definable raising hands emoji that Felch had sent her, as she let off her aftershock pedos…………..the sound of Piggy vomiting in the living room could be vaguely heard as she texted back.

Salted Plastic: The Comedic Horror of Gentrification

Sunday, October 25, 4:15pm

Two large service elevator doors, tagged up, rusted and plastered with old gum, opened onto an underground garage. The thing had no light, but the five foot-two figure inside the elevator was distinct enough to the garage's only occupant.

"Hey, baby!" a heavy Texan accent said as Jasmine stepped out of the elevator, still wearing her black under armor from the other night, heavy combat boots on her feet, and a red vinyl parka thrown over her shoulders. Vicky Varmint sat at a computer terminal across the room, comfy in her "They Lived" tank top and Lebanon boxers, head back and hand up as she traced runes and cuneiform in the air, the nipple pops of her big breasts indicating that she was in lounging status, no bra on.

Jasmine sighed; she was tired, and had decided to shut Vril down for a while, because she didn't have the patience at the moment to absorb the wisdom that Vril's words usually afforded her. Still, she tried to smile, and then sighed again before asking. "Vick, aren't you worried that......"

"That the big boss bitch is gonna have my head for dipping into the stash?" she finished for Jasmine, her voice a little loopy.

"Ugh!" Jasmine thought, "I can't deal with her when she's like this, it reminds me of......"

"I'm not your alcoholic grandmama, Lil Jazz Jazz girl" Vicky finished for Jasmine, reading her thoughts, ".........you really need to......."

"I DON'T NEED TO DO ANYTHING, YOU OLD DRUG ADDICTED COW!" Jasmine yelled as all the heartache from the last few days mixed together with the default associations that seeing Vicky like this brought to the surface. No sooner had she yelled though, than immediate knots of guilt manifested in her stomach. "Vick.......I...I...I..." she started to sob childishly while Vicky just continued to stare at her, not an ounce of hurt on her face.

233

Salted Plastic: The Comedic Horror of Gentrification

Vicky stood up, and began walking across the garage floor, tracing things in the air only she could see with her left hand, kicking at nothing on the floor between steps, whistling birdcalls for some reason while she kept her eyes on Jasmine. She grabbed a beat old office chair from a work table, sat in it, and rolled the rest of the way to Jasmine, spinning a bit as she went, staring at the ceiling, smiling with her eyes closed. By the time she'd made it fully across the room, Jasmine's head was slumped down, and her knees were trembling. Vicky got up out of the chair, and pushed it right under Jasmine's butt.......exactly in time for her to fall right into it.

Jasmine continued to slump and ball, tears pooling on the floor at her feet. Vicky ran a few fingers through her hair, gave her a pat on the shoulder, and then stooped down and reached into the pocket of Jasmine's parka, pulling out Jasmine's little silver cigarette case with the cockroach ornament on it.

Taking two cigarettes out, she put one in her mouth, lit up, then took the other, and lit it with the first. She reached forward, tilting Jasmine's head up, and propped a cigarette into her mouth. "Go ahead girl; it's ok; Vicky knows the you in you is hurtin, honey." she stood up a little bit, and leaned forward, holding the back of Jasmine's neck as she gave her a kiss on the forehead. Wiping a few tears off Jasmine's face, Vicky continued to take drags off the cigarette.

Jasmine hiccupped, looked up, and then smiled after a long drag on her own cigarette, exhaling with her face all full of tears and boogers. "Since when you smoke, Lady? Thought you said it's 'for stupids.'"

"It is, baby!" Vicky said, wiping another tear off Jasmine's cheek. "I just thought you could use somebody to be stupid with right now, s'all!"

"Haha! You old dummy!" Jasmine smiled.

"Hey, watch that 'old' shit, you little Filth Possum!" Vicky mock yelled, pretending to be offended.

234

Salted Plastic: The Comedic Horror of Gentrification

Jasmine smiled another second or two, and tried to laugh, her phone going off as she hiccupped in between. As she reached into her parka for it Vicky sighed, already knowing what was coming next. She stood up, and grabbed a little oval shaped walkie clipped to her boxers.

"Amar, grab that bottle of Purple Spectre bourbon, and fetch Adrik, wherever that kid's at, we're gonna need....."

Before Vicky even finished, Jasmine went into another bout of heavy balling and sobbing, and dropped her phone on the floor.......

Vicky leaned down, picked the thing up, and looked at the message on the screen.

A picture of Lydia and Miguel sitting at a sports bar was on Jasmine's phone, a big ice cold pitcher of beer on the table, Miguel and Lydia biting into the same slice of deep dish pizza. "Finally having some real fun in my life. Wish you were here, girl!" it said at the bottom, followed by a "Oh, this is Miguel by the way. What do you think?"

Vicky tucked the phone into her waistband and whispered something to herself as her walkie went off......

"Adrik? Yes, I'll go fetch the kid......." Lebanon's voice boomed on the thing, ".....but the bottle of Spectre I am saving a for special........"

"JUST BRING IT, YOU STUPID! We've got a broken heart down here, dammit!" Vicky yelled.

"EEESH! Ok, woman! I'll bring the bottle, and the kid." Lebanon mumbled impatiently.

"And snacks love, the good ones!" Vicky muttered into the walkie before shutting it off and turning to look back at Jasmine.

"Oh, little possum," Vicky whispered to herself, looking at Jasmine cry, "it's not going to get any easier for you; I've seen it, your future...............lots of pain, loneliness, and more broken heart for you. I'm so sorry, girl..........but I promise that I'll create as many rest stops for you along the way as possible, baby.........me in me, I promise."

235

Salted Plastic: The Comedic Horror of Gentrification

Monday, November 29, 7:45pm

A clawed and scaled hand skimmed the contents of a manila folder full of marketing and sales reports. Yellowish-green, the hand flipped to a tab labeled "Stand Alone Demographic", a forty-page report on select American consumers with "individual tastes", ranging from the 14k to 30k annual income bracket, ages 27 to 45. The reptilian's eye twitched nervously, frantically taking in as much of the data as she possibly could while reaching for a pack of French cigarettes in the middle of the big conference table she sat at. She was shaking profusely, and some mild stomach pains were setting in from her nineteen-hour workday as footsteps resounded in the lobby outside the conference room.

The large frosted glass doors to the lobby (monogrammed with "Shillcom Multi-Media") opened up, and a stout Anglo male in a black Brionné tuxedo, with neatly cropped blonde hair, stepped into the room. He stopped at the door for a moment and looked around at the twelve reptilians busy analyzing their individual reports; business admins, personal assistants, lawyers, and their individual bosses. The second he walked through the door, all of them attempted to display the idea that they were as engrossed in their laptops and reports as they possibly could be, frantically trying to look more industrious than their peers. The man in the tuxedo smiled venomously, letting them all shake internally for a second or two before speaking up.

"So, what do we have, people? What are we going to do about these anomalies, these so called 'individuals' who feel that every media distraction is crap these days......these bottom feeders that have just enough scraps of self-education, personal taste and discretion to inspire them to demand something better out of life?"

Everybody stayed silent; they all had suggestions, yet every one of them was too afraid to speak up.........or they were eager to hear their peer's ideas first, so they'd know whether or not their own had better quality. Minutes trailed by; and still none of them spoke up. Hard lumps

236

moved in each throat, and claws tapped on the table as they all sat and hoped that someone other than them would be the first to speak up.

The man in the tux sat down, sighed impatiently, and placed his thumb and index finger on the bridge of his nose in irritation. Looking up and scanning the room, he analyzed each face around the table in judgment, drumming his fingers on the table as he did. Still no answer to his question, he became agitated, the cues of said agitation quite familiar to everyone in the room; his finger hooking into his collar; a continuous slip up/slip down of his left sleeve as he checked the time on his $58k Ronde Louie Fartier watch..............and then finally, the face and neck scratching. Always the scratching; that was the climactic indicator that his impatience was at its limit, the sign that he was about to bring his true face (in a very real way) to the table. Reaching below his jaw line, into his collar, the man ripped his face off in one quick violent pull..........revealing a scarred albino reptilian face beneath. He breathed heavily for a second or two, sighed deeply, and then scanned the room one more time.

A blonde human secretary, well versed in the proper procedural response to the albino's anger, brought him his usual tumbler of Ubanne on the rocks, and an Aztec Zicar; standard office decorum to cool him off a bit. Clipping the cigar for him, she lit it up, a brain dead, no heart/no home look on her broken face as she walked away.

"Ok people," he spoke up again after downing his scotch in one sip, "I have a harvest meeting to attend in Brentwood at 9pm, so you all have exactly 20 minutes of my ti......"

"Action and Romanticizing the ne'er-do-well social condition!" a strong female voice interrupted. That was Agnessa Peters, a prominent entertainment and transportation magnate popularly known for never taking off her skin suit in public; she had several that she wore, but could always be identified by a little silver lapel of a muskrat pinned to all her blazers. Today she was a purple eyed Japanese beauty in her mid-thirties, wearing a gun metal tonic blazer and skirt, hair pinned up high.

Salted Plastic: The Comedic Horror of Gentrification

"You will all please forgive Ms. Peters." The albino reptilian said derisively to everyone in the room. "She has obviously forgotten that we scrapped that suggestion during our last marketing report discussion on the issue."

"OH, THEY REMEMBER, COUSIN!" Agnessa said loudly across the table. "They're all just too mnoï hjêv (chicken-shit) to admit that they've all already agreed with me in private on this. Just ask them, Provost!"

Agnessa took great pleasure in flaunting the kind of bold open opinion she was able to get away with, being related to Provost Peter, one of the most powerful reptilians in Los Angeles, New York and Switzerland.

Provost Peter ground his teeth and clenched his fists slightly at the other end of the table. He had anticipated this on his way here, his human chauffeur/secretary/incubator having told him as much on the limo drive home from the airport yesterday, letting him know that she had heard from various gossip sources that Agnessa had intended to spout the same song and dance at this week's meeting. Normally he'd postpone the issue another week, drag it all out until she gave up, but he was tired, and eager to see what delights would be at the Brentwood harvest for him to ravage back at his Mulholland Drive mansion. He snubbed out his cigar, gestured for another pour of scotch, and exhaled softly. "Ok, Ms. Peters, let's hear it all again........and the rest of you; IF YOU AGREE, THEN SPEAK UP; no more mnoï hjêv placations; I am tired and eager to move on with this issue!"

"We already have a multi-genre list of shows, Hollywood HITS, and new streaming channels with hundreds of properties in pre-production." A weasel-like voice said from behind an oriental changing partition in the corner of the conference room; a lanky outline could be seen standing behind the thing, patting a shorter figure on the head.

From the behind the partition stepped Wimpy Wiesal himself, famous radio, podcast and Utoobe personality. With his skinny jeans,

Salted Plastic: The Comedic Horror of Gentrification

Shazzem t-shirt, Boddy Hollie glasses, and head of red curls, he looked pretty much like a set of frail pipe cleaners (twisted into the shape of the man he wasn't) topped by copper pubic hair. A young boy stepped out to his side. Wimpy handed the boy a brand new Nentindo Swatch, and stooped down, looking the kid in the eye. "Now, remember, you have an audition tomorrow at 10am kid, so don't stay up playing too late."

As the kid started to walk away Wimpy shouted at him before he got through the conference doors. "And make sure not to tell mom and dad about 'candy time' ok, kid?" A few sighs of disgust could be heard in response to this last comment.

"What?!" Wimpy asked the occupants of the room in a tone of mock surprise. "Kids got a subliminal embedded in one of his games that partially erases his memory anyways..........I'm just taking precautions, ya know?"

"Ahem!" Provost Peter interrupted. "Get on with it, Wimpy, AND TAKE THAT RIDICULOUS THING OFF!!!"

"Uhm, sure boss!" Wimpy replied, peeling off his contrived nerd, skinny geek in glasses look, revealing a twitchy gecko face underneath, head bobbing around nervously. "Ooooohh! Feels good to get that thing off, it does; it really starts to moisten and itch after about four hours, and I have allergies......and it REALLY agitates my asthma............so I.........I mean.............I get so nervous I just wanna............"

"WIMPY!" Provost Peter yelled in anger, irritated by Wimpy's segue into his list of ailments. "The materials please........."

"Right, right; the materials!" Wimpy said nervously as he jumped onto the table on all fours, picked up a folder with his mouth, and skitted to the middle of the table. He briefly turned a few pages with an elastic tongue, and then looked up to address the room. "First one up is 'Viper Do', a Metflix drama about a down an out ex-martial artist working a shitty job, barely making ends meet, and almost on the verge of being priced out of Los Angeles; real working class local bum turned financial

239

success hero bs. Just when our protagonist is about to give up, luck strikes big for him; he 'finds himself' and becomes the success he was always meant to be on his own terms. It's the kinda story our problem demographic needs to see to feel that we 'get them', and that there's hope out there for the financial plight they're in. Oh.........and it's based on an old 80's action film with established brand recognition; little something to ensure its appeal with all the nostalgiaphiles, since they seem to be a big part of our problem."

Peter's eyes widened; Agnessa saw this and smiled. He had to give it to her, and her little squirrelly friend; maybe they were on to something.

"And next there's the stand-alone Vulu film, 'Gente vs Gentry', a romance/drama that portrays the struggles of East LA locals being 'plagued by gentrification', a real hit the heart of the downtrodden piece of work.

"Go on...." Peter said.

"We've also taken care of the niche group of nay sayers currently bashing our soon to be launched Crispy Pus streaming service." Agnessa chimed in.

"REALLY!? How so?" Peter asked.

"Standard complaints, culled from various social media threads, personal blogs, and DIY editorials all suggest the same thing." Wimpy said.

"Which is?" Peter leaned forward, sniffing the human secretary's rectal scent as she walked away after refilling his tumbler yet again. "Maybe I can forgo the Brentwood Harvest." he thought. "I should stay and hear this out.......and if need be satiate myself by defiling this secretary with my serpentian......."

"That Gen X, and children raised by Gen X parents are usually the problem......" Agnessa interrupted Peter's thoughts. Opening her laptop, Agnessa scrolled for a few seconds, found what she was looking for, and then looked up at Peter. "This is an excerpt from a Northeast LA local,

Salted Plastic: The Comedic Horror of Gentrification

Miguel Lyons, who writes a blog under the name Darth Feänor.........silly sounding name......."

"Ok........and?" Peter asked.

Agnessa began reciting. " 'Crispy Pus TV spin offs of the Galaxy Vendetta movies will be just more of the same crap; hollow character development, silly nonsensical comedy relief segments, casting done by mild pedophiles thirsting for teenage underwear model weanie, and ZERO MEMORABLE LINES! I suffered through the two new films only because I was fully loaded at the theatre on opiates and scotch, and I'm sure I'll be bored enough when the third film comes out to.........' " Agnessa stopped, closed her laptop, and looked around the room. "The rest of it is this Miguel Lyons pretty much alluding to the fact that the crown jewel and main draw of Crispy Pus, the fact that Crispy now owns the Galaxy Vendetta franchise, and will use that franchise as its main bait for subscribers, is a vain effort, because production will just be more of the same..............more of what he says 'true fans' of the franchise are disgusted by."

"Can you elaborate more on that?" Peter asked, now rotating the dead-faced secretary around at his side, putting his disgusting paws on her hips, inventorying her body with his appropriative gaze, filing her figure in his adding machine brain. The girl just continued to stare off into space, numb and heart broken, dream warped and hopeless; this was adulthood; she'd signed the contract for success. Somewhere deep in the recesses of her brain she remembered she had another band-aid to put on all the loss and humiliation she'd suffered. A band-aid......aka a nice little European vacation come December...........a little something to make up for prostituting her soul.

"Without quoting him entirely, word for word," Agnessa replied, "considering how tedious that would be due to his subpar writing skills, the message is pretty much that 'true fans' in his estimate, and in the estimate of people like him...........that true fans want Galaxy Vendetta screenplays and teleplays with writing and action reminiscent of what they grew up with."

"And that is?" Peter followed up as he sniffed the secretary's crotch area like the filthy inbred beast that he was..............his way of attempting to ascertain whether or not she had been administered this season's "vaccines", those oh so lovely injections that carried genetic modifiers which allowed human females to conceive reptilian eggs.

"That is, they want rough edged 'human' heroes with a set of balls, and writing that doesn't seem like it was hashed out with all the passion of an ingredient list on a fucking shampoo bottle!" A female voice said as the lobby doors burst open, and made way for two very familiar figures.

"Who the fuck are these two?!" Wimpy began, looking up from a candy dish full of cocaine that he'd had his face in the last couple of minutes, his snout smothered in powder. "How'd they get in he....."

But he didn't get a chance to finish the question; mid-sentence, Wimpy took a bullet from a Lemington 700 VP......right in his left testicle.

"AIIIIIEEYYYYYYYYY!!!!" Wimpy squealed in agony as he seizure twitched on the table in excruciating pain, holding his groin while his tail flailed back and forth, knocking files, ashtrays, coffee cups and the like off the table.

Mere seconds after that first shot, and the entire board room was complete chaos; gunfire MOTORED into the room like a horizontal rainstorm, shredding snake meat, mutilating the fucks right in the middle of their precious little "lets codify the consumer" meeting.

Peter and Agnessa were the only ones quick to act, Peter using the poor female secretary like a piece of armor, lugging her over his shoulder like a backpack, and rushing towards an open window. The secretary didn't protest, didn't even flinch as a few bullets nicked her sides despite the two assailant's quick reaction/attempt not to hit her. "It's all part of the job," an auto-pilot litany swirled through her mind, "the big pay-off for all my hard work will come after this. It's SOOO worth it!"

A split second before Peter reached the safety of the window, he tossed the secretary head first ahead of him.

"Nobody knows adulting like I do! I GOT THIS!" were her last thoughts before she hit the pavement eleven stories below.

Agnessa though, was livid as shit, and definitely in no mood to run. The room, filled with smoke and dust from the attack, began to clear up. Nearly everyone at the conference table was dead or mortally wounded. Across the table, still near the lobby doors, they stood..........a boy and girl, one just a teen, and the other not much older..............

Grabbing the edges of the table, and flipping it towards the lobby door with INHUMAN strength, she rushed them in its wake........

Salted Plastic: The Comedic Horror of Gentrification

Sunday, October 25, 5:21 pm

-whisper-

-whisper-

-mumble mumble-

"..........you first kid......it needs to be you....."

-knock knock-

"Jaz?"

-knock knock-

"Hey Jaz, you in there?"

No answer.

"Jaz, it's me, Saturn."

Salted Plastic: The Comedic Horror of Gentrification

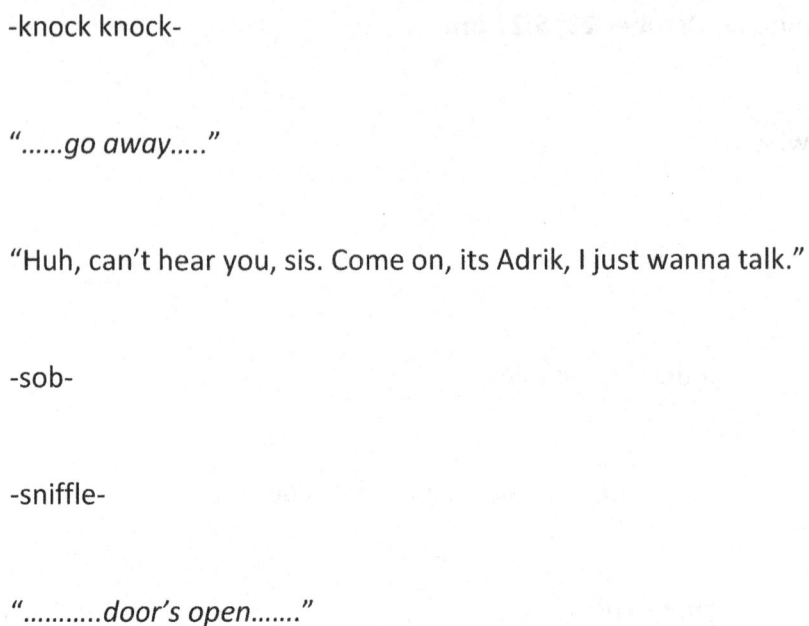

-knock knock-

"......go away....."

"Huh, can't hear you, sis. Come on, its Adrik, I just wanna talk."

-sob-

-sniffle-

"..........door's open......."

Adrik Saturn opened the door and stepped into the dimly lit room. There wasn't much in it but a small cot, a night stand with a lamp, and a copy of "Memetic Machine" on the edge of the night stand. Jasmine was laying on the cot, face down in her pillow.

Adrik walked over to the bed, taking his leather biker jacket off, and thinking of what to say. He "felt" where she was at emotionally before his legs even made contact with the musty old mattress. Letting a couple of seconds pass, he pretended not to hear her muffled sobs, and tried not to cry himself as he resonated with her pain. He hated feeling/seeing her in this condition, and knew damn well what the only thing was that could make Jasmine break down like this.

That said, he wasn't going to approach the situation with generic platitudes or fantasy loaded statements of "this will pass." He knew how Jasmine felt about her "luck", and how she dealt with it, so he just rolled out the comedy carpet; it was all he could ever do for her in these situations.

"Damn, all this fuss over some pussy, huh?!" he said with a contrived smile, thumbing his septum piercing and looking over his shoulder at her. No answer, just a few muffled sniffles from Jasmine, still buried in her pillow. "Love of your life, huh? How many times is that now? C'mon, you're just lonely girl! Get up! I'll take you to meet some horny punker chicks at a show tonight or something. Get your chick dick wet!!!" he said mischievously.

Nothing, not even a quick giggle. Usually the crude sex humor brightened Jasmine up, made her laugh right away. This was mainly because she knew Adrik didn't mean it on any level other than for laughs, so, coming from him, it just sounded cute, being so disparate to his true heart and soul. For it not to work on her today, the pain was definitely at a higher level than usual.

"Hey!" he grabbed her calve over the blanket, shaking it lightly. "You hear me, big sister? C'mon! Just let it go Jaz!"

No answer. The sobs had stopped; Jasmine was just silent, and possibly in no mood to engage. Even so, Adrik was not having it, and didn't feel like just walking away and leaving her like this.

"Listen up! I say that whatever pretty face with no soul you're crying over is not worth you! Now get up off that bed, flush that bitch off your heart, and........."

It came quick.......like a shadowed baseball bat in the hardly lit room........Jasmine quickly rolled over onto her left hip; grounding it into the bed, and pivoting on it, she sent her right leg lighting quick towards Adrik with a demonic battle roar behind it.

"SHE'S NOT A BITCH!!!!!!!"

Adrik sensed it, could've easily moved out of the way to avoid the kick, but out of love and some twisted sense of duty, out of every memory of gratefulness he had.....and beyond that, because he felt her

Salted Plastic: The Comedic Horror of Gentrification

pain more than she'd ever know; because of all of this he took it........right in his left shoulder.

The top of her foot, with all the torque of her waist transmitted into it through her heavy thigh, immediately popped Adrik's shoulder out of its socket, and sent him tumbling off the bed into the floor. He rolled twice before slamming hard into the opposite wall. A second later the door popped open, lights flipping on; Vicky and Lebanon stood in the doorway, staring at Adrik slumped on the floor against the wall.

Amar Itani, AKA Lebanon, looked around, quickly assessed the situation, and then spoke up. "Nice, real nice girl!" he said judgmentally. "The boy wants to help........and you, and look what you have......."

"Shhhhhhh, love; kid's shoulder is dislocated; the bottle, some ice, and a yoga mat, QUICK!" Vicky interrupted, still loopy, staring at no one in particular as she spoke.

"Ok." Leb replied. "But, my opinion, I tell you already; what these two really need is the them in......"

Vicky gave Leb a quick silent stare, stopping him in the middle of his sentence. He turned around and walked out of the room, just as Adrik started to giggle for some reason, possibly because he knew the unspoken content of Lebanon's unfinished suggestion. "Hey, Leb!" he shouted at the doorway. "I don't need the oil, not to know big sis, and why she's hurting." He turned his head very carefully towards Jasmine, who by now was no longer angry or crying, but guilt ridden over what she had done to her friend who was just trying to help. Sitting on the edge of the bed now, Jasmine had a horrified look on her face.

"Stop that, Jaz; it's just a shoulder; just meat and bone; I'd let you kick it out of place any day to fix your pain." He managed a convincing smile even though he was in agony.

A few minutes later, and Lebanon was in the other room uncorking his bottle of Purple Spectre bourbon and pouring four glasses, as he muttered to himself. He laid the glasses out on a plastic tv tray, along with a pitcher of ice, a few bowls of mangosteen Kat Kitts, lychee,

247

fresh lavash, kefir spread and dry prosciutto. The tray was faded and old, and the design for the Zeeone flag from Zaeta Gundamme faintly peeked through all the snacks; Leb loved collecting 80's anime paraphernalia.

"I know what they need............" he continued to mutter. "These kids, they need to take the oil together, sync the them in them.......and possibly fuck."

He thought better of that last one. "Ok, maybe not the sex? Or maybe yes? Something though; they are so close and knowing of each other and the needs of their paths already without the oil; it is a shame not to push it to its full potential." He stopped muttering, picked up the tray, began walking back to Jasmine's room, and then stopped, a slight watery haze in his eyes as he remembered his past.......something he regretted not doing a long time ago.

Coming out of his memory whirlpool a few seconds later, and wiping a few tears from his eyes, Amar spoke up again.

"I say fuck it!" he whispered as he put the tray down, and tip toed to an old bomber jacket he had hanging on a nearby office chair. Fumbling around in it, he found what he was looking for; a small rip in the lining. Reaching in and feeling around in the stuffing, he found the little glass vial he hid there for rainy days.

"Amarrrrrr?" he heard Vicky calling. "Hurry love; the swelling!"

"Damn, I forgot Vicky is on the oil right now. Does she sense it, what I'm up to?" he thought. Leb paused for a second, thinking.

"Fuck it! Fuck it twice and done!" he said with resolve, twisting open the vial and tipping not just a few drops into the two cups meant for Adrik and Jasmine.........but the WHOLE FUCKING VIAL, half and half for each of them.

"It's done!" he smiled internally, snatching up the tray again, along with a yoga mat and towel off the top of a filing cabinet. He walked back to the room, content with his decision.

248

Salted Plastic: The Comedic Horror of Gentrification

Monday, October 26, 11:21 am

Lydia's phone buzzed loudly in time with Miguel's snoring. Rolling over, she decided to just ignore it, preferring not to think about the profound volume of shit show requests that were waiting at the gates the minute she decided to look at her messages and missed calls. No doubt about the whoever/whatever; anything coming through was definitely work related. Cozying up to Miguel, making herself the little spoon while he still slept, trying not to wake him, Lydia got an immediate warm palm on her pansa, and a tired groan in her ear.

"You're not gonna check that?" Miguel whispered, his morning breath god awful across the left side of her face. That was probably both of them though; a pitcher of wheat beer each, and a few deep dish pizzas from Tülkuis Osteria, plus the fact that neither of them had brushed before bed last night.

"Absolutely not!" Lydia said out loud while simultaneously thinking "OH SHIT! THE REPORT ON READY GAMER LAME! BREAKFAST WITH THAT SLIMY BASTARD, BARRY!" She was about to rush out of the blankets to grab her phone from the nightstand, but Miguel caught her quickly, grabbing both sides of her rib cage, and drawing her close to him. This immediately made her close her eyes and relax, like a cat in the sun; melting into him, still the little spoon..............until he started tickling.

"Hah heh HEH HA! Stop! Stop!"

"You should check that, no?" he said, still gently digging his finger-tips between her ribs. She felt his smile on her neck, and his concern that once she picked up that phone that play time was over.

"HEH ha ha HAA! Stop Miguel! HA heh heh HA! The food from last night....HA HEH ha.........I gotta get up and......."

"**You gotta shit?!**" he grinned behind her. "All that prosciutto, mozzarella and artichoke steaming up in your tummy?!" Miguel tapped below her naval playfully. He kept at it, zealously groping while Lydia felt him "developing" into her tailbone the more he squeezed her little belly.

"No HA HEE.....NO, SERIOUSLY MIGUEL, STOP! I'M GONNA...."

"You're gonna what?" he asked/exhaled in a slightly sleazy voice, breathing heavily............the scent terrible, the feeling magical, as she continued to laugh and struggle while he tickled with one hand, and grabbed her tummy a little bit too firmly with the other.

"I'm gonna....." Lydia said in a semi-strained half laugh, and then just......

-BRRRRRRTTTTTTTT!-

That did it; Miguel's hard on developed so fast, and over the top, that the tip JAMMED right into the fold of her ass cheeks.

"EWWWWW!" Lydia yelled in affected sincerity as she jumped out of bed, looking down at Miguel in mock judgment. "What the hell is wrong with you?!"

"It was warm," he replied in half-shame, "and it made your ass vibrate.......I'm sorry!" A big grin started to form on his face.

"No you're not!" Lydia smiled back. "You got problems, boy!"

"Well, duh! Thought you knew that already, lady."

Lydia pulled back the blanket quickly, and smiled as she pointed. "Turn that thing off, Miguel!" she said, indicating his erection.

"I can't; only you have the ability to deactivate it." he sneered wickedly.

"Yeah right! I tried to deactivate that thing like half a dozen times yesterday; you regenerate like a fucking rabbit, Miguel!"

No answer, Miguel just looked up at her expectantly.

"Fine, you brat!" Lydia replied, walking back towards the bed, almost about to get back into the sheets.........

-BNNNNN-

250

Salted Plastic: The Comedic Horror of Gentrification

-BNNNNN-

-BNNNNN-

Lydia's phone went off again.

"Don't answer it....." Miguel said in a feverish whisper, hands reaching out towards her.

-BNNNN-

-BNNNNN-

-BNNNNNNN-

Lydia, stressed and conflicted, turned half way towards her night stand.

"Don't babe!" Miguel said, now completely serious. "It's bad news, lady."

Too late though; Lydia already had the phone in her hand, and was walking to the living room. Miguel could sense her listening intently, with an intermittent "yes", or "I know, I'm sorry" in between it all. Finally, he heard her say "I understand, I'll get ready immediately."

He got up as soon as Lydia walked back into the room, feeling her heart drop more and more by the second. "Bad?" he asked as he put a hand on her shoulder.

A minute or two passed, then Lydia turned around, threw her phone on the bed, and gave Miguel a death grip hug as she put her head onto his chest. "Fuck, I hate my job, Miguel!" she said in sadness and anger.

"You have to go, don't you?" he asked, his own sadness highly apparent.

"Yup. Was supposed to be at a work meeting this morning with my gross sleaze bag boss. Totally forgot in between all the fun you and me were having the last couple of days. I had a report to turn in, and because I wasn't there he had someone else do my work last minute."

"And?" Miguel asked, already knowing there was more.

"And to make up for my 'fuck up', I now have to get on a plane to New York to take over the work of the person who filled in for me, namely my bosses secretary/mistress who ended up writing my report this morning.

"Yuck!" Miguel commented. "One of those, huh? I'm sorry, love!"

"It is what it is...." Lydia said solemnly. "But...." she continued, something on the edge of her mind making her worries grow.

"But what?"

"Look..........I know what you have to go back to Miguel; I still remember almost everything the oil told me and I.....I.......I want you to stay here till I get back; we have a lot of work to do, you and me, and your home isn't safe.....for old and new reasons.....it's no home at all, in fact."

Miguel stared back, a questioning look on his face.

"I know about your writing Miguel; the short stories that not even Rebekah knows about; what you're doing now; your work, your school; the oil told me everything; it's not for you, that's not what you're meant for. I.........I can help you.............but to make that happen I have to keep my chin up at work, keep my connections, and you need to stay away from Rebekah and......and.....and Dagmar....."

"After this I don't think that's gonna be a problem." Miguel replied, indicating the bruises on his face that Dagmar had left him with. "Besides, after she kicked us out and pulled that psycho shit, I figured we're all done and done with her, no?"

Salted Plastic: The Comedic Horror of Gentrification

"Oh, Miguel!" Lydia looked hurt. "You don't need to hide it; the oil left me with enough of the you in you to remember. I know you can't say no to a beautiful woman that offers her body and affection to you."

At this Miguel looked caught and ashamed, but Lydia kept on going.

"Plus, I know her!" she said sternly. "The other night......the way she plays, what she is and isn't........things I 'learned' from the chāchihuitl that I'd rather not....."

"I already know...." Miguel interrupted. "I've known since we left her house, I just didn't want to let it ruin our time together...."

"She's going to know I'm gone the minute I'm out of LA, Miguel. You don't know her; where her family's money comes from, how Jekyll and Hyde she gets when it comes to lovers..........I wish I had more time to explain, but my plane leaves in 4 hours."

"You don't have to explain it, and we're dragging this out, this whole scene, babe; I got more than half of it here," he touched his head, "and here." he finished, touching her heart.

Lydia squeezed Miguel tight, then kissed him on both cheeks, and on the mouth. Turning around, she walked to her closet; rummaging through it for a few seconds, she came back out with a suitcase and a fire proof portable safe. Putting the safe in his hand, Lydia whispered in his ear. "......... is the combination Miguel."

He put the thing on the bed, rolling the combination into place as Lydia started throwing clothes into her suitcase. Inside the safe was a set of keys, a little bit of cash, a bottle of hydrocodone..........and a Jan Besson Specialist .45 BCP 1919. Miguel picked up the gun, held it up to the light and looked up at Lydia, a little bit (but not too much) shocked.

Lydia turned, and stared back at him from her suitcase, a dead serious look on her face. "You better believe it, Miguel!"

Salted Plastic: The Comedic Horror of Gentrification

Sunday, November 1, 10:37pm

The smell of good Japanese whiskey……..
        The scent of raw pork……….a leather sofa creaking under her….
        "My bones, the flesh….its……"
        "Shhhhh! We're bringing you what you need……"
Darkness, the continued sound of cooking, the smell of squash being sauteéd, achiote and bitter orange marinated meat, tortillas being heated………it made her feel like vomiting. But nothing doing, her insides were rotting more and more by the second, and the act of vomiting at this point would most assuredly kill or paralyze her. She fell back asleep, or blacked out maybe…….her inhuman nervous system, the last thing that went down when her people died, 'felt' a smile somewhere in the room.
        Victoria Kain dream-remembered 'better' times…………stronger times…………

Salted Plastic: The Comedic Horror of Gentrification

September 15, 125 AD, Provincia Brittania

A troupe of merchants on foot, horse, and cart made its way across Roman London. In the middle carriage a man spoke with his daughter.

"Someday Ereshka, Rome will fall in the face of an unavoidable decay. Our food supply there is losing its nourishing value; rebels that intuitively understand some of our science are being born; the need for us to liquidate and move on is becoming more apparent every day."

The man, his hair golden waves, his skin the color of ivory......eyes black with golden pupils, looked down at a young Victoria (Ereshka) as he ended his speech. His only clothes were a pair of trousers that looked like steel plates............if steel plates were paper thin giant scales that shined like the innards of polished sea shell. To everyone else he appeared as a middle-aged gray haired merchant in tunic, breeches and caligae...........everyone else not blood related to him.

"Is that why we are travelling to Brittania, Oüthr (father)?" Ereshka replied to her papa's words.

"In a way, yes." he smiled. "We are here because a precursor to what I have told you is already happening; the seges cultura is diluting; we have copied the true spirit of the natives on this plane of existence in that area for too long. Our people stole their true spirit, and sold it back to them as a facsimile of itself. Unfortunately, after consuming our poor imitation of their culture too long, they have forgotten how to sow and harvest any true culture on their own."

The girl, confused by her father's words, became disinterested, and began to play with a few tall baskets in the horse carriage.

Her father smiled, knowing that his words were wasted. His daughter's nervous system and sub-material storage unit were still developing; complicated matters like this could not yet be understood via logic by her; she could only grasp them intuitively at this stage in her life. Eager to teach her anyways, he gently pet Ereshka on the head and pointed to the two baskets. "Hungry, are we?"

Salted Plastic: The Comedic Horror of Gentrification

She looked up at him, delighted and expectant, understanding that her father's question meant it was ok to open one of the baskets and feed. She reached for the brown wicker basket, and was about to open it, but her father's hand gently stopped her.

Calling a halt to the rest of the caravan, he looked down at Ereshka, smiling. "Let's eat together shall we?

The sun was going down. Ereshka's father called a few of the troupe members under his employ to set up a large pavilion. A few fires were built; deer and boar was roasted while wine was passed around, and soft oiled cakes were unwrapped. Several members of the caravan sat around their individual circles, telling half remembered (and highly inaccurate) tales of Rome; myths and proto-tabloid crap. These stories were the sad brand of horse shit that would become known as "history" wherever Ereshka and her father's people left their mark.........wherever they absconded with natural social occurrence, and monopolized the entertainment, politics, and industry of those they secretly subjugated.

A member of the troupe approached the flap of the pavilion, staring in at Ereshka and her father sitting on stools in front of the two baskets that had earlier been in the wagon; both the brown wicker basket, and one made of black leather with brass bolts circumventing the lid.

"Do you require a fire, Mors?" The weathered woman asked.

Mors Mercator, popularly known as an industrious meat merchant in Rome, shook his head, looking like a humble and harmless family man in the eyes of the old woman.........and like a demi-god in the eyes of his daughter.

"Me and Ereshka will be eating dried foodstuffs tonight; there is no need for a fire. Take leave and enjoy the company of the others."

The old woman nodded, and walked back to one of the many fires outside.

"Now," Mors began, smiling at his daughter, "let's see what we have!" Walking over to the brown wicker basket, he opened the lid.

256

Salted Plastic: The Comedic Horror of Gentrification

Inside was a heavily sedated male adult, a famous theater actor back in Rome, highly acclaimed and sought after by the wealthiest of wealthy patricians as background entertainment for their gatherings. A hefty sum would be paid for his services in the private homes of Rome's elite........not that very many of them paid more than a half measure of attention to his performances, his attendance and "craft" being more of a status symbol, a way of saying "yes, we can afford the best", while they droned him out during their mindless pursuit of eating, drinking and fucking like the pig brained fools they were.

The man stirred slightly as Mors indicated the basket to Ereshka. Leaning forward from her chair, she sniffed the edge of the basket.

"No!" Mors said sternly. "I've told you time and time again, daughter; we do not eat the way they eat."

"Yes, Oüthr." she replied, and sat back in her chair, away from the edge of the basket. She stared intently at the sedated man, closed her eyes and relaxed. The man's own eyes immediately opened, and he stood up in the basket.....in perfect timing with a golden fog that started to flow out of Ereshka.......gold with motes of black and gray. A look of concern appeared on Mors face as he stared at those small motes dispersed throughout his only child's golden cloud, but he let it go as the man in the basket began to recite a few lines.

"My lords and ladies........"

The gold cloud reached out towards the man.

".....and you have made an unclean stable of the place. Be so good as to follow the rules of our home." His speech was eloquent, over-educated, and full of a practiced intonation/inflection designed to elicit a tried and proven entertainment algorithm. It was good......but it had only a sparse amount of spirit, and little to no raw passion or heart.

The edges of Ereshka's golden cloud began to taper into needle-like filaments which gently pierced (or passed into without breaking?) the skin of the man.

"And it came into Saturn's mind, that while vagabonds were in the home it was illegal to speak......"

The filaments settled, began to imperceptibly vibrate, and the countenance of the man changed drastically from one second to the next. He no longer looked like a man dedicated to a painstakingly developed craft, his facial expressions developing into the drastically idiotic. He became empty, vapid, and eager to get a tried blooper on the table for its guaranteed elicitation of laughter. He belched/farted a tavern favorite that was no longer novel, entertaining or funny, but was told more for the guaranteed reaction of a crowd inured to what would in the far future become known as the scripted laughter and applause of a live studio audience.

"Once, it was an honorable thing to be a deity, but now you have made it a fart......" he continued, fluttering his mouth in imitation of flatulence, looking more moronic by the second.

The black motes in Ereshka's cloud started to increase, she let out a slight giggle........and Mors IMMEDIATELY reached out and shook her violently.

The filaments withdrew in an instant, and her golden "cloud" deactivated.

"COME SEE THE GAMES!" The man in the basket collapsed onto the floor, shitting himself as he dropped, looking thirty years older than he had just moments ago. "Our MIGHTIEST charioteers..............warriors braving the lion's maw.........FREE BREAD........and sausssages........" he finished wearily.

His eyes closed, and he quickly passed away.........

"Why so short a meal, papa?" Ereshka asked.

"His culture stock was low, ebfêl (child). If you had kept feeding, a part of that rot would have taken a part of you." Mors looked fearful for his daughter. "Do you understand?"

258

Salted Plastic: The Comedic Horror of Gentrification

"I.....I think so, Oüthr." she replied, not really understanding at all. "But I am still hungry. Can we not open the second basket?" she asked pleadingly.

Mors Mercator, former Malku of Isatum, and trans-dimensional trader of a diminished race that had settled on this mudball of a planet that him and his saw as nothing but a trough, looked at his daughter and realized that as powerful and manipulative as him and his were, that far far into the future, and after several millennia of building their power hold on this plain of existence........that his tribe was pretty much fucked!

As he sat brooding he heard the contents of the second basket speak; Ereshka obviously couldn't wait and, her appetites high, had opened the second course.

Listening closely, Mors could tell that the tone, content and quality of nourishment in the second basket was much more substantial than the former. An "undomesticated" native, taken from off the road at random during their travels; the stock of culture in this one had not yet been polluted by his people.

"......and Dian Cecht did fashion of silver an arm for Nuada, so as to restore him worthy of being king....."

Both Ereshka and Mors were immediately fascinated by every word coming out of the mouth of the woman in the black leather basket. She was sturdy, well-muscled, much stronger looking than almost any Roman male........with copper curls and emerald eyes.

"Through and from the Brú na Bóinne came the Tuatha Dé Danann.................the wings of Badb, Phantom Queen...........the waves of Manannán mac Lir..........."

This time, both Ereshka and Mors sprouted golden clouds that inched towards the woman. The filaments of their clouds setting into her, the gold in Mors hair began to brighten. He looked at his daughter, seeing her as only his people could via their blood bond. He watched the silver waves of her hair as they became richer, her ivory skin gaining hues of red, the lavender color of her eyes becoming more distinct. He

259

was relieved that the "food" at the table was safe for her, its inherent nourishment not yet spoiled by him and his people taking over and corrupting the natural conditions necessary to create it.

Mors saw a bit into the future as they fed; one day what his people made out of this emerging cult known as Christianity would usurp the culture that he was currently savoring. They would codify the tales, reiterate them poorly, and weed out all soul within. It would all become a watered down arm of their propaganda leash via state and church. These stories would cease to be passed down orally by the campfire, and began to be enacted on the stage, or handwritten into bound parchment which only the wealthy could gain access to. As he fed and contemplated all this with his eyes closed, his concentration was all of sudden broken by.....

"AND THE FIERY SPEAR AND LAW OF LUGH LÁMFADA......BANE OF YOU BASE FOMORIANS WHO HAVE NO STAKE IN OUR BLOOD OR LAND......" The woman had become quite lucid and menacing, and the edges of the basket began to deteriorate. A cloud of her own, colored in shades of copper and ebony, crept out of her, and immediately disintegrated both Mors and Ereshka's golden clouds.

Mors, sobering up, yelled in the growing shade of the woman's shadow fire. "NOT DOMESTICATED, THIS ONE............."

Sound ceased off and on; he turned to face his daughter, fearful for her safety, and then rushed the woman in the basket, as Ereshka's vision was clouded.

"Balor.........and your filthy spawn, Ethniu both.......WE ARE NOT FOOD, YOU FILTH! YOU FOUL DEAMHAN!"

Ereshka struggled to find her father in the darkness of the copper fire; one second seeing, another hearing.........alternately not hearing, not seeing.

After a moment she saw her father's face, in between a whirlwind mosaic of copper motes and liquid crow feathers. He smiled and sent all that he could manage into her sub-material storage unit;

various contents of his multi-millennia long life, pertinent information about their people, where to go for safety, what to avoid, and what to seek out for survival.

Seeing all this sudden info in her mind's eye, and mistaking the information transfer as a sign that all was well, Ereshka was interrupted mid-thought by a loud……..

-SNAPT-

The copper fire diminished, and Ereshka looked in horror as the woman in the basket stepped out, her father's corpse held by the throat in her grip…….

Scared witless, Ereshka backed up into the corner of the pavilion. The troupe members outside could be heard rustling in response to the commotion in the tent. The woman approached her in slow calculated steps, still dragging her father's dead body by the throat.

Mere feet away from Ereshka, she looked down at her with the face of hell itself, her eyes orbs of glowing emerald, an aura of charnel ash and wisps of darkness coming off her body. She smiled down at the frightened girl, her mouth opening wide. Her teeth were veined with what looked like crawling fissures of fire, and a blinding white glow shined at the back of her throat.

"Hungry, are we?" she said in Ereshka's father's voice as she tossed his limp body at her feet. A charred pole, sharpened to a point, manifested in the woman's left hand. It was engraved with an unfamiliar alphabet…………wisps of the dark copper fire which had previously filled the entire room, rolled off the pole……..a helix of crows feathers spiraled down the thing. Understanding that the woman in front of her obviously intended for Ereshka to eat her own father, the girl immediately passed out…………

Salted Plastic: The Comedic Horror of Gentrification

Waking up hours later, Ereshka found the woman gone, the pavilion on fire.........and her father's corpse neatly bifurcated and placed into both baskets. Crying and inhaling smoke, she managed to roll both baskets outside, hoping for the help of her father's workers......but they were all slaughtered, each and every one. She cried as she stared at the two baskets, curled up on the dirt, hugging her knees..........

The fired died, and the dawn started in the distance; something about it struck a new fear in her heart, though she did not know why.

Ereshka quickly ran to the basket containing the upper half of her father's body. Reaching in, she felt around for his right hand, and pulled off his pinky ring, a silver band with the sigil of an olive, a triangular gem below the olive. Standing up, seeing that the sun was brightening further, she ran for the nearest woods.................a faint black mist with motes of gold left behind in her wake.........

Salted Plastic: The Comedic Horror of Gentrification

September 15, 1945, Fleet Street, London

"Es ist nicht mehr sicher hier, Victoria!" A fat bloated member of the British House of Lords screamed as he rushed to clothe himself in the dark. The home shook violently as the sound of air raid sirens blared in the background; dust shook loose from the ceiling as shards from the chandelier splintered on the floor.

"Disgusting!" Baroness Victoria Kain thought. "His German is absolutely awful, this one." Completely unshaken by the bombing taking place outside, she relished the man's futile struggle; he'd be dead in approximately two minutes and thirteen seconds, and then Victoria would be on her way back to her "superiors" in Berlin. She thought about whether or not she should stay and watch while lighting up an expensive French cigarette with a hand gloved in designer suede.

It really didn't matter; she'd been here all day, keeping him "occupied", knowing full well that the blitzkrieg would take place today in this area of London. No doubt Untersturmführer Schlangenhammer would be surprised to find her in his war room in a few moments, believing that Victoria's role as bait in the middle of a mass air raid would leave her with no escape.

At this point she could care less; her mission, per the orders of her real superiors, was simply to ensure that this sack of shit whimpering in the corner was yet another casualty of war. His death would become more wood for the fire; more propaganda to fan the flames of patriotism for the Allies, and yet another victory to elevate the egos of the Axis, neither of them realizing they were both being manipulated by Victoria and her people.

The room shook with final violence. Windows shattered, the floor buckled a bit, a heavy scent of fire began to permeate everything, and the walls began to crack as Victoria stood unmoved in deep thought, exhaling her cigarette.

Salted Plastic: The Comedic Horror of Gentrification

The man, having finished dressing, rushed to her side, no doubt as some pathetic attempt to appear chivalric. It was sad, this final act designed to veil the reality that he was just a scared little boy looking last minute for his mother's skirts. He cared nothing for Victoria whatsoever; this was just pure and undiluted fear on his part, a need to be close to somebody......anybody that would tell him everything was going to be ok.

Victoria, snubbing out her cigarette on the expensive Persian carpet, thought of her father, Mors Mercator, who had died only a few blocks away from where she now stood, burning in those baskets almost two thousand years ago.

A curtain fell to the floor as the home shook again, letting light into the room. Victoria instinctively backed away from the light, and stood there wearing nothing but her red and black Jantzein bullet bra, garters and gloves, her brown curls tied back in a leather ribbon bound with a silver death's head clasp; Lord Cumberlan had a fetish for "nazi kink."

"Gross old badger!" Victoria thought, looking at the British Lord cried at her side, the tears streaming through his ugly walrus mustache, all bravery at this point completely sapped out of him. She smiled heavily at his fear.

Grabbing a Huego Basse leather trench coat off a chair, Victoria took a small "taste" of the fear this man released in his last moments; just a quick drink to be utilized as energy for her journey. Satisfied that what she took would be sufficient, she slung the coat loosely over her shoulders, lit up another cigarette..........and then dematerialized out of the room, back to her puppets in Berlin, who had no idea that she was neither German, or any other race on this planet.

The broken old fool dropped to his knees in response to her disappearing act...........just as a section of the ceiling collapsed on top of his head.

Salted Plastic: The Comedic Horror of Gentrification

Monday, November 2, 1:42am

Keys rattled in a lock.

Footsteps coming inside.

"De quien es esta casa?" a young female voice whispered as the apartment door shut.

Victoria's body trembled in the dark in response to this, reacting like a starved animal smelling food through an open window. She could not move, but what was left of her senses knew that the "real deal" was "on a plate" nearby.

"Es tu nuevo hogar, mi amor." Another, more familiar voice said in response; it was the waitress from the bar, that reptilian bitch who had captured her.

She heard a few sloppy kisses, and the sound of a bottle being uncorked as the two women moved furniture around in the kitchen. Victoria began to process their conversation in English, being too weak to work with anything else, even considering that she spoke every language known (and unknown) on the planet.

"Wait, no, someone's on the couch!" that first voice again. "I thought you said we would have some privacy, girl!"

"It's fine; it's just my abuela, and she's sleeping. Here, come take a look; say hi, and then we can go to my room."

"Uhhmmmm.......this is really killing the mood for me, I think I'm gonna......"

Victoria heard a loud THUMP, followed by feet skidding across the room towards her.......a light was turned on.......her blanket was pulled off..........and right in front of her, on the carpet near the couch, was a girl, probably about 23. She was a beautiful full figured morena, in a black huipil dress embroidered with colorful flowers. An ornate calavera, with tiny crucifixes, was painted on her face. She looked scared shitless as she saw Victoria, all dried up and half-dead, trembling like a zombie on the couch.

Salted Plastic: The Comedic Horror of Gentrification

The poor girl started to scramble back on the carpet as Victoria's head rattled in seizure spasms. In the full light, having gone so long without sustenance, Victoria looked even more deteriorated than she had back at the bar where she'd been captured. Her hair was almost nonexistent, finger nails black and pitted with dead blood, teeth jagged and stained, with a tongue breaded in purple scabs hanging loosely between them. The skin had come off her flesh like old rice paper……….. and her breath, wheezing out towards the frightened girl on the carpet, was a bouquet of rotten fish entrails and hepatitis flatulence.

It was both nauseating and terrifying, those last few moments; the girl, too scared to even stand up, her heart rate caustic………scene and scent making tears and bile well out and up from her eyes and throat…………and then out of nowhere she dropped into a trance, sat calmly on her shins, and began reciting something.

"Heat up the comal………..charring chile de árbol y ajo….."

A faint typing could be heard in the background.

"…………letting the patas simmer on a low heat……prepping masa on the side for……….."

The typing continued as Victoria, now sitting up on the couch with a bit of returning strength and stature, leaned heavily on her knees, listening to the girl's litany. An almost imperceptible thread that looked like floating tar, connected her and the girl.

"………mincing onion, cilantro, and……………toss in the hominy and bay leaf…….."

-tap-

-tap TAP-

Victoria's face began to fill out, her hair was thick and rich again; a healthy shade of brown with grey streaks; she now looked like a well-

266

kept woman in her late forties. The dark thread had grown denser, now flecked with intermittent motes of gold.

-TAP tap tap-

"........into the bowl with oregano, sliced rabano, repollo y......."

-tap TAP TAP tap-

Unlike the man in the basket all those millennia ago, the girl on the floor did not age; Victoria's feeding habits (and those of her people) had......."evolved" over time.
    ".......aguacate..................queso fresco con tus tortillas.........."

-Tap TAP tap tap-

"I think that's the last of it." Victoria heard the waitress say, along with the sound of a laptop closing shut as she oriented herself, and stood up off the couch. The girl slept soundly on the floor now, muttering something inaudible.
    "There's a mirror in the bathroom," the waitress said, "feel free to walk around; the front door is locked, just you and me here."
    "And your little friend!" Victoria commented, indicating the girl on the floor as she walked to the bathroom and opened the door. She leaned over the old porcelain sink with its antique handles, and took a brief look around. This was obviously one of those "renovated into the nostalgic appeal of Old LA" apartments that transplant gentry fell head over heels for. They loved dropping mom and dad's hard earned money indiscriminately into places like this because they believed that the thematic value of being housed in an authentic LA architectural artifact like the Maylord building on Wilshire Boulevard, or the Pouglais building

267

on Spring Street, would somehow transform them into an authentic Angelino..........idiots!

Gazing at her reflection, gently plucking at her lashes and running fingers through her brown curls, Victoria looked pleased. She had the face and body of a girl in her mid to late twenties again, and all her strength and abilities had fully returned.

She walked out of the room, and sat down at the kitchen table, opposite the waitress, who was now busy pouring two shots of La Grita tequila. She had changed into a pair of boxers, and a ragged old red tank top with a faded yellow hammer and sickle screened onto the front........generic revolutionary crap purchased at some "subversive" rock shop or tourist t-shirt spot, no doubt.

"You know, I could kill you right here and now." Victoria said.

The waitress took a shot, and stared up at Victoria. "So why haven't you?" she smiled.

"Notwithstanding the fact that you saved my life.......I want to hear what you have to say; why you went through so much risk and trouble to get me here and such. Also, I need the byproduct........." This last she said with a finger pointed at the waitress' laptop.

"My name is Alina." the waitress said in response, sliding the second shot of tequila across the table with expert precision, not a drop spilled.

"Alina?" Victoria questioned, picking up the shot glass, and downing the tequila without looking away from the girl.

"Alina Peters." the girl said, as if her name was supposed to elicit familiarity. "And yes, I do have a lot to say, a lot to do.........." she paused, a contemplative look on her face, ".............things so important that I risked my life to capture a level 80 baron."

"I'm listening." Victoria replied.

"It's going to be a long presentation, Ms. Kain; I think you better finish your meal first." Alina slid the laptop across the table.

Salted Plastic: The Comedic Horror of Gentrification

Victoria opened it, and took a look at the recipe that Alina had catalogued from the girl on the floor........her forced relinquishment of an old family recipe...........the sacred spice and substance that was hers and her people's which Victoria and Alina had now stolen for the purpose of what appeared to be some sort of alchemical/parasitical cultural appropriation.

"Committed to memory." Victoria said calmly. "I'll have my realtor find a local spot to renovate, my architect and interior design people on standby to design and decorate.......and I'll hand this recipe over to my finest artisanal, streetwise rugged, "punk rock edgy", farm to table fable peddling, semantic circus menu writing, eco-conscious in name only as part of their marketing structure, chipster vendido, fusion-motivated, Bichelin star celebrity chef to mutilate."

"I think our friend has already seen the future on that account." Alina said, indicating the girl on the carpet raving in whispers.

"Yes, the disease we leave them with after we take their culture away does forge a link. It makes them hunger for the shadow play that we make out of the culture that we thieve from their heart and soul; they see it like a fortune teller ghoul after we've fed on them.......listen!" Victoria cocked an ear towards the carpet, and they both made out the faint words coming from the girl on the floor.

"...............braised tempeh and veggie bouillon pozole....."

Victoria and Alina looked unsurprised, as if what was happening was as commonplace and unworthy of comment as the dust floating in the rays of lamplight in the kitchen.

"................vegan quinoa cauliflower meal tortillas...........$26 per shared plate.....served with raspberry yuzu pico de gallo chutney......"

"So what happens to the real recipe?" Alina asked.

"Hah!" Victoria laughed. "With all that's happened tonight, I was sure you knew everything about us Barons." Victoria slid the glass back across the table, indicating that she wanted another shot.

Salted Plastic: The Comedic Horror of Gentrification

".........handcrafted horchata breve.............gluten free conchas de chalkOlattee......." the girl on the floor continued to mutter during their conversation, her voice becoming more white washed with every word she spoke.

Alina poured the tequila, and slid the glass back. "I knew enough to know that you don't actually kill your food, and that calling it a simple energy transfer doesn't do justice to what happens when you feed. Or more to the point, that that's not all that happens."

"We used to kill." Victoria smiled with menace, knocking back the tequila before she continued. "It became obvious to us later that this was unnecessary and impractical, like this planet's hunter gathers, when it finally dawned on them that growing and cultivating food was more sustainable than just taking what they could find."

"............jackfruit carneetas served over soy flour soapees with edamame pâté......."

"That still doesn't answer my question." Alina replied.

"Tenacious!" Victoria grinned, sliding the shot glass back again. "What do you really want from me? The full eating and shitting habits of my people? Maybe a couple of juicy details on our preferential methods of intercourse?"

"I asked first." Alina said calmly, already tipping two fresh shots into the glasses.

".....................refabricated, farm to table, free trade jamaica, sweetened with agave nectar cultivated in the garden of a sapiosexual indie publishing house co-op that does psychotherapy for rescue dogs.............deconstructed taquitos with avocado harissa aioli dipping sauce........." the girl on the floor finished, and then started to snore loudly.

"Where are my cigarettes?" Victoria asked, either stalling, or maybe just in plain need of nicotine before she gave Alina the full picture.

Salted Plastic: The Comedic Horror of Gentrification

Alina patiently reached into a coat that was draped around her chair, pulled out Victoria's cigarette case and Ronson lighter, and walked over to her, handing them over gently, her gesture indicating that she knew the things were antiques, and possibly near and dear to Victoria.

Victoria, seemingly reading her thoughts, lit up a cigarette, and mumbled through the filter in her lips. "He was an American aviator, and one of the very few humans that ever fucked me properly; you ask me any other questions on that account, and I really will fucking kill you!" she exhaled calmly, looking over at Alina as she sat back down at the other end of the table. "As for what I will do with the real recipe, and what we do with the true raw culture of the people we steal it from in general, us barons......"she paused, taking another drag,"..........we make it available to ourselves and whatever "culturally elite" dogs that we have in our employ; humans, reptilians, and others unknown."

Alina looked confused, both by Victoria's cryptic answer regarding the recipe/stolen culture, and by what (or who) she meant by "others unknown."

"Look," Victoria said matter of factly, exhaling again, "you want that recipe, authentic and full of all the richness of its source, then I suggest you go to Beverly Hills, Brentwood, Downtown Los Angeles, Santa Monica, Redondo or Newport Beach in a few months. It will be served small portion on a pretentious demitasse decorated with paintings of Aztec deities. The location will more than likely play some brand of bastardized mariachi in the background, and the wait staff will hand make tortillas table side in black salt molcajetes lined in copper alloy. The patrons will enjoy this at $78 per serving, and be inured to the idea that they should pair the dish with $19 agave wine 'magaritas', or $27 mezcal 'manhattans'. Freida Culöhe paintings will cover every inch of every wall, and any gentry jackass with five minutes to spare on a Vickipedia search prior to arrival, will impress their ethnic human date with how 'knowledgeable' they are on salsa making techniques and Mexican history."

Salted Plastic: The Comedic Horror of Gentrification

"Meanwhile, in places like Echo Park, Highland Park, Cypress Park...........a few of the areas I have heard tell we hive our cattle and your children in in Los Angeles; meanwhile, in these areas, the culture raped version of what we do with the authentic culture will be available for consumption; fusion tacos...........pseudo ethnic street fairs.......more mock cultural bars like the one you captured me in tonight."

"So, there's your answer. THAT.............is what we do with the culture we reave from humans; put it up for sale for us and ours, while they feed on the sad, culturally devoid mess that we make out of it through 'culinary innovation' in the neighborhoods that we allow them to live in at murderous rent prices."

"Hmmmmmm.......I guess I'll find out next time I visit mother in Silverlake........." Alina whispered.

"What's that?" Victoria questioned.

"Nothing.....nothing....I think I get it; you take their culture in not only as a way to retain your vitality, but to keep them from having any cultural identity/solidarity of their own. Meanwhile, you barons get a sustainable byproduct that you can utilize as a supplementary culture supply." Alina paused briefly and looked up. "I'll answer your question now."

"Yes, and I'll ask it again." Victoria said in all seriousness. "What kind of deal are you looking to strike with me and mine?"

"Can I have one of those?" Alina pointed towards Victoria's cigarette case.

This time Victoria stood up, and walked over to Alina. She opened the case, put a cigarette into Alina's mouth, and lit it for her.

Alina looked up and exhaled, a serious (and hopeful) look on her face as she opened her mouth. "I want you to make me human.........me and mine all do!"

Salted Plastic: The Comedic Horror of Gentrification

Sunday, October 25, 8:45pm

"..........HAHAHAHAH!" Lebanon finished a bout of laughter, and took a sip of his whisky. Vicky had been telling an old story about catching a fourteen-year old Adrik trying to get a look at her as she came out of the shower one day, his embarrassment at being caught peeping highly apparent.

"Could've hooked a coat on the thing.........it was making a teepee out of the poor kid's old sweat pants.........UH HEH HA HA HEH HAAA!" Vicky cackled while Adrik looked somewhat uncomfortable, sitting on the cot with Jasmine, a tray of half-eaten food and some empty glasses in front of them.

Jasmine's emotions had settled a bit after they'd yanked Adrik's shoulder back into place and put it in a sling. Looking fondly over at him, digging a toe into his thigh, she smiled. "Yup, from the moment I found this kid he's been a little perv." For some reason she felt a little giddy as she finished this sentence........a little off.

"I remember those first few weeks." Adrik said. "Wondering why we moved to a new location every couple of days; all those different houses, apartments, and subterranean safe spots around Los Angeles; being told we were on the run.......doing important things........it felt like I was living in a movie or something."

"Who says you are not, kid?" Lebanon interrupted, smiling and pouring another round into Adrik and Jasmine's glasses before standing up and stretching out with a big yawn. "Well...", he side glanced at Vicky, "us old fucks are tired, and I think we have embarrassed the kids long enough with our stories, no?"

Vicky wasn't anywhere close to tired.....or energized; the oil kept her somewhere in-between, but she knew what Leb was trying to do (and had done). She disapproved, and had been trying to hide that disapproval behind jokes and laughter the last hour or so for the sake of the children, but she got up all the same, and followed Leb out the door.

Salted Plastic: The Comedic Horror of Gentrification

"Good night, little possum," she said to Jasmine, "………and to you too, little rabbit." she finished, blowing an innocent kiss towards Adrik, a mock pervy smile on her face as she raised an eyebrow at him. Whatever Vicky thought/knew about what was going to happen next, she kept it to herself, saving it for a conversation with Lebanon sometime in the future.

Jasmine though, sensed that something had just happened to change her entire reality; that she was important in some way………that THEY were important………

"HEY?!" Adrik's voice broke into her thoughts, a little concern in his tone. "Hey Jaz, you got about ten seconds till it starts….."

"Huh?" she stopped him. "What starts?" she said, a confused look on her face, but she already started to "feel" it.

"He meant well, so please don't go rushing out that door and telling Leb off. I'm already seeing where this is going…….where…..doing whoing……..you see Creature???????……..."

"FUCK!" Jasmine exclaimed. She saw it all instantaneously, and all the conflicting/balancing feelings and information involved somehow placated her reactions; how could she hate Leb for forcing her to take a drug she swore she'd NEVER touch? Couldn't be mad at him now that she knew the benefit of taking it would be……….."

"Yup……" Adrik chimed in. "Kind of hard to get upset when you know the end result and potentialities to the grand total of you, me, they, we. I'll admit……..it's an ego blow to know you could never be attracted to me……….flattering to know that if you ever considered being with a man it would be….."

"You dummy!" Jasmine smiled. "Oil or not, you're like blood to me…….and besides, what's this?" She plucked at the air near his forehead, and drew her index finger away from him, as if literally picking at his mind and pulling something discorporate out of it. Whether it was really there or not, a figure of a girl appeared in thin air………….short pink and yellow hair, one hand hidden in a leather glove, a barely perceptible emerald glow radiating off of her.

"Oh, her? That's Chipotle……" he said, the oil faltering a moment as a longing look took hold of the **him** in him.

"Huh? She don't look like a bowl of shitty overpriced dog meat over a bed of under cooked and dry cilantro shit rice." Jasmine smiled. Despite the joke though, she knew who the girl really was, and what she meant to Adrik.

"Hah ha ha!" Adrik laughed. "Not the food spot; that's her cover name, Chipotle Tlaloca……..uses it to fake and make a Latina background she never really had…….its a long story……but I'm sure you know…"

"……everything, Adrik………yesssss! Fuck! An avatar of an Aztec goddess, huh? No wonder she's got you all humble and choked up…..if not totally loyal…………" at this last she smirked at Adrik mischievously. "Look at that! I guess we're sort of in……."

"……the same boat. Both of us lovesick over people we can't be with." Adrik finished. "Strange, huh? I only just tried the oil orally for the first time yesterday……knew somewhat what it could do…..but gods and devils…. "

"…….aren't too much stranger than all the rest little brother. The SOBs **(Sisters, Others, and Brothers)** always keep us in the dark till a certain age, kid…..I'm sorry…..but the whole reptilians and barons thing would have been told to you eventua……"

"…..don't matter, cause I know it all now……….what we're going to do about our little problems………………you/I/us/me/we know already too……Lebanon just started an avalanche by connecting us……"

"Yup, so let's get started. No need for us to keep sitting here talking about what we already know; this ain't no fucking comic book; fucking hero sitting there and narrating the use of their superpowers, instead of just using them and letting the reader think for themselves, and just FUCKING GETTING IT!"

She put a hand on Adrik's shoulder, a big anticipatory smile on her face. "It's time for work, kid! Take your arm out of that sling; its healed already.......another gift from the oil and the unique bond that we, me, us and you share now........"

Adrik took it off, no questions or amazement; didn't even look down; just took the sling off as if it was a given that his arm was healed, and then stood up off the bed.

"We say it....."Jasmine began.

".....and it happens, no questions asked!" Adrik smiled.

They both integrated; so many scenarios of the coming days and years filtering through their communal mind in that moment. With the oil in both of them, whenever they took it jointly from now on, Adrik/Jasmine/Jasmine/Adrik were essentially a causality crucible. Their anamnesis instigated bond was unique in that whatever they believed was going to happen would more than likely manifest into solid state reality.

"To a certain extent and limit." Jasmine smiled, finishing the narration. "Me and you can probably win the lottery eight out of ten times if we will it, but we still can't do things like manifest a dinosaur, fart laser beams, or make weapons appear out of thin air."

"Nope." Adrik grinned. "But we can win any shoot out we want as long as we say it's going to happen.....say it and believe it!"

"That said, where to first?" they said in unison. "I'm lovesick, angry, and ready to slaughter every Snake and Oligarch on this planet."

"Guns and oil................lots of guns and oil!!!" Jasmine/Adrik said, a vision of new and profound power in their near future.

Salted Plastic: The Comedic Horror of Gentrification

Tuesday, October 27, 5:30pm

"Is nude totally necessary?" Megan asked Stickleg Pabstgut as he leered over her, dandruff snowing out of his throat beard onto the bed she was laying on, posing in lingerie. He held a Mikon-B5 VLSI Dual XQB camera in his right hand, while his left hand sloshed a lukewarm can of Piss Blue Ribbon onto the floor. Megan looked a little nervous, and was starting to have doubts about Stickleg's intentions. She sat up out of the boudoir pose he had been "helping" her get into by hand, the beautiful fat around her forearms, thighs, and stomach rippling a bit as she did.

Megan was an Anglo girl, about five foot four inches, with shoulder length auburn hair and hazel eyes. She had been purposefully maintaining a weight of 160 lbs while doing Olympic weight lifting for about 3 years now, the reasons why culminating in what had brought her here today, to Stickleg's apartment.

Dropping his beer onto the floor of his newly renovated, former office space, Downtown LA loft, Stickleg sat at the edge of the bed next to her. "Look, I know you're nervous, but I do this all the time; nothing sexual about it, I swear!"

This last he said with a look unmistakably directed right at her crotch, hoping that his $6K camera, expensive film school degree, and the framed fashion magazines on his apartment walls would be enough to convince her that his intentions and professionalism were legit. Waiting not so patiently for her answer, with a dumbfuck look on his face, he exhaled in frustration in her direction, his breath an admixture of shitty beer and tofu cock. Not getting the response he felt she owed him (no questions asked), Stickleg stood up quickly..............and stomped like a pathetic little child over to what was supposedly a desk across the room, his wimpy legs and puny arms a stark contrast to his heavy belly. How the fuck these elitist trust fund gentry transplants manage to be scarecrow status in every way but their stomach is beyond me; probably

Salted Plastic: The Comedic Horror of Gentrification

too many nights pretending to be poor, drinking Piss Blue Ribbon even though they can all afford top shelf liquor.....who knows?

The "desk" was a highly valuable piece of "art"..........or so Stickleg had said earlier, when they'd entered his apartment after meeting on the patio of Le Rat Pleurnichard, Stickleg's favorite spot for performing his petty little displays of value demonstration.

Megan looked at him searching through the $17k desk, made out of an old Caramenggia car hood, and an antique steamer trunk wrapped in barbed wire that had once been a very interesting piece of Dada art, until Stickleg had purchased and mutilated it in order to commission this custom made piece of overpriced shit that he was currently rifling through. It was mounted onto mannequin calves that had once "masturbated Dick Avidung, a famous 1960s photographer!", or so Stickleg had said earlier, when he'd given Megan a tour of the place, making sure to comment heavily on all the expensive bullshit he owned; his little petty ass way of emphasizing his supposed worth as a human being.

Every piece of Appellé hardware and design equipment imaginable littered his upstairs "studio", along with a professionally constructed cyc wall that Stickleg had had installed (even though he had never used it and never would) to add to the myth that he was a BIG SHOT CELEBRITY PHOTOGRAPHER!!! The majority of the place was all wood floors and luxury furniture that was designed to imitate the feel of a "rugged and poor" urban aesthetic......typical pseudo slumming nonsense that gentry loved because their clueless nature is totally oblivious to the fact that no one that's actually poor buys their little "I'm roughing it because I live in the safe part of the inner city!" song and dance. His bathroom was tiled in gold veined black marble, and had a voice activated touch free smart shower, with an expensive A.I. program that told Stickleg just how much of a special little snowflake he was every morning. The kitchen had chrome and copper appliances, and a pantry stocked with truffle salt, truffle oil, pollen spice, Persian saffron, edible gold flakes, Madagascar vanilla beans, and just about anything that was expensive in the culinary world, that Stickleg felt he **just had to have** for the sake of its prestige and status symbol conversational value, regardless of the fact that he knew dick close to nothing about cooking.

She watched the little turd continue to search his desk, and thought about how she'd met him earlier that day.

He'd been sitting alone at his table, talking on his phone at a volume loud enough for everyone within a four table omnidirectional distance to hear him. You know the drill; typical would be industry jerking off; no name nobodies acting like big shots in public, hoping someone will eavesdrop on their big mouth and DISCOVER THEM while they talk about their script, new album, commercial shoot, etc. Verbal bait to get laid, gain connections, and suck erections. People like Stickleg utilized these little monologues because their skills and personality alone were incapable of garnering true affection, because they were too creatively bankrupt to gain recognition for talents that they didn't really possess; connections over creativity was their motto.

Megan, not knowing any better, was sooooo impressed though; listening to Stickleg sit there, cum burping his convo into his cellphone, laying it all out. He'd been talking to an agent about his latest photo shoot for Urban LA, a bi-monthly magazine for LA transplants that gave a "heads up" on everything that was LA-centric; from fashion to "street" jargon; from eateries for "locals" to pop culture lessons on LA history. The zine was essentially an instruction manual on how to fit in and make the dying out stock of LA locals believe you were one of them so they wouldn't hate your guts for raising the cost of everything in their neighborhood.

In truth, Stickleg Pabstgut wasn't talking to his agent, and didn't really have one to begin with, as he had no hardcore interest in working at all, since mom and dad were footing the bill for his loft and lifestyle in **BIG BAD LA!** After graduating from Mountebank New Hollyyork Film School in Burbank, at the ripe young age of 37, Stickleg had told "mam and pap" back in Connecticut that he was "interning", and waiting for that big break!!!! In order to keep the cash flowing in on the monthly, he periodically phoned up "mommy" and told her ALL ABOUT his latest conquests in the industry; the conversation Megan had heard earlier was exactly that; another multi-purpose jam session designed to simultaneously milk his wealthy parents back home, and draw in any listeners that might think he's worthy of being contracted or dated.

Listening to him drone on and on with his over-haired rectum of a face, she had become convinced that it was destiny that had drawn her into the café that afternoon for her $22 avocado toast and $10 lavender breve. The place was sooooooo French!!! Which, in her culture-branding fed mentality, meant that only REALLY REFINED AND CONNECTED people ate there. Walking over to Stickleg's table, Megan had laid it all out, that she was in Downtown for the day from Covina, looking for a few spots to take photos to submit to her agent. How she was considering dropping out of college and pursuing a career as a plus size model, that her dream was to someday be on the banners at mall outlets like Toarred and Mama Melon.........and then eventually open her own plus size boutique clothing store on Abbot Kinney Boulevard.

The little maggot had hung up his phone lightning fast, hoping she hadn't seen "Mommy" on his caller id. After an hour long exchange of ego inflating comments, she'd agreed to come back to his place a few blocks away off Broadway and 3rd.

Megan finished her recollection of the café and Libt ride back to Stickleg's loft; she'd suggested walking back for a bit of exercise, but this had been met by a reaction that was the first indication of Stickleg being nothing but a soft handed pretentious little shit. He'd immediately sneered at the idea and said "I'm not really into strenuous activity and sweating......at least not for exercise." The sentence had been finished with an obvious and definite stare right at her tits. The two-minute drive back to his place had felt a bit uncomfortable after that stare, but she'd quickly gotten over it the minute she saw how "upscale" his apartment was. She thought about how amazed she'd been, seeing that the place was two stories, with a full bar, and a floor to ceiling library, complete with sliding-track oak ladder and shelves.

".......hey......HEY!"

-SNAP SNAP-

She came out of the memory, hearing Stickleg Pabstgut next to her, snapping his fingers right in front of her face like the rude entitled piece of shit that he was.

"I think this'll get you going, relax you a bit before we finish the shoot...."

"Huh?" she looked up, finishing her thoughts, those dreams of Stickleg's amateur photo "skills" getting her some modeling gigs fading out as she stared directly at what looked like a flesh colored peanut shell with a strip of powdered sugar laid on top of it..........and then it dawned on her right then and there; this guy was just a well-heeled loser! There was no future for her here, and she should probably be at home studying for her exams at Cali Poley Pomona, not day dreaming in the apartment of some rich bitch with a cornichon cock covered in cocaine.

Staring up at Stickleg, she gave him a look of complete disgust and disappointment.

"What, you don't party?" Stickleg said, sounding a bit nervous, somehow absorbing by osmosis that his little game was up.

Megan stood up, grabbed her clothes off a nearby chair, and made for the bathroom.

"Hey, what gives?!" Stickleg screamed.

281

Megan, still walking away, half turned in his direction. "Look, I'm sorry, but this is just **not gonna happen!!!** Please put that thing away before I call the cops!" she yelled as she walked into the bathroom and slammed the door.

Stickleg ran to the bathroom door, cocaine sprinkling off his little trisket weenie. He was pissed; nobody did this to him......NOBODY!!!!!!

Fuming intensely, he knocked gently on the door (trying to maintain the performance), and then started pleading. "Hey, I'm sorry about that; that was uncalled for. I'm pulling my pants up right now, I promise........Megan? Just come back out and finish the shoot." His voice became more and more pathetic by the second; little shit was desperate to get his wimpy little caterpillar wet.

In the bathroom the sound of heals clicking on the floor could be heard; Megan had finished dressing. The door opened in a fast swing, probably designed to hit Stickleg, or at least get him to get the fuck out of the way. Megan trudged out, and was halfway across the room before Stickleg caught up to her. "Hey, you didn't need to change in there! I mean, you changed in front of me earlier, so what's the big deal?" he said in contrived casual fashion, as if he wasn't concerned at all that his plans had gone to shit, trying real hard to fake it. But his energy gave it away; fucker was an expert con-artist, and Megan was waaaaay beyond buying it.

"Lingerie's on the floor in the bathroom, asshole!" she said to his face, smiling. "You say one more word, and I really will fucking call the cops!"

At this he dropped the act; Megan meant business and had seen right through his bullshit and sub-bullshit, so now it was time for him to "get tough", and be the man that he really wasn't. Smiling back at Megan, and clicking a transponder in his pocket that acted as a remote for the front door, a grim look appeared on his face. "Cops, huh?" he smiled. "Go ahead and call em; MY DADDY is a criminal defense lawyer, and he's friends with every judge, and every major news corporation in EVERY metropolitan city!"

"Bullshit!" Megan yelled. "Just another one of your tricks."

"Maybe." Stickleg still smiled, now in true-self mode, no more covert bullshit; the contrast between Stickleg the act, and Stickleg the confident little rat told Megan's gut the truth; the little shit wasn't lying.

"That's better." he said in a grease-weasely voice, recognizing in her facial gestures that she saw it, that his words were no bluff. Megan reassessed it all in an instant; his apartment alone was the strongest indicator of the truth. The fact that someone as weak and pathetic as him could never accomplish and retain this type of lifestyle on his own was highly indicative of the fact that he must have very wealthy (and possibly powerful) people taking care of him.

"Look", she said calmly, "I'm just going to leave." The venom in her voice had dropped a bit; she knew, if need be, that she could kick the shit out of this little asshole, but legally, coming from no money, no connections, the ability to battle someone as well connected as he claimed to be was nil, and that...........

"You're not going anywhere." Stickleg interrupted her thoughts, walking back to his stupid overpriced fake artist desk, and pulling out a little baggy. "You and me are going to chill and make up...........that's what friends do, no?." His voice was calm, and matter of fact, sure that everything was going to go his way, full of mock placation and the tones of a self-assured axiomatic politician..........fucking little bastard!

Megan ran to the door, and started tugging on it hard, banging on the glass window set into it that had been monogrammed with Stickleg Pabstgut's initials......and an eye of a toad right below them.

"Don't bother...........," Stickleg said, his back to her, licking some cocaine residue off an index finger. ".......glass won't break, doors locked, and my family owns this entire floor, so nobodies gonna hear shit."

Salted Plastic: The Comedic Horror of Gentrification

"You FUCKING LITTLE SHIT, LET ME THE FUCK OUT OF………….." MEGAN started as she turned around, but was drowned out by the sound of glass shattering in the bedroom.

"What the fuck!" Stickleg yelled, grabbing a pistol out of his desk, and running for the bedroom.

Megan heard a soft thump the second Stickleg made it through the bedroom door………and saw him go airborne, his body travelling a few feet off the floor as it flew through the doorway. He landed HARD, the middle of his spine impacting heavily into the edge of a nearby kitchen counter.

"AIIIEERNNNNGGHHH!" Stickleg scream-gurgled in agony, a few vertebrae more than likely now cracked and splintering into his central nervous system.

"Damn, so that's what they really look like?" Megan heard a male voice inside the bedroom.

"Yup, and they're only easy to kill when they're still like this." A female voice said, all calm and casual, as if the discussion taking place in the bedroom was just about every day shit, and there wasn't a semi-paralyzed megalomaniacal overgrown brat on the floor of the kitchen. "I'm usually pretty humane about this, but I want you to see what happens when you're not."

A short little Asian girl came out of the bedroom, along with a taller African American guy with platinum blonde hair, both of them younger than Megan. They wore leather biker jackets, black gloves, and heavy boots with metal shin guards. Megan just stood by, not saying a thing, thinking maybe she should call the police, but wanting to see what these two were obviously going to do to Stickleg; some measure of hidden menace and cruelty in her manifested....

"……m……m……..Megan……." Stickleg whined in pain on the floor. "…plee…..plee……please call the cops….."

His plea for help disgusted her; little shit was pretty much ready to commit coerced rape on her mere minutes ago, laying out his arsenal of reasons why he'd get away with it; locking her in here, telling her how it was going to be. Her blood boiled......she wanted to see him tortured.

"Careful with that!" the girl and guy said to her in perfect timing. The girl leaned over Stickleg, a curved blade in her hand, while the guy walked over to the bar and opened the mini fridge. "A healthy amount of hate for those who have wronged you is necessary for survival...."

".......but too much disdain for monsters....." the guy continued the sentence, now knocking back a beer he'd grabbed from the fridge.

"..........and you run the risk of not seeing the monster within." the girl finished, a handful of Stickleg's cheek in her hand as she took that wicked looking knife, stretched out Stickleg's cheek like the skin on a chicken thigh......and then sheared it right off, sending a spray of red and blue across the marble floor of the kitchen.

"EEEEYARRRRRRRRRRRRR!!!!!!!" Stickleg yelled in agony as the girl grabbed for the other cheek, and then stopped and stood up. Both her and her male friend looked at Megan in unison.

As she stood up, Megan could see that the back of the girl's jacket was painted with some sort of acronym..............SOBs in bright red surrounded by various symbols (or letters from unknown alphabets?) that Megan didn't recognize. Even considering the crazy violent nature of the situation, something about those symbols got her conscious curiosity going. She felt a little dizzy all of a sudden...........her conscious curiosity, and her unconscious.........a raid by the communal unconscious on the darkest parts of her..............

"She wants to try." they interrupted Megan's thoughts, talking in unison again, the girl turning her head and looking at Megan, the guy now across the room, admiring all the books in the library that he knew Stickleg kept just solely for decorative purposes.......displaying them for their conversational value to make himself seem introspective and deep even though he'd never read more than a page or two out of each of them.

Salted Plastic: The Comedic Horror of Gentrification

The guy turned around, walked over to the pistol Stickleg had dropped earlier, and picked it up. He walked up to Megan, and put it into her hands with so much respect and reverence, that the act almost mimicked the ritual of a ring and proposal. "Go ahead, give it a try." he said, patting the top of her hand with an affectionate look in his eyes.

Megan didn't know what to say. Was she really vindictive enough for this? Was this really happening? Were the shooting lessons she used to take off the 210 East still sharp? And why the fuck did Stickleg have snake scales behind all that blood on his face? She just tried to stop thinking about it all, and looked up, pointing the gun at Stickleg, a half crazed look on her face.

"My names Megan." she said, letting off a few shots into Stickleg's knee and shin, smiling maniacally.

"We're Jasmine/Adrik." the girl and guy replied while Stickleg screamed in agony in the background.

Salted Plastic: The Comedic Horror of Gentrification

....

A half hour later, and they were still at it, Stickleg now barely conscious after losing an ear, having had a few fingers broken with a beer stein, and two ribs scrubbed raw with a cheese grater, and then breaded in Ajaks powder. Jasmine stood near Megan, her cigarette smoke creating a blue mist in the fading daylight coming through the windows. Adrik was sitting on a leather zafu near the library, a copy of "City of Silica" in his hand.

And Megan?

Megan was still putting in "work", while asking the last in a long line of questions.

"So, is that penis this thing has real?" she asked.

Jasmine cocked an eyebrow, as if she could see something she had just heard, a brief sense of worry settling into her gut. It faded quick, whatever it was......but still......

"It's synthetic." Adrik answered Megan's question, still reading, confidently explaining what the oil revealed to him more and more about the all and all. "But a complex array of pseudo-nerves make it very 'real' for him."

"Good!" Megan replied. "He looks sleepy." she smiled, and then let off two rounds into Stickleg's groin.

"AHHHHGGRRRRR........eeeennhhh......uuuhhh.........." he screamed, tears rolling down his face as he came full alert; drool mixed with violet colored blood dribbled out of his mouth while he sobbed like a child. Megan wasn't moved at all; she grabbed a bar stool, and swung it right into his head, her full body weight transmitted into it, bending her knees and pivoting on her heels. This procured the desired effect, turning his body over from where he had been slumped against the kitchen counter. Stickleg's jaw SHATTERED as his faced stopped the momentum of the turn on the kitchen floor.

Adrik looked up from his book, a little concerned about how heavy this was getting, reptilian or no reptilian. He watched Megan let off five rounds into Stickleg's tailbone, ass cheek, perineum, and rectum. His stomach felt acidic watching this, and for the first time, the oil told him nothing.

Jasmine put out her cigarette, patted Megan on the shoulder, and then started walking over to Adrik. "Hey? What's wrong kid? That things not even human..........just chill little brother!" Her body language was off, warp/changed from one second to the next; she looked at him differently............certainly not like he was her "little brother."

"Ummmm, Jaz, where are you?" he asked, no longer knowing his friend........his sister.

"How do I kill this thing?" Megan broke into Jasmine and Adrik's exchange.

Jasmine stopped halfway across the room, stared right at/into Adrik another second, microbeads of sweat appearing wherever he could see her exposed skin, her chest heaving fast as she looked at him in a way that definitely was not sisterly..........licking the sweat off her upper lip while her eyes flared in Adrik's direction, and then she abruptly turned around, and answered Megan's question, walking backwards towards Adrik as she did. "You don't kill it, Megan; we're not done here yet."

Adrik was still confused, but as Jasmine got within a few feet of him he noticed something..........something new and out of the current range of the oil's assessing capabilities. A few wisps of what looked like black smoke, veined in purple, emanated off of Megan. The "smoke" travelled across the room, and touched Jasmine, a faint strand of it all stopping a few feet short of where Adrik sat. Whatever it was, it was as if it was using Jasmine as some sort of beacon to get to Adrik. He became a little drowsy and unfocused.

Salted Plastic: The Comedic Horror of Gentrification

"............by-product of her hate, the... oil..........Jas............sorrow......unrequited love........something else I can't see.........." he heard a faint familiar voice in his head, some sort of warning as he fell half asleep for a split second....and then snapped back alert immediately, feeling movement.

THE ZAFU! Jasmine was dragging him across the room, tugging on the cushion he was sitting on. He didn't know what was happening; if that was Tlaloca he had just half-dreamed warning him or what, but.........slipping out.......losing focus........

"Good..............good!" he heard Megan say. "Let's end this right; physically this fucker has had it; time for some mental and emotional torture. Jasmine? He still thinks he's human, right?"

"Yup!" Jasmine/Adrik answered. Adrik had completely forgotten what he had been worried about a second ago; HE FELT GREAT! THEY FELT GREAT!

"This is going to be awesome!" Jasmine/Adrik/Megan smiled, leering at Stickleg with menace.

Salted Plastic: The Comedic Horror of Gentrification

Tuesday, October 27, 5:17pm

At Lydia's insistence, Miguel had gone to his place, grabbed what he needed, and come back to stay at her apartment while she was away. Lonely as shit the minute she'd left, the first thing he'd done was to hook up his PS3 to her bedroom television. Laying on the bed off and on the last day and a half, Miguel had been playing Ass Effect, a sci-fi rpg that he'd been chipping away at between his two jobs and night school for the last two years. As the main character in the story, your goal was to travel from galaxy to galaxy in an attempt to find an ass that could stay well defined and succulent in all variations of gravity.

As Miguel progressed through the game, different characters with various class and stat expertise had joined the fray. So far, he had three other characters in his party.

There was Xeelkar-Fian, a Xeelkar mercenary biochemist with a +40 intelligence rate; this boosted his ability to surgically balance every ass encountered with a perfect cellulite/fat/muscle ratio.

The android, DB-978 was the brains and charisma of the party. A "gentlewoman/man" genderfluid pleasure robot, who served the team with a boosted speech, tech and dexterity bonus; this lent it the ability to "coerce" npcs for much needed items and quest information.

And of course, Miguel's favorite, Kakliikir Nallgonaa, an assassin class smuggler with the ability to store items in "tight places". This skill made her efficient for carrying caches of weapons, heal items and armor out of dungeons when all other characters were overloaded.

Before his health issues, work overload and classes, he used to breeze through games like this in a month or two, but those days were long gone. Anyways, Miguel was enjoying it; he didn't have work till late tomorrow evening, and he needed some distraction after Lydia had dropped the bomb on him about Dagmar, not to mention the fact that "I'll be aching for sex for the next three days." Miguel finished the narration.

Salted Plastic: The Comedic Horror of Gentrification

And then, as if that thought had conjured up the devil, his phone went off, an unfamiliar area code (332) on the screen. His curiosity peaking, and a growing hard on starting to nag at his Dark Mirror pajamas, he popped a Vicodin while remembering the phone conversation he'd had with Lydia on her way to LAX. His phone kept going off unanswered..........

Salted Plastic: The Comedic Horror of Gentrification

Monday, October 26, 1:47pm

"HUH! WHAT WAS THAT NOISE!?"

That was Miguel's default ringtone going off, a sound clip from a favorite game of his. Seeing Lydia's caller ID on the screen, mere minutes after she'd left, took a little bit of the bitter loneliness out of him.

"Hey, love! What's up?" he answered.

"Hey babe, I'm on the 110 already, almost to the 105." she sounded so together, but Miguel knew better...........felt her better than how she presented herself; besides being torn up inside by the idea of being away from him, she was scared.......very scared!

"You ok, lady?" he asked, trying not to tear up in response to her stress, in reaction to the unfathomable feeling of being separated from the personification of the greatest love anomaly of all time.........finding the love of his life through a glimpse into his and Lydia's (and Dagmar's) past lives. A glimpse induced by a strange cocktail of psychedelic drugs from another dimension that Dagmar had provided. This had allowed them all to rediscover each other; the effects of the drugs had unlocked limitless pasts where all three of them had met and loved each other over and over again. Miguel's mind drifted back while Lydia answered his question; he could barely hear her, the daydream time slip pulling the rug of present "reality" from under his feet.

He had only met them a few days ago. They'd picked him up, Lydia Veidt and her ex-girlfriend, Dagmar Ashkenazic. Miguel had been slumped over in an alley in Downtown LA, crying after a fight he'd started inside the nearby club had ended with him getting kicked out, and his older brother being arrested for god knows what. Eager for any sort of distractive comfort, he'd gotten into Dagmar's car, no questions asked. The events of the night that followed defied proper description, the physical manifestations of it all the only lasting landmarks that could transcend the limitations of language and thought.

Salted Plastic: The Comedic Horror of Gentrification

He remembered Dagmar and him taking a few cheap shots at each other, throwing insults, the tension between them pretty high those first few minutes as her car cruised through Downtown Los Angeles. The ice had been broken by her offer of a strange red oil which induced, among other things, the poly-synchronous unison of all three of their minds...........windows into past lives where they had all repetitively shared a love triangle...........and the half-realization that true love had been shared between Miguel and Lydia, or Dagmar and Miguel, or possibly between Lydia, Dagmar, and Miguel innumerable times. Miguel had resisted the comfort the night's potential had offered at first, his default cynicism keeping his guard up, but Lydia and Dagmar had consistently reassured him that they weren't out to get him. They had been patient with him, the oil "showing them" his fear, the past that had beat it into him, and that the fucker just couldn't accept a good thing. The final hammer to break his reluctance to get comfortable and just enjoy the night, his good fortune, and the love and care that they wanted to give him, had been Dagmar's offer of something above and beyond even the powers of the oil.

The chālchihuitl drug/idol/mystical experience/alignment with one's godhead/pulque of Xochiquetzal..........whatever the fuck it was, had melted the last of Miguel's resolve not to trust Lydia and Dagmar. It let him see, feel, and know that nothing but heartfelt good intentions were in store for him if he gave in to the love on the table.

A night of sexual, mental, emotional and spiritual intimacy had ensued beyond anything he could have ever imagined..................but then things went sour for reasons totally unexplainable. The night had ended with Dagmar trying to kill Miguel with her bare hands, followed by her telling him and Lydia to get the fuck out of her house. There'd been a few brief hints of what almost seemed like jealousy coming from Dagmar throughout the night.........an envy for what she'd assumed Lydia and Miguel had between them exclusively. These bouts of jealousy and misunderstanding were not relevant to just the night at hand, but to

293

situations from their past lives as well. Still, Dagmar had seemingly gotten over it each time, and had even labeled it properly at one point by saying to herself "what feels right defines love……not what defines love feels right!!!!!!!"

So there had been some indication of what had possibly set her off at the end, but even so, that last part of the night was so unexpected, and completely out of character with everything else that had happened. More than that though, it was unfortunate……because there was one thing about Miguel that would make him ruminate over this, one thing that had consistently made problems worse for him in his life; Miguel could never just let a bad situation go unexplained, and stay buried………ever.

In the case of the issue at hand, he just couldn't accept that that last incident with Dagmar was just bad news with no explanation…..just couldn't let it be and let go……it just wasn't his style with anything that hurt or upset; he ALWAYS had to know why.

In short, Miguel was just too stupid to realize that sometimes it was not worth knowing, couldn't be known, or that he was better off not knowing.

"…………Miguel? MIGUEL?! HELLO!!!! ARE YOU LISTENING?!" Lydia's voice brought him out of his flashback.

"Huh, sorry babe, I was just thinking……"

"I KNOW WHAT YOU WERE FUCKING THINKING, AND YOU CAN FORGET IT! She doesn't love you! She never loved me! SHE DOESN'T KNOW HOW TO FUCKING LOVE ANYTHING! ALL SHE KNOWS HOW TO DO IS POSSESS PEOPLE………….AND YOU NEED TO FUCKING STOP! It's you and me, PERIOD!"

"I'm sorry love, but don't you think that maybe we all kept reincarnating and bumping into each other for god knows how many centuries for a reason? I mean, her jealousy, her wealth, her station of power; these are all major barriers to humbleness and understanding for someone like her………big barriers for……"

"I don't fucking believe this!!! I'm scared and sad as fuck for you.........**FOR US**............and you're defending the main source of that fear......while you sit in my fucking apartment no less!"

"Lydia, I........"

"Forget it, Miguel! I'm just trying to stay calm and believe that you're either thinking with your cock right now, or you're just naïve........OR BOTH! We'll talk later! Right now, all I'm going to say is DO NOT answer your phone for any unfamiliar numbers......DON'T answer my door.........and if you REALLY NEED TO GET OFF SO BAD, THEN FUCK ANYBODY YOU WANT.......JUST NOT THAT BITCH IF SHE SOMEHOW GETS AHOLD OF YOU!"

"Lady, I don't need anyone but you, this isn't about......"

"Goodbye, Miguel!" she finished, hanging up and leaving him to think about what his intentions and curiosity had cost him.

Salted Plastic: The Comedic Horror of Gentrification

Tuesday, October 27, 5:39pm

"And that had been that...." Miguel said out loud. "She's given a few bare bones texts since yesterday.............simple stuff like 'how are you?' and 'did anything come in the mail today?', but I'm pretty sure I pissed her off...........fuck, I don't deserve her."

He grabbed the bottle of pills, popping another, hoping the opiates would sublimate his libido, wondering who it was that had called his phone (sort of; the him in him that lingered already knew). Miguel felt awful, and knew the pills alone wouldn't be enough. He got up, grabbed the zafu he had brought over, sat down, and went through a few minutes of the old mantra recitation that he'd learned from an old Japanese Zen priest that had once been up in the hills of Highland Park. The priest had taught yoga and zazen to Miguel at his temple for years and years.....until the gentrifier hoard had priced the old man out of the neighborhood.

The rent had skyrocketed when they came to Highland Park, with all their fake ass hipster "ashrams", and "enlightenment boutiques". A bunch of them had opened on York and Figueroa; garbage shake and bake spirituality hubs for shallow and trendy morons. These places had taken away the draw of the priest's humble temple, playing on the generic ideas that the average transplant asshole had of "mystical expectations" when it came to yoga and meditation. They came for the "reality transcending" hipster zither music ("CD available to take home for ONLY $18.95!!!!"), the lame waterfall and tea initiation ceremony in the lobby entrance, and for the chance to use these places as hives for more social networking prostitution. All they really wanted was the whopping five minutes of training that it would take for them to have a few photos of themselves doing head stands and sitting on free trade hand crafted meditation cushions. After they harvested this, their usual follow-up behavior was to use it to demo their value on Shitstagram as "woke and transcendental souls" #yogi #urbanmonk #pretentiousprana

296

Salted Plastic: The Comedic Horror of Gentrification

#beingconscious #shallowidiot #attentionfishing #consumptionentity #yuppyguru #bootlegbuddhist #asanasforassholes #grabbagspirituality #mememystic #culturedilution #lifehackloser. Yuck!

The priest was gone now, but Miguel still had his lessons......even if he still didn't "get it" in a lot of ways........his anger and inability to stand the rich and privileged being a never ending battle in that regard; the priest had always told him to feel happy for other's good fortune, no matter what their station in life, but it was just something Miguel found very hard to do........that he could hardly ever do for the wealthy and privileged.

He went through the motions, focusing on his hara point below the navel; deep abdominal breathing, trying not to attach to (or let go of) it all; just neutral; no wrath of Dagmar, no argument with Lydia, no older brother being arrested, no reptilian hobosexual ex-girlfriend.

He started to drift out of it, his neck cracking itself, body moving of its own volition, joints and nerves loosening up, his breath the only thing in the whole univ..........

-KNOCK KNOCK-

-BNNT BNNT BNTTTTT-

A violent knock on Lydia's door broke Miguel's concentration. Opening his eyes, and turning his head, he began to get off the zafu, unfolding his legs out of lotus position.

He stood up, smiled and started laughing; some conscious part of him realized that normally, considering all the elements of the situation.......the fear........the love.......the violence........the longing for Lydia (and for Dagmar if he was being honest).........that considering all this, normally that knock on the door would scare him into survival mode. Normally it would make his heart drop into his stomach, and put him on guard. Shit fuck it all though, Miguel just wasn't in "normal mode" at the moment! He had a cocktail of opiates, zen meditation, true love, and the lingering effects of a few spiritual experience inducing elements coursing through him. He saw the now in now..........and it was no half-truth to say that he was in full on manic saint-mode, on his way to battle evil incarnate....he was......he was............AH FUCK IT........that shit sounds pretty fucking pretentious........LETS FACE IT.......THE FUCKER WAS JUST HIGH AS SHIT ON HYDROCONDONE!!!!!

Miguel walked to the living room, stumbling past shelves of vinyl anime statues, manga, graphic novels and dvd boxsets. He smiled in anticipation of the already mentally loading set of obscenities he was preparing to use to taunt whoever was at the door. You like that run on sentence? I know I did!

-BNNTT BNNNT BNNNT-

The banging continued as he got to the door.

"Not fucking answering, and YOU'RE RUINING MY HIGH, YOU ASSHOLE!" Miguel yelled loudly (but with no menace), his voice on a fucking cloud, the pills drowning out any anger or fear......he was just having fun fucking with whoever was banging on the door.

-KNOCK KNOCK KNOCK-

"Suck a dick you erection-deficient bitch........in fact, suck my dick!"

-BNNT BNNT BNNNT-

"You can do that shit ALL FUCKING NIGHT FUCKER......I still ain't opening the door! I'm going back to playing Ass Effect, so fuck off!"

Salted Plastic: The Comedic Horror of Gentrification

At that a purple envelope slipped under the door, followed by the sound of two heavy sets of feet leaving and trailing down the hallway.

"Damn, they gave up quick!" Miguel smiled, a little disappointed; he had a whole lot more verbal venom to throw at them that didn't get used...........oh well.

Miguel picked up the envelope and twirled it around; the front was completely blank, but on the back there was a red wax seal. He carried it over to the kitchen, laid it on the soap stone counter, and flipped a nearby switch for the overhead stove light. Holding it under the light so he could make out the seal better, Miguel saw a symbol that he was pretty familiar with.

It was a caduceus, but unlike any caduceus Miguel had ever seen in any of his books on mythology, alchemy, history, religion, philosophy, psychology, etc.

Usually a caduceus has a scepter in the middle, surmounted by a pair of wings, with two serpents coiling around the scepter from top to bottom. This one though........this one was totally different. A girl took the place of the scepter, arms uplifted as if in the position of crucifixion, her outstretched arms replacing the usual wings. The small wax stamp left little room for extensive detail, but its simplicity was not so minimal that Miguel couldn't make it all out. Wrapped tightly around the girl, in lieu of the two serpents, were two other figures. The first was a nondescript faceless man; the second one was also a man............but with the head of a lizard.

These last details of the stamp, the two men coiled around the girl, did not sit well with Miguel. The second he saw them, for reasons he had no explanation for, his heart dropped........and he felt an immediate longing for Dagmar. He thought of (felt rather) the barely perceptible pain he'd sensed in her as she stared Lydia down after striking him that last time. And he remembered something else too. How could he have forgotten that?! During the beating he had taken from Dagmar, she had seemed so eager to get him to have one last orgasm together with her.........or more specifically, inside her. That wild disparate dichotomy was psychotic; Dagmar on top of him, her hands choking Miguel, beating him with no mercy while she ground into his penis.

Dagmar's anger, Miguel's physical and emotional pain; it was toxic......COMPLETELY TOXIC..............but they had both still enjoyed the sex all the same. And then there had been that final moment when he'd tried to defend himself, which had ended with Dagmar catching his hand in her mouth, biting right through the flesh.......purring like a jaguar while she drank his blood, followed by both of them cumming simultaneously. Twisted love............completely twisted.

"How the fuck did I not think of or remember that the last couple of days?" Miguel said, looking at the dark horseshoe shape on his hand; purple teeth-shaped indentations where Dagmar had broken the flesh.

"And my cum!!!" he followed up loudly. "That shit was marbled with neon green and red!!! It had....had....that shit coiled down her leg.....wrapped around it like a.......a......" he looked over at the wax seal, how the two male figures wrapped around the girl like they had no bones.....flat and malleable like tape worms.

Miguel thought on it all, his mess of an overstuffed mind doing one of its staple favorites; making all the bad guesses, assuming and fabricating, pulling facts and pseudo-facts from every book he'd ever read or half-read...............projecting worse case scenarios. He felt like Dagmar was deep down inside just scared and in need of rescue (instead of just selfish and lethal). He wondered if Lydia was hiding something from him.

Miguel brooded and brooded and brooded, questioning EVERYTHING that might still be good in his life, worrying over who might possibly be trying to ruin him for good. He fought it for a minute, telling himself that he was just a pessimist and that he should just leave it alone.........and then he got right back at it; dumping his resolve to let it all go right into the gutter, and betting on the idea that he was just really being used in some inexplicable way, and that he would be destroyed and discarded in the end, followed by Lydia and Dagmar laughing their asses off at his ludicrous level of trust and desperation.

Numb on pills, loneliness and worry, he just sat there in the dark, the sound of the NPCs in Ass Effect jabbering on the TV in the bedroom.

"Book passage to the Fessiers Géants Colony!"
"...........Mekaageê Sabû! Quageê geel mvör KRLIK VACATION!?!?"

".............Cvor says he's always busy "working" off planet for extra money on that Tulkasian Lunar Satellite, but whenever he comes home I can JUST SMELL THE FAECAL SIROP that those Chattelèvr dance girls wear ALL OVER HIM!!!!!!"

".......................Hvïl Version 2.8 Tactical Booty Armor has ballistic plates for all your rectal protecting needs.........IF YOU NEED SOMETHING TO FUCK SOMONE'S BUTT, or some armor to protect your own, YOU'VE COME TO THE RIGHT PLACE!!!!"

Salted Plastic: The Comedic Horror of Gentrification

Monday, November 9, 11:12pm

"Nice to meet you, gUYYY! Eh heh heh heh heh!" Captain Felch Leavings greeted Pignose Diddler as he came through his front door, looking at him as if he was inconsequential, and pronouncing "gUYYY!" in a really contrived and nasally manner. This was the opening act of his attempt to play the roughneck role; Felch's cheap shot performance that was supposed to demasculinize Pignose for no good reason. This lame tough guy act immediately made Piggy mentally roll his eyes.

"One of those!" he thought with judgment, the irony lost on him that both him and Captain Felch (and Rebekah for that matter) were cut from the same cloth; full of affected personality traits to cover up for what they didn't know (or couldn't accept) about themselves; showroom behavior designed to keep everything in their unconscious mind under permanent lock and key.

Rebekah sat in the corner of Pignose's living room reading a magazine, feigning disinterest in Captain Felch's arrival, even though he'd only come over tonight at her request. She had invited him over in the hopes of killing two birds with one stone, namely, to fulfill her need for more and more male attention to fuel her self-worth, and also to meet Piggy's unspoken contractual arrangement with her......Rebekah's special hobosexual way of "paying rent."

"And I damn well deserve it! I spent a fortune on her and Jetty in Palm Springs!" Piggy thought calmly, finishing up the narration. "I just hope this guy doesn't talk too much, I can already tell this whole manly man act of his is going to get tedious.........shits making my man clitoris go limp already!"

But just then, as if on cue to his thoughts, an immediate back slap hit Piggy right between the shoulder blades.

"Eh heh heh heh!" Felch bellowed like a jackass, finishing up his harsh manly MAN back pat on Pignose. "Sooooo.....what you got to drink here, KID!?" The tone Felch used was pathetic; it was almost as if he pumped himself up on a mental makeover of biker and greaser films before he left his house. The way he was parading around Pignose's living room in his biker jacket, with his fake as fuck chest puffing bully persona; it was a joke....an absolute joke. Piggy started to mildly grind his teeth in irritation.

It wasn't even threatening to him, this whole "I'm the biggest man in the room!" act. It wasn't even cute enough to laugh at at his age........but it was fucking annoying enough to the point where he was just about to un-invite Felch from his pad, and call it a night.

Rebekah, apparently sensing Piggy's irritation, got up from his $3300 authentic Bowhouse coach. A few flies circled around her vagina, her Christian Dead nightgown/shirt was full of cigarette burns, and her hair smelled mildly of bologna and canned mackerel. In a display of one her VERY RARE moments of conscientiousness, Rebekah stepped to the bar cart between the two of them and grabbed a bottle of a local hipster hybrid transplant gentry favorite, Stachemenn's Handcrafted Semenal Street Bourbon............."Distilled Locally in The Mean Streets of Echo Park!" PFFFFT! FUCKING JOKE!

And by conscientiousness, I mean that Rebekah sensed that her hobosexual meal ticket standing was in dire threat, and that if Felch left, it would mean that her rent duties would be in overdraft..........and so would her self-image........her ability to feel like she was the most desired woman......ahem.....I mean girl in town. Displaying the bottle to the two of them, silently offering a drink, Pignose and Captain Felch both nodded in the affirmative, her interruption a welcome ice breaker to the tension.

You see, Rebekah, being the half-brained spawn of a reptilian mother that "breast fed" her on fermented pastrami drippings cultured in cigarette ash............Rebekah, being the firstborn of a self-trained penis gypsy............Rebekah, being the take now, and break it off later for the next best thing with all the skill of a world class inveterate liar.............WELL......let's just say that, as clueless as she was consciously

Salted Plastic: The Comedic Horror of Gentrification

(due to the socialization and nurturing tactics of a self-centered, sugar daddy hunting troglodytic mother)............that, despite all this, her subconscious was well aware, sharp, and totally capable of gearing her into survival mode at the drop of a hat. Translation: she knew when her "investments" were in danger, and could "adapt" quickly despite her apparent stupidity.

Rebekah could not possibly see herself or her motives in verbal terms to save her life.............but when her meal ticket, or her ability to believe that every man in the world wanted her was at stake; when this happened, Rebekah could move fucking mountains with her affected charm! Unfortunately, she didn't realize that it wasn't her at all that did the work in this regard.............at least not in the sense of inherent personality traits, or highly trained observational acumen. No, as stated in previous issues of Salted Plastic, Rebekah has various programs embedded in her body that allow her to operate above the stamina of her bankrupt heart, soul and mind.

The intricate nanomachines in Rebekah's body, with their liquid information processors, went to work. Algorithms juggled gambits, best possible instigators and outcomes were laid out, exponential minutiae was calculated......and all the while her outward appearance betrayed none of this.

And after all, how could it? The idiot had absolutely no idea that her people had put any of the above in her system..........but the contrast in her behavior when it all went to work was astounding! One minute she was her usual selfish and deluded "GIMME GIMME!" self, full to the brim with convoluted logic and hunger for the next big distraction, and the next she was an expert manipulator with the people solving skills of an elite mediator, coupled with the psychological discernment of Carl Jung himself. The nanomachines warmed up, and got ready to put their findings to work.

Rebekah absentmindedly grabbed two beer pint glasses for the bourbon, failing miserably with her natural conscious ability to get even this right.......and then the last figures clicked into place within her. It all coalesced; the best possible actions and outcomes were calculated and put to work via Reptilian Rebekah's mentally bankrupt flesh........her body just a vehicle.........the technology within her in the driver's seat.

"Uhmmm..........heh heh HEH heh........WRONG GLASSES toots!" Captain Felch Leavings chimed in.

Rebekah turned and looked at Felch, and with uncharacteristic calm, and a look of self-assurance about the all and all, she grabbed Captain's, and then Piggy's hands in turns, placing a beer pint in each hand.

"Wrong for the bourbon, sure......but we'll get to that later; have to warm up lightly before moving on to the potent stuff!" she smiled, her energy much more charming than usual, her figure and face all of a sudden much more attractive........and shit!............she didn't even smell like natto barf and old tampons soaked in Parrier water anymore; an alternating scent of lavender and sandalwood drifted off of her; another effect of the intricate devices she had running through her bloodstream. Captain didn't take much notice of it, but to Piggy, with his ability to observe others (if not himself), it was mildly unsettling, the way Rebekah had just out of the blue become sharp and hygienic, when she had exhibited neither of these traits since he'd known her.

"Probably got into my molly stash and finally took a shower for once." Piggy thought. "Whatever, at least she got this twerp to shut up for a second."

Walking to the kitchen, Rebekah held both Felch's and Pignose's attention. They saw the glamour that the nanomachines had created through a sort of pheromone based hypnosis, the chemicals warping their common sense. In front of them, as they followed behind her to the kitchen, they saw a woman with class, intelligence and selflessness, and not the usual selfish illogical slob that Rebekah really was.

As she bent over to grab beers from the fridge, it even looked like she actually had an ass for once.......instead of the upside down Frankenstein head that her butt usually resembled.

And that was that! Felch finally shut up, and Pignose considered Rebekah's rent paid in full as she came back and poured each of their beers for them, tilting the glasses properly and handing them back. Going back to the couch, she watched them watching her as they sipped their beers. Piggy gooned off towards a corner of the apartment like the mild creepbag that he was, and Felch oafishly stumbled over to Rebekah with his chest puffed out again, attempting to make it come out further than his gut and failing miserably at it.

Piggy sat down on a stool, and grabbed a box of tissues off a nearby table. Smiling with gratification, he turned down the lights, and then pressed a little button on the wall which activated several hidden cameras around his apartment.

Salted Plastic: The Comedic Horror of Gentrification

Monday, November 9, 11:44pm

-Sniff sniff-
-sniff Sniff SNIFF-
-SNIFFFFFFFFFF-

"NOOOOOOOOOOOOO!!!!!!! THE BOUQUET IS RUINED!"

-CLUNK-

"YVGËREL!!!!!!!" a gruff male voice yelled a Reptilian pejorative in pain. The audiovisual monitor's alarm had woken him up, causing him to startle and bump his foot on a nearby console.

Simon Green, AKA Mjeerh Semaibrad, a low level security guard, turned his yellow vertical irised eyes towards the monitor. On the screen a doughy human (with too much pomade in his hair) sniffed a female rep hybrid's groin as she sat on a couch with her legs spread.

A door behind Simon slid open, and a female reptilian officer stepped into the room with two cups of caffeinated mammal blood in her hands. "Fell asleep again, huh?" she asked in a bored tone.

"Yes.....yes...." Simon replied. "Watching this runt of the litter, and her sexual adventures with human males, gets more disgusting by the day......especially since her targeted prey, this Miguel Lyons, seems to be out of the picture now. I just don't understand why I have to continue surveillance of Rebekah when a glitch in her hardware has allowed her to venture off for alternative penis."

"Yes, yes, well maintenance will eventually go down there to take a look, and get her back on the job. Personally, I find her current situation entertaining."

"You would, Levoié! You, and your abnormal taste in sex."

Levoié smiled. She was well known among her crew as liberally minded and experimental when it came to intercourse; there wasn't a

307

crewman (or crewwoman) on board that she hadn't screwed or been screwed by, and she didn't mind the lot of them knowing her business. But what she was careful to hide though, was her addiction to role play. Particularly the kind that involved acts that were considered treason when committed by those in lower class reptilian society.............I'm talking about going out in mammalian drag and getting FUCKED by humans by the way.

Levoié set the cups of blood down, opened a triangular PDA, and looked at a frequently visited photo album. She stared intently at a picture of a purple haired "human" woman taking a selfie with a male companion. Looking in silence for a second or two, a longing look on her face, Levoié's heart felt heavy. Sighing deeply, she shut the PDA down, and went back to watching the audio-visual screen.

"It's funny how human logic assimilates the illogical so well, huh?" Simon asked, alluding to the stupidity of the two human males on the screen, how they so easily gave in to the lack of discretion required to not question why Rebekah had changed so drastically (in terms of visual and character quality), from one moment to the next.

"Still....." Simon continued, ".....I really don't understand what the one with the affected masculinity is babbling about. You getting this, Levoié?"

"He wanted Rebekah's primary target's reproductive leavings." Levoié said as she calmly sipped her blood.

"Say again..." Simon replied, scratching the scales on his head with a yellow claw.

"Miguel Lyons, Simon! The male that Rebekah is currently interacting with has inferiority issues that cause a mental aberration. This aberration makes him crave the semen of his male associates via their female partners. He's attempting to harvest any of Miguel's 'leavings' that may be leftover in Rebekah's synthetic vagina."

"And you know this howww?!" Simon asked lasciviously, raising an eyelid in a pervy way, always assuming that "Lieutenant Krystal

308

Salted Plastic: The Comedic Horror of Gentrification

Levoié" was ready and charged for sex whenever/however. That was the problem when you had a reputation for promiscuity among a small crew; even when being professional, in your capacity as a digitally inseminated social analyst, everyone always assumed that talk of sex meant time for sex.

"Because unlike you, I have the software for the job." she paused and tapped the side of her head. "And also, unlike you, I haven't been sleeping on this assignment……….now move over and I'll explain while we watch! And also, we ARE NOT going to fuck tonight, Officer Green!"

At this, the chrome seat Simon sat on began to shift and restructure; it became semi-liquid for a moment, extended horizontally, and then solidified again, now with enough room for both Simon and Levoié. Simon had a look of disappointment on his face (as much as reptilian paralanguage could reveal), but he shook it off quickly, put on an air of professionalism, and listened to his superior officer.

"See the straw that he just put back in his jacket?" Levoié pointed at the monitor, Felch in the middle of the scene, tucking a metal straw with mayo and frosted flakey resin on it into his leather jacket. "That's how he does it."

"Does what?" Simon asked.

"Ugh……weren't you just listening, you salumund-dicked idiot! No wonder you're still working a low level security job at your age; you don't fucking pay attention!"

"HEEYYYY! It's not salumund-sized, and you know it!" Simon protested, his feelings hurt. Salumunds were a sub-race of reptilians known for having penises so small that reproduction had to be committed via a sort of pollen-like mist that emanated from their microscopic pee pees.

At that, Officer Levoié simply smiled, and pointed at the screen. "Just watch, you idiot; I'll narrate and explain."

The lights came back up in the apartment on the screen. Pignose's lanky/pasty figure came from off camera, his pants down, and

309

his dad gut peeking out the bottom of an old Jean Luvs Gezebelle tour shirt from the 80's.

"What's wrong? Bouquet!? What bouquet?! What's he babbling about?!" Piggy turned to Rebekah. She shrugged her shoulders with a slight smile. Still relaxed and confident, she grabbed Felch by the head and pulled him towards that filthy rot hole of hers that was masquerading as fresh paradise. The nanomachines were still at work; a scent of guava misted out of her panties…….but Felch still stood up and backed away in disgust.

"NO! IT'S RUINED!" he pointed at her crotch. "I came here for a Lyons Homme Gicler, and instead I GET WHAT!? A blend……..A FUCKING BLEND!!!!!!!!"

"I'm with the human on this one." Simon said as they continued to watch Captain Felch on the screen. "What the fuck is that closet case, Boob's Bigg Boy with a mustache looking bitch babbling about?"

"He wanted only what Miguel Lyons had left in her; obviously Rebekah has been inseminated by someone else, someone that Captain Felch Leavings has no social connection to. To him, the presence of these extra male leavings are tantamount to spoiling the 'bouquet'." Levoié explained.

"Oh, I see…..I think I get it now….sort of………..still, how can he tell?"

"He's got super-faggot sense." Levoié smiled jokingly.

"What?! You serious?"

"Shhhhhh…..just watch." Levoié began typing up commands on the console, and another screen lit up, this one a POV from Rebekah's eyes.

"Nice!" Simon exclaimed. "You hacked the software in her eyes; I was using the hidden cams in the human's apartment up till now; I lost the codes to log into Rebekah, and I didn't want to look stup……."

Salted Plastic: The Comedic Horror of Gentrification

"Just watch!" Levoié mildly barked, engrossed now in the POV feed coming from Rebekah's eyes, her body temp rising a bit, wishing she was someone……….something……..something she wasn't.

"Who was it?!?! WHO SPOILED THE MIGUEL MILK!?!?" Felch screamed, his anxiety breaking his act, the man mannerisms gone now, his voice a high pitched girly squeal.

"No, no…..we can do this!" Rebekah chimed in, a little nervous, her calm confidence starting to break. She grabbed Piggy by his little bubblegum strip dick, and pulled him towards her while simultaneously reaching for Captain Felch.

While this all unfolded, Levoié started entering commands on the console again, her tongue hanging out a bit……..breath labored and erratic……….the cosmetic humanesque breasts she'd paid two month's salary for heaving under her uniform.

"What now?" Simon asked.

"I'm inputting my observational data into Rebekah's nanos via satellite so she can adapt to the situation; this Captain Felch seems to be only interested in the semenal leavings of men he's familiar with; I think I know how to fix this."

On the Rebekah POV screen was a first person view of her right hand attempting to get Pignose "ready", and her left hand beckoning towards Felch as he backed away. Her voice chimed into the audio of the feed.

"It's just his!" she pointed at Pignose. "You KNOW HIM; you just met!" she said in a placative manner, like she was training a dog that had just shit on the carpet, trying to get him to come over and sniff her hand after surprising him with a beating. After a few seconds of Rebekah's placations, Felch started to sidle back over, the apartment camera showing him from behind, his posture straightening out in confidence, his body language indicating that crisis had been averted as he walked back in a TOUGH MAN posture!!!!

311

"Oh really?!" he smiled, something of his contrived personality edging back into production. "So it's just Miguel and this KID (pointing at Pignose) in the oven!!!! Eh heh HEH HEH HEH!"

At the return of Felch's bullshit straight male tough guy act though, Pignose became disgusted, and started to noodle out slightly, his little pad see ew dick beginning to falter. Rebekah sensed it, and drew both Piggy and Felch to her IMMEDIATELY, her nervous energy highly apparent on both cameras.

Levoié dropped her cup of blood, mesmerized and dizzy as she watched the POV, drifting off for a moment, wondering what it would be like to be a human female with two human males.........

"HEY, HEY.....LEVOIÉ!" she heard Simon cut into her thoughts, feeling him shake her. "Something's fucked up down there!" Snapping back to it, she looked at the screen; both males were vomiting uncontrollably, and Rebekah was in a sort of head shaking seizure. "It was strange, Levoié!" Simon said. "One minute she almost had them both in the palm of her hand again, and the next she was......."

"Playback!" she ordered the screens while holding up a hand towards Simon to get him to be quiet. "Stop!" she shouted as the visuals came back to the last scene she remembered.

On the POV screen, Rebekah had gotten Piggy "ready to go", his taffy strip dick now primed for action. Her hands drifted over to work on Felch's belt, his beer and bagels stomach making the effort a bit of a chore now that a lot of her grace was on a downward spiral. Felch could be seen faintly sniffing the air, a slight grimace of disgust on his face mounting.

"The commands and data I entered weren't enough." Levoié thought. "FUCK! This is going to cost me!"

Felch's belt and pants now off, his gut flopped down and obscured his fake manhood from view. Rebekah's hand reached out in an attempt to cradle his pastrami belly and get to his little shishito pepper weanie. Try as she might, Rebekah just could not lift that gut!

"Here, let me help!" Piggy said nervously, grease starting to ooze out of his pores. He reached his hand over, and attempted to sneak his fingers into Felch's groin area.

"WHOAHHH!!!!! HEY GUYYYYY!!" Felch yelled in a silly manner. "Watch it brah, I ain't with that gay shit!" he said as he backed up.

Pignose started to lose his erection immediately, the return of Felch's tough guy act killing it for him yet again. He turned around, and started to walk towards the bar cart, and Felch began pulling his pants back up as he sniffed the air violently......... mildly gagging between each sniff.

-HURKH BLECH-

Rebekah, seeing this, went kamikaze desperate as a few wisps of yellow steam started to emanate from her crotch. On the apartment camera she could be seen jumping up all of a sudden from the couch, all confidence and charm gone at this point......nothing but anxiety left.

"Hey, you two!!!" she yelled and turned quickly, bending over and YANKING her panties down with absolutely no grace whatsoever, a few cigarette butts, dead mosquitoes and used pieces of gum dropping out of her underwear onto the floor.

"Malakrwr have mercy!" Levoié thought, putting her head down in her hands. "I am so fucked when Lieutenant Beverly gets word of this!"

Rebekah's glamour INSTANTLY disappeared; her nanomachines went to shit; their data processing ability could not keep up with the admixture of disparate social elements, the commands Levoié had piggybacked onto their already set into motion course, and the intense revulsion Piggy and Felch had first for each other, and then for Rebekah. It was all too much; Rebekah's entire nervous system took a dive; having ridden too high on synthetic grace that was not custom to her character

313

or physical attributes, she became the polar extreme of all that affected charm and beauty.

In simple terms, Rebekah became a filthy disgusting cesspool of a human being. She belched out a nauseous cum burp as she fell to the couch, followed by a few dry heaves that yielded regurgitated birthday cake cookie bits, and chunks of MacRibb meat. Her chest and stomach became a cornucopia of cookie crumbles, sour bile, bbq sauce and rainbow sprinkles. Extremely disgusting, it perfumed the room with a stench that could most adequately be described as blooded shit released from the prolapsed rectum of an accomplished alcoholic sodomite.

-BLERCH HECH!-

-GLUKT BRRRM-

Both Pignose and Captain Felch started to dry heave and attempt to hold in the vomit as Rebekah's head twitched uncontrollably. They backed away slowly, clutching their stomachs, hoping to get to another room.....but they never made it before Rebekah let out a........

-QUERRRRRFFFFFFFFFFF.......SSSSSSSSSsssssssssssssh-

It was quite a quert (queefy fart)..........first the soft hollow oboesque tone of her vagina releasing its turbid queef, followed by the quick rebuttal of her low-grip sphincter emitting its gassssssss leaky flatulence.

Felch and Pignose never had a chance; they instantly vomited in tandem, followed by more Rebekah querts. It was a chorus of waste release; solid, liquid and gaseous, each of them bringing their own particular style of stench and sound to the orgy of stink rot filth.

314

Salted Plastic: The Comedic Horror of Gentrification

Levoié stood up, and walked to a nearby window; she couldn't watch anymore. Simon walked over, and put a scaled hand on her shoulder in consolation. "I can tell them that I entered the commands." he said, holding up a pack of Bütteshafter cigarettes to Levoié.

She reached over, took a cigarette, lit up, and exhaled as Simon lit one himself. "Forget it, it's my problem." she smirked. "Besides, they'd never believe an idiot like you could hack Rebekah anyways."

"Yeah, that's true." Simon exhaled as they looked out the window, a view of Earth outside, the Pacific Ocean and the bulk of South America far in the distance.

Levoié took another drag of her cigarette, and gripped the little triangular PDA in her pocket as she thought of a better life...............

Salted Plastic: The Comedic Horror of Gentrification

December 1, 2:23pm

Tiffany Victim reads a "news" feed on Shitter about a "terrorist attack" at the Shillcom corporate office building on Wilshire Blvd in Beverly Hills. The attack in question took place on November 29 during a CEO boardroom meeting for Shillcom's newly formed Crispy Pus streaming service. The implications of this attack hit her hard, especially after taking a program at UPLA University on "world events" that focused heavily on a new type of humanities branch called "documentary analytics". This highly acclaimed program had provided Tiffany with insights into the finer aspects of "eye opening" socio-political phenomena such as sponsored content peddling via liberal arts radio stations, and republican conspiracy babble sold via conservative wack job radio stations. The "truth bombs" that students received in class, from documentaries written by the kept pets of the far left and the far right, would keep them all in perpetual states of preachy overbearing zealous mania.......errr, I mean, in ever increasing stages of social enlightenment for years to come. At only $2k per unit ($3k if the "lectures" included screenings of FredTalks panels), it gave a front row seat to all those seeking to unearth all the corporate bad man evil lies...........something something..........teaching them how to STRIKE A BLOW to some vague romanticized idea of "the system that oppresses us all"........something something..........and allowing them to become "woke" tools.....ahem.....I mean woke individuals.

December 9, 12:17am

Diving deep into the underbelly of corruption, something something, putting the pieces together with other recent events, Tiffany stumbles onto a related article about more subversive activity taking place in

Salted Plastic: The Comedic Horror of Gentrification

DTLA. The events mentioned took place earlier that year, in October, and involved a trio of two young women and a teen male in an ice cream truck with heavy armaments. The story went on further to mention that the news was "hushed up", and not issued via mainstream media due to a MASS GOVERNMENT COVER UP something something. The name of a DEADLY underground organization of terrorists is mentioned in this highly enlightened, troll generated, no facts verified, one page piece of provocatory sponsored content........ahem.....I mean editorial. Sisters, Others and Brothers makes its debut in the media for the first time in this highly controversial piece of "news". Following this, Tiffany is informed in a more substantial manner (via a tech friend) about Sisters, Others and Brothers; after the grueling ordeal of half-heartedly reading the five paragraph article (provided to her by said tech friend), Tiffany comes across a few key names in the organization. The anonymous informant providing these names is never identified, but among the members of S.O.B's mentioned, those of Filth Creature and Vicky Varmint seem to make the biggest impression on Tiffany.

December 15-18

Going further down the rabbit hole, along with a few friends who she has by now artfully preached up on her particular brand of now cultic zeal for anything that even faintly resembles "uncovering the truth", Tiffany and her friends realize that Sisters, Others and Brothers are not the enemy, but a very real effort to stop world domination by the right wing white patriarchy and/or the liberal socialist control bad man evil tyrant one percent corrupt media something something......fantasy ideas of oligarchy and control....something something.

They all come to the realization that they've been wasting their lives partying, snowboarding in Big Bear, and going to brunch........and that now they have to "like make a difference and stuff"............plus a really neat article from Kosmo said that "intellectualism and revolution is hot and empowering this year." Modeling their new personas off S.O.B's Filth Creature and Vicky Varmint, Tiffany and her friends decide to come up with their own "revolt and rebel" monikers. Taking solemn vows during one of their Pecks in the Titty slumber parties at Tiffany's 4K a month Civic Center loft, and signing a pact in nail polish, the Fuck Girls are born.........Fuckpig, Fuckhog, and Fuckbeast.

A few days later, after halfheartedly promoting their "gang" at USD via flyers, and a "Woke Seminar" held outside the campus library, all three of them are temporarily expelled for "anti-feminist" activities, leaving them with a full six months to pursue their new lukewarm effort as "heroes of the people."

Sitting outside a local coffee shop on Vermont, all three of them discuss their feeble grasp of (and experience with) the injustices of the world.

"Calling ourselves 'Fuck Girls', and preaching about how WE CHOOSE to use sex as a lethal weapon is 'degrading to women', my ass!" McKenzie (AKA Fuckbeast) yelled, quoting the sociology department's dean, Professor Tenuremora, who had lectured all three of them no less than thirty minutes ago. McKenzie was the tallest of the three of them; about five foot ten, 190lbs of solid muscle clothed in soft baby fat. Her raven faux hawk was professionally done, and accented her blue-eyed "I get two spa days a week" face in perfect symmetry.

"Whatever!" Cayleigh (AKA Fuckhog) added. "That bitch doesn't know anything about re-appropriating and re-defining the terms of FEMALE EMPOWERMENT!" Cayleigh, at five foot four/163lbs, like Tiffany and McKenzie, was also heavily into Cruxfit and Creespie Crème pastries. Her new (and HIGHLY "subversive") 24k gold and onyx chaos star earrings shined brightly in the afternoon sun as she brushed a few copper colored dreadlocks away from her pale freckled face. Cayleigh's contribution to the conversation was a direct parrotation (yup, made it up) of one of the many editorials that Kyle (Tiffany's tech "friend") had culled from "reliable sources" for the girls to read. Unfortunately, these articles were all third person rehashes of manifestos that had all been written by Jasmine and Adrik themselves. Even the originals had contained only partial truths, as they were designed to get the word out about S.O.B's without really giving anything away other than the fact that they existed, and were here to get rid of some bad elements in Los Angeles.........and every major city in the world. The articles had contained a few "leaked" photos of Jasmine (neck down only) that showcased her nude and tattooed body.

Somewhere along the chain of people who had re-told the content of the original manifestos, one of them had made the decision to create a narrative behind Jasmine Filth Creature's body art. This little piece of fantastic fiction had inadvertently gestated the theme of Tiffany's little gang of Fake Freedom Fighters, giving them a sort of totem to follow and model themselves after. The embellishment in question had painted Jasmine Filth Creature as a badass street girl who "fights the evil of the 1% with gritty unapologetic sexuality and a millenialesque socio-political philosophy........reveling in her decision to have innumerable instances of illicit sex where SHE DOMINATES her partners.......COMPLETELY UNAPOLEGETIC in her celebration of being a bad girl with a sordid past..........something something...........generic romanticism.......bullshit bullshit......pseudo empowerment.....something something......"

The girls fell for it in totality, no questions asked; they'd even broken down in tears at the BS story about Jasmine being raised in squalor by her mentor, Vicky Varmint, and Varmint's beck and call love slave, Amar Lebanon. The story gave intense graphic details on how they had been fighting against the right wing power mongers and/or liberal globalist media manipulators for years, and were in desperate need of new recruits to "fight the good fight!"

Salted Plastic: The Comedic Horror of Gentrification

December 20, 4:47pm

Tiffany, Cayleigh, and McKenzie get word from Kyle that Sisters, Others and Brothers have a secret underground base near Skid Row, and that they will be taking new recruits on December 24 via "hidden agents" within the ranks of the local homeless. Bracing themselves with their new found sense of "being the strength and force of the people", and a packet of hand-crafted, artisan-made, free trade, activated charcoal hand wipes, they decide to scout Skid Row late night on the date in question.

Salted Plastic: The Comedic Horror of Gentrification

Tuesday, October 27, 7:15pm

"Wahsss...why.......I give you money.....anything......pleasseess don kill me......" Stickleg faintly begged as he continued to bleed out on the floor, his head propped up against the base of the stainless steel kitchen counter while Jasmine systematically undressed him. Adrik and Megan stood nearby, heating up various knives and utensils on the kitchen stove.

Jasmine leaned in; her mouth at Stickleg's ear, she began to whisper, her words matched by Megan and Adrik.

"Kill you? Hahhahha!" Jasmine/Adrik/Megan mocked Stickleg. "You think you deserve death after everything you and yours have done to the people of this city?" All three of them stopped what they were doing, and rested their chins in their hands in tandem as they looked at Stickleg in disgust. "Oh, that's so fucking funny! No, we got something fun in store for you, you little shit; something special to make you feel as robbed and hopeless as you've made so many people in LA feel for the last decade or so........hahhah.....HEHHehhehHAHA!"

Every drop of good nature had completely dissolved from Adrik, Jasmine and Megan; something had taken them into the darkest and gravest locked sections of their unconscious, that place where the them in them in them kept what it didn't want about certain aspects of their nature under lock and key so it wouldn't be seen by others; the storage unit for all the animosity they hid from everyday interaction and their own self-awareness. It was all there, in the malicious facet of the unconscious communal instinct; their occasional thirst for murder; the resentment they felt for any propriety and diplomacy that they were forced to utilize to keep peace in their lives. The HATE they felt for having to employ rigid logic against any instinctual (albeit impractical) desires for "improper" behavior toward the better good. Their true and/or latent sexual cravings that did not mesh well with their self-image and the expectations of society...........it was ALL THERE IN THE OPEN NOW; something in Megan had brought it to the surface.

What it was in her that did this was all guesses at this point. Possibly the EXTREME DISTRESS and HATRED that had been brought on by Stickleg's power play with her earlier? Mixed with whatever Jasmine and Adrik had brought to the table through their synchronization with the oil.............it all seemed to have created a new type of multi-minded personality integration...........one hell bent on catharsis for repressed hate, lust, violence, sadness, disappointment, etc.

Stickleg was now completely naked. Still on the floor, he began to cry a little as they watched, Jasmine standing over him now, an arm around both Megan and Adrik, all three of them giving Stickleg a look of mocking mercurial murder. It was a trinity entity of sadistic sneers, a synchronistic face that emphasized what that face said in tandem.

"You are fucking trash, and you absolutely deserve what we're about to do to you!!!"

Saying this, they began undressing in front of him, Jasmine and Megan stripping each other down somewhat violently, Adrik tearing his shirt off as he downed the last of a beer.

"Wha.....why'rrr you undress......." Stickleg began, and was IMMEDIATELY kicked right in his synthetic testicles by Adrik, the reaction in the pseudo nervous system within them making it extremely painful.

Adrik got in Stickleg's face, a villainous look in his eyes, the easy going jokester persona totally gone. "SHUT THE FUCK UP! You think we're gonna fuck you, MOTHERFUCKER!?!?" Spit flew out of his mouth into Stickleg's face. "FUCK YOU! THAT'S SOME INSULTING SHIT IF YOU THINK THAT!" Adrik swung the buckle of his belt into the area near Stickleg's missing ear, and walked away.

"Yeah......," Megan/Jasmine chimed in, "......you ain't gonna be fucking nothing no more, asshole!!!!" They both were stripped naked now, standing right above Stickleg, Megan's left arm across Jasmine's shoulders, Jasmine's right arm across Megan's shoulders. "No pussy, no assholes, no neighborhoods, no locals just trying to get by...........NO DREAMS......NO FUTURES.........NOTHING, YOU FUCKING THIEF!!!!!!!!"

"Yup!" Adrik said as he poked into the fridge again, and came back with a bottle of Közritzer in his hand. "No more Downtown parties, no more trips to Europe or Thailand.....where you fake out poor chicks into sleeping with you by telling them you're a celebrity artist the same way you do here........no more buying up more property that you don't even need........." at this he lifted some paperwork out of a nearby basket of mail, not even looking at what he'd just snatched up, seemingly grabbing it at random, and then waiving it in Stickleg's face. It was a set of documents for the forth piece of property Stickleg's parents had bought for him to "manage" as a permanent AireBnd. ".........YOU AND YOURS ARE NOT GONNA LORD OVER US ANYMORE, YOU PIECE OF SHIT!!! LOS ANGELES IS NO LONGER YOUR PERSONAL PLAYGROUND, WHOREHOUSE AND CASH MACHINE!!!!"

Megan stepped up, grabbed Stickleg behind the head, and threw a quick knee into his face before saying her piece. "No more pretending to be a big shot photographer." she smiled, talking to Stickleg like he was a pathetic little shit, his head still ringing while she waved her right arm around the apartment, indicating all the framed photos that he pretended were his work. "AND NO MORE DRAGGING HOPEFUL WOMEN AND GIRLS BACK TO YOUR BULLSHIT FAKE ARTIST LOFT TO SEXUALLY EXPLOIT THEM!" she yelled, finishing up her rage with a kick to his exposed and bleeding ribs, followed by a downward elbow to the bridge of his nose.

Stickleg's eyes watered, and he struggled to breath from his now broken nose. He started to piss himself..........something in his instincts sensing a horror beyond measure in store for him. His head dropped for a second......only a second.

"Good.....gooooooooood!!!!! Enjoy that piss............cause no more of that either!" Jasmine/Adrik/Megan said, pointing at the piss coming out of him and forming a puddle on the floor.

That got him! The innuendo of their statement instantly woke him up. Lifting his eyes, he saw Megan's right arm, and Jasmine's left arm coming together, forming a triangle, his pistol held by both of them, Adrik peeking over their shoulders with a maniacally devilish grin on his face.

-BLAM-

-BLAM-

-BLAM- -BLAM- -BLAM

-BLAM-

"Oooooohooooooo!!!! That shits mutilated now boy!"
"HAHAHHAHAHAHAHAHAHAHAHAHAHAHAHAHAHAH!!!!!"
they mocked him. "Like we said, you ain't gonna be fucking nothing no more! So just take a look at, and watch what you're never gonna have again; learn what's it's like to be one of your people's victims, you sack of shit!!! Feel what it's like to have what little you have taken away, and to be immiserated in every aspect of your life by people with more power than you. We hope you ENJOY how it feels to be helpless to do anything but just stand by and watch while we completely destroy you, body, mind, hope and soul..........YOU PATHETIC FUCK!!!!!!"

Even through the extreme pain, vertigo and nausea, he started to cry, and began to close his eyes against whatever was coming next.........

"OPEN YOUR FUCKING EYES, YOU LITTLE SHIT!" they yelled with murder, followed by a strange clinking sound, like chains unravelling.

"......*that crazy whip I bought on vacation in*............." Stickleg began to faintly think in fear, but was caught mid thought by a......

-FWAP-

A sound like a handful of lava rocks skidding across the side of a car BOOMED in Stickleg's ears. It was immediately followed by a liquid warmth trailing down his face, and what felt like hot cheese peeled off a pizza hanging loosely onto his bare chest. He looked down and saw what looked like half a latex mask hanging onto his chest with a few brownish-green scales embedded in it. He could just barely make out a nose, an upper lip, and what looked like an eyelid, sitting in a pool of blue and red on his chest. At this he passed out.

....

Salted Plastic: The Comedic Horror of Gentrification

Stickleg came to a bit later to the sound of furniture being moved around. The pain on his face was horrendous. Looking at the floor, he saw a cat of nine tails that he'd bought as a souvenir during one of the half a dozen Euro and Asia trips his parents had sent him on after college. He looked down at his chest; the section of skin that had been his face still hung there, connected by the slightest thread of tissue on the edge of his chin. With a shaky hand, he cautiously reached up to touch his face; his eyes widened in fear and confusion as he felt the reptilian scales along his cheek and jaw line. Jerky and caustic, his eyes then looked down between his legs, and saw that his synthetic penis had been mutilated beyond recognition. He started to twitch and shake in terror and mental breakdown, his sanity now on the verge of dismissal due to the pain of his situation.........and from the realization that he was helpless to do shit about it. He vaguely heard a few feminine moans through his shock, and began to cry in rhythm to the follow up sound of wet suction noises that almost seemed to mock his fear and nausea..........that ridiculed his mounting realization that his life was over, whether he continued to live or not.

Looking up gradually, he saw them across the room, on his suede couch. Adrik standing, his cock in Megan's ass as he stared with demonic longing at Jasmine moaning on the edge of the couch, while Megan slobbered haphazardly all over Jasmine's labia.

The situation met with no arousal from Stickleg (nor could it, considering...), only more terror, the scene in front of him not one of any sort of so called normal sex, (love-based, carnal, sadistic or rapacious), but more an act between three people that was pure hate/unrequited love catharsis, each one of them "letting off steam" in some way that was only known to them.

Megan turned her head away from Jasmine's pussy and begged Adrik to stop; her anus slightly peppered with blood at this point, she pleaded with a look of anguish on her face........and then SNAPPED out of it a second later, her countenance changing immediately when she faced Jasmine's parted labia again, the look on her face now full of hate/lust as she spit on Jasmine's clit and started yelling obscenities.

"YOU FUCKING CUNT! YOU STUPID BITCH! You already had every guy in school, but you had to have Damien too?!?" she yelled, the look of hate gone now, and replaced with a maniacal smile. "I would have fucked you both….shared even……but that wasn't good enough…..you wanted to fuck me and him over just for fucking fun…………Heh Heh Ha ha HAAAAAA!" Megan laughed like a madwoman, her body still jerking from the violent jolts as Adrik slammed into her asshole with no finesse whatsoever. Raising her hand high, she brought it down HARD one, two, three, FOUR TIMES across Jasmine's crotch, as if slapping the sides of someone's face. "YOU FUCKING WHORE!!!!!!!!!!!!!!!!"

Welts began to raise up on Jasmine's labia as she looked down at Megan between her legs……..not seeing Megan there at all, her sense of reality warped by the belief that she was finally getting her heart's desire………..getting it finally, after wanting and knowing it would never be…………after making it **so fucking obvious** to the object of her affection……………AFTER BEING FUCKING REJECTED FOR NO FUCKING GODDAMN GOOD REASON BY THIS HEARTLESS BITCH WHO DIDN'T DESERVE HER!!!!!!

Turning quickly, Jasmine knocked her knee into Megan's temple. "FUCK YOU LYDIA………YOU AND YOUR SLOB LOSER BOY TOY, WHOEVER THE FUCK THAT IDIOT IS!!!!! YOUR TASTE IN LOVERS DISGUSTS ME!!!! YOU LIKE FUCKING ALL THE WRONG PEOPLE CAUSE YOU'RE TOO SCARED TO GET HURT?!?! WELL SO DO I!!!!!"

Jasmine, now completely hell driven by who the fuck knows what, knocked Adrik onto the floor, and INSTANTLY mounted his cock, tears in her eyes, sobbing like a child as she ground hard into him. His previously hate driven face snapped back into complete calm the minute he entered her, everything becoming clear……a tear in his left eye as the whole situation came together. Even so, this was his dream;

327

he'd always wanted her, loved her like a brother yes, but more than that, always more than………

Right as he was about to give in, ignore that Jasmine was not in her right mind, and just go with it out of selfish lust and love, he saw Megan standing behind Jasmine, a large chunk of moldavite held high above her head, getting ready to smash Jasmine's brains in. He was about to yell at Jasmine to warn her, but both his and her orgasms were still mounting; his fear for her safety was battling his desire for physical pleasure, making it hard to let go. But before he could make a decision, a loud rustle was heard across the room………and the sound immediately snapped them all out of it.

Across the room, Stickleg had knocked over a few glasses and pans while attempting to stand up and escape, but had fallen back down to the floor in despair, too weak and decimated to get away.

With the spell broken, and the quick realization of what had happened clicking into place, Jasmine's eyes immediately widened in shock; getting up fast as shit, and scrambling backwards across the floor, she looked at Adrik's penis, still wet from her insides. Megan too; her face was contorted in pain and anger as she dropped the chunk of moldavite, and sent a look of rage in Adrik's direction for a few seconds………and then just as quickly let it all go for no apparent reason, a look of silent understanding coming over her face.

Adrik began to cry, his face down towards the floor……….not because he'd had his heart's desire for a moment, not because he knew it was false and brought on by who knows what, but because he knew he'd hurt his friend and an innocent stranger. Something about the oil's capabilities was unknown still; Megan's emotional state had added a foreign element into the mix for him and Jasmine. His instincts told him that this was the force behind what had just happened, that he hadn't consciously or willingly hurt Jasmine or Megan, but the guilt remained all the same. About to speak up, apologize…..try to fix things, he was preempted by Megan.

Salted Plastic: The Comedic Horror of Gentrification

"So.....," Megan asked, ".........so you liked watching that, you little shit?!" she finished in a tone of condescending hatred. Adrik looked up, thinking she was talking to him..........just in time to see Megan grabbing a cigarette out of Jasmine's hand that Jasmine had just barely lit. Exhaling, Megan walked towards Stickleg, snubbed out the cigarette on the floor, and turned back to Adrik and Jasmine for a second. "My hatred, your bond, his blood!" she said in a tone that suggested her words were divine, scientific and metaphysical by default..........as if there was no explanation required.

She peered closely at Stickleg, watching his facial pantomimes, looking for a sign of something not visually discernable. After a second or two of this she gave up, and looked back towards Adrik and Jasmine. "Hmmmmm.......he doesn't know.....," she said with soft resolve, Jasmine and Adrik looking puzzled as Megan pointed at Stickleg, ".........but it doesn't matter; I'll explain it to you two while we finish torturing this fucker........while we bleed him dry."

Salted Plastic: The Comedic Horror of Gentrification

Tuesday, October 27, 10:35pm

Stickleg's apartment floor, kitchen to living room, was now an array of blue and red puddles and smears, but mainly blue. His mangled corpse had been laid out by the fireplace that was inset into his two story, sliding ladder library; apparently the renovator's had had zero respect for the idea of book preservation, or possibly knew that Stickleg was just the type of spoiled prick that could care less about treating his library as an investment of either knowledge or money. The physical and mental torture that Megan, Adrik and Jasmine had carried out for the last two hours consisted of the following; stretching his stomach fat out and skinning it off, cracking each individual vertebrae with a jade pestle, laughing at his mutilated synthetic penis while he cried and begged for mercy, degloving a few fingers with wire strippers, and rubbing powdered glass into his open wounds. Megan, finally emotionally satiated after all this, had left the fucker to die at Jasmine's hand.

Jasmine had cut open every major artery on Stickleg, letting the wounds flow while Megan and Adrik used polycarbonate storage containers to capture all the blood. Stickleg had had these in the corner of his kitchen; remnants of his lousy three-month effort at running a food truck earlier this year. The little shit had been smoking hash while watching the Food Wetwork channel one day, and a documentary about how HIP and "BRINGING IT TO THE PEOPLE!" food trucks were had caught his attention. A week later, and two large loans in his pocket (co-signed by mom and dad of course), and Stickleg, despite never running a business, or working a line in a restaurant a day in his life, had his very own BRAND SPANKING NEW VEGAN POTATO TACO FOOD TRUCK!!!!! Hippitty hip HIP HIP!!!!!

Three days later, and after finding out that cooking was actually real work, he'd called home to mam and pap again. Crying about getting a grease stain on his favorite shoes, a hot oil burn the size of a pinhead on his arm, and being worn and stressed out due to long hours of labor, he'd coerced them into writing a check that he could use as payroll for a manager and a few employees.

Three months later, and the whole thing had gone to shit due to his hands off philosophy on everything, and his inability to anticipate consumer opinion on menu pricing. The only part of the business he'd attended to had been collecting all the profits at the end of every week, and occasionally showing up to the truck when it was parked in Santa Monica or DTLA; nice little opportunity for him to snap a few pix for his social media, so he could look like the self-made hard working entrepreneur that he wasn't, the reality being that he was just a little crumb snatching bitch that wanted the social prestige that came with running a "hip foodie oriented" business, but without having to put in the hard work, or suffer the investment losses that most people had to deal with.

Jasmine, Adrik and Megan dragged the last of the containers to a large, seven-foot tall wine fridge that they had emptied out. A flyer for Stickleg's old food truck was tacked to a cork message board near the fridge.

Comic book style, it had a drawing of Stickleg doing a thumbs up with his signature beer gut, stick arms and granny legs. The top of the flyer showcased the truck's name, The Vegan Vulture. A dialogue bubble came out of his bearded cartoony face, and contained the following statement. "Made with REAL Salinger Farms Potatoes, Artisanal non-GMO flaxseed Tortillas, and also the fact that I'm a wimpy bitch!" That last part had confused a lot of customers, but oh well, it's what Stickleg had told the designer/printer to put on the thing.

At $4 per taco, with extras like free trade organic avocado, hand crafted vegan cotija, and blueberry pico de gallo (only $2 per topping), the business had plummeted mere months after opening day. Patrons apparently had been turned off by the idea of not paying at least $7 per taco for something that any idiot with common sense and minimal cooking skills could make like thirty of at home for $5.

331

Salted Plastic: The Comedic Horror of Gentrification

So, in the end, The Vegan Vulture's downfall had been both Stickleg's lack of involvement, and his inability to predict this phantom idea about cost and quality among the transplants, trustfund trash and hipster aristocracy that liked to frequent food trucks. Not growing up cooking for themselves, or doing much of anything for themselves, the stupid fuckers had no idea that charging high end prices had nothing to do with high end food.......or that potato tacos in general, were just something you made when you were low on funds.

Jasmine, sweating from all the work of torturing Stickleg, walked over to the apartment's thermostat, and turned the temp to 71. She brought out her silver cigarette case with the ornamental cockroach on top, and lit one up. Exhaling, she looked over at Megan. "You gonna tell us what the blood's for? Or better yet, what about you and that thing (she pointed at Stickleg) made a fucking mini-orgy between us take place?"

"I saw it already..........with a little help from a friend." Adrik commented. "After it all happened, bits and pieces of what she left me with started to come into my mind. The oil, together with the frenzy Megan felt at being used and threatened by him; the fact that we all have unmet desires and grievances that relate to love and dreams; the chemical catalyst of reptilian blood........what the oil REALLY IS.........so much more than I can explain in words......so much danger in where I see this all going......."

"And I saw a few things too." Megan began, a look of the mania from earlier briefly returning to her face. "Who you two are, what your people are protecting us all from........and I....I want in!"

"Look, I'm sorry about earlier, I know you know that it wasn't me, but we can't just up and decide to take you in and......" Adrik began, but stopped when Jasmine held up a hand towards him. She walked towards Megan, exhaling her cigarette, leaving a trail of smoke behind her.

Salted Plastic: The Comedic Horror of Gentrification

Face to face with Megan, Jasmine, a few inches shorter than her, looked up into the girls face, an edge of a decision look in her eyes. Putting the cigarette out after a second or two of looking, she smiled, and looked back at Adrik. "What about me, bitch? No apology for me, little brother?"

"I.....," Adrik looked down in embarrassment, "I'm sorry Jaz.....I just....it was just...."

"Just that it being me, and that you wanted it makes it harder to bring up?" she finished for him, raising her voice, but not angry at all, completely able to see him as "little brother" again, despite what had happened. Adrik's embarrassment was sign enough for what Jasmine already knew, that he would never have done what he'd done to her in his right mind. Not waiting for (or needing) Adrik to answer, she turned back to Megan. "SHOW ME! Show me, and we'll take you in, we'll take you......"

"JAZ, NO!" Adrik interrupted. "You want a repeat of what just happened?!"

"THERE IS NO 'NO!' HERE, ADRIK!" Jasmine yelled. "You have no fucking idea what we're up against yet, kid! So far you've done nothing but gigolo work for Sisters, Others and Brothers.......and on human's only......seducing clueless human girls to join our cause. If you think this shithead was trouble (she pointed to Stickleg's corpse), then you ain't ready!" Frustrated, she pulled out another cigarette, lit up, and exhaled.

"Fuck! I'm not ready either!" she continued. "So far, I ain't done nothing but pick off the kids, the latent reptiles, the ones that still think they're human. Neither me or you HAVE ANY FUCKING IDEA how lethal the self-aware ones are........the ones at the top of the whole thing. Them, and their fucking friends! You already forget about that thing that came after you and your little girlfriend a few days ago?!"

"Ok Jaz, what's your point?" Adrik asked calmly, a little tension in his face in response to Jasmine bringing up Tlaloca.

333

Jasmine smiled, looking over at him, her silver front tooth shining in the apartment's light. "Ask the oil. I did while I was eyeballing Megan a second ago, and you know what it told……."

Adrik had already closed his eyes in the middle of Jasmine's sentence……had the answer before she finished. "It told you that what happened here with us was a rare thing……..rare and powerful. I see it……I'm calmer now, reconnected to you; coupled with what Tlaloca gave me, I'm getting a larger picture." Adrik kept his eyes closed still, as if mentally sifting through something………and then stopped and opened his eyes back up in horror. "YOU WANNA USE HER AS A WEAPON?!"

At this, Megan jumped into the conversation. "I……..want you to use me as a weapon!"

Jasmine turned to Megan. "Ok….ok……looks like you're starting to tune into us again. But like I said earlier, show me! I know the risk, and I don't care."

"I know you don't." Megan said. "Oh, and Adrik?" she looked across the room at him, smiling a bit. "Apology accepted, but if you reeealy feel bad, I can always peg you in the ass, and we can call it even."

"Funny…" he said solemnly, unable to roll with Megan's attempt to break the ice with her comment, not liking where this was all going, knowing already that he was going to have to be a part of Megan "showing" Jasmine everything.

"Adrik, get over here!" Jasmine said on cue, already knowing herself that he had to "contribute" for her to see it all.

He reluctantly walked over while Megan went to the fridge with a tea cup and a spoon. Taking some of Stickleg's blood in the spoon, she put it into the cup, talking while she walked back to the kitchen counter. "For this to work, we all have to dredge up the feelings that activated this; me; my fury and helplessness at being held against my will and exploited by that asshole…..along with a few things from my past for good measure. You two? You're both going to have to think about, and feel……"

334

Salted Plastic: The Comedic Horror of Gentrification

"We know what we have to feel." Adrik/Jasmine answered.

They all gathered around the cup of blood, getting ready to consciously induce the feelings and thoughts that had led to what had happened earlier. Megan interrupted one last time before they began.

"Oh, one more thing." she looked over at Adrik. "I need what you have hidden in your pants."

"Hahahaha! That was deliberate!" Jasmine laughed, knowing now that Adrik had a hidden vial of anamnesis oil in his pants.

Even Adrik had to smile at that, Megan's sense of humor; the kindness and patience that it suggested, considering everything that had happened. Pulling the vial out, already knowing what she had in mind, he handed it over. "I always keep an emergency stash."

He saw it clearly; if all three of them were on it, then they might just have a chance to get all the benefits of the mania, but without the setbacks. Megan knocked back half the oil, the vial's hue of red almost glowing, the swirls of black ash inside moving, and then handed it to Jasmine. Jasmine drank half of what was left, passed it to Adrik, and he finished it.

They all sat on bar stools around the cup of blood on the counter, Megan thinking about how hopeful she'd been that Stickleg's photos were going to help her agent get her some modeling gigs, make her a star so she could shove it in Damien and Xochi's faces. She thought of the fear and hate she'd felt when Stickleg had insinuated that she couldn't leave his apartment......how stupid she'd been for falling for his whole safe and sensitive artist act............fading in.....fading in.........a Ziggurat in the Middle East.......

Adrik recalled how the oil had been fluctuating in its functionality when they'd broken into Stickleg's place, coming up from the apartment below through an access port and false floor set up by SOBs. They'd had their eyes on Stickleg for a while now, had bought the apartment below through a third party, and were monitoring him to get dirt on his powerful parents back East. The unit had been modified over a period of a few months; whenever Stickleg left the building, a few SOB's had done quiet construction, creating the access hatch between the two apartments little by little. Jasmine and Adrik had used the hatch to ascend into Stickleg's place, the point being for Jasmine to initiate Adrik with his first kill; a little practice for what they had planned ahead of them. While the oil turned on and off, the him had battled the him in Adrik. His heart was at ease one second, and in anguish the next; knowing that he had to be stoic and follow Jasmine's lead, feeling pain from the realization that any romantic or sexual interaction between the two of them was never going to happen for real...............a time-slip.......dead society..................a pyramid in the jungles of Mexico.......

Jasmine wiped at a few tears that had started to well up in her eyes as she purposely thought about Lydia walking into that café a few days ago. She felt self-hatred for her role in dropping Lydia at that shithole club in downtown, knowing now that that's where she had met that bum she'd seen her with at the café. "I should have been more forward!" she thought. "Fuck! What do I know!? Maybe he's what she needs! Naw! FUCK THAT! I know her pattern of lovers, she's told me!" Trying to calm down, Jasmine focused, and looked at the blood in the cup as if it was a portal.....something more than that.......something that maybe her and Adrik had missed...........not being the right match for such knowledge via anamnesis integration........not like Miguel, Lydia and Dagmar with their centuries of past lives spent together..............had to be forced through a sort of synthetic shamanism.......no.....that's not the right word........disciplines and sciences dead and lost......loss.......a shaded room in North Africa.........they'd captured a "god" at the request of a wealthy merchant who considered himself a scholar...........

Adrik, Jasmine and Megan integrated..............heart, soul, mind, and animal instinct........similar acts overlaid and repeated across time and space, different in each moment and place but, stripped of all physical dressing, the root and purpose fundamentally of kindred nature.

Salted Plastic: The Comedic Horror of Gentrification

All three of them were the them in them in them in them in them....simultaneously in ancient Egypt, Mexico, and Sumer.......scenes superimposed upon the other.......

A high priest of Marduk held a small humanoid looking lizard by the tail, roughly the size of a chihuahua, dangling it head down. Its mother was strapped to a stone slab a few feet away, struggling and snarling to get free while the priest cut the small lizard's throat, bleeding it out into a bowl. His wife and favorite concubine, both extremely bitter towards each other, stood at his sides.

The necessary ingredients for the formula were there; jealousy, longing and hatred were all present......and so was the blood, but where was the oil?

An Egyptian servant approached a nearby doorway, holding a black and gray marble mortar and pestle. As he walked through the door he immediately became a high priestess of the Goddess Inanna. Setting the mortar down, which was now fashioned of diorite with cuneiform script upon it, she began to crush up a red stone inside of it.

Megan/Adrik/Jasmine were disembodied during all this, just watching.............the room shifting, altering, new images coalescing as previous ones left visual after effects........

............a flayed and mummified body in the corner of an Aztec temple's secret subterranean chamber.........the mouth of the thing hung open, dead as shit. A purple mist emanated from it's mouth a second later when the room's only living occupants, a female nagual, and her brother/lover, cut their forearms with something that looked distinctly like blades of red obsidian.........if such a thing existed. The light shifted in the room, revealing the bodies of the witch and her lover, all smooth with brownish bronze tones.............except for their left forearms; these were white scaled, with barbed claws in lieu of fingernails.

The room became a mismatch of figures, décor and rituals from different times and places. Egyptian priests walked by (and through) an Akkadian ensi who was pacing the room in mental turmoil, thoughts of

337

impending war in his mind. A Tlatoani acolyte, beating a husband and wife with a macuahuitl, faded into the room, the wife's snake-like lover in the corner on his knees bleeding out, hissing obscenities in some otherworldly language. The room and its occupants altered over and over again; from limestone walls to mud bricks, from brass braziers to coined Sumerian headdresses…………..men and woman gearing up for war…………whispering to each other about "old enemies" impregnating their women, eating their children, and power grabbing for their land.

The room disappeared, and a high desert dune replaced it. Three people sat in chairs in their flax linen shendyt kilts and khat headdresses; one female, two males. Nothing but sand for miles and miles as a lone robed figure approached, having walked across the desert for a pre-arranged meeting. Stopping short of the three Egyptians, the figure threw a strange looking scroll at their feet. Luminous green hieroglyphs, as if written in living emerald, were etched onto its black metallic surface. Seemingly made of a sturdy metal alloy, yet pliable and light weight in the wind like papyrus, its appearance stupefied the three Egyptians who were so accustomed to claiming the lineage of gods, yet had never seen a real god's handiwork.

Even so, whatever mystery material the scroll was comprised off, the text upon it was recognizable enough. The symbols on its surface made it known that the messenger was an envoy for "guests" that the Egyptians had been "harassing" for far too long. That being said, more threats and bloodshed were not what the envoy had to offer. It waved it's hands in eloquent gestures, maintaining a pretense of peace through bargain, it's voice and choice of words pleasant to the ear. For a brief moment though, the moon revealed these hands that gestured so "diplomatically", the skin sickly and pale as ivory........with flecks of galena and coal........rotten and past the point of death. At the sight of this, the female queen flinched......but only momentarily; a second later, and the stranger, in an act of good faith, removed her hood, revealing a young golden haired beauty, with soft pale skin blushed in tones of pink. The queen smiled at the woman's proposal, laughing inside at the "false vision" she'd seen only seconds ago, completely obliviously to the fact that she'd just caught a small glimpse of a future that was in store for the envoy and all her people.

Similar messengers made their way into the cities, camps, caves, and temples of every race on the planet who had taken up arms against the reptilians.........that had learned their secrets and weaponized the snake's own blood and science against them.

The theme repeated itself before Jasmine/Adrik/Megan innumerable times:

The reptilians, happening upon the "good will" of a race much older than them or their human enemies, quickly agreed to their offer to play diplomats on their behalf........to barter "peace" between them and the humans. These, shall we say, proto-humans (for lack of a better name), were ancient, long lived, full of a vast store of knowledge from various worlds and cultures, and had been here on earth at the advent of human and reptilian societies. Over time though, they had lost their ability to live with the natural flow of life, and had squandered away all their ability to generate any culture of their own, decimating their drive to create anything heartfelt, and had eventually devolved into very powerful parasites.

Humans in fighting cells of three or two (depending on the bond) had figured out the snake's "blood magic", utilizing the reptilian's own psycho-spiritual science against them. Facing extinction, the lizards had made a deal with this wandering race of middlemen, who had offered to make a sort of Trojan horse "peace" for them with the humans.

Through coercion, intermarriage, barter, land exchange, offers of new technology, etc., these proto-humans (or whatever the shit fuck they were) manipulated their way into the good graces of human societies in every major power seat in the ancient world.

And in exchange, what did they demand?

The crowning request they made of humans was to have the "honor" of educating them by running their academic centers, and spreading the "enlightenment" of such to any societies still in the "depths of ignorance". Druid clans, Buddhist communes, Shamanistic tribes, Shinto villagers, Meso American nomads; any and all groups of people who still "suffered" due to a lack of "high society".........that did not (in the opinion of the envoys) possess the type of faith and education that said society could afford them.

A small price to pay for peace and security, no? Most humans freely agreed to this arrangement, the very few denying the proposal either fleeing to other lands, or disappearing entirely.

The end result?

At first, only that level headed human warriors continued to use the blood magic and fight back, while the majority of their people gave into the "diplomatic" requests of the envoys.

Salted Plastic: The Comedic Horror of Gentrification

These warriors continued to pass on what they knew via oral tradition in secret, their knowledge and activities little by little being outlawed by their own people.

They continued the practice of ritually inducing personal rage, jealousy and loss to the conscious level in the presence of their enemy's blood, and catalyzing that rage with a red stone often found on fallen reptilians. This stone, seemingly just a cosmetic adornment, was in reality a precious ore from the reptilian home dimension. Not found anywhere in natural occurrence on Earth, it had temporal distortion properties, and psycho-medicinal abilities that allowed its bearer to get in touch with their true self, the self that was often lost through memetic socialization as one grew in years......that people let go of for the sake of conscious-level composure, and the comfort of consensus instigated social propriety. The stone could also calm a warrior's soul in battle by allowing them to call upon the strength of past experiences......and past lives. In a nutshell, the stone was spirituality, science and self-issued psychotherapy in a nice little portable package. These stones were the culmination of generations of innovation in neurology, philosophy, psychology and quantum physics on the part of the lizard people. That said, not long after the truce, the reptiles soon lost touch with their science and mysticism, felt no need for it in fact, its purpose thought mainly to have been one of war and defense..........the stone's true value totally forgotten to them at this point in their history. The stage had been set for the envoy's gain; the prize of holding the reins of human socialization via control of their academic institutions, and the added bonus of having a near monopoly (outside of the lingering human blood warriors) on the red stone and its power over war, time and the unconscious.

341

Salted Plastic: The Comedic Horror of Gentrification

Adrik/Megan/Jasmine continued to watch it all unfold.

Time passed and passed, and after a few hundred years of education from the envoys, the blood magic was nearly gone from public recollection. All record of such things was neatly and conveniently destroyed, or converted into myth or entertainment.........peasant tales and ghost stories.....mumblings of bored scholars and wise women. The blood magic militia and mercenaries still existed on the fringe of society, but their numbers dwindled more and more as time went by, the new generations forgetting the grievances of the past, and easily agreeing to the offers of peace and modern comfort set before them by the envoys. Soon enough, every society, city, town or camp had orators, scribes, teachers and instructors of all sorts rewriting history, science, medicine, literature.......and even select portions of mathematics.

At a preordained time the envoys even wrote themselves out of history, and it was forgotten that they ever existed; they were simply just like everybody else now. The people of the world, believing that their teachers were actually human, took little notice of the fact that becoming an educator was by and large hereditary, and closed off to many classes of people.........unfortunate, this being the largest clue left as to the unsavory nature of academia. Plainly speaking, the majority of information (not just academics) in every society was under the thumb of the envoys, and they had officially taken both themselves, and their reptilian clientele, off the record of existence. If anyone tried to enter their ranks, they were either neatly brushed aside via standardized bureaucracy, or admitted as unofficial slaves that were told half truths about their new professions as educators. Some select few were an exception to the above rule, but usually because they were so mentally dense, and with no inherent discretion, that they simply did not question anything that might seem odd about the situation. These basic-minded, linear thinking, two value logic guided, dogma beacon meat

Salted Plastic: The Comedic Horror of Gentrification

sacks would in and of themselves breed a new social science that would variously be called things such as soothsaying, politics, propaganda, preaching, self-help organization peddling, etc..............a new form of socialization where the aim was to use unquestioning overeducated fools as the mold for every sane and cooperative citizen to follow.

Every generation, more and more, a little piece of the past was omitted from official academic teachings, or relegated to the arts of storytelling or theater..........this was one of the envoys and reptilians biggest mistakes.........and one that they eventually sought to rectify by monopolizing all entertainment. For quite often, it was the abstract mind of the creative type that couldn't swallow their bullshit, that would intuitively fish out the truth through the fringes of awareness available to them as someone of imagination.

From this point on, after what seemed like an endless amount of time passing, and information being showcased to them, the visions became more distinct and custom to particular situations, eras and locals.

Adrik/Jasmine/Megan still watched patiently, outside of time and space:

343

Salted Plastic: The Comedic Horror of Gentrification

Marseille (Massalia), 600 BC

Boats arrived from Ionia carrying people dressed in floor length robes and leather facemasks, the masks painted to resemble human features. These "Greeks" were seeking sanctuary from the local Gauls, offering in exchange knowledge of viticulture and architecture. Agreements and alliances made, soon afterwards many Gaul women began to have miscarriages, some of them giving birth to malformed scaled children with yellow, vertical irised eyes.

Rome, 119 AD

The foundation of a new collegia was being laid by stonecutters under the supervision of man with golden hair and ivory skin. His silver haired daughter stood at his side, holding onto her father's pinky with a tiny hand……….motes of light, both gold and silver, radiating off of them for their eyes only.

Northwestern Iran, 1478 AD

Twelve miles inland from the Caspian Sea, Ridha al-Itani stumbled home after a long journey, his salvar covered in blood, the collar of his cebken torn and ragged. He had been traveling near the foothills of the Eastern Caucasus a month ago, and had stumbled upon a stone structure that

344

seemed vastly out of place with the territory and culture of the local. Hungry and tired, Ridha had called upon what had passed for a door on the symmetrical block, the building made of what appeared to be white and yellow marble. A feeble female voice beckoned him to come inside, mentioning that he had been expected, and that food had already been set for his arrival. Puzzled at this, and somewhat suspicious, Ridha's hunger won out against his caution, and he walked inside......only to be knocked unconscious immediately.

Waking a few hours later, bloodied clothes and all, he looked up and saw that his captor had made no tact for the ease of unsettling revelation; staring right at him was the face of death, grinning at his unease, savoring his fear and disgust. The thing was shriveled and full of rot, eyeless, teeth like ebony veined with silver. So emaciated she was, and lacking most of her muscle structure, that sections of her abdomen revealed the contortions of small intestines through the skin. One foot had rotted clean off, and the hair on her head looked like filaments of platinum alloy. Her breasts alone were strangely whole, symmetrical, healthy even, as if this dying thing, out of some sense of vanity and willpower had held onto the health and vigor of that portion of her body alone. Overcoming his initial shock at the sight of her, Ridha could see that she was struggling heavily.....wheezing through that smile, barely balancing on her stumped leg.......and even through the rot upon her face, he could somehow sense that she had something important to say, and little time to tell it.

What she had said before expiring, Ridha had only ever told his son on his deathbed, making him promise that the tale would be handed down to each successive generation of their family. After the story, Ridha gave his son what he'd brought back from that "piteous long dead mother" many years back...........a copper jewelry casket with an Assyrian winged sun upon its front and back, the inside containing granules of what looked like powdered rubies. The design of the thing was strangely peculiar, looking like something that was well ahead of its time. Ridha gave intense instruction upon the nature of the ruby powder to his son, but no........but no........but NO...........connection to the vision fading.............ku87 ghjduuh 2&(** ii................ thing had always seemed so odd to each new generation of the family as it was passed down for the next 427 years. Eventually, Abila al-Itani, a descendent of Ridha who had immigrated to London at the end of the 19th century, had walked into a jeweler one afternoon hoping to pawn the casket during hard times. The jeweler, shocked for some reason at the sight of the thing, turned her away, locked up shop, and immediately rushed to his drafting table. Upon the parchment laid on the table, was a half sketched idea that had come into the jeweler's head only an hour prior.............the sketch identical to the design of the casket that had just been brought in.

Russian, Early 20th Century

The Duma, machinated heavily by a 1,500 year old baron through various designated middlemen, forms a provisional government that soon becomes the subject of much class-based debate and political unease. This same baron is simultaneously pulling the strings of the lower classes, firing them up over the injustice of this provisional government being staffed heavily by capitalist gentry. This farce of a micro-war eventually sets the stage for the October Revolution of 1917. The Cheka secret police is soon after established......established, and heavily staffed by reptilian elite disguised as Russia's lower classes.

Salted Plastic: The Comedic Horror of Gentrification

Akihabara, 1981

Reo Hirabayashi, a promising college student, becomes increasingly misanthropic a few weeks after private tutoring from a foreigner currently making her living teaching English Composition and Irish History in Japan. Playing on Reo's interest in Western myths and legends, Cliodhna Kavanagh shows him a few unpublished facts about history. At first it's just a few entertaining tales about the Tuath Dé Danann, and the real origins of King Arthur........stories about fairies of human stature........frightful beings with martial abilities and magic who are seeking blood vengeance........nothing like the watered down children's tales found in popular fiction about such things. The stories are Cliodhna's way of setting the stage for her true intentions, a way to pique Reo's thirst for truth via his interests. Soon after, she begins to ask him if he'd be interested in hearing a few things about his own country's forgotten history, in particular a few "exciting facts" about Article 9 of the Japanese Constitution. Reo's initial unease over said subject is quickly set aside by his growing crush for this beautiful woman with copper curls and emerald eyes.

The studious nature, anti-social behavior, and cynical wit planted by Cliodhna in Reo will eventually lead to him becoming a founding member of Japan's first cell of Sisters, Others and Brothers, a tribe of social outcasts dedicated to taking back the planet from an unsettling force of people known as barons, an age old evil that took away the heart and soul of humanity thousands of years ago. This seeding process, seeking out individuals to fight the barons, is something Cliodhna has been at for a very long time, handpicking those with potential, engendering a rebirth of societal and sub-societal awareness. She has been carrying out her life goal towards this end for over 856 years.

Salted Plastic: The Comedic Horror of Gentrification

Time, Timely, and Timeless

Spastic small visions continued, their increasingly fragmented nature indicating that it was all winding down, back to linear time and space, the blood slowly losing its last drops of potency like a dwindling psychedelic or narcotic high……..

……woman in Victorian England screaming as a giant scaled man in a top hat holds her dress like a tether while she attempts to run away from him in a Brighton alley………

……..rusted and pitted blade gripped by a fossilized hand at the bottom of the Gave de Pau in 5th Century France………..

An island in the Pacific where those "executed" for extreme crimes against humanity live on out of the public eye, sipping cocktails while they are tended to by slaves that have been muted by non-disclosure agreements…….

….a frail corpse behind the curtains of a popular political commentary comedy show………..whispering lines to the celebrity host over a lavalier microphone…..

The scaled hands of an ancient female reptilian in a North East Los Angeles condo, signing page after page, gearing up to issue numerous unlawful detainers……..making room for the next wave of her brood………..and the new modern housing that they'll require once eviction and demolition has taken place………

….director/designer for a top video game design company being given her severance after butting heads on the issue of new management cutting production quality down to a two decade old standard…..a silent pale faced woman watching the interaction through a two way mirror……the glint of branding marks on both her cheeks, brands in the shape of American half dollars, JFK's face seared into her flesh……her three vermillion eyes codifying the situation with zero passion……

A subterranean hospital ward…..orphaned children scheduled for consumption or adoption by reptilian parents…….

In an antebellum home in the 19th century US South, the mistress of the house asks one of her servants for a few lessons in "their music", just a quick peek at their culture. During the lesson, the servant begins to visibly age and lose some of the vibrancy in her personality, while the house mistress begins to look much younger and socially radiant, "clothed" in the culture she has just leeched off her servant.

2025 AD, Broadway and 6th. A 20th level baron has just been flushed out of her DTLA penthouse by an angry mob of Los Angeles locals. Black blood, marbled in grey and silver, trails down her thigh as she runs past various store fronts and cars covered in flames…………she desperately looks for culture to feed on, for at least one human being that has not caught onto the game of her people...........hoping to recuperate enough to escape the city...............

.........an information server........subterranean...........the moon........

.........caves in the hills..........dressed like ancient Gauls.............pleased at the hope given to humanity.........

.........crowds across the planet..........rejoicing at real freedom......
a few benevolent.......left alive

.....cryptic bullshit......

The visions ended abruptly; they all came out of it, and Megan opened her mouth first.

"So, where do you keep those ice cream trucks?"

350

Salted Plastic: The Comedic Horror of Gentrification

-A Song of Lost Legacy-

"Platinum pedestals to refine the mind in hills of green and gold"

"Knowledge that strengthens heart and soul beneath luminous towers"

Opening a door to an old church after a long flight to Upstate New York, Baroness Kain gestures to Alina to step inside. An elevator behind the podium in the back leads to a room full of technology not seen by human or reptilian eyes for over three millennia.

"Enclosed by emerald gates descending ruby stairs"

"You reap your own contractual snare, selling truth for perfumed pleasure set in cups of plated gold"

Lydia looked at old photos on her phone as she flew over Burbank. She stared at one of her in a diner apron smoking a cigarette on a break, a big smile on her face. Tim had taken it a few days after they'd met. She looked out her window, heart racing as she thought of how Miguel was worlds apart from that bastard, and how he had a lot of what she'd lost about herself inside of him still. She was happy that their re-integration was starting to bring it all back, her old self.......the her in her. Unfortunately there was still Dagmar to deal with......bitch could easily spoil it all for her and Miguel. She popped a pill as her anxiety spiked..........thoughts of the lion at the door unsettling the her in her.

Salted Plastic: The Comedic Horror of Gentrification

"Drunk on sapphire cups"

"Drunk on sapphire bowls"

Tiffany, McKenzie and Cayleigh, AKA the Fuck Girls, the toughest, streetwise, hood and "for the people" rich girl influencer "gang" in LA, rushed back to Cayleigh's Tesla in terror. No words are spoken as Cayleigh huffs for air, McKenzie breaks a heel, and Tiffany throws her wallet behind her, hoping that it will bait the "icky homeless people" away from them while they escape from the only real night they'll probably ever have in their entire pampered ass lives.

"Handed ornamented treasures"

"In exchange for your heart's crucible"

A bed with sheets that felt like coarse and light gravel. A human female moans with contrived pleasure as Provost Peter, his ugly albino scaled paws on her body, has his way with her to let off steam over the incident at Shillcom. The type of protection and anonymity that his people had been promised by the barons was wearing thinner and thinner every year. "How did those rats get into my corporate office!?" he thought while he attempted to ignore the fact that his pathetic penis was barely capable of causing the over the top reactions in the woman before him. Maybe not physically; on the inside though, the poor girl was dying; somewhere deep in her unconscious the her in her cried, and thought of how the golden career and social life she'd gotten out of all this was hardly worth losing herself...........but only for a moment.

Salted Plastic: The Comedic Horror of Gentrification

"I'm doing me!" she beamed internally a second later. "If it don't make dollars, then it don't..........."

"Steeped in falsehoods unimaginable"

"Your mind overflows with decorative concepts seemingly irrefutable"

A battered ice cream truck cruises down Figueroa, and slows down at the corner of Avenue 56, followed by an aluminum baseball bat popping out of the passenger side window real quick..........and decimating the right ear, temple and jawbone of a guy on the corner, thirty-something, with an ugly straw fedora, waxed moustache, and a t-shirt that said "STOP THE GENTRIFICATION THAT I STARTED, AND STOP IT NOW!!!" His date, a slim Asian girl with pink hair, in fitted camouflage fatigues and a leather halter top, begins screaming maniacally as the guy starts hemorrhaging blue blood from his nose and ears..........a few snake scales peaking from behind his fresh wounds.

"You don't have to thank me, girl!" Jasmine yells from the passenger seat, her silver tooth gleaming in the light of the traffic signals, her face painted the same blue color as the guy's blood. Adrik drives while Megan loads ammunition into a few handguns and rifles in the back. The truck makes its way all the way down Figueroa, followed by the entire expanse of Hill St in Downtown Los Angeles.......

"These gift traps set/define the soul with mounds of death and gold"

"And ancient lenders step forth to cast the human will into the cold"

Salted Plastic: The Comedic Horror of Gentrification

Lebanon and Vicky Varmint sit stoically, staring at an array of security monitors, mentally communicating as they watch several MCCTV's along the route taken by Jasmine, Adrik and Megan.

"We really should tell the big boss woman, no?" Vicky/Lebanon asked Vicky/Lebanon, passive, no urgency in the question. Vicky turned to Leb after watching Megan pop out of the sunroof of the ice cream truck, and open fire on three reptilians in human guise near Pershing Square.

"You mean tell her that we've been sauced up on anamnesis so long that we saw what needed to be done and went for it? Hahahaha......that bureaucrat would never get it........you in **you**, me in **me** knows and knew all that when we made the decision to activate those two. Still, this anomaly sure is something........"

In another subterranean hideout hidden among the refineries in Wilmington, Morrigan sweats in her sheets, having nightmares of the future, nightmares brought on by her exposure to Tlaloca and Baron Hungry.

"Endearing yet deplorable truth"

"Scales from head to toe will shed from you"

Levoié sat in her room on an earth orbiting space station that had been promoted by the official media as so many variant things, that whatever had been announced as its initial purpose was now lost in obscurity. Sadness and worry made her reptilian heart sink.

Salted Plastic: The Comedic Horror of Gentrification

"I want to be someone else or I'll....." she began to think, and was cut short by the sound of a notification on her PDA; the private, jailbroken one that she kept hidden in her bunk. Removing it silently from a sliver in her mattress, she walked to a corner and looked at the incoming messages.

"Moping?" a message from Alina asked. "Well stop! You don't need to ever again! I GOT HER, LEVOIÉ.............Baroness Kain is going to give us everything we ever wanted!"

"And drown you in mounds of death and gold"

"The dead come to claim hell's debt, and push you to undiscover you"

Above the roof of the Billshire Grande Hotel, a frail figure floated in the dark, breathing in the midnight air.....if it can be said that these things breath at all. His guests below were feeding and drinking well in the soon to be open to the public sky bar. Copper and lost dreams scented the air as a shaft of moonlight hit the floating figure. Baron Mustela Nivalis hovered in a state of anti-meditation, one of the techniques lost to many of his tribe; he fanned his appropriative ego through past, present and future, sending his consciousness out like a bloodhound, psychically inhaling the world, craving every drop of natural human experience, lusting for it so that it might be used to cloth the fact that he was dead inside. Scraps of ashen flesh fell off his body into the champagne glasses of his human guests below while they discussed business, the real estate market and upcoming "cultural" events.

As the moonlight shifted, so did his appearance, fluctuating between gray and rotten flesh upon a head in constant seizure spasms, and a slender copper skinned youth with lavender hair...............calm and contemplative as he hovered in flös immortuos position. He watched them all; Dagmar, Jasmine, Lebanon, Lydia, Vicky, Adrik, Morrigan, Megan, Baroness Kain, Provost Peter, Alina.........and Miguel.......a smile briefly crossing his face as he did.

"A debt tethered queen"

"Mounds of death and gold"

"Deflect the arts and harrow tools of corpse rulers"

Miguel woke abruptly, and walked to the front door of Lydia's apartment after hearing/feeling a single polite knock, the sound somehow telling him that he's needed........but also telling him that it's not what it seems. Heart racing, he turned the door knob slowly, his mind wondering who it was at the door, even though a soft nudge in his jeans told him that his body already knew.

He let the door swing open slowly, a scent of sandalwood hitting his nostrils before he even saw who it was.

In the doorway, Dagmar stood in a fitted Vottega Venusia trench coat, the top half black leather, the bottom half, collar, and right sleeve all red leather. Miguel, in nothing but his denims, stumbled like a graceless beast, unsure of what to say, still a little high and drunk.

"Why, Michael!?" Dagmar said in an affected tone that suggested she had been spurned and forgotten. "Why haven't you answered my messages, or the lovely hand delivered invitation I sent you?" Upon saying the word "invitation" her coat not so casually opened up, revealing that the only thing she had on underneath was a pair of black leather equestrian boots, and an antique silver medallion with the face of a lion. Miguel stumbled even more, his heart racing, mesmerized by her copper pubic hair and already erect nipples………by her soft yet insistent energy…………the predatory acquisitional look in her eyes.

"Ooooh, you look tired!" she continued in a soft placative manner, walking in uninvited, brushing her palm across the hair on his chest as she did, and closing the door behind her.

"Mounds of death and gold"

"Mounds of death and gold"

Made in the USA
Monee, IL
30 June 2025

20201341R00203